Bruce

C000174974

Murder at the Bridge

Detective Inspector Skelgill
Investigates

LUCiUS

TROUBLED WATERS

AN ATTEMPTED MURDER in the United States ... a tragic road death in a Cumbrian forest ... an old photograph stolen from an ancient coaching inn. Unrelated events – until a midnight drowning below Ouse Bridge exposes a connection. After two decades, has a killer returned to Cumbria to ply their trade? Does a suspect hide in plain sight among loose acquaintances? Who is truthful and who is lying? Skelgill must patiently circle ... until finally he picks up the scent.

BRUCE BECKHAM is an award-winning author and copywriter. A resident of Great Britain, he has travelled and worked in over 60 countries. He is published in both fiction and non-fiction, and is a member of the UK Society of Authors.

His series 'Inspector Skelgill Investigates' features the recalcitrant Cumbrian detective Daniel Skelgill, and his loyal lieutenants, long-suffering Londoner DS Leyton and local high-flyer DS Emma Jones.

Set amidst the ancient landscapes of England's Lake District, this expanding series of standalone murder mysteries has won acclaim across five continents, with over 1 million copies downloaded, from Australia to Japan and India, and from Brazil to Canada and the United States of America.

"Great characters. Great atmospheric locale. Great plots. What's not to like?"

Amazon reviewer, 5 stars

Text copyright 2023 Bruce Beckham

All rights reserved. Bruce Beckham asserts his right always to be identified as the author of this work. No part may be copied or transmitted without written permission from the publisher.

This is a work of fiction. Names, characters, places and incidents either are the product of the author's imagination or are used fictitiously. Any resemblance to actual persons, living or dead, events and locales is entirely coincidental.

Kindle edition first published by Lucius 2023
Paperback edition first published by Lucius 2023
Hardcover edition first published by Lucius 2023

For more details and Rights enquiries contact:
Lucius-ebooks@live.com

Cover design by Moira Kay Nicol
United States editor Janet Colter

EDITOR'S NOTE

Murder at the Bridge is a stand-alone mystery, the twentieth in the series 'Detective Inspector Skelgill Investigates'. It is set in the English Lake District, at an ancient coaching inn on the shore of Bassenthwaite Lake, close to the outfall of the River Derwent, and its crossing point known locally as Ouse Bridge.

If you are familiar with the exploits of Daniel Skelgill, you may notice some allusions to his emergence; a score of adventures later (an anniversary of sorts), a journey of justice and discovery, your loyal company is wholeheartedly appreciated.

And, please be assured, Skelgill has not yet reached his destination; he has more lakes to paddle, more fells to climb, more crooks to catch.

THE DI SKELGILL SERIES

Glossary

SOME of the Cumbrian dialect words, abbreviations, British slang and local usage appearing in *Murder at the Bridge* are as follows:

Ah – I
Alan Whickers – knickers (Cockney)
Arl – old
Arl fella – father
Arl lass – mother
Alreet/areet – alright (often a greeting)
Any road – anyway, besides
Barney – argument, trouble (Cockney: Barney Rubble)
Bathers – swimming costume
Blow the gaff – reveal a secret
Bookie – bookmaker
Chore – steal
Deek – look
Donnat – idiot, good for nothing
Dwam – trance, reverie (Scots)
FLO – Family Liaison Officer
Gattered – inebriated
GP – General Practitioner (doctor)
Gubbins – paraphernalia
Guddle – feel for fish with bare hands
Hank Marvin – starving (Cockney)
Happen – maybe
Haver – talk foolishly (Scots)
Hefted flock – sheep habituated to a certain fellside
Hikey-dykey – hedge-hopping
Hoik – uproot, pull
Hoying – throwing (heavy rain)
Howay – come on

Hump (take the) – to be offended
Jug – ear (Cockney: jug of beer)
Lamp – punch
Mash – tea/make tea
Marra – mate (friend)
Mithering – annoying
Monkey suit – man's dress suit
Neb – nose; pry
Nicht – night (Scots)
Nobbut – only
Nowt – nothing
Owt – anything
PHV – private hire vehicle
Pike – prominent peak
Playing away – having an affair
Rod, perch, pole – antiquated surveying measure of 5½ yards
RP – received pronunciation; Queen's English
RTC – road traffic collision
Scotch (adj.) – inanimate object of Scottish origin
Scran – food
Snout – police informer
Steeyan – stone
Stotting – pelting (rain)
Summat – something
Syling – heavy rain
T' – the (often silent)
Tapped – crazy
Tarn – mountain lake, usually in a corrie
Thee/thew/thou – you, your
Tod – fox
Us – often used for me/my/our
Willylilt – sandpiper
Yatter – talk
Yersen – yourself
Yin – one/person (Scots)
Yowe – ewe

THE DAA COMMITTEE

CHAIRMAN, **Sir Montague Brash**, 58 – married; landowner, Brash Hall Estate.

SECRETARY, **Georgina Graham**, 43 – divorced; HR director, Servill Consulting; lives Swinside Barn, Derwentwater.

TREASURER, **Anthony Goodman**, 45 – single; director of finance, Fellview Nursing Home, Bothel; lives Keswick.

Jackie Baker, 37 – married; hotelier, Applethwaite House.

Stephen Flood, 47 – widower; quality supervisor, Cumbria Water; lives Cockermouth.

Ruth Robinson, 39 – married; Kirkthwaite Farm.

Jay Chaudry, 42 – single; IT entrepreneur; lives Salford Quays, Manchester & Castle How Farm, Orthwaite.

Kyle Betony, 45 – married; independent financial advisor; works & lives Cockermouth.

Lucy Bedlington, 37 – single; general medical practitioner, Keswick; lives Bewaldeth.

Professor Jim Hartley – retired historian; Braithwaite.

Alice Wright-Fotheringham, KC – retired barrister and judge; Keswick.

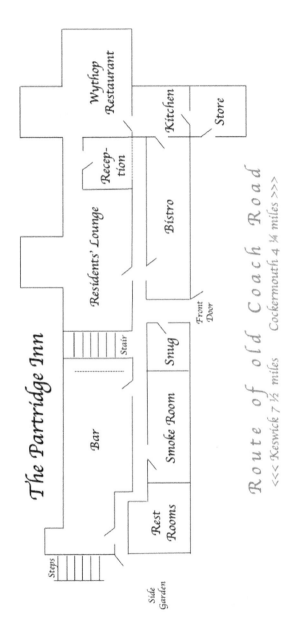

The Partridge Inn

Steps

Bar

Stair

Residents' Lounge

Reception

Wythop Restaurant

Rest Rooms

Smoke Room

Snug

Side Garden

Front Door

Bistro

Kitchen

Store

Route of old Coach Road

<<< Keswick 7 ½ miles   Cockermouth 4 ¼ miles >>>

11

QUOTATION

"In human affairs of danger and delicacy successful conclusion is sharply limited by hurry. So often men trip by being in a rush. If one were properly to perform a difficult and subtle act, he should first inspect the end to be achieved and then, once he had accepted the end as desirable, he should forget it completely and concentrate solely on the means. By this method he would not be moved to false action by anxiety or hurry or fear. Very few people learn this."

From *East Of Eden* by John Steinbeck

PROLOGUE

Article in 'TRUE CRIME HUNTERS MONTHLY' magazine

WHERE ARE THEY NOW?
WOULD-BE KILLERS
WHO MIGHT BE YOUR NEIGHBOUR
FEATURED THIS MONTH
SUSPECTED WIFE-POISONER
TOBIAS JUBB

When Jolene Jubb woke in the passenger seat of her husband's pickup she couldn't believe her eyes. Deep in mountainous Missouri woodland, the vehicle teetered on the edge of a ravine. Crazily perched on the hood was a four-gallon jerry can with its screw cap dangling loose. Beyond, through blurry eyes she glimpsed the figure of her husband Tobias, hunched over their child's buggy, pushing it hurriedly away, up and out of sight along the dry track. Jolene tried to call out, to move – but her voice would not come and her limbs felt heavy, her muscles numbed. Her nostrils were filled with the pungent smell of gasoline.

What was happening to her? To her child?

Slowly, laboriously, Jolene's survival instincts kicked in.

Somehow, she managed to push open the door.

She tumbled out and half-crawled, half-scrambled away from the vehicle.

Fighting a yearning to sleep, battling dizziness and stupor, she lurched drunkenly in the direction her husband had taken their daughter.

Reaching a bend, she heard voices. She froze, clinging to a tree for support, her breath coming in erratic gasps, her heart pounding in her chest.

'Where's Momma?'

'She's coming sweetie, Daddy's just going back for her now.'

'I want Momma!'

'You're safe here – Daddy's going to fetch Momma from the fire.'

'I don't like fire!'

Jolene crept closer, and watched from cover as her husband wedged the buggy between two saplings and checked that the straps holding the child were secure. He took from his pocket the multitool cigarette lighter she had given him for his thirty-fifth birthday. Then he jogged back down the hill.

There was no time to lose.

No animal in the jungle is more determined than a mother with her cubs – and Jolene reached deep into her reserves of will power.

She staggered across the track, unclipped her daughter, lifted her free … and plunged into the brush.

At the wheel of the truck, Tobias came roaring back.

He slewed the automobile to a halt in a great cloud of dust.

Jolene did not wait to watch what happened next.

Imploring her child to stay silent she pushed on into the thick understorey – her babe in arms she bore insect bites and stings, and thorns and briars to escape the terror that lay behind, that filled her mind with dread. Despite her debilitated state, Jolene was sure of one thing: she could not trust Tobias.

She toiled on, tired, thirsty, unnaturally weary – but eventually she came upon a clearing – and a small isolated homestead. A middle-aged woman was sweeping the porch. Exhausted by her ordeal, Jolene could only hand up the child to the surprised countrywoman. She collapsed. But they were safe. The woman's husband was the local deputy.

The county sheriff was doubtful at first – he believed he had a garden variety family tiff on his hands. But when Tobias Jubb never turned up at the family house that evening – *suspicion began to shift.* And when Tobias Jubb never reappeared at all, and his pickup was found abandoned next day at St Louis Lambert International Airport – *alarm bells began to ring*. And when it was discovered a few weeks later that Tobias Jubb had, without his wife's knowledge, taken out a multi-million-dollar insurance policy on her life – *the police began to take notice*. And when, in searching his personal possessions left at the family home, the police found a supply of a strongly sedative benzodiazepine – *the FBI were called in*. And when Jolene Jubb began to relate the strange sicknesses she suffered, and her inexplicable tiredness sometimes lately when they went out for family picnics, often falling asleep before they arrived at their destination – *the FBI notified Interpol*. And when a hunter came forward, remembering he had seen a man fitting Tobias Jubb's description looking into the ravine a week earlier – *Interpol issued a worldwide Red Notice for his arrest*.

And where is Tobias Jubb now?

A decade has elapsed and no trace has been found of him. Jolene Jubb says he was British – and she wonders if he has returned to his native land.

Perhaps one of our readers holds a clue to the answer.

IN NEXT MONTH'S EDITION: an exclusive interview with the estranged wife of disappeared British murder mystery writer Hugh Dunnett, who tells how she almost became the real-life victim of one of his fictional plots, *Dead Reckoning*, a nautical tale of a sabotaged lifejacket.

1. DEDICATION TO DUTY

Bassenthwaite Lake – 6.04 a.m., Sunday, 19th September

'Wakey wakey, Skelly – six a.m. alarm call.'

'George – I'm in the middle of Bass Lake. It's Sunday. Tell me you're just bored.'

'Sorry, lad.' The desk sergeant's disembodied voice softens: as a fellow fisherman, there is a note of compassion in his tone. 'You've got another body on your patch. Possible drowning. Suspicious circumstances, by all accounts.'

There is a long pause, in which the solitary sound in the still morning air, heard but ignored by both parties to the telephone call is the cackle from the reeds of a drake mallard, only now it seems getting last night's joke.

For his part, Skelgill does not look amused.

Sergeant George Appleby breaks the silence.

'Owt you want to know?'

Skelgill stares at his left hand, his long fingers splayed.

'Where. When. Who. What. Why.'

He intones flatly, as though to himself, no question marks needed; a practical version of Kipling's six honest serving-men, in which 'what' puts in a double shift on behalf of 'how'. The detective's rap.

The sergeant emits a half laugh.

'I can give you the 'where' – starter for ten. The rest's above my pay grade.'

'Very funny, George.'

But Skelgill's inflection invites his associate to be forthcoming.

'Washed up at the Colonel's Pool – just above Isel Bridge, if I recall. You could probably row there quicker – if you can get yersen under Ouse Bridge.'

Skelgill makes an indeterminate noise. Maybe not in the dark; although dawn is breaking. And he has done it before in this boat, albeit with saving a life in mind.

The sergeant adds a rider.

'Oh, aye – and it's a male in his forties.'

'Why suspicious?'

The operative word earlier uttered has not escaped Skelgill's attention.

'Apparently, he's wearing a dinner suit.'

Skelgill takes the point. A Barbour jacket, say, like his own, though probably in better condition, would seem more apposite; an angler who put a foot wrong and tumbled into the rushing river.

'Any cause for urgency?'

It seems Skelgill is hedging his bets; his colleague understands.

'I can raise Alec Smart, if you like. Ruin his lie-in – *hah!* But I thought you'd want first dibs. I hear young Emma's on her way.'

There is a note of advisory caution in the desk sergeant's voice.

'Nay.' Skelgill's response is a little abrupt. 'Like you say, George, it's a stone's throw. Who needs a double-figure pike on this cracking morn?'

George Appleby produces a sympathetic intake of breath.

'Caught owt, yet?'

'Reckon I was just about to.'

'Ah well, bigger fish to fry now, lad.'

Skelgill reels in and turns his boat. He takes a bearing off Skiddaw Little Man; keeping the false summit dead astern will send him arrowing into Peel Wyke, the tiny hidden wooded inlet that has echoes of the wild oarsmen that once ruled these parts, literally the 'Wyke-ings', the Norse 'baymen', who left their mark on today's maps with descriptors that abound, like beck and dale, fell and pike, gill and skel.

*

When Skelgill slows to cross Isel Bridge he sees a lanky uniformed constable, bent over in close confab with a fair-haired young woman, strikingly dressed, and who looks out of place – so it takes him a moment to realise it is DS Jones – perhaps the sight of her distinctive yellow hatchback tucked into the verge behind a marked patrol car is what brings her into focus. Skelgill gives a pap of his horn, although there are no two cars in Cumbria like his. He catches a glimpse of blue-and-white police tape stretched across a stile. He passes the pair and shunts his shooting brake into the rear of the line; the lane is narrow and bordered by a dressed stone wall that is a continuation of the bridge parapet.

His colleagues seem to be sharing a joke, perhaps of the black humour variety that pervades police work – though it would not be like DS Jones to be disrespectful. Then Skelgill remembers that she and Kenneth Dodd were contemporaries, alumni of Penrith Academy, a decade later than he. Despite the interval, Skelgill and Jones had even shared some teachers, albeit not grades. Although Skelgill still holds the school record for throwing the cricket ball – worth an A-star, in his book. You can't bring down a fleeing criminal with an English A-level.

DS Jones breaks away and comes alongside, as if expecting him to lower his window. But rather peremptorily he pushes open the door and she has to step back.

'Howay – you'll freeze like that.'

Never expect the expected. DS Jones must be tempted to say, "And good morning to you" – but she knows him too well to be offended.

She also knows there are layers of questions beneath his critical observation of her rather skimpy outfit. She watches as he prises himself from the car, his bulky fishing garb impeding easy movement.

'I was at a hen party in Carlisle – I'm sure I mentioned it on Friday.' She gives him only a second, in which he does not react, before she continues. 'I passed an RTC coming down the M6 and switched on my radio in case I could help. That was when George got onto me. He'd just received the report of a body.'

Behind DS Jones the early autumn sun is breaking over the skyline of the Skiddaw massif and Skelgill is squinting at her, his front teeth bared in a way that reveals some consternation. Natural bronze strands glint in her paler locks; more artificial is mascara that delineates her large hazel eyes.

'Was there a stripper, aye?'

DS Jones cannot suppress a chuckle. She turns and completes a modest pirouette. Rather coyly she brushes away a wisp of hair that has fallen across her face. Her full lips retain the hint of an enigmatic smile.

'When I tell you it's two girls getting married, I'll leave the answer to your imagination.'

The suggestion seems to stymie him – whether it jams the microprocessor of his mind's eye – or perhaps he is satisfied, and he just wants to get on. He steps past her, towards the stile where PC Dodd stands sentry, the latter looking a little sheepish now, as if feeling outranked for the loyalty of his female colleague. Skelgill nods to the constable but strides on, to the centre of the bridge. Beneath, the river flows true and deep, an oncoming conveyor, its surface smooth enough to reflect billowing white cumulus clouds. As always he watches the water before raising his sights. The right-hand bank is reed-lined and runs into gently shelving meadows; the steeper left is lined by alders and willows, but he can make out a white-painted farm cottage through a gap in the vegetation.

DS Jones seems to know when to narrate.

'Apparently there's a shingle bank just upstream of the far bend. The woman who lives in that cottage had let out her dog. It didn't come back in when she called. Then she heard it barking and went to look. She found the body washed up on the exposed stones. I don't think there's any chance she's connected. She's been asked to stay indoors until we're done. We've closed off the footpath – and besides, this early on a Sunday I don't suppose there'll be many people out here.' She looks quizzically at Skelgill. 'Anglers excepted.'

Skelgill shrugs, as if she reminds him of his forbearance in the face of such a distraction.

'We'd better have a deek.'

*

A sandpiper – a willylilt in local parlance – draws Skelgill's eye, bobbing at the water's edge as they approach, before taking flight with a characteristic *twee-wee-wee*, a refrain known to all anglers, if not always its origin. The river swings around the broad shingle bank, as if in deference to the corpse that lies unmoving. This is the slow water of the Colonel's Pool, a renowned salmon beat. But Skelgill continues to stare at the point from which the wading bird took flight.

'The level's still falling.'

DS Jones does not respond; for her part, the late human presence is too compelling for such an incidental detail to wrench away her attention.

They approach.

'The woman from the cottage said she didn't move him.'

Skelgill nods. The man lies supine – as advertised wearing a dinner suit, and patent leather shoes. It is plain that he is dead – but were it not for open eyes and the obvious absence of vital signs, perhaps a reasonable conclusion would be that here is a person who, under the influence of alcohol, has absconded from a country house party and found somewhere to sleep off the effects.

So much so that the first thing Skelgill does is to stoop beside the corpse and feel the cloth of the jacket. The black colour hides the fact that the material is soaked through.

'He doesn't look like he was long in the water.'

DS Jones, two yards back, casts about.

'Do you think this is a natural point for him to have been washed up?'

Skelgill remains crouched; he squints pensively.

'Aye – and I'd venture he's been there above six hours.'

DS Jones realises he has performed some calculation – an equation that conflates local knowledge with the laws of physics. The Derwent is reputedly the fastest-flowing river in Europe. It is one of Skelgill's aphorisms, that rain which falls on the Scafell pikes at breakfast can be in the Irish Sea by teatime: the corollary that the level can change quickly – and that Skelgill knows the formula.

Skelgill is cautiously patting the pockets of the man's jacket.

He rises, with a small haul: a set of car keys attached to a Ford fob; a wallet; a small folded sheet of paper. But there is no mobile phone.

'Here.' He hands the wallet to DS Jones.

She wastes no time.

'A driver's licence. Credit cards. They're all in the name of Kyle Betony – does that ring any bells?'

But Skelgill has carefully prised open the sodden notelet; she realises it is of more significance to him.

'What is it, Guv?'

'Look.' He displays it for her to read.

It is a printed menu on headed stationery. "Derwentdale Anglers' Association. Annual Committee Dinner." The date and time are of the last evening.

'The Partridge?'

'Aye – that's where they hold their meetings.'

Then Skelgill makes an exclamation of disgust.

'What's wrong?'

'Pan-fried perch. What's Charlie thinking of?'

DS Jones flashes him a sideways glance, but Skelgill seems to be serious. She humours him.

'Perhaps they had a themed dinner and ate fish they'd caught to order?'

Skelgill is grimacing.

'That's scraping the barrel. I'm glad I'm not on the committee.'

'Are you a member of the club?'

He looks surprised that she asks.

'Aye – most folk hereabouts are – fisherfolk. Jim Hartley's on the committee. And Alice Wright-Fotheringham.'

'What about –' (she consults the wallet) 'Kyle Betony?'

Skelgill shakes his head. He doesn't know.

'I don't have owt to do with it. I just pay my subs and fish.

They send out a newsletter, but I only look at the latest catches page – to see what's about, like.'

There is something in his rider that hints at a more competitive motive, but DS Jones does not allow the notion to divert her.

They stand in silence for a moment; they might almost be mourners at an unconventional funeral, the sort that takes place alongside the Ganges; there is enough sun-bleached driftwood for a pyre at the higher tidemark, last winter's biggest flood, and still dried strands of stained sheep's wool and ochre-coloured bracken woven into wire fencing that marks off the adjacent pasture land.

From the willows a chiffchaff beats out its swansong, an avian rendition of Chopsticks that lacks the vim of its spring version, and laments of an imminent departure. The alders are still green, though the willows are turning, and occasional yellow leaves drift past. A couple of swallows, also fattening for their southbound return to Africa, hawk above the surface for late-hatching olives and sedges.

Skelgill, watching the antics of the graceful hirundines, is thinking that the end of the season is slipping away, but DS Jones must be more profoundly affected, for she suddenly shudders.

Skelgill begins to shrug off his waxed-cotton coat.

'Here – put this on.'

But she has spotted an all-male group approaching, and they her. Led by PC Dodd are two paramedics bearing a stretcher and two white-suited scene-of-crime officers, one toting a camera on a tripod.

'Guv.'

There is a note of caution in his colleague's lowered voice and Skelgill sees the uniformed constable and his little entourage. The sight seems to spur him into action.

'Howay, lass. There's nowt more for us here.' He glares at the body of the man they believe to be called Kyle Betony. 'Hardly owt for them either.'

23

But some record of the scene is necessary before the corpse is extracted, while significantly more informative will be the autopsy that may now ensue.

'Where to?'

Skelgill checks his watch. He still has hold of the menu. He brandishes it.

'Charlie's normally up by six. We can ask him if anyone choked on a perch bone.'

*

They drive separately the four miles from Isel Bridge to The Partridge, passing no one and reaching the secluded coaching inn seeing no soul abroad. Skelgill gets out and surveys the broad sweep of redundant tarmac. Large cars damp with dew glint in the morning light, their magnificence perhaps a reflection of the price of accommodation in the Lakes these days. But he makes no judgement in this regard; it helps him in what he is looking for.

He stalks over to a car that stands out inversely as more modest than most, a small blue Ford saloon. But when he points the remote and presses its buttons there is no response.

DS Jones has drifted across.

'Maybe his car's elsewhere.'

But Skelgill does not give up so easily. He glowers at the small device; it is likely waterlogged. He releases the key, a switchblade mechanism, and inserts it into the lock of the driver's door. When he twists it there is a satisfying clunk.

He casts a glance at his colleague, looking pleased with himself.

But when he opens the door, the alarm goes off.

He does not flinch but, so close, the blare is painful and DS Jones instinctively presses the heels of her hands over her ears.

A face appears at an open window just above the rustic porch – which Skelgill knows belongs to the most prestigious guest room, the Skiddaw suite. It is a rather imperious-looking man, perhaps in his late fifties, suntanned, hair slicked back – and sneering it seems, as if in looking down his prominent aquiline beak he considers the ill-suited couple and their inadequate means of transport to be not only literally beneath him. He could be about to protest – but perhaps Skelgill's fierce countenance foretells of the likely rejoinder. Instead the man retreats, ostentatiously shutting the window and pulling the curtains together.

Skelgill mutters something under his breath and slams the door.

To his relief – and no doubt that of those others in their beds just above – the alarm stops.

But now, too late, the door of what was once a stable but is now the kitchen store bursts open and out tumbles a rather corpulent red-faced man with curly ginger hair wearing a bloody butcher's apron and brandishing a meat cleaver.

'Danny?'

The man stops in his tracks, the implement held aloft.

'Alreet, Charlie.'

Charles Brown, joint-proprietor of The Partridge Inn, looks bewildered.

Then he begins to curse – but realising he is in female company he morphs his words into an inarticulate grumble.

'Do you always keep one of them handy?'

Skelgill sports a macabre grin. The hotelier lowers the cleaver rather sheepishly. He straightens his overall and presents himself for inspection. His intonation becomes more measured, when there is surely a West Midlands accent straining to get out.

'I'm cutting lamb chop portions. Chef's making Rack of Herdwick with Bleaberry Sauce tonight.' Now he looks apologetically at DS Jones. 'But we did have an attempted break-in to a Porsche a couple of weeks ago.'

Rather to her surprise, Skelgill makes a belated introduction.

'Charlie – you know Detective Sergeant Jones.'

It is neither a question nor a statement – rather more it seems a means of moving on the conversation – and it appears to have the desired effect. Perhaps it is the use of her formal title.

'Are you on duty, Danny?'

Given the detectives' respective attire the man would be excused for thinking otherwise. By way of elaboration Skelgill inclines his head towards his colleague. She produces the driving licence.

'Do you recognise this person?'

Charles Brown squints doubtfully at the small pixelated image. It would be a long shot at the best of times.

'I can't say I do – why do you ask?' He shoots a glance at Skelgill.

Skelgill has no reason not to be candid. Now he produces the damp piece of hotel notepaper.

'We think he was at your dinner last night. He was wearing a DJ and this was in his pocket. We weren't able to ask him.'

But the man still seems a little perplexed.

'Why not?'

'He's been found this morning. Looks like he fell in the Derwent.'

The penny drops.

'Dead?'

Skelgill nods.

Charles Brown wipes his brow with a bare freckled forearm. It can only be a gesture of momentary displacement; the air is still cool. Then he glances up anxiously to see if any of the bedroom windows are open. There is eavesdropping and Tripadvisor ratings to think of. But he seems to understand that some explanation will be appreciated.

'I was only here until eight. We've got the wife's sister and her teenagers staying and we phoned for a Chinese takeaway. I know – ' He makes a face of small guilt. Then he turns to DS Jones. 'We live in the cottage in the grounds at the back – it's only a minute, so I'm on hand if need be. The night bell comes through to me.'

Skelgill flaps the menu.

'What was the arrangement for this?'

'They met in the bar – seven-thirty for eight. They had the Wythop Restaurant to themselves – we didn't take any external bookings and residents who wanted an evening meal ate in the bistro. There were eleven covers booked – but there was one no-show. Chef was miffed about that – it was the only vegetarian and he'd created a pea-and-lentil fishcake in the shape of a leaping salmon.'

Skelgill looks like he has to suppress some unfavourable comment; he casts about the parking area.

'Are you full?'

The innkeeper shakes his head.

'Nine out of fifteen rooms occupied. All couples.' He makes a loose gesture with the meat cleaver to take in the prestige marques lined up along the front of the ancient building, as if they serve as proxy for the biographical details of his guests. He notices that Skelgill seems to be counting the vehicles; there must be more than a dozen, excluding those belonging to the detectives. He adds a rider. 'Drinkers sometimes get a taxi and come back for their car next day – plus we get anglers parking here.' He flashes a wry grin at Skelgill.

But Skelgill is not diverted from his line of thought.

'Did any of the committee stay?'

'No. At least, no one had a reservation. But I would have been notified if someone wanted to stop over.'

'Are you aware of any incident – disturbance – argument – drunkenness?'

At this a frown creases the brow of Charles Brown, although his blue eyes remain amiable. He does not, however, give any indication in his response of the sentiment that has troubled him.

'Nothing that was reported. Again – anything of note, I would have been called. The girls are all briefed – not to feel they have to handle something untoward by themselves. There were two waiting staff on – females – but Colin's always in the kitchen until ten, and you wouldn't mess with him. Especially not after the vegetarian fishcake.' The man pauses, and looks as though he rues that this particular employee is not to be messed with under other circumstances, too. 'Last one here would have been Saskia – she was manning the bar until closing time.'

Skelgill is on bantering terms with the girl; or, rather, she has on occasion humoured his questionable wit.

Charles Brown seems to understand that the detectives might

have work to be getting on with, as does he.

'The waitresses have gone home – but Saskia's got a room in the staff quarters. It's her day off. Want me to get Angie to wake her?'

Skelgill ponders for a moment.

'Leave her just now. We've got one or two things to do.'

He refers to the menu page.

'When was this all booked?'

The hotelier again furrows his brown, more reflectively now.

'It's been in the diary since the turn of the year. They hold their committee meetings in the Smoke Room, last Tuesday of the month. Sir Montague Brash is the Chairman.' He hesitates, and flashes a sideways glance at DS Jones. 'It was his, er – secretary that made the arrangements. After that I only really know Jim Hartley and the lady judge – you know, Alice – with the double-barrelled name? Oh – and Jackie Baker – she's on the Society of Hoteliers' committee. She runs Applethwaite House. I can't say any of the rest drink here.'

Skelgill nods.

The isolated location of The Partridge means it is not a 'local' in the sense of a typical English alehouse; indeed its location is anything but, being situated on the old coaching route between Penrith in the east and the coastal ports in the west, and built in an era when the velocity of long-distance travel was barely above pedestrian, in that horses could pull a carriage for about twenty miles a day. Now bypassed, the section of old road, encroached upon by weeds is to the main east-west A66 what an oxbow lake is to the Derwent, in its tree-lined arbour a sun-dappled oasis of calm. Within, the small public bar is often quiet, despite its extraordinary seventeenth-century charm. Diners may divert for a pre-prandial pint of cask bitter, but after-dinner coffee and liqueurs are served in the more refined if chintzy Edwardian surroundings of the residents' lounge.

Skelgill is thinking that they will certainly need to take statements from the serving staff, and soon, while the events of last evening are still fresh in their minds.

Charles Brown interrupts his thoughts.

'Want me to organise you some breakfast?'

When a bear-and-woods order of reply might be anticipated, DS Jones is surprised that Skelgill declines. Instead, he instructs her to take down contact details of the staff. As she turns to follow Charles Brown beneath the creeper-shrouded portico, Skelgill diverts to his car.

A few moments later he loiters mid-corridor. The building is long, low and rudimentary in its design. His colleague waits at the cramped reception for the information she requires. At the opposite end of the single passageway are the restrooms; in between, facing the front, the bistro, the main entrance, the Snug and the Smoke Room. To the rear are the residents' lounge (through which the Wythop Restaurant is reached), the staircase to the upper floor, and the bar which, despite its comparatively diminutive size, has two doors exiting to the corridor, suggesting it once comprised two even smaller apartments. The kitchen area and stores may be accessed from the bistro and the restaurant. At the back shady gardens run into mixed woodland, where the semblance of a stream seeps along to Peel Wyke.

Skelgill turns away as DS Jones approaches. He has over one shoulder his clanky rucksack. She notices he checks his watch.

'Walk this way.'

She grins; surely he affects a swagger.

But she is puzzled, for they pass the bar on their right and the Smoke Room on their left and seem to be heading for the toilets. Then she realises that the corridor jinks right then left to approach a door marked both 'Fire Escape' and 'Garden'.

They emerge from the end of the old building with stone steps to their right, and ahead between raised beds and rockeries a small secluded sunken lawn. A collection of wrought-iron garden furniture is roped off from the damp and wild undergrowth beyond. Picked out in a shaft of sunlight, a spotted flycatcher launches itself to intercept a passing gnat – Skelgill hesitates, and watches the bird return to its rope perch, admiring its aerobatic prowess. But then he moves on, through a gate in a yew hedge topped with an effort at topiary that might represent a partridge but which looks rather more like a dishevelled pheasant.

This takes them to the front of the inn. Skelgill keeps walking, past their own vehicles, and in the opposite direction from the nearby inlet where his boat is moored.

*

Skelgill marches on. From The Partridge it is a comparatively short distance to Ouse Bridge, where the reconstituted River Derwent drains from Bassenthwaite Lake. He walks steadily, rather than with his regular urgency, and notes the time taken. On the bridge itself he inspects the tarmac, in particular the fine sharp gravel at the margins. He dwells over a skid mark – but it was clearly made by a bike tyre, perhaps where a cyclist had abruptly pulled up to avoid an oncoming vehicle, or just realising there was a view to be had.

Then he notices a spent match, and collects it in a small plastic evidence bag.

'Do you think he would come this far to have a cigarette?'

Skelgill glowers.

'I wouldn't. I doubt he even smokes – he didn't have a lighter on him – or owt to smoke, come to that.'

He leads the way around and down to the river bank, in the shadow of the bridge. He unpacks his gear and casts down a fold-out foam mat, indicating that DS Jones should sit.

She watches as he scavenges for combustible flotsam. A double-handful secured, he demonstrates his expertise with a battered vintage Trangia stove and the strange smoking contraption that is his Kelly kettle. Being self-sufficient in food and drink is a state of affairs he swears by.

So is not jumping to conclusions.

Equally, the death is suspicious. Moreover, Kyle Betony has not been reported missing. And it is evident that he left the inn on foot.

She understands it will serve them well to assume the worst –

albeit that most such incidents prove to be accidental. It can be no coincidence that Skelgill – despite his characteristic reluctance to speculate – has brought them to what is probably the nearest practical point of entry to the river. Peel Wyke might be equidistant, but she can deduce that there is inadequate flow upstream of the bridge.

She turns her inquisitive mind to the structure, its imposing double stone arch something that goes unappreciated by the passing traveller, for whom it is a mere utility, a bump in the road.

'Why is this called Ouse Bridge? I thought the Ouse was a separate river.'

She piques Skelgill's interest.

'Aye – you're half right there. It's a hatful of rivers. There's the Ouse through York – the Great Ouse in the Fens – and the Sussex Ouse, they get monster sea trout.' His expression becomes wistful, as if he is reflecting upon some Grand Tour. He sighs. 'Ouse – it just means "river" – in Old English, summat like that.'

'Like avon? I think that's Celtic in origin.'

'Aye.'

'And so when people say "River Avon" they're saying river twice. The same for "River Ouse". It's a pleonasm.'

Skelgill regards his associate wryly. She seems to have a glint in her eye.

She casts a hand languidly.

'Perhaps it's because the Derwent *oozes* out of the lake just here?'

Skelgill does not demur. Indeed, the notion clearly prompts some reflection. He rubs the knuckles of one hand against the stiff stubble of a jaw that seems to jut even more than is usual. His unblinking gaze is fixed upon the outfall from the lake. He doubts he would have got his boat through. But here, beneath Ouse Bridge the water is deeper; safe enough to jump in, if not dive. Thus there remains the question as to why a person would not swim – or even wade to the nearest bank; the Derwent might be swift, but it is not in spate, and in scale it is hardly the Mississippi.

'It was right here that you first showed me that thing.'

Her words rouse him from his conjecture. He looks puzzled, until she gestures to indicate his Kelly kettle. Perhaps he misreads her tone, for he seems to take offence, like a dog owner when a disingenuous admirer refers to their pet as "it".

'It's an essential piece of outdoor kit. Wait till North Sea gas runs out – then folk'll be queuing up to buy one.'

He glances to see that she is smiling – but now the device lives up to its generic moniker of volcano kettle and begins to erupt – he swoops to lift it, cantilevered by its handle and tilt-chain, and fills their enamel mugs.

DS Jones watches; he is deft, well-practised, not spilling a drop.

She goes again.

'It doesn't seem like ten minutes since we were last here. The case at Bewaldeth Hall.'

Skelgill concentrates upon setting down the kettle so that it balances on the shingle.

'I feel like time's standing still.'

She regards him pensively.

'The eternal present.'

He looks up sharply.

'What?'

'It's a literary device.'

'What – like a typewriter?'

She laughs.

He grins.

But he has been operating on his haunches, and now he rises with a grimace and flexes his spine, turning away to stare beneath the main arch down the lake. Irregular patches of grey-white stratus have begun to slip across the pale morning sky and the sun is presently obscured. He looks displeased – but an involuntary sound from DS Jones causes him to turn.

He sees the goosebumps on her bare shoulders.

Now he pulls off his jacket in earnest.

'Here – you should have taken this before. You've got chilled.'

This time she accepts – and then cups with both hands the tin mug that he proffers.

She sips cautiously; Skelgill's functional temperatures would be found at the upper end of the Three Bears' scale. Notwithstanding her delayed reaction, she responds to his reproach in an even tone.

'I didn't want to attract attention.'

Skelgill harrumphs.

'You couldn't attract any more attention.'

She eyes him knowingly over the edge of her mug.

'But there's the wrong and right sort.'

He is about to argue when he realises she has the more persuasive of the two points of view. But he shrugs, all the same, as if he would have thrown caution to the wind.

He settles down a yard apart from her; there is a convenient rock seat, and they both drink in silence. Before them small dark birds in pursuit of insects put on a mesmerising display. After a while, Skelgill speaks musingly.

'You never know when you've seen your last swallow – not at the time.' DS Jones does not answer, but she keeps watching the birds. 'These could be our last. Except I reckon they're sand martins.'

'How can you tell?'

Skelgill makes a face.

'We'll ask the Prof – he's a bit of a twitcher.'

2. THE PROFESSOR

Braithwaite – 8.08 a.m., Sunday, 19ᵗʰ September

'Oh, certainly they could be sand martins, Daniel – although it is getting rather late. They tend to be the earliest to arrive in spring and among the first to depart in autumn. They winter in the Sahel. But there are river cliffs hereabouts where they excavate their nest tunnels. It is a Holarctic species – the Americans call it the bank swallow.'

Skelgill nods enthusiastically. Their host being a renowned home baker, he munches on a rib-sticking treacly confection, oaty parkin.

'However, methinks you have not come to pick my brains about ornithology.'

He has the good grace not to suggest a post-angling snack as an alternative reason for the impromptu dawn visit. Skelgill certainly looks like he has been fishing, and DS Jones, having donned a hoodie and jeans from the boot of her car, could just feasibly be an accomplice.

Skelgill inclines his head towards his colleague, an indication that she will explain.

They are seated at the solid oak table in the cosy stone-flagged kitchen of Jim Hartley's Braithwaite cottage. DS Jones now has the dinner menu and the driving licence in clear polythene evidence bags, and she lays the exhibits carefully before their host. Angular shafts of morning sunlight penetrate a small casement window to illuminate her display and the fine smoke of steam that rises from their mugs.

'Earlier this morning the body of a man was found beside the River Derwent.' She places a carefully manicured finger first on the driver's ID card and then upon the menu. 'We believe him to be

Kyle Betony – and that he attended this dinner at The Partridge Inn.'

The professor raises both hands in alarm and rakes bony suntanned fingers into his unruly shock of white hair. He pores over the licence, and then looks up, clearly shaken, first at DS Jones and then at Skelgill.

'But – Daniel – young lady – I was there. I am on the committee. I saw him – only last evening.'

Skelgill nods in a confirmatory manner, that he knows this, and here is the purpose of their call.

The professor is clearly lost for what to say; and Skelgill requiring to gulp tea. DS Jones continues evenly.

'We need to establish what were Mr Betony's last movements. There is no CCTV at The Partridge. We guessed you might have been at the dinner. We thought you could tell us who else was present.'

The professor's expression is one of great concern; but he appears to gather his wits.

'Certainly – I can print off a copy of the committee members' contact details – that ought to save you some time. But, what on earth can have happened? He seemed perfectly fine when we left.'

DS Jones politely picks up on the ambiguity in his reply.

'When you say "we", Professor Hartley?'

The retired academic looks up in surprise.

'Please – call me Jim, as your boss does.' He grins, a little sheepishly. 'You rather remind me of a former student and I feel like I should be critiquing an essay. I never liked to disappoint a person.'

Whether there is the implication that he thinks he will disappoint them, he is no more forthcoming. He glances interrogatively at Skelgill.

'You know Alice Wright-Fotheringham, of course – and that she is also on the committee?'

'Aye. Good old Alice. She still holds the Derwentwater sea trout record.'

Jim Hartley turns back to DS Jones.

'Alice lives in The Heads – at Keswick – and so must pass here. She habitually gives me a lift to committee meetings.' He makes a subdued murmur. 'We old codgers have to stick together. This morning she has a commitment at her church – she wanted an early night. That suited me just fine – you know how it can be awkward prising oneself away from these gatherings? So, we left at ten p.m., immediately after dessert was served. The others – Kyle Betony included – were all still seated in the restaurant.' He stares intently at the formal dinner menu, his bushy white brows knitted. 'The thing is – I didn't even speak with him – because of the seating arrangement. And I'm not even sure that Alice did – neither of us was next to him, you see?'

Skelgill now interjects. He is perhaps a little more forthright with his acquaintance of long standing.

'Jim – can you give us a quick low-down?' He waves a hand in a circular motion. 'Seating plan – who's who.'

'Of course. Of course.' The professor bows his head obligingly. It seems he joins the underlying dots. 'And I suppose it must be possible that he said something to someone that will help you.'

He sees DS Jones reach for her reporter's notepad and he waits for her to flip to a blank page before pronouncing, the lecturer in him so accustomed.

'It was a single long table. It was originally set for five either side and one person at the head – I suppose that was going to be the Chair – but Lucy Bedlington sent her apologies late in the day and it was reorganised so that no one was an orphan at one end.

'I was at the top, so to speak, on my side, and Alice beside me on my right. So, opposite me was Monty – Sir Montague Brash – you would know of him, of course, a substantial landowner. He has been Chair for the best part of a decade, I should say.

'On Monty's left was Georgina Graham – she is Secretary – very efficient. I think she may be a personnel manager – quite high-powered – she's always jetting off to New York or Hong Kong or Abu Dhabi or some such far-flung place. Yet she always has the minutes out the next day – give a busy woman a job – as the saying goes. Oh – and some kind of Scrabble champion, I believe.

'Beside Georgina was Ruth Robinson – she and her husband farm at Kirkthwaite – they've had the tenancy for many years. Naturally they have an interest, in that we anglers use their land.

'Then there was Anthony Goodman – he is Treasurer. He works at the private nursing home at Bothel – I think in an administrative role. Charming fellow – and highly competent.' Jim Hartley gives a shake of his head, as though he rues his own failings. 'Finally, on that side was Jay Chaudry – he's an interesting character. A businessman – has his own IT company in Manchester. He bought Castle How farm over at Orthwaite and has it under management – I think he's keen to assimilate into the rural community. He has made a couple of sizeable donations to the club.

'Opposite to Jay sat Stephen Flood – he's actually a Scot but he's lived in the area for some years. Archetypically dour, but a useful chap to have on the committee – he's some kind of surveyor for Cumbria Water. It means we get the heads-up on their schemes, hair-brained or otherwise, so that we may represent our position.

'Then coming back up the table it was the said Kyle Betony.' The professor pauses and stares for a respectful moment at the driver's licence. 'I know little of his background – I've never actually had a one-to-one chat with him. Quite often we turn up just in time to begin – and generally Alice and I leave directly afterwards. I actually have no idea what he did for a living.

'And finally –' He glances at DS Jones's page as if to check for completeness. Aside from the names, she is making notes in rapid shorthand, and she turns the pad for him better to see the table layout that she has drawn. 'Yes – that just leaves Jackie Baker, who was sitting beside Alice. Jackie and her partner run Applethwaite House. The connection for her is that they get a lot of anglers as guests – and she is also on a hospitality committee – which is handy because we generate a good share of our income from visitor permits, which they promote through all of their members.'

He watches while DS Jones produces additional hieroglyphics, more or less keeping pace with him.

'I think that covers us all.'

But DS Jones has noted an omission.

'You mentioned – a Lucy Bedlington? The one who didn't attend.'

'Ah, yes, Lucy – I suppose for completeness.' He frowns, as though only now appreciating something. 'I believe she lives over towards Bewaldeth; she is a GP – I assume she was on call, and that was the cause of her late unavailability. She, too, is otherwise a mystery to me. In fact, now that you are asking me, I realise I know precious little about the lives of my associates.'

DS Jones does not appear disconcerted. She gestures at her notes with an open palm.

'You have a good proportion of women on the committee.'

The professor seems intrigued that she has noticed.

'Believe it or not we have a quota – equality – the Chair excepted. It was a resolution passed at an AGM some years ago. Quite progressive for a stuffy old angling society, don't you think? Of course, it doesn't really reflect the profile of the membership, and it would be fair to say that at times there has been some proxy attendance – but it makes for more amenable committee meetings – and our junior section has blossomed with perhaps more thought given to the encouragement of youngsters. A far cry from days gone by.'

He looks inquiringly at Skelgill, as if inviting him to agree. Skelgill's cheekbones perhaps redden – three decades ago he was a rare beneficiary, thanks to Jim Hartley's tutelage and patience, and the gift of a spare fly rod when Skelgill's family could certainly not afford such a thing.

DS Jones takes advantage of the hiatus to delve a little deeper.

'I know you said you didn't speak with Mr Betony. Did you form any general impression about him – about his behaviour – that with hindsight strikes you as unusual?'

The professor ponders. But after a few moments he shakes his head.

'I should not say unusual – and neither do I wish to disparage – but he is – he *was* – the pushy sort. Now I don't mean self-aggrandisement – rather that he was always full of ideas. You see, in most respects we're rather set in our ways.' The professor regards his audience a little apologetically. 'Don't get me wrong – the committee takes its task seriously – but these are volunteers who give up their own time. They may each have a small vested interest in the access or status being on the committee gives them, or just being in the know – but there is also an element of a cosy club, of meetings with like-minded folk – you know what I mean? To make suggestions in others' areas of expertise or responsibility carries with it an implied criticism that they are not doing their job well.

'Kyle Betony was the most recent member to join the committee – just over a year ago. He had moved into the area and had been involved with an angling club somewhere down south. The purpose of our annual dinner is to foster team spirit. It is a sort of reward for the year's attendance. But I perhaps did get the feeling that Kyle was up to his normal thing, ruffling a few feathers – a leopard can't change its spots, as they say. But I don't think there was any acrimony in the air – at most an aura of resigned frustration emanating from those around him.' He regards DS Jones more pointedly. 'My apologies – that was a long-winded answer to your question.'

But it is Skelgill that responds.

'How about drink, Jim – was there a lot of that going down?'

'Well, for my part I had a half-pint of Jennings when we arrived and eked out a glass of Chablis with the meal. Alice – nothing at all – alcoholic, that is. But you're wondering about Kyle Betony, in particular, I don't doubt. Well – it was lively, but merriness rather than drunkenness – and of course I have no idea of how late they might have stayed.'

He regards Skelgill shrewdly, although he seems to be holding back from speculation. Skelgill moves to relieve any pressure his old friend may be feeling.

'Most likely, Jim – he wandered off at the end of the night to clear his head. Leaned too far over Ouse Bridge and fell in. We'll get an autopsy – but probably not until tomorrow. It's best we hold fire, while there's nowt concrete.'

The professor nods reflectively.

'Was it at Ouse Bridge where he was found?'

Skelgill shakes his head.

'Nay – it was well downstream – happen he floated the best part of two miles. There's a big shingle bank on a bend where the current slows, just shy of Isel Bridge.'

'The Colonel's Pool?'

'Aye.'

But the professor is suddenly animated. He does not immediately speak, however.

'What is it, Jim?'

The older man seems a little reluctant to elaborate. He moves both hands in a calming motion, aimed it seems at himself.

'Well, merely that it rather puts the cat among the pigeons.' His tone is questioning, as if he half expects Skelgill to know what he might be talking about. He looks now at DS Jones. 'You see – the Colonel's Pool – a renowned salmon beat – is on Kirkthwaite land farmed by Ruth and Jack Robinson – and part of the Brash Hall Estate.'

DS Jones glances at her superior – but his expression is typically inscrutable – it is unclear whether this is news to him, or otherwise. Either way, he does not immediately comment. It is left to the professor to state the obvious.

'An unfortunate coincidence.'

Skelgill seems unruffled. He reaches for another slice of oaty parkin.

'These things happen all the time, Jim. My middle name ought to be Coincidence.'

3. MRS BETONY

Cockermouth – 11.11 a.m., Sunday, 19th September

Cockermouth – 11.11 a.m., Sunday, 19th September

'Want me to do the talking, Guv?'

'Aye – you can. But it's not like we've got to tell her he's dead.'

Skelgill looks as if he might just be a little conflicted by his colleague's offer. Nonetheless, there is an underlying note of relief in his voice.

DS Jones has another question.

'What did the FLO say?'

Skelgill has rejoined her in his car; she has been finishing off a call to headquarters. They are parked on double yellow lines on a steep rise in the old town centre, close to Cockermouth castle. He has been in confab with the Family Liaison Officer and a local uniformed constable who had awaited their arrival, and now handed over to them.

'They took her to identify the body. There's no bairns involved. She's much younger – from Thailand.'

A rat-a-tat-tat of facts. A panoply of broad detail. Skelgill turns to regard his colleague – she seems a little unsettled.

'How much younger?'

'Twenty-four.' Skelgill answers a touch cagily.

DS Jones cannot suppress a small involuntary raising of the eyebrows.

'He was forty-five – according to his driving licence.'

She senses his scrutiny, as though he tries to read how she calibrates this information.

She covers all bases.

'People can be mature for their age. And young at heart.'

Skelgill makes a scoffing sound. He has not fully closed the driver's door and now, with a glance at the wing mirror, he pushes it open. With a simultaneous heave and a groan, he begins to rise.

'I used to be old for my age – but I grew out of it.'

He hears a snatch of hysterical laughter as he slams the door. But the street barely takes two vehicles and he does not linger in the way of traffic. Instead he rounds to the shelter of the front of the car. He flexes his spine and grimaces as he surveys the property towering before him, a grand if neglected Georgian house, part of a continuous stuccoed terrace that gives on directly to the narrow pavement. They have established that Kyle Betony worked as an 'IFA' – an independent financial advisor – from a small office above an estate agency just a couple of minutes' walk along the contiguous main street. He had no criminal record and no judgements of debt against his name. Legally speaking, a clean bill of health.

Having volunteered to take the lead, DS Jones proceeds to ring the doorbell.

Over her shoulder, Skelgill prepares himself.

A new person, an unfamiliar dwelling – such a door opens to release a wave of first impressions like a dam bursting. It is easy to be overwhelmed by this flood of stimuli and notice nothing. Equally, to try too hard – to penetrate the advancing wall of the deluge – is perhaps to look for something that is not there, perhaps to imagine it is, or to mistake one thing for another – for example, fear for anguish.

Yet the small, slender, dark-eyed girl with long black hair defies Skelgill's expectations – her foreign appearance aside – for in her demeanour there is little to fasten onto, be it repressed upset or casual indifference. She greets them in a manner that seems neither thankful for their presence nor resenting their arrival. Skelgill is made to think of a well-schooled housemaid of old. But he reflects that shock can operate in mysterious ways – such as eliciting a paradoxical rush of energising elation in place of paralysing horror, perhaps the body's primal defence in times of crisis; no point in crumbling and also being eaten by the sabre-toothed tiger.

At once it is apparent that the newly widowed young woman's

English is excellent, and that her accent – if there is one – barely discernible, vaguely American. Perhaps the only clue to some essential disquiet is the way her gaze shifts frequently from one to the other of them, as though she scans for subtle messages that might pass unspoken between the two law officers. Her name is Jasmine.

They are led through a high-ceilinged windowless hallway past sitting rooms on either side, past a broad staircase with a traditional wrought-iron banister that curves out of sight, taking the eye to ornate plaster cornicework, and into a large back kitchen now merged with what was once the scullery, beyond which a small walled-in yard with double gates that would admit a car is visible through a mullioned window. There is a striking aspect. The place is clean and smells artificially freshened, but lacking in harmony, identity and personality. It reminds Skelgill of a slightly shabby holiday home and he immediately reaches the conclusion that this is a furnished rental property.

She seats them at a table and offers drinks, but for once Skelgill declines on their joint behalf – but when DS Jones puts in a supplementary request for a glass of water he joins her, much to her surprise – she has only ever seen him drink water from a mountain stream. And then he gulps it down, somewhat ostentatiously.

Settled, DS Jones reprises their roles and the purpose of their call. Perhaps knowing it can be unwise to ask how a person is – inviting a relapse into grief – against her better nature she proceeds in a businesslike mode.

'Mrs Betony, we do not yet know the exact cause of your husband's death. It appears to have been the result of an accident, and we have no reason to believe otherwise – but I'm sure you will understand it is important that we establish that fact.'

The woman is calm, and remains hard to read. She has some herbal tea. Skelgill stares – the drink is alien – but perhaps he is in fact registering the steady hand. DS Jones continues.

'You may know something – even that you have noticed inadvertently.'

But Jasmine Betony shakes her head with certainty.

'I would immediately have said.'

DS Jones nods amenably, but effectively ignores the closing off of the subject.

'Did he give any indication of why he might have left the hotel but did not just drive home? He didn't call you, for instance – to say that he would walk?'

Although speculative, this is the crux of the matter as far as the detectives are concerned. What drew Kyle Betony to the water's edge? It seems improbable that he would take on several miles of back lanes in pitch darkness. In the absence of his mobile phone, they rely upon her.

The question produces another shake of the immaculate head of raven hair. But she seems to grasp the underlying train of thought.

'He was a light drinker. I do not drive – he was always careful. Besides – he did not really like wine – and he thought the local beer is too warm and flat.'

Discord emanates from Skelgill – but he holds his peace.

DS Jones moves on swiftly.

'Did he mention that he was meeting anybody?'

'Just that it was the committee dinner. No person in particular. Although I don't really know who is who.'

'How did he seem – about attending the event?'

'He was a little excited. They dress up.'

Now there is perhaps the hint of a smile at the corners of the wide mouth with its full lips. It appears she was pleased for her husband.

'Did he speak of what they might discuss?'

The woman turns out her bottom lip; she looks perplexed.

'I don't believe there was a meeting. Kyle did not take anything with him.'

'At what time did he leave?'

'Seven o'clock. He was eager to arrive early.'

DS Jones pauses. By the fastest route it is a ten-minute drive to The Partridge – probably fifteen, door to door.

'Did he say what time he expected to be home?'

'Just that he might be a little later than usual – that I should not wait up.'

'And you didn't.' DS Jones intones evenly, knowing she is stating the obvious.

'I went to bed after the BBC World Service news at a quarter past ten.'

DS Jones frowns at her notes, as though she is dissatisfied with something she has written. But Skelgill can tell she is trying to appear casual; she has reached a decisive moment.

'And you noticed him missing – this morning?'

If there is any reaction, at most it is the semblance of surprise that she is being asked this question.

'It was your officers at the door – they woke me.'

Now DS Jones allows herself to sound a little curious.

'That was the first you knew?'

'I thought he must already have got up. It was his routine, to rise early every day – most of his work is with private clients, so they are equally responsive to correspondence at weekends.'

But now she volunteers a rider.

'I wondered – when he did not answer the door.'

DS Jones pushes the envelope a little further.

'Is it usual – that he could come home without waking you – and get up again, the same?'

'No – it is not usual – but it can happen.'

'How long have you been married?'

'Almost two years.'

'And how did you meet?'

'At a financial services conference in Bangkok. Kyle was based there. We began dating and then we married.'

'From Thailand – what made you come to Cumbria – Cockermouth?'

'Kyle often spoke of how he wanted to live in the Lake District. That he used to visit for holidays as a boy – from his home in London. That it is the most beautiful part of England.'

DS Jones detects Skelgill shifting a little in his seat. It is the sort of thing about which he would have something to say – probably irrelevant – and she is relieved that he again contains himself.

'Mrs Betony – how about you – do you work?'

'Oh yes – I –' She folds her hands, one over the other upon the table surface. They might be the hands of a child, were it not for nails immaculately manicured and lacquered in a subtle shade of lilac. 'I am a translator. Thailand's economy depends on exports, and many companies require their websites and communications in English.'

'So you're home-based?'

She nods.

'All I need is my laptop.'

Perhaps the declaration that she is footloose prompts DS Jones's next question.

'Do you think you'll stay – you're a UK citizen?'

The woman does not appear ruffled that such a question might be asked of her at this early juncture.

'I have dual nationality. But I have little reason to remain.' She seems faintly apologetic. 'This house, it is rented. We have been looking for a place to buy. But now – I am alone.'

Despite that Jasmine Betony still is so matter of fact in her manner, DS Jones cannot suppress her innate sororal compassion. The woman – the girl – is two years her junior. She regards her earnestly.

'Will you be okay?'

But the rejoinder is unexpected.

'Our wills and life insurance policies were made in one another's favour. It was Kyle's profession – so he took care that we were both well protected.'

It seems she has interpreted the question in purely pecuniary terms.

DS Jones judges that she should move on.

'Your husband – do you have a digital photograph that shows him clearly? It would be helpful, since we will be asking people at the hotel if they saw him leaving.'

'Yes, one moment.'

She rises and returns with her mobile phone. She has already found an image. She presents it to DS Jones for approval.

'It was taken here, in his study?'

Skelgill, too, leans forward better to see. The man is seated, turning to look over his shoulder. The contrast to the pale, lifeless countenance they witnessed earlier is stark. Here Kyle Betony appears dark and rather swarthy; there is something of a Machiavellian grin, a rather goblin-like face. But perhaps it is more representative of the man described to them by Professor Jim Hartley.

'Can you transmit it to me?' DS Jones manipulates her own handset. 'That's the Bluetooth on now.'

'Yes, of course.'

She does it easily. DS Jones checks it is received. She continues to look at the photo.

'Did you husband smoke?'

'No.' Jasmine Betony's answer comes quickly. 'I did not approve.'

The reply is interesting in several respects. DS Jones chooses one.

'You mean, he used to?'

The young woman gives something of a resigned smile.

'In Bangkok, it seemed like every man smoked.'

DS Jones nods.

But now Skelgill interjects.

'Mrs Betony, would you mind if we had a look at your husband's study?'

'Not at all, sir. Now?'

'Aye, please.'

She leads them back the way they came and lightly up the staircase to a landing that runs longitudinally through the house. The study is a room at the front, overlooking the street. The terrace opposite seems to loom uncomfortably close. Substantially overdue for a clean, the windows are grimy on the outside with dust and the dried salt spray cast up by traffic.

The desk is set into an alcove, rather than before the window, and the room is busy with filing cabinets and shelves. There is a printer and a small photocopier, a flashing modem, and a lot of paperwork and lever-arch files; though all seems well organised.

Skelgill backs away, and leaves it to DS Jones to make something of the arrangement; but she takes only a moment to cast her eyes over the work station. There is a black lever-arch folder marked DAA Committee Meetings on its spine. Its contents are divided into sections, standard sub-headings such as Agenda, Minutes, Chairman's Report, Accounts, Projects and AGM. She turns carefully through its pages, but it seems nothing more than a well-organised file packed with dreary minutiae.

'Would your husband have told you if there were any issues – any financial or legal difficulties?'

The question is ambiguous; DS Jones may be referring to the committee – or it could be the man's private life. Jasmine Betony regards her coolly; there is an impression of maturity beyond her years.

'His personality – he did not keep problems to himself. I would have known if he was troubled.'

DS Jones glances around. Skelgill has been perusing a low shelf on which there are lined novels and textbooks, business and fishing, crime and thrillers, and some periodicals. But when he might have been expected to pick up Trout & Salmon she sees that he is reading a true crime magazine. The cover puffs lurid stories – not least a special feature about the Moors Murders. Skelgill's expression is at once pained and vengeful. But he senses DS Jones's attention, and he looks up sharply, and inclines his head in the direction of the street.

DS Jones addresses Jasmine Betony.

'Unless it is for something essential, it might be best if you could leave everything in here as it is – just for the time being. A day or two.'

The woman nods compliantly.

'I have my own laptop, as I say.'

Skelgill is backing out of the room. He jerks a thumb over his shoulder.

'Mind if I use your bathroom? That water's gone right through me.'

Jasmine Betony responds with a rather submissive bow of her head.

'Of course, sir. It is the door facing, at the far end of the landing.'

Skelgill glances at his colleague.

'I'll catch you downstairs.'

*

They loiter in Skelgill's car, as if waiting for some inspiration to strike. DS Jones eventually breaks the silence.

'She doesn't come across like a mail-order bride.'

Skelgill gives a little sarcastic laugh.

'Is that what you thought I was expecting?'

'It is the cliché.'

'You know what they say about clichés.'

It is a throwaway remark, but she calls his bluff.

'That they are truths that no one believes.'

She surprises him with her retort, when he was just casually chaffing.

'Do they?'

'Yes – and an idiom is just a metaphor with a fan club.'

Skelgill stares ahead; he appears to force a grin. He knows enough of his colleague that she will say something provocative to get at his thoughts; but it is a tactic that relies on him having thoughts that are sufficiently formed, and the inclination to share them.

'Can we get back to the mail-order bride?'

DS Jones nods pensively. In part, she sticks to her guns.

'She certainly didn't have mail-order English.'

Skelgill can at least concur with this assessment.

'Aye – she's got her head screwed on.'

'She wasn't inquisitive about his death.'

Skelgill inhales, as a precursor to a caveat.

'Mind – she has been to see him. I reckon we can take it that part was covered.'

But DS Jones does not look entirely convinced. She offers a different take on her observation.

'If I had to guess, I'd say it's perhaps not the worst thing that's happened in her life.'

Now Skelgill looks questioningly at his colleague – but if he has something to say, no words materialise, and after a moment she speaks again.

'I wonder – how close they were.'

'They sleep together.'

'Ah!'

She regards him with a glint in her eye. She had suspected him of snooping, but not quite to go so far.

'Three bedrooms – two out of action. One's stacked floor-to-ceiling with removal boxes, the other's tiny and the bed's just a bare mattress. The master's got a king-size bed and personal stuff on both nightstands.'

Sympathy for the young woman does not prevent DS Jones from developing Skelgill's point.

'It seems odd to me – that she didn't notice his absence.'

Skelgill adopts a flippant tone.

'Can you kip for that long?'

His colleague shrugs, a little resignedly.

'As a student I could sleep for England. I still can, left to my own devices.'

Skelgill frowns; but it might be that he struggles to reconcile what is a widespread habit with his own proclivity for wakefulness.

'I find the only advantage of sleeping is that I catch bigger fish.'

DS Jones grins.

'I think we all do.'

Skelgill glances at her acutely – but she does not give him time to dwell upon her meaning.

'We only have her word for it. What if she didn't expect him to come home?'

Skelgill looks doubtful.

'It was hardly a late-night knees-up. And they weren't booked in.'

DS Jones nods pensively, she is ever conscious of Skelgill's antipathy for conjecture that might be wildly off track. But the young Thai woman's bearing has affected her more profoundly than it has her superior. She voices her surmise.

'If Jasmine Betony thought her husband were having an affair – I'm not sure she would tell us.'

She makes eye contact with Skelgill, in a small way defying him to gainsay her.

But perhaps he reads that this is gut feel and not logic, and thus in a perverse way it is an approach he cannot decry, groundless as it may be.

Notwithstanding, he turns away with a half-shrug and an exhalation of breath that is at best non-committal.

When he does not answer, DS Jones retreats to firmer ground.

'I got the impression that Professor Hartley was being diplomatic – that Kyle Betony was more of a busybody than a dedicated angler.'

'I'd need to see his kit. He read the right magazines.'

DS Jones watches Skelgill for a moment or two; she knows well enough that he operates more by gradual osmosis than sudden fits and starts.

'What did you think about those true crime magazines?'

Skelgill slumps back in his seat and folds his arms.

'There's plenty of folk interested in that stuff.'

But he sounds as though it is a circumstance that troubles him.

DS Jones offers a supportive observation.

'I don't know why they have to keep rehashing the Moors Murders. It was the Sixties. They caught them. They died in prison.'

But Skelgill remains disparaging.

'Because justice wasn't done, was it?'

'What do you mean?'

'Justice is like offence – to be effective, it needs to be taken as well as meted out.'

DS Jones nods pensively.   She responds in kind to his reasoning.

'Guilt and psychopathy – they're like oil and water.'

'Is that the title of your latest essay?'

DS Jones, it is true, is undertaking continuous professional development. But she gives a little ironic laugh.

'Not exactly.'

When she does not elaborate, Skelgill presses her. He inclines his head towards the Betony house.

'Reckon she's a psychopath – is that what's bugging you?'

DS Jones looks for a moment as though she will contest the assertion that a 'thing' would bug her. She shakes her head.

'It's said one of the first signs of a psychopath is that they are over-endearing, ingratiating.'

'No danger I'll be mistaken for one, then.'

DS Jones chuckles – it is a rare flash of self-appraisal.

He starts the engine and jams the car into gear, drawing a protest from the long-suffering transmission.

'Howay, lass – let's see if Charlie's Saskia's still kipping for England.'

4. POST MORTEM

Police HQ – 12.22 p.m., Monday, 20th September

'The nippers think it's marvellous, Guv. I can't believe we ain't discovered it before. Gets you out and about – fresh air – adventure – take your own picnic. And it don't cost an arm and a leg.' DS Leyton, seated beside Skelgill's tall grey filing cabinet, throws up his hands animatedly. 'Take our lot to the multiplex and I've had me pocket picked for the thick end of a ton before I've drawn breath. How am I supposed to afford that every weekend? I'm a one-man cost-of-living crisis!'

Skelgill is regarding his subordinate a little smugly, as if he takes some credit for DS Leyton's newly discovered family hobby of geocaching.

'Find some treasure, Leyton. Kill two birds with one stone.'

'Yeah – but it ain't actual treasure, Guv – it's little trinkets, toys, crystals, collectibles – stuff you can swap over that don't cost a packet. I reckon it's even educational.'

Skelgill is just about to speak when instead he holds up a warning hand.

There is a male voice and the click of heels approaching in the corridor; the door is ajar.

Then the footsteps accelerate to a little crescendo and the door is pushed open.

It is the besuited and gaunt form of DI Alec Smart.

He leans in with a leer.

Then he transfers his attention to the corridor.

DS Jones appears, bearing a tray of drinks and other materials; it is evident she has been accosted en route, the chivalrous DI Smart clearing her path.

He remains at the threshold, keeping the door open as though it

53

were sprung, which it is not.

DS Jones hesitates, then makes a face of resignation and plunges past him, closer than she would wish.

She crosses to Skelgill's desk to deposit her load.

DI Smart pats the seated DS Leyton on the shoulder. 'Alright, cock?' He makes brief eye contact with Skelgill. 'Skel. Nice day for it.'

Skelgill merely glowers.

DI Smart is not discouraged.

'I see you got a conviction in your Ambleside case. The Wicked Witch of Pendle, they're calling her.'

Skelgill permits himself a limited reaction, a slightly superior sideways glance; his subordinates, taking his lead, remain subdued.

DI Smart grins. He rubs his hands together in the fashion of a baker rolling a ball of dough into a sausage.

'Almost didn't recognise you in that press photo in a suit on the court steps, Skel.' He laughs a little manically and turns his gaze with its hint of a strabismus upon DS Jones. 'The bunch of you looked like you were rehearsing for a wedding.'

There is something of a pregnant pause; it is never easy to discern DI Smart's motive; more often it is to sow discord or wreak embarrassment. Today, however, the usually disingenuous note seems absent from his Mancunian drawl. Certainly, an outsider overhearing the mainly one-way conversation would wonder what he has done to deserve such an unreceptive hearing.

'Nice one. Sound. Nice job, Team Skelgill.' He tugs at the lapels of his designer suit – and perhaps he even sighs wistfully. 'Love you and leave you.'

And he backs out and pulls the door completely shut behind him, further uncharacteristically eliminating any potential for eavesdropping.

Skelgill's sergeants share bemused looks.

Skelgill, however, remains distrustful. He addresses DS Jones.

'What was it you were saying yesterday – about psychopaths?'

She raises her eyebrows in the affirmative – she sees what Skelgill is driving at. But she does not develop the point. Now that they are left to their own devices, she rises from her seat to hand out the teas.

It is DS Leyton, somewhat in the dark, who picks up the thread.

'Are we on the trail of a psychopath?'

Skelgill sups from his mug before he answers.

'Leyton, we might not be on the trail of owt much at all.' He turns again to DS Jones. 'What's Herdwick saying?'

DS Jones has her tablet in one hand; she raises it illustratively.

'Any moment. I spoke with his assistant – the draft PM report is just being proof-checked.'

DS Leyton now chimes in.

'So it's a geezer in a monkey suit and a late-night dip that's gone down the Swanee?'

His rather ill-construed idiom is perversely apposite, although Skelgill looks at him askance, before referring the matter to DS Jones.

'Did you get Leyton's wording – for the Coroner's report?'

DS Leyton looks a little sheepish. However, he mounts a defence.

'I'm just going by the hearsay. Sounds like he's had a skinful and gone for a sly fag. Missed his footing in the dark.'

DS Jones is nodding in a more collaborative way: that they have considered this line of thinking. However, she outlines their contrary finding.

'His wife insists he didn't smoke. At least, it sounds like not since they were married.'

DS Leyton gives a weighty shrug of his broad shoulders.

'From what I can gather, there's no such thing as a retired smoker. Only resting.'

The idea of an accident fits both Skelgill's initial instincts and the statistics that underpin such incidents – but he has an objection.

'Leyton – the nearest point from the pub to the water – Ouse Bridge – it's a good few hundred yards. If you wanted to smoke there's a garden with seats – right on the doorstep.'

He rises with his mug and turns to look at his county map. It is not of a scale conducive to support the case he has just made, but it does contain the ambit of Derwentdale Anglers' Association. 'Derwentdale' is a construct that has always troubled him, for he knows his maps (and the district) off by heart, and there is no such place. It seems that when the 'DAA' was established in the post-war period, there was already a rival club, and the more suitable epithet of Allerdale was taken (the 'AAA'). So the rebels and renegades had the idea of forming an association that would fish the entire length of the River Derwent, from its source in Sprinkling Tarn beneath the black cliffs of the Scafell pikes to its silt-streaked confluence with the Irish Sea at Workington, taking in the great bodies of Derwentwater and Bassenthwaite Lake, through which it flows. Derwentdale was born. The logic is infallible, although unlike, say, Haystacks, the name never caught on, and is known only to club members.

He stares introspectively, drawing back his upper lip to bare his front incisors; he is uncomfortable even with his own small contribution to their collective uncertainty.

And then, a notification.

It is DS Jones's tablet.

She pounces upon the device.

'Here it is.'

Her eyes scan rapidly. DS Leyton watches with a certain admiration as she skims the pages. Skelgill casually resumes his seat.

DS Jones's expression becomes conflicted.

She looks directly at Skelgill; she knows he wants the abridged version.

'Cause of death, asphyxiation through drowning. Blood alcohol level 78 milligrams – just within the legal driving limit. No trace of other intoxicating substances.' She allows just the merest of pauses, suggestive of drama to ensue. 'Blunt force trauma fracture to the back of the skull – limited contusion. Time of death estimated between ten p.m. and two a.m.'

'Someone's walloped him one!'

It is DS Leyton that reacts with jubilation; but Skelgill is looking grim.

He addresses DS Jones.

'And?'

She nods – she is ready for this and taps the tablet with her fingertips.

'He's added a note – he gets it that we would home in on the injury. I'll read. "The nature of the fracture suggests a rounded object with a point of impact of two to three inches across, such as a large elliptical pebble or the smooth edge of masonry. It is not possible to determine between rock-to-skull, such as in a blow inflicted, or skull-to-rock, such as in a fall. It can be inferred from the limited contusion – restricted subcutaneous bleeding – that the impact shortly preceded cardiac arrest, and is likely to have been sufficient to render the subject unconscious."'

She glances up at Skelgill to gauge his reaction, but he has already moved on.

'Two a.m. – what's he playing at?'

'Ah – there is a footnote. It states that the time of death is problematic because of uncertain duration of submersion in the water. He refers to something like putting a body into refrigeration.'

But Skelgill is shaking his head.

DS Leyton probes his superior's reaction.

'You reckon he died earlier, Guv?'

Skelgill shoots an accusing hand in the direction of DS Jones's tablet, a proxy for the police pathologist.

'Else what was he doing Leyton? The report says he weren't gattered – and he sustained the injury just before he drowned. There's only so long you can wander round in the dark.' Skelgill's tone is indignant. 'Any road, the river had dropped – by a good five or six hours' worth.'

DS Leyton nods, accepting the wisdom of his superior's watercraft.

'What have we got on his movements? Any CCTV?'

He glances from Skelgill to DS Jones; she obliges with the answer.

'There is no CCTV. Professor Hartley stated that Kyle Betony was at the dining table when he left just after ten. The female running the bar, Saskia, told us that everyone had either left the inn or gone to bed when she locked up just before midnight. If you recall, the reception desk is not in view of the front door but tucked away at one end of the central corridor – besides which, it is only staffed as required, by a call bell. PC Dodd interviewed the two waitresses who were serving in the restaurant, but they finished their shift at ten p.m. One of them did remember that Kyle Betony was late sitting down to eat – he sent his fish soup back to be reheated. The girl Saskia was ferrying drink orders from the bar; she says the bistro where residents were eating cleared out by nine-thirty and she confirmed that the angling dinner didn't begin to break up until after ten. Thereafter there was a mixture of diners and residents having coffees and after-dinner drinks in various of the public rooms, including some who hung back in the restaurant. Her impression was that people went home or up to bed in dribs and drabs – and that the dining party certainly didn't depart as a group.'

She leans back and crosses her ankles; she is wearing a close-fitting sports outfit with trainers and appears to be sockless, although a sharp eye would pick out the hem of trainer socks snug around her tanned ankles.

DS Leyton has listened carefully; but now he turns to Skelgill and changes the immediate subject matter.

'What do you reckon to the injury, Guv?'

Skelgill regards his sergeant pensively.

'If he went over the bridge, backwards – he could have cracked his head on the pier.'

'What about rocks in the river?'

But on this point Skelgill looks doubtful.

'Aye, there's rocks under the surface – but I reckon they'd be too deep.'

DS Jones chips in.

'People do get knocked out diving into swimming pools. How deep is the water beneath the bridge?'

Skelgill frowns.

'Saturday night – maybe six foot.'

It is inconclusive as a theory.

DS Leyton leans forwards, resting his palms on his ample thighs.

'Or some cove coshed him and hoiked him over? Chucked the rock in after him.'

Skelgill flashes a sideways glance at his sergeant – perhaps that he has employed a local word, and not entirely accurately. But he refrains from splitting hairs. And DS Leyton distracts him with a rider.

'What are the odds of it being some randomer?'

Skelgill reflects for a moment.

'I can't see it Leyton. These lanes are dead at night. No lights. Nowhere to hang about. Long, is the answer.'

Now DS Leyton cranes his neck, looking up to the ceiling and speaking musingly.

'If it were an accident, Guv – if he leant over the bridge and fell – skull-to-stone – frankly, our job's done, right? But if it's the stone-to-skull variety – then ain't we looking at one of your fisherfolk?'

It is of course the elephant in the room – it has been the elephant in the car and the pub and everywhere else that Skelgill and DS Jones have been since they breakfasted at Ouse Bridge early yesterday morning.

There ensues a silence.

After a few moments, Skelgill begins to look around his desk, as if he is wondering where are the biscuits; so close to lunch, DS Jones has not for once brought any. Rather reluctantly, he raises his mug and drains the contents.

DS Jones takes advantage of the question that hangs in the air; she hands out a trio of stapled pages. The first is a photocopy of her notebook, the information gleaned from Professor Jim Hartley, including the seating plan; the second is the list he supplied of the DAA committee members' contact details. There is a final sheet that contains the names and telephone numbers of hotel guests, recognition that she has not overlooked this aspect. Indeed, supplementary notes indicate that DC Watson has been assigned to follow up the latter, once the go-ahead is given, and that all DAA committee members have been informed both of the incident and to expect further inquiries.

She waits for Skelgill to pronounce.

'We can rule out the Prof and Alice.'

He states the obvious, in that this couple left while Kyle Betony was still in his seat – but there is an authoritarian note in his voice: that they would be above suspicion, in any event.

DS Jones is nodding – and now quick to make a suggestion.

'If you look at the seating plan – see how Stephen Flood was at the end of the table on Kyle Betony's right? I think he would be the person most likely to have engaged in conversation with him.'

Skelgill is unconsciously biting at the nail of the thumb on his left hand; he stares seemingly unseeing at the page before him. But when he speaks it is clear he has made an assessment.

'I'll talk to the Chairman. Leyton – you take the three other blokes.' He turns to DS Jones. 'That leaves the three women. You can drop me at Brash Hall – if you leave Ruth Robinson until last, I'll yomp along the Derwent and meet you at Kirkthwaite. Happen I'll drop in on the sheepdog that found him.'

DS Jones regards Skelgill quizzically; she would love to know by what logic he has allocated the interviews. The riverside stroll might not be the only factor in the equation.

But there is an intervention – a visible jolt from DS Leyton. He raises a finger, in the manner of a boy scout testing for the direction of the wind.

'What if he were dumped, Guv – on the river bank, I mean?'

There is a flash of the grey-green eyes and a contraction of features that might just be self-reproof on Skelgill's part. He folds his arms. His thoughts revert to his initial conversation with DS George Appleby – when he learned of the incident. "Washed up at the Colonel's Pool"; these had been the desk sergeant's exact words – and Skelgill had taken them at face value. Of course, at the scene he had checked carefully for signs of disturbance, and there were none. But the shingle was firm, and would not easily accept tracks.

But he is a little less candid with his colleague.

'Leyton – the spot's three hundred yards from the lane where Isel Bridge crosses the river. There's a fixed stile to climb over. That's some job to shift a dead weight in the dark.'

DS Leyton is phlegmatic.

'Just saying, Guv. It would be easy enough to drive him along in the bucket of a tractor – across the fields, like.'

Skelgill senses that DS Jones is staring at him. They both know that DS Leyton has inadvertently touched upon the fact that Kyle Betony's body was found on land farmed by one committee member and owned by another.

But speculation, that mortal enemy of the detective, threatens to run amok. Skelgill drops his elbows onto his desk, intertwining his long fingers. He looks at DS Leyton, seated opposite.

'We're talking witnesses not suspects, right?' His tone is insistent.

DS Leyton nods obligingly. Skelgill turns to DS Jones. The sun has emerged from behind a cloud and he squints as the light flares about her, igniting bronze highlights in her hair.

'Make sure the press office stress that it's an accident. And no need to mention the name of the hotel – or the exact location of the body.'

DS Jones, too, nods in accord.

Skelgill relaxes his grip and gently, perhaps subconsciously, he punches his left fist into his right palm.

'And be on your guard with Smart – if he's got wind of this, I don't trust him not to gum up the works.'

5. MONTY

Brash Hall – 2.04 p.m., Monday, 20th September

'ait!'
    'What?'
    'Duck!'

Skelgill – just as he was about to open the door, has instead slid down into the passenger seat of his colleague's car, as best the cramped space will allow his gangly form. DS Jones, perplexed – but understanding the principle of his order – bows her head against the steering wheel.

It is possible that, at a glance, the car looks empty. They each have their windows partially open, and there is the crunch on gravel of slow footsteps that pass in the middle distance; to their relief they do not halt or waver, but disappear from earshot. They are parked on a sweep of driveway that curves around beneath ancient limes to give them a view of the linear sandstone pile that is Brash Hall; it could almost be half a street in Georgian Bath or Edinburgh, or one side of London's Grosvenor Square. The way continues to what looks like stable blocks at the rear. DS Jones turns to glimpse her superior – evidently he had spotted the person responsible for the footfalls and did not want them to be seen.

After a moment, Skelgill cautiously resumes a normal position.

He stares at his colleague interrogatively; it is clear he is processing some revelation.

'Yesterday morning at The Partridge. When the alarm went off. The bloke who opened the window – did he see you?'

'Well –' DS Jones hesitates. She is unsure of what answer Skelgill is looking for. Of course the person must have seen her.

'Your face, I'm talking about?'

'I don't think – no – I had my back to him. I didn't realise there was anyone there until the window closed. The alarm was so loud.'

When under most circumstances Skelgill would have been dismayed that she is unable to corroborate his inquiry, it seems he is in fact satisfied with her response.

'It was him.'

'What do you mean – who?'

'Sir Montague Brash – in the bedroom at The Partridge.' Now he gestures towards the country house. 'He just walked past.'

'Ah.' It takes her a moment to get her bearings. 'I assumed that you knew him. Through fishing, I mean.'

But Skelgill shakes his head, glowering a little.

'I reckon we don't exactly move in the same circles. Like I said – I'm just a member – I don't get involved in social events and the like. And the angling club's not like cricket – it's not as if you play as a team and practice together twice a week. I might not see another member from one year to the next. Suits me down to the ground.'

DS Jones nods pensively. In her estimation Skelgill's lone wolf tendencies extend to the otherwise collaborative summer game; as a fast bowler he stalks in from the distant boundary to hunt his prey, and return unsung with scalps in his belt.

But she is quick to see the corollary of his assertion about Sir Montague Brash.

'So – someone did stay over?'

Skelgill now looks conflicted – almost a little cheated.

'There's no way Charlie wouldn't have told us.'

DS Jones accepts Skelgill's assessment of his hotelier friend.

'Charlie wouldn't have to know.'

Skelgill scowls.

'What's Brash doing – staying at The Partridge when he lives here – a quarter of an hour's drive.'

'Maybe he drank too much and just decided to crash out – if a room were unlocked? He's obviously familiar with the place.'

'Do you think that?' His tone is leery.

DS Jones smiles.

'Well – I can think of a more scandalous explanation – but I know you don't like idle gossip.'

Skelgill forces a perfunctory grin.

He stares coldly at the house.

'You'll need to interview him.'

'Pardon?' This represents a sudden change of plan.

'He eyeballed me on Sunday – he looked right at me.' He squints at her appraisingly. 'Put your hair in a band, or summat.'

DS Jones regards her boss reflectively.

'You mean – we – *I* – don't ask the question – why did he stay at The Partridge?'

Skelgill nods.

'Exactly. Play it as if we didn't know. If he's got nowt to hide, he'll tell you.'

'And, if he doesn't?'

'Leave it be.'

DS Jones's expression becomes rather musing – possibly even amused. But she goes along with Skelgill's approach. She produces a hair band from the door pocket and gathers in her fair locks. Skelgill watches with some apprehension; carrying the legacy of long summer days, it is a striking feature that could give her away. But he is reasonably confident; the man had glared at him, correctly identifying him as the cause of the commotion. Moreover, he had withdrawn himself quickly, in a manner consistent with the sudden realisation that he was unwisely exposing his presence.

Skelgill gives an involuntary shake of his head – a caution against such post-rationalisation.

DS Jones has a clipboard. On top is a printed sheet, an empty table headed "Witness Report", designed intentionally to convey to an interviewee their status in the eyes of the police. It suits their purposes.

'I'll stick to the list. Will you just wait?'

Skelgill suddenly seems a little vulnerable.

'Aye – I reckon so.' A thought strikes him. 'Leave us your keys – in case I need to beat a retreat.'

'You would probably be better off in the driving seat.'

Skelgill grimaces.

'You're in the driving seat now, lass.'

She taps her clipboard decisively against the steering wheel and turns to flash her even white teeth in a confident smile.

'Leave it with me.'

*

Skelgill is indeed in the driver's seat when DS Jones re-enters the car a good half-hour later. In the absence of distractions it has been a rather agonising wait and perhaps he drives away as much to release the coiled spring within him, as to take no chances of being identified. He wonders if the car is watched from a window and thus the watcher will know that DS Jones has an accomplice. A little earlier, a young woman, blonde, had passed on horseback, and he had again taken cover below the dashboard.

For her part, DS Jones knows not to wait to be asked, or to beat about the bush.

'He didn't come clean.'

Skelgill makes as if to speak – but then allows her to continue.

'But he was very clever – and he has that way, you know?'

Skelgill declines to be drawn – her suggestion is far too subtle, and he dislikes the implication. He stares ahead.

But now DS Jones is momentarily reticent. For the upper-class charm and handsome looks of Sir Montague Brash had been turned upon her full beam – and she is not intending to give Skelgill a blow-by-blow account – if she did, she can imagine him performing a U-turn in order to deliver a blow or two of his own. Such is life.

But she had held her own. Though it was not easy, she had risen to the challenge. Moreover – and notwithstanding her police status and (latent) feisty nature – she had been the one with an ace up her sleeve. The Knight of the Realm must have, if not suspected that she knew, then at least felt in thrall to his secret. Beyond the grand sash windows of the sitting room, and a mown grassy ha-ha, a broad stretch of the River Derwent bisected rough grazing meadows; Sir Montague Brash had constantly glanced that way – DS Jones could not escape the sensation that he feared a badly weighted corpse might any moment bob to the surface.

'He said he left The Partridge at about eleven fifteen and arrived home at eleven thirty.'

'So he outright lied?'

DS Jones ponders, a knowing smile forming at the corners of her mouth.

'Look – we agreed I would let him choose his own length of rope?'

'Aye.'

'So, I didn't press him. I suspect if it came to the crunch and he was forced to confess, he would insist that he had meant Sunday a.m. and not Saturday p.m. A white lie, maybe.'

Skelgill raises his head to show he understands. Not so much a white lie as dark grey – but he does not comment.

'So, my next question was whether Kyle Betony was still there, and if not when did he last notice him. Or, indeed, did he see him leave? His answer was that he himself had not left the dining table – he had remained seated, in conversation with Georgina Graham. If you recall the seating plan, Sir Montague Brash was at the end opposite Professor Hartley and she was beside him. He says he is not sure what time Kyle Betony left the table – that he wasn't paying particular attention. But he and Georgina Graham were the last two remaining, and they left directly from the restaurant; they parted just inside the front porch. She went out to a waiting taxi and he visited the gents', after which he saw no one. Presumably he sneaked up the stairs instead of leaving.'

But Skelgill has another idea.

'Did you notice that flight of steps that comes down by the garden door? It's the fire escape from the first floor. If that were left unlatched he could have gone out by the toilets – and back up on the outside. Even less chance of being spotted, and anyone seeing him would have thought he was leaving the same way we did.'

DS Jones considers the suggestion; it would be the kind of simple practical expedient that comes naturally to Skelgill. But she offers nothing further.

'And?'

His prompt seems to surprise her.

'Well – to be honest – that's just about it.'

'What took you half an hour?'

'Was it half an hour?'

Skelgill gives her a sideways glance and then has to make a sudden adjustment to his steering; the narrow lanes demand continuous concentration. The near miss with the verge and its wobbly aftermath provides a small respite for DS Jones to recover her composure. She had seemed momentarily compromised, and now Skelgill appears to be driving faster.

DS Jones reverts to her clipboard.

'He's fifty-eight. Married. Four children. About to go riding with his daughter.' She pauses as though to give particular emphasis to these facts. 'And a little arrogant. I would say that as a landowner he considers that being Chairman is an entitlement – and that he sees himself above most of the committee and no doubt the members – and that he probably doesn't greatly dirty his hands with the club's business.'

Skelgill, now focusing upon the winding lane, seems a little mollified. But he waits for her to continue.

'Obviously, there were the formalities – completing his personal details. And he did express concern for Kyle Betony's connections. He asked whether there was anything the committee could do by way of help or comfort – he said he didn't know him well, but he was aware that he had a young foreign wife.'

'Did you ask him how come Betony joined the committee?'

She nods.

'I did – but he referred me to the Secretary – Georgina Graham – she handles the formalities of appointments.'

Skelgill seems to be brooding over this point.

'Jim mentioned he'd been in a club down south – but we know he was in Thailand two years ago.'

But they do not speculate further.

'What about the fact that Betony turned up on his land?'

'Well – firstly, I did ask whether he knew of anything that could shed light on the accident.' Again, she hesitates before continuing. 'You know – for a moment I thought he was going make a joke about it. He said he must have a word with his gamekeeper – as if he had been over-zealous. Then I realised he meant it was remiss of his keeper not to be the one to discover the body.'

Skelgill is reminded of boyhood escapades in the very area, of playing hikey-dykey with a former keeper in hot pursuit.

'He did however quip that, if this were a detective novel, someone would be trying to make him look like the guilty party.'

Skelgill's retort is sharp.

'You told him it were an accident?'

'Of course – it was the first point I made, and I stressed it again. That we are working on the assumption that Kyle Betony fell off Ouse Bridge, drowned and was subsequently washed up on the shingle bank.' She hesitates reflectively. 'He rather made light of that, too – he said he might have to think about renaming the Colonel's Pool in his memory.'

Skelgill makes a face of disapproval.

'So – what's your summary?'

DS Jones is not expecting the question. She sinks back into the passenger seat. Perhaps Skelgill is beginning to trust her intuition as much as her facility for logical analysis. But her intuition had been strained by a succession of subtle attempts to charm her, artfully concealed as good breeding.

'I would say he went to some lengths to act with supreme casualness – but that it was not about the corpse in the river. More likely the room at the inn – assuming it were he.'

Skelgill forces the small car around a tight bend; his eyes are unblinking. He dismisses the caveat that undermines her certainty.

'It were him, alreet. I'd recognise that great beak a mile off.'

DS Jones glances across, the hint of a smile on her lips; a small case of kettle and pot.

But Skelgill now takes the initiative. He slips his mobile phone from his shirt pocket and hands it over.

'Let's see what Charlie's got to say.'

DS Jones understands what to do. She manipulates the screen. 'Would it be "C"?'

Skelgill gives a bow of his head.

She grins. Handy shorthand until you know two Charlies. Then there are Juliet, Mike, Oscar, Romeo and Victor.

'Shall I put it on speaker?'

'Aye.'

She fixes his handset into her holder.

The hotelier evidently recognises Skelgill's call.

'Danny – how's it going?' Understandably there is an apprehensive note in his voice. Skelgill skips any preliminaries. Though he does show a certain sensitivity.

'Nowt to worry about, Charlie – are you in the office?'

'I'm at reception, yes.'

'Saturday night – what was the name of your booking for the Skiddaw suite. That's the room over the porch, aye?'

'Er – yes.' He sounds surprised – but obliges. 'Hold on.'

There are the clicks of a keyboard, and hems and haws under the breath. And then a little sound of revelation.

'It was a Mr and Mrs Smith.'

The man's tone carries just a hint of resignation – that, in tandem with the detectives' inquiry, the predictability of his finding is telling. For their part, Skelgill and DS Jones exchange a brief knowing glance. DS Jones takes up her clipboard and frowns at the guest list – the so-named couple ought to have jumped off the page – albeit the details were supplied without indication of room allocation.

It is Skelgill that responds.

'We thought it might have been them. Did you see them?'

There is a considered intake of breath from the hotelier.

'Can't say as I did. But that's not unusual. I don't generally do check-ins or service. Plus we had private visitors, like I said.'

Skelgill is nodding, accepting the point. He stands by his earlier assertion that his good acquaintance would not hold out on them. But he tries one more time.

'Put it another way – did you recognise any of your paying

guests on Saturday night?'

'No – is there someone I should have?'

'More like someone you would have.'

'Ah.'

He seems to understand he is not going to learn the identity of the mystery person at this juncture.

Now DS Jones interjects.

'Charlie – it's Sergeant Jones. Can you tell anything from the booking – Mr and Mrs Smith?'

There is a short pause and more clicks.

'Not directly. It was made through an online booking aggregator. They took the payment. We don't see it – but there must be a credit card in their system. Your boffins could get at it, couldn't they?'

DS Jones agrees – but she avoids being drawn further.

In any event, the hotelier seems distracted.

'Is there any news on the chap who drowned?'

'We're still proceeding on the basis that it was an accident. We have just begun taking witness statements from the committee members.'

'I see.'

Now Skelgill chips in.

'There'll be a press release. We've made sure there's no mention of The Partridge – it's not necessary. The request for eyewitnesses refers to the vicinity of Ouse Bridge.'

'Righto.'

There is a note of relief in the man's voice – though perhaps just a tinge of disappointment, on the old principle that no publicity is bad publicity.

Skelgill signs off.

The detectives drive in silence for some moments.

It is DS Jones, scrutinising the list of Derwentdale Anglers' Association committee members, who finally poses the question that is on both their lips.

'So, who is *Mrs* Smith?'

6. WITNESSES

Afternoon – Monday, 20th September

Afternoon – Monday, 20th September

KIRKTHWAITE FARM, 3.07 p.m.

Ruth Robinson, 39, looks like she enjoys the cakes she bakes – and indeed has wasted no time in tucking in to the treacle scones that she has placed before her visitors, seated at a substantial oak table in the airy, somewhat untidy and disorderly but welcoming farmhouse kitchen. Pots bubble on a hob, and despite the home baking the smell is of boiled cabbage and evokes for Skelgill school dinners – but no less hunger. A Lakeland Terrier, initially guarded, has quickly worked out that Skelgill is its best bet and sits to attention at his side. It may not be apparent to another person that one is a dog owner, but there is no hiding it from their pooch.

'I said to oor Jack – I said – it would've been a sight better if he'd got himself washed up on t' other bank. I should think Sir Monty's livid.'

DS Jones, who has performed the necessary introductions, appears to conceal what might be reasonable consternation that the farmer's wife has exhibited such an offhand reaction to the fate of a fellow committee member. It might almost be as if they have borne the news that a neighbour's heifer has inconveniently drowned on the Robinsons' land.

For his part, Skelgill chews phlegmatically. Given the handbrake turn at Brash Hall he has decided to stick with DS Jones. There is also the practical expedient that they have only the one car between them. They have taken the nearest call first, when it was their previous plan eventually to rendezvous here at Kirkthwaite.

Moreover, there is the 'Mrs Smith' conundrum. On the

assumption that there actually was such a person with whom Sir Montague Brash spent the night, then – with the proviso that it might be a red herring as far as their investigation is concerned – Skelgill is of the view that he ought to see DS Jones's next three interviewees. And, while he is shrewd enough to know that his colleague is far less likely than he to be hoodwinked by female guile (even if he wouldn't admit it), he does perhaps possess the advantage of being able to see the candidates through Sir Montague Brash's eyes.

Accordingly, he has already reached the conclusion that Ruth Robinson is not Mrs Smith.

The woman is a curious mixture of what he thinks of as 'sheep' and 'hawk'. Medium-length mousy blonde curls and prominent rosy cheeks bat for the former, offset by a rather predatory arrangement of arched brows and curved nose. Chestnut eyes and a mouth of average proportions play neutrally.

His judgement may be a harsh one, and neglectful of facts such as her geographical proximity and subordinate relationship to the esteemed landowner. But there it is. Gut feel. If Sir Montague Brash drops in on horseback from time to time when Jack Robinson is mowing some distant meadow, Skelgill's guess would be that the output of her oven is the draw. Or is that an excess of personal bias creeping in?

While Skelgill keeps his own counsel, DS Jones immediately picks up on what is more than a nuance in the woman's lament.

'Mr Brash certainly expressed his concern – but why would he be upset – in the way that you describe?'

Perhaps Ruth Robinson realises that she must sound heartless; however, she makes no apology for her sentiments as expressed. On the farm, life goes on, death being part of it.

'I mean – no offence to the family, like – but it would be crocodile tears – I hardly knew the chap myself. But what I'm saying is, Sir Monty had that trouble a few years back – with the poacher that got blown up?'

Her inflection infers an assumption that they know of the incident – but the detectives shake their heads in a trained way that is both bland and designed to elicit further explanation.

'He'd broke into the keeper's bothy and tried to light the gas burner? No?' The detectives appear to remain in the dark. 'Bang! The gas went up – he lost a hand. Sued for compensation. Can you believe the cheek of it? Sir Monty had to settle out of court – cost him quite a packet, so they say.'

She has Skelgill's attention. He knows nothing of the case – but then, if the police had not been called – and the legal action was settled – why would he? However, despite that pointed questions jostle for prominence in his mind, he resists the temptation to enter into what would be a secondary digression.

DS Jones employs the matter at issue to get them back on track.

'We believe that Mr Betony fell into the river at Ouse Bridge – outside the boundaries of Brash Hall Estate. As you'll be aware, there is no easy access thereafter until Isel Bridge, and he was found upstream of that.'

Skelgill casts a sideways glance at his colleague. She has skirted the other possibility – DS Leyton's suggestion that the river bank may be reached from the farmstead, via a network of gated tracks.

Ruth Robinson's route home would have taken her across Ouse Bridge and on via dark lanes to Kirkthwaite. She seems perhaps a little quick to address this aspect.

'I surely never saw him. Not on my way home. I never saw a soul – didn't even pass another car.'

'You drove?'

'Aye – I didn't want to be late – Jack were getting up at five for milking – though I slept int' spare room so as not to disturb him.'

'Can you recall at what time you left The Partridge?'

'It must have been – I don't know – about twenty to eleven? That's right – the weather report was on the car radio when I arrived back – that's just before the eleven o'clock news.'

'Before you left – can you recall what Mr Betony was doing? Where he was, whom he was with – after the meal? In fact, did you speak with him yourself?'

The woman looks blank.

'He were sitting next to Jackie Baker – but I don't remember him being in our conversation – I think he were mainly talking with the men at his end of the table. There were a block of four men – and then a block of four women. The men talk about cars and football. You know what they're like.'

She looks at DS Jones and then at Skelgill – as if first she sympathises with DS Jones and then in a way that does not overly blame Skelgill for something his gender cannot help. Albeit cars and football rank low in Skelgill's repertoire of subjects on which he may hold court.

'Ooh!'

Suddenly the woman seems animated. But she has taken a bite of her scone and now must keep them on tenterhooks. She has a swig of tea – holding up a palm in apology at the delay she has caused.

'We went through for coffee – me and Jackie – into the residents' lounge next to the restaurant, you know? We were talking about Prince Andrew.'

She looks at DS Jones as though this would be the most natural subject of conversation. DS Jones nods encouragingly.

'He came across to us – he butted in.'

'Mr Betony?'

'Aye.'

'What time was this, would you say?'

Ruth Robinson looks a little surprised that this aspect can be more important than the topic of her chat. However, she yields and furrows her brow.

'Well – I couldn't say exactly – but if I had to guess it was, like, in between coffee and us leaving. We left at the same time. Jackie couldn't be late either – they're booked solid all month and she'd got to be up early to do breakfasts.'

DS Jones pulls it back to the crux.

'It seems that the meal ended at just after ten o'clock. So would that mean Mr Betony spoke to you at approximately – what – twenty past?'

She frowns again.

'Happen it were a bit later. The nice old professor and Miss

Alice, they announced they were leaving – so Sir Monty made a little speech – thanking everyone, like, for their service on the committee in the past year. It might have been ten past ten by the time we got us coffees.'

DS Jones makes an adjustment to her notes. The last sighting of Kyle Betony could prove to be the most crucial information they will glean from their interviews. Now it has been pushed back a little, to circa ten twenty-five p.m.

'You say he interrupted you. Was there something urgent?'

Now Ruth Robinson makes a face suggestive of impatience, the raptor gaining ascendency over the yowe.

'Oh, he's got – he *had* – a bee in his bonnet about selling more fishing permits. I mean – I know you shouldn't speak ill of the dead.' She makes a hand gesture that might be of self-reproach, and the sheep makes a brief appearance before the hawk returns and she promptly breaks her rule. 'He would keep mithering folk about it. He was a bit obsessed with money-making schemes. You see, with Sir Monty's ownership and our tenancy, we control a prime stretch of the Derwent, a good two miles. And Jackie's got her hotel contacts. Now, that's all very well – but it's Jackie that would have to do all the sales and marketing – and the likes of us that would have folk traipsing about leaving gates open and scaring the stock. Besides, Sir Monty keeps all the best beats and time slots for his school pals from London. Stockbrokers and hedge fund managers. He went to Eton, you know? They say he has some wild parties in the fishing lodge.'

DS Jones has listened evenly.

'Did Mr Betony seem particularly exercised over his scheme on Saturday night?'

The woman shakes her head.

'No more than usual. He said summat like, "Ladies – we must work on Sir Montague, make the business case" – like he thought we were all for it and only Sir Monty objected.'

'And how did the conversation turn out?'

Now she looks a little perplexed.

'I think he went away. Jackie and me – we looked at each other like: we'll be gone before he comes back round to us, thank heavens.'

'You mean he was canvassing members of the committee in turn?'

She nods.

'Perhaps, aye. I didn't really think much about it. Maybe he went off to bend Sir Monty's ear.'

DS Jones is completing her shorthand notes when Skelgill casually interjects.

'Mrs Robinson – I'm in the club myself. I've been in it since I was a junior. I've often wondered about standing for the committee.' He does not flinch when he senses DS Jones shifting in her seat.

The woman, who perhaps to Skelgill's minor annoyance has paid almost no attention to his presence, and certainly no deference to his rank, fixes him with a somewhat interrogative stare. Then she breaks into a rather lopsided smile that reveals crooked ovine teeth.

'Well – you'd always be welcome to try. I could propose you and Jackie would second. I can ask Georgina when the next elections are due?'

When a person might be expected to answer diplomatically, her forthrightness thus far suggests her words require no pinch of salt. Skelgill's bluff has been inadvertently called, and now he has to act out the charade.

'What are the pros and cons, would you say?'

She regards him more benignly now.

'There's no real cons, if you don't mind turning up for a meeting once a month. It's only if you're an officer that there's actual responsibilities – like doing the minutes and the accounts. And you don't even need to know owt about fishing – so you wouldn't have to worry on that score.'

The hint of a smile trying to escape her lips, DS Jones sneaks a surreptitious glance at Skelgill – knowing he will find it hard not to correct such a misapprehension. But Ruth Robinson emits a robust cackle and continues.

'Oor Jack – he always says I wouldn't know a rod from a perch from a pole!'

Skelgill knows this old anglers' saw – or perhaps it is more of a riddle – but he rather doubts that the woman understands what she repeats. Again, before he can muster a rejoinder, Ruth Robinson has more to say.

'I'm no fisher, myself, you see. It would be Jack – but there's only so many menfolk allowed on the committee.' She chuckles again, in part to herself, but then she turns to DS Jones to enjoin her in the joke. 'Just as well, eh, love?'

Skelgill grimaces, and while the two women trade artful smiles, he slips a quarter scone to the terrier.

PENRITH TO MANCHESTER BY ZOOM, 3.16 p.m.

'How's that, sir – can you hear me now?'

'Spot on, officer – I think you were on mute.'

'Cor blimey – if I ever get the hang of this, it'll be gone out of date.'

'I shouldn't worry, officer – it's my business and *I* can't keep up with it.'

'And I ain't speaking to you with Mickey Mouse ears – anything like that?'

'No, no – I have you clear as crystal – how about your end?'

DS Leyton grimaces into the computer screen. Not only is technology not his forte, but neither is an online interview his cup of tea. "I prefer to see the whites of their eyes, Guv" was his lament in discussing his schedule with Skelgill. But the latter's insistence that they mop up all the pertinent DAA committee members before close of play has meant for him a virtual meeting with Jay Chaudry, who has returned to his IT business in Salford's MediaCityUK. Now, he takes a moment to consider what he can determine. DC Watson's pro-forma tells him the man is aged forty-two and single; but that his home address is given as Castle How Farm, Orthwaite – on Skelgill's wall map the speck of a settlement near the small lake known as Over Water. He wears a striped shirt and a flamboyant jungle-pattern necktie; his regular features are cleanshaven and his black hair cut short in the modern style. But the image resolution is moderate, at best, and the man's dark eyes appear as black pools (no whites to be seen). His accent is only slight, Midlands perhaps. His manner is entirely cooperative, and DS Leyton, having himself begun in self-deprecating terms, maintains his disarming tone.

'If you don't mind my saying so, sir – you don't look like most of the farmers I meet.'

Jay Chaudry chuckles.

'I'm still learning to wear that hat, officer. Skip a generation and believe it or not I hail from an agricultural background – but a very meagre one, and the only way I was ever going to get back there was by making some money first. And, as I don't doubt you've heard, there's no fortune in farming.'

DS Leyton has trailed at Skelgill's heels long enough to appreciate there is some merit in this case, although agriculture, like many walks of life, is plainly not without its class system, the haves and the have-nots; but it is a debate for another day.

'What brought you to this neck of the woods, sir?'

'To be honest, it was by chance. I wanted a place within two hours' drive – I have an apartment here in the Quays – and Orthwaite was right on the limit. But the land agent that was on the lookout for me heard that the neighbouring farmer was interested in a joint venture. That made it perfect – Castle How Farm came with a hefted flock of three hundred Herdwicks – the sort of commitment I could never have taken on – never mind not having the first clue about sheep.'

DS Leyton is nodding. He congratulates himself that he understands what the man is talking about – the hefted flock being one of Skelgill's regular lectures. But there is a technical lag developing, and he is reminded he should get to the point before the screen freezes or the line drops out entirely. He approaches his object carefully, however.

'And how about the fishing, sir – where does that come in?'

The man raises both hands in an apologetic manner.

'Well, I'd be the first to admit I'm neither the most prolific nor skilled angler – but I had made a donation to an appeal to rebuild the bridge over Dash Beck that had been swept away by floods. I mean – don't get me wrong – it wasn't entirely altruistic – the lane was cut off to the south of the farm. I was asked along to a DAA committee meeting – I thought just to thank me – but they had a vacancy at the time and they seemed quite keen to co-opt me.'

'How long ago was that, then, sir?'

'It will be six years next January.'

'So, Mr Betony – he joined well after you?'

The man draws breath self-reproachfully – as if to acknowledge there is a more portentous matter that he has rather glibly avoided.

'Yes – he was the newest member – he came on board about a year ago, I should say.'

'Did you get to know him, at all?'

Jay Chaudry shakes his head – an action he perhaps exaggerates for the purposes of the camera.

'I can't say I did.'

'I thought he was the outgoing sort, sir?'

'Oh, well – yes, he was that. But for some reason I didn't personally click with him. He was perhaps a bit full of his own agenda – preoccupied, if you know what I mean? He never really stopped to find out what you were about. Whenever you met him he was straight in with his latest scheme.' The man pauses, it seems as if to ponder what has been an instinctively drawn sketch. 'When I think about it – Stephen Flood, for instance, is a bit of an introvert, and yet I feel I know him much better. And Anthony – Anthony Goodman – he's a chatty sort – but he's interested in other people for their own sake.'

DS Leyton is nodding along – in part wondering where this is going – but it provides enough of a bridge.

'Well – as you can imagine, sir – we're trying to understand whether there was anything that might explain what happened to Mr Betony. Can you recall when you last saw him?'

The man frowns, before responding more tentatively now.

'Well – speaking of Anthony Goodman – we were seated beside

one another for dinner. We went to get a coffee together from the lounge. Anthony had a look out in the corridor to see if the fireside chairs in the Snug were free – they were, so he bagged them and I followed him with the coffees.'

'What time was that, about, sir?'

'Maybe ten past ... a quarter past ten.'

'And was Mr Betony still at the table?'

There is a further hesitation.

'I think he was – he would have been talking to Stephen Flood, who was next to him. Yes – I think they were both still at the table. Oh, wait – were they? You know, you'd better not quote me on that – I'm not a hundred percent sure now.'

'And are you saying you didn't see Mr Betony again?'

'No, I can't say I did. I sat the whole time in the Snug with Anthony. I left at just after eleven.'

'You didn't get up for any reason?'

'No – I mean – we did have one for the road – a small Scotch – but Anthony fetched them from the bar. He seemed to think it was his round from the last committee meeting. Maybe he saw Kyle?'

DS Leyton does not indicate whether he already has such information.

'Going back to the dinner, then, sir. Was there anything that came up – anything that Mr Betony said – that would give you cause for concern – with hindsight – in view of what happened to him?'

Now Jay Chaudry looks plainly conflicted.

'Well – I'm sure he wasn't drunk, if that's what you're asking.' (DS Leyton scowls as though he has not heard properly, and waits until the man continues.) 'And he was certainly his usual talkative self – but I don't recall anything that made me think, wait a minute, this guy's going to jump in the river.'

DS Leyton jerks back a little. The turn of phrase is suddenly rather stark – but of course the idea of suicide is a natural conclusion to reach. And, while not entirely palatable, it suits the police who wish to justify their interest when a more sinister explanation might underlie their inquiry. However, DS Leyton edges closer to this latter possibility.

'There wasn't any argument – anything along those lines that might have upset him?'

For the first time the man looks a little alarmed – his eyes widen and now there are discernible whites.

'Oh, no – nothing like that, I'm sure. Besides – I'd say he was as thick-skinned as they come. He didn't seem to take offence if you knocked him back.'

'Can you recall what you discussed – as a group?'

He seems keen to answer – but gives the impression of grasping at the first thing that comes to mind.

'Well – we talked about football. Stephen Flood was winding the rest of us up. I'd managed to get the Wi-Fi working on my phone – and England were playing Liechtenstein in a World Cup qualifier.' (DS Leyton is nodding – he had bitten his nails through the dire performance.) 'I mean – they won 1-0 with a last-minute penalty – but we should be putting double figures past a side like that – population, what, about a third of Carlisle? Of course – Stephen's a Scot and he was loving it.' He reflects for a moment. 'That said – I don't think Kyle was interested in football – he didn't seem particularly engaged.'

'Was there anything he did bring up – about the club maybe?'

Jay Chaudry lifts a finger, as if the prompt has helped him.

'Well – I was seated at an angle to him – I wasn't entirely tuned in. But now you mention it there was one thing that struck me – actually, I thought it wasn't a bad idea.' There seems to be an element of surprise, the revelation on reflection. 'He said something like he'd being doing his research and there used to be an annual fishing match between us and the AAA. That's the Allerdale Angling Association – our local rivals, you might say. He was suggesting that we resurrect the fixture – and that we should be looking to merge with them.'

DS Leyton's antennae now twitch – not that here is a startling fact in the case – but rather it is surely a scoop that will interest Skelgill. Advance warning of a matter close to his heart. The interview has been rather unproductive, but at least he will be able to demonstrate his diligence in winkling out this intelligence.

While DS Leyton is pondering such serendipity, the man continues, now a little absently.

'Come to think of it, the subject must have changed – maybe someone said it's one for a committee meeting – or perhaps the dessert arrived and distracted us. But there's merit in it. What's the point of the DAA and the AAA bidding up the prices of the best beats when they could all be under one big umbrella? Put them together and you'd save money *and* be able to charge more for a better offering. If you brought in business consultants it's probably the first thing they would say.'

DS Leyton is nodding – but having reminded himself that he has not got far with the inquiry (unless he counts the elimination of Jay Chaudry as a witness to Kyle Betony's last movements) he racks his brains for some sort of killer question – when the Cumbria Police internet goes down.

APPLETHWAITE GUEST HOUSE, 4.11 p.m.

The next logical port of call for Skelgill and DS Jones, the hamlet of Applethwaite, despite its relative proximity to the Derwent, offers a very different picture to the river valley, the broad agricultural floodplain. Tucked away on the lower slopes of Skiddaw, and extensively wooded, there is an altogether different atmosphere. Such contrasts always give Skelgill pause for thought – a game he has often played with himself – what is his natural habitat, that for which he feels most affinity? Half an hour – three-quarters, maybe – could see him first paddle across the flat, almost Arctic expanse of Bassenthwaite Lake, insulated from any hint of civilisation; to beach the boat and clamber beside a rushing beck in dense oak woodland, with whining gnats and avian echoes and tropical undertones for company; thence out onto the open fells, striding through the heather with the sweet scent of bog myrtle in his nostrils, the wind in his hair and the skyline ever beckoning him. It is a conundrum which he knows he will never bottom; but one he can live with.

As they alight from the car, however, he is somewhat rueful of the change of plan. DS Jones would have been right in assigning a small ulterior motive to his intention to go on foot from Brash Hall to Kirkthwaite. For the riverside is another first among equals; an ecosystem easy on the eye and brimming with wildlife; plants that grow nowhere else; the ubiquitous alders that attract redpolls and siskins; spinning clouds of mayflies; and the magical quality of movement through the landscape, the unseen flow of fish, and flies and leaves on the surface; the flyway that is the exclusive province of kingfisher and dipper and goosander, an experience that can only vaguely be replicated by canoe.

'Guv?'

DS Jones breaks into his reverie; albeit the sensation for Skelgill is less cerebral and more visceral. He gives a little start and turns his attention to the dwelling before them. Applethwaite House is an appealing slate-built edifice, perhaps originally the country residence of some rich Lancastrian merchant, raised on the foundations of the cotton trade, a reviled anachronism; a clue to its earliest purpose are the non-native sequoias and western hemlocks that number among the surrounding trees. Such properties lend themselves to conversion into guest houses, with their generous public rooms and servants' quarters and ample sculleries. The present incumbents have gained something of a reputation for their cuisine, and have got themselves on the gourmet map of the Lakes, a notional publication entirely alien to Skelgill – indeed used by a class of visitors that together with their caprice are anathema to his way of seeing the world. Though no inverted snob, he does wonder how some people will pay a small fortune for so much bare white china. His benchmark for keeping his feet on the ground is the reaction to any such unwise boast in his local. "Thou paid 'ow much? Thou must be tapped, Skelly, lad!" (Expletives deleted.)

He follows a few paces behind his colleague as she approaches the freshly painted white door that sits between symmetrical projecting windows, beneath a slate-tiled porch that extends to form the roof of each of the bays.

It opens hardly a second after she presses the bell.

'Hello – yes?'

'Mrs Baker?'

'Er – yes, I'm Jackie Baker.'

While DS Jones completes their introduction Skelgill makes a casual assessment of their second female witness. The first thing that strikes him is that she does not look like a committee member of a traditional angling society. While Ruth Robinson was of rather indeterminate but probably stocky build, her form largely disguised by a long loose-fitting floral smock dress that had seemed apposite in the farmhouse kitchen, Jackie Baker's figure is plain to see. Clad in smart skinny blue jeans and a close-fitting plain black t-shirt with a subtle *AH* logo embroidered in silver (Applethwaite House?) it is a youthful physique, indeed a schoolgirlish appearance enhanced by straight, shoulder-length fair hair and finely boned features. She is thin-lipped with small eyes a little close together that dart about as though they follow a hover fly. She is holding a yellow duster and an aerosol can of some proprietary household cleaner, and she has answered their knock so swiftly that she must surely have been polishing the brass on the inside of the door.

She seems anxious – as if she is expecting guests to arrive at any minute and still has much to do. But as DS Jones fills in the regulation gaps in their knowledge Skelgill begins to form the impression that she is just slightly manic. She cannot keep her eyes on DS Jones for more than a few seconds at a time; she sporadically checks her wristwatch, and she seems to keep noticing things around them in the driveway and the flower beds that trouble her. It is as though her action list is growing by the minute. She does nod urgently from time to time, but not exactly at the right places in DS Jones's discourse. And she inserts inapt phrases, "for sure" and "absolutely" and even "it is what it is".

It does not appear to occur to her to invite them inside, and when DS Jones reaches the point of her first question of substance (what time did she last see Kyle Betony?), Jackie Baker folds her bare arms across her narrow chest, the duster and spray can rendering the pose uncomfortable-looking.

'It was about a minute before half-past ten.' DS Jones takes a note; a very specific response. The woman gives another glance at her watch. 'I'd promised Kirsten that I would be back at eleven – I had just checked my phone.'

Looking on, listening, Skelgill concludes that not only do Ruth Robinson and Jackie Baker differ in appearance, but also in provenance – the former speaks with a strong local accent; Jackie Baker has rolled the 'r' in "Kirsten" and is surely Scots. But they do have in common that neither has seemed resentful of the interrogation, nor made any great expressions of sympathy.

DS Jones is onto her next question.

'How did Mr Betony seem?'

Jackie Baker appears a little baffled.

'Just, er – normal – as much as I knew him.'

'We understand he had a conversation with you and Mrs Robinson about a fishing permit scheme he was trying to get off the ground?'

'Not exactly.'

The eyes dart about again, but now between the detectives, and her tone sounds more guarded.

'What do you mean, madam?'

'Well – he did briefly mention the permits idea – but it wasn't us that he wanted to speak with.'

DS Jones is taking rapid notes – and her pen hesitates over her pad as she tries to make sense of this answer. Jackie Baker seems to appreciate that her response has a logical flaw.

'It was after the meal. He was in the corridor – that is, he peered round the door into the residents' lounge – as though he were looking for someone. He saw us having coffee. I was facing him. Then he turned his head and I assume saw someone else – and made as if to go after them. Then he changed his mind and came across to us. But he just said something along the lines of, we must talk later. Then he went away.'

'Which way?'

'Back out into the corridor.'

'Definitely not into the restaurant?'

'No – I presumed to catch up with whomever he had seen.'

'He didn't say who – or why?'

She gives a small quick shake of her head – and checks her watch once again.

'No, he didn't.'

'Which way did he go – in relation to reception?'

'Away from reception.'

'Did you see him again?'

'No. Ruth and I left shortly after – at a quarter to eleven.'

Skelgill is content to remain in the background. This woman might be more highly strung than her counterpart, but it seems in her nervous birdlike attention to her surroundings she makes a far better witness. But she perhaps makes less good company, lacking concentration upon the other's conversation. That said, he feels a certain kindred spirit, in a way that he does not really understand, or can even begin to particularise.

DS Jones moves the interview on.

'I believe Mr Betony was seated next to you at the dinner?'

Jackie Baker understands that her questioner anticipates more than a simple affirmation.

'Yes – although he didn't pay much notice to me.' There is the hint of a frown and a brief reflective flicker of her eyelids. 'I was opposite Ruth – and the four chaps at the end seemed to be engrossed in their own conversation.'

'Were there any arguments?'

This raises a look of alarm – as a question it touches upon the implication that the police inquiry covers the possibility of foul play – and it seems that the woman has not hitherto considered this. She looks questioningly at the detectives in turn.

'Well – no – not really. Disagreements, maybe – as would be normal. But nobody fell out, if that's what you mean? I would have noticed that.'

Skelgill is thinking that she probably would have; despite her erratic manner – in fact, because of it – and indeed, now she suddenly stiffens, and she leans to one side to gaze past DS Jones to the point where the driveway curves out of sight behind a stand of rhododendrons. She has heard an approaching vehicle.

Skelgill turns to see, heralded by the slow crunch of wide tyres on gravel, the emergence of a large new-looking Range Rover with a private registration plate and, affixed to its roof bars, a brace of Hardy fly-rod tubes.

He senses that his colleague's eyes are upon him – he gives a small jerk of his head, a suggestion that they should leave. In the action of folding over the cover of her notebook, DS Jones signals to Jackie Baker that the interview is concluded.

'Onwards and upwards.'

She grins – her first smile – a nervous expression of relief, it seems, and another platitude to go with it. But she takes it that she is freed of their custody and steps to one side and stoops to deposit the yellow duster and spray can behind a stone planter in which grows a neatly trimmed box. She stands to attention and tugs down her t-shirt at her sides and smooths the stretchy material over her flat stomach. She is now preoccupied entirely by the new arrivals, and the two detectives are able to drift across without further ado to clamber into DS Jones's car.

They watch for a moment, perhaps both curious in their own ways: Skelgill wants to see if the anglers look as competent as their tackle; DS Jones has perhaps a more subtle interest in people watching. A smartly dressed couple emerge from the Range Rover, good-looking and glamorous – and perhaps counterintuitively Skelgill watches the male and DS Jones the female. There seems to be a short discussion about what they should do with their bags, but Jackie Baker indicates towards the guest house. She leads the way and ushers them inside – and for one last time her attention suddenly switches, and she glances across at DS Jones's car, a momentary expression of anxiety distorting the girlish features. The door closes.

'What age is she?'

DS Jones knows the answer.

'Thirty-seven.'

'Young, then.'

Skelgill continues to stare at the white door, unblinking.

'Definitely.'

A small silence ensues before Skelgill speaks again.

'She referred to a Kirsten.'

'I think that must be her partner. I expect it will say on their website.'

'You mean business partner?'

DS Jones gives a little rock of her head. She checks the factsheet compiled by DC Watson.

'We've got her down as married.'

Skelgill ponders reflectively.

'Bit hyper.'

'Yes.'

'I don't reckon she or Ruth Robinson stayed the night at The Partridge – looks pretty certain they went home.'

DS Jones eyes her boss with a hint of amused intrigue. There can be two bases for his conclusion, and he may have conflated them for politically correct purposes. It is reasonable to say, though, that both women appear to have departed as they have suggested. And their almost-matching accounts of Kyle Betony's brief post-prandial appearance are lent a certain authenticity by small discrepancies.

COCKERMOUT SEWAGE TREATMENT WORKS, 4.26 p.m.

As DS Leyton swings his car between industrial wire gates he experiences a premature sense of dusk. At this time of year the afternoon sun never seems to tarry; he imagines it as a comet plunging towards the western horizon; silhouetted against the golden sky flocks of small long-tailed birds are swooping in to roost. Skelgill would probably know what they are, or at least claim to. The existence of the site is a novelty to him – it is concealed from the main road by a dense row of poplars, perhaps to spare the townspeople's blushes – but he supposes there must be these places everywhere.

He can see an arrangement of round ponds with rotating booms; the idea of a "sewage farm" – the suggestion of the cultivation of effluent – is somewhat stomach churning; moreover, the air is redolent of boyhood mudlarking near the Millwall docks; it was never England's most auspicious tidal foreshore, and when torrential rain overwhelmed the capital's Victorian sewers poor Old Father Thames was inundated.

But someone has to do this job – and it is at the convenience of Stephen Flood (who has given his title as Area Supervisor, Water Quality) that Cockermouth Sewage Treatment Works has been agreed as a rendezvous. And now the man in question – DS Leyton assumes it is he – emerges from the barnacle cluster of portacabins close by which he has parked. He approaches to within about two yards and, planting his feet apart, stands his ground.

'Mr Flood?'

'Aye.'

Although the response is not suspicious in tone – more grudging – DS Leyton displays his warrant card. He knows from DC Watson's report that Stephen Flood is aged forty-seven, widowed (not strictly relevant) and has his home address nearby – although it seems his employment takes him to facilities spread across the northwest quarter of the county. His role must be more administrative than hands-on, for like DS Leyton he wears a slightly ill-fitting business suit. There is further affinity in his short, squat stature – a passing motorist glimpsing them might get a flash of Tweedledum and Tweedledee.

But DS Leyton has come prepared, on Jay Chaudry's say so, for an introverted Scot.

Accordingly, he begins in jovial terms.

'What is it they call us, sir? *Offcomers* – and that's the about the most printable name my guvnor uses for me.'

The man merely glowers; might he be suspicious that such endearment is a mere tactic? DS Leyton makes a small adjustment.

'Opposite ends of the country, mind.'

Neither does this suggestion elicit much in the way of a reaction. The square-jawed features seem to be set in a permanent state of concentration, as though a mild inner straining is taking place, the eyes narrowed. DS Leyton wonders if his choice of subject matter is missing the mark. He is aware that the implication that England and Scotland are part of the same nation state is not universally appreciated. He recalls a reprimand he received from Skelgill on their last trip north of the border, and determines not to misuse the word "Scotch". But he does give it one last go.

'Which part of Scotland are you from, sir?'

'Dourness.'

The voice is gravelly and DS Leyton is none the wiser, and is beginning to regret his line of engagement. He could mention his recent visit with the family to the famous Blacksmith's Shop at Gretna Green – but for all he knows Dourness and Gretna are deadly rivals in caber tossing. He pivots to a marginally more pertinent aspect of the man's provenance.

'Have you been down here long?'

'Twenty-two years.'

Perhaps this is the explanation for Stephen Flood's apparent disinterest. There is a sudden atmospheric disturbance, a zephyr that raises dust from the unmetalled ground, and an invisible waft of something like ammonia and sulphur envelops them. DS Leyton looks longingly over the man's shoulder at the sanctuary of the huts. But it seems no invitation will be forthcoming. Stephen Flood, despite his bulbous whisky-drinker's nose, must be inured to the stench. DS Leyton inhales through clenched teeth. It is all the incentive he needs to make short work of the interview. He trots out his standard introduction – their wish to get to the bottom of, number one, Kyle Betony's last movements and, number two, his demeanour on Saturday night – although he does not hold out any great hopes.

But now Stephen Flood surprises him.

'After dinner I went tae get a drink. I sat down in a corner of the bar. A few minutes later Kyle followed me.'

The bald facts are plainly stated, with no hint of innuendo. But DS Leyton takes it upon himself to join the tentative dots.

'You make it sound like you were avoiding him, sir?'

The remark evidently touches a nerve, for there is the first hint of animation in the man's granite-like countenance.

'Ach – he'd been havering all the nicht. Someone put me next tae him.'

Whatever is havering, it was plainly a source of irritation; and DS Leyton doubts that Stephen Flood would suffer fools gladly.

'Did he want to speak about something in particular?'

But now the man merely shakes his head.

'He didn't say anything that struck you as odd – that might cast some light on what happened to him?'

'He said plenty over dinner, but I wasnae listening.'

'Your associate Mr Chaudry mentioned there was something about a merger between, what is it – the DA and the AA?'

The man turns his head slightly and there might just be a glint of amusement in the reptilian eyes – that DS Leyton has inadvertently abbreviated the abbreviations.

'Aye – he was full of hare-brained schemes.'

There is no further elaboration.

But it is clear to DS Leyton that he is not being evasive – merely that his views need to be prised limpet like from the submerged rocks of his stoicism. Surprise is the trick, for limpets.

'In the bar – was he worried, excited, nervous, angry?'

Stephen Flood appears reluctant to choose – though he seems to weigh the relative merits of DS Leyton's options.

'Nearer agitated.'

DS Leyton feels a small flush of success.

'But he didn't say what about?'

'He didnae.'

'And – so – what happened?'

A heightened belligerence grips the stony features; the man seems to be recalling the moment.

'I went tae the gents. He'd nae got a drink, and I thought he might clear off.'

DS Leyton is now getting the hang of his role – each prompt only produces so much information.

'And did he?'

'Aye. When I came back, he was awa'.'

'Did you see him after that?'

'I didnae.'

'What time was that – can you recall?'

'If the clock over the bar was right – it was at the half-ten mark. That's the time I'd decided tae leave.'

'So you were keeping your eye on the time?

'Aye.'

'And that's when you left – about ten thirty?'

The man nods.

DS Leyton ponders a further question – but there is the breeze again, and with it a particularly diabolical gust of gas, almost debilitating – such that his knees weaken and he cannot suppress an exclamation.

'How long does it take to get used to this smell, sir?'

'Smell?'

When irony might be anticipated, Stephen Flood appears offended – as if suddenly DS Leyton has resorted to a criticism of his professionalism. DS Leyton decides it is time to bank his gains.

'Probably my imagination.' He folds away his notebook and slips it into his jacket pocket. 'Thanks for your time, sir. I think you've given me something to go on. I'll leave you to your business.'

SWINSIDE BARN, 5.16 p.m.

'I didn't think we'd have a *Georgina* in the family.'

DS Jones turns to look at Skelgill. He peers somewhat critically through the car windscreen at the restored stone property that rises before them; cutting along the contour of the fellside it would once have been a combined farmhouse and barn; where hay was pitched beneath a great oak lintel an immense picture window provides what must be a breathtaking view across Derwentwater.

'Guv?' Skelgill's observation does not make immediate sense.

'The arl lass – she's a Graham.'

'Oh – of course.' He means his mother. But while many of the Grahams they come across on their travels bear some clan affiliation, after Wilson and Smith, Graham is the third most abundant surname in the county, and Skelgill cannot be related to them all.

DS Jones refers to the information sheet that DC Watson has supplied for each of their witnesses.

'She's a divorcee. It doesn't state whether or not Graham is her married name.'

'How old is she?'

'Forty-three.'

Skelgill gives a little uplift of his head.

'Happen I'll recognise her soon enough.'

DS Jones wonders if the rueful note in his voice means he still clings to the outside hope that there might be such a tastefully converted residence in the extended family.

But now Skelgill cranes around to look at a covered recess between the near end of the main dwelling and a separate outbuilding. A Land Rover Discovery with last year's plate is parked nose first.

'Looks like she's in.'

DS Jones raises the page of notes illustratively.

'It says she holds an international post – Director of HR for Servill Consulting. I think they're just outside the Big Four. She works primarily from home.'

Skelgill does not indicate whether he understands; he stares again at the property, and then his gaze tracks across to their left, to the view. The early autumn sun is setting out of sight in the west; already the property is in shadow, but across the lake the oak woods, determinedly green, shimmer in its last rays; above, the bracken-clad fellsides are burnished bronze beneath pale grey screes.

'And why wouldn't you?'

DS Jones nods. Then she speaks reflectively.

'Would you get bored – I mean, with the same view every day?'

Skelgill seems a little perturbed by the challenge, but his rejoinder is swift.

'Not when there's a lake in it.'

DS Jones chuckles. Water, to most people a blank sheet, is a whole textbook in Skelgill's eyes.

But now their attention is diverted back to their immediate vicinity.

Just ahead of them a stack of massive stone steps, more like a mounting block (for which they perhaps once doubled) marks the main door of the property, though in its ancient practical design it has neither an obvious front nor back – and now the door swings open and a tall woman with a striking head of carefully coiffured blonde hair emerges into view. She wears high heels and a blue floral ruched mini dress, sleeveless with tie-straps and a ruffle hem that displays what would be considered a sought-after figure, the naked flesh on show evenly tanned. Without being over-revealing, it is an arresting get-up – and certainly not the casual attire of the modern-day home-worker. She looks more like she is about to head out for dinner than someone who has been at the computer in her study.

They have not agreed times with the witnesses – much to the frustration of the general public it is not a practical commitment the police can easily make. This would have been DS Jones's first call, were it not for the unexpected development at Brash Hall – and so perhaps Georgina Graham has been waiting for some time, and does indeed have an assignation.

Certainly the woman is looking at them in a way that suggests she has been anticipating their arrival. Though she does not deign to descend the steps, she holds open the door in a manner that invites their approach. Her face is a little long to qualify as a natural beauty, but in the regular features – prominent cheekbones, wide full-lipped mouth and large pale blue eyes beneath even brows – she exudes the confidence of a woman that is accustomed to being regarded as attractive, a subtle arrogance that elevates her above the average mortal.

They identify themselves and are led into a capacious stone-flagged hallway from which they ascend via a broad curving staircase. The stair opens directly into a large thickly carpeted sitting room with a casual dining table in one corner, but she directs them to an arrangement of lounge chairs around a coffee table in front of the big picture window. The view is framed like a vividly coloured Wainwright sketch, and it is easy to see why the living accommodation has been elevated to the first floor.

There is a smell of fresh coffee and without asking them she momentarily disappears through into what must be an expansive kitchen – there is partial sight of another table that would seat a good ten people – and she reappears with a tray on which there is a brushed steel percolator and stylish Italian cups and a small plate of almond biscotti.

DS Jones knows Skelgill can be fickle when it comes to coffee – and certainly snacks that fall outwith his regular local repertoire – but when she glances at him she sees his eyes appraising not the tray and its contents but its bearer. And rather meekly, she thinks, he acquiesces to the offers of coffee, cream, sugar and even the questionable hard-baked sweetmeat.

DS Jones decides that small gaps in their factsheet can wait.

'Madam, we are trying to piece together Mr Betony's last movements on Saturday night.' In her wording – and indeed in her tone – there is the implication that they are already well-informed, and that anyone adding to such knowledge would be well advised to tell the truth; however it is a sentiment that lies beneath the surface, and just about succeeds in not giving cause for offence. 'Could you please tell us what you can remember in that regard?'

The woman has spoken comparatively few words – if anything demonstrating a self-assuredness that conveys she certainly has nothing to hide – but now she is more forthcoming, and in the process dispels any final chances that she might be a local Graham. Her accent is decidedly RP. Her voice is deep for a woman, throaty – perhaps a little affected.

'I am ashamed to say I did not mix at all.' She glances at each of the detectives in turn, as if to check the reaction to this subtly worded negative; perhaps trained HR skills are being brought to bear. 'I was seated next to Sir Montague at dinner, and opposite us were Alice Wright-Fotheringham and Professor Hartley. We inadvertently although I suppose inevitably formed our own little clique – for the purposes of conversation – and when the meal finished and the group began to break up, I remained at the table talking with Monty. His youngest daughter has a place at Oxford to study International Relations. We were discussing the possibility that I could perhaps organise a summer internship in one of our overseas offices.'

She gives a bow of her head towards the papers in front of DS Jones; the top page is the partially completed pro-forma and her move is an acknowledgment that she knows they are aware of her status.

DS Jones glances at her notes.

'Were you at the table for the whole evening?'

The woman smiles and directs a mildly conspiratorial look at her questioner.

'Apart from powdering my nose – just once.'

She says it in the time-honoured way – the suggestion that, for the fairer sex, to visit a public convenience is always something of a last resort. But DS Jones remains focused.

'What time was that?'

Now Georgina Graham hesitates. To get her ducks in a row? She must assume that they have already spoken to Sir Montague Brash – indeed she might well know the fact.

'Well – it was certainly after the meal – I couldn't say for sure what time.'

'If you had to make an estimate?'

The woman seems reluctant to do so.

'Perhaps – I don't know – ten-thirty?'

'Was Kyle Betony still at the table?'

'No – by then it was just Monty and me.'

'Did you see Mr Betony when you went out?'

Now she surprises the detectives with her response.

'To be frank, I had spilt red wine on my dress.' Her hand moves to her thigh as if she is subconsciously covering the location of the stain. 'I rather put my head down and scuttled through. I had a general impression of there being a small scattering of people in the various rooms – I believe Ruth and Jackie in the lounge, and perhaps I noticed Stephen Flood somewhere – but also I didn't want to keep poor Monty waiting on his own.'

DS Jones accepts the explanation without query.

'At what time did you finally leave?'

Now her answer is entirely definitive.

'I had an Uber booked for eleven fifteen. It was probably a few minutes later, because it was already parked outside and Monty said just to go ahead – we parted company at the porch.'

DS Jones nods amenably.

'So you arrived home by – what – something like eleven thirty?'

A witness to events at The Partridge might reasonably wonder at the reach of such a question. But if Georgina Graham is hiding the fact that she stayed the night at the inn, she shows no adverse reaction.

'Well – I suppose it must have been. Certainly, I was in bed before midnight. I had a report to write to be on a desk in Sydney first thing this morning Australian time. I set Alexa for seven a.m. Sunday – and I remember the display was still showing twenty-three something.'

DS Jones takes the response in her stride.

'Sir Montague – you say he remained behind? Did he say why?'

The woman gives a little purring laugh. For a moment they might think a disclosure is on the cards.

'His exact words were that he had to see a man about a dog.' She smiles a little coyly. 'I took it that he meant to visit the gents' toilets.'

'Of course.'

There is a small hiatus in the questioning, and now Georgina Graham makes an interesting move.

'Do you suspect that something untoward happened to Kyle?'

Her manner is businesslike, even authoritative. DS Jones regards her with a hint of caution. In work terms, in relative rank this woman is probably on a par with their Chief; two decades of people management under her belt. She must see through their thinly veiled approach. It occurs to DS Jones that Skelgill would probably resort to sarcasm – *"Untoward? A bloke in a dinner jacket dead in the Derwent?"* – but instead she picks up on the finer point, that Georgina Graham used her fellow committee member's first name.

'How well did you know him, madam?'

If anything, the woman now seems to row back a little. Indeed, her answer is somewhat oblique.

'I imagine you are aware that he only joined the committee last year – it was in August.'

'How did he come to join?'

'It was on his own initiative.' She smiles, and inexplicably casts a knowing glance at Skelgill, which rather catches him off guard. He manufactures a slightly sheepish grin. 'Unlike most members, it seems that Kyle read the papers that were circulated in advance of the AGM. Typically, the only attendees are the committee. In these days of electronic communications club members don't wait for the AGM to come around to voice their grievances. And they know that otherwise as an event it is a turgid rubber-stamping exercise. Why waste a summer's evening when one could be out on the water?'

She gives a second glance at Skelgill; it seems she reads him like an open book – and she has him at a natural disadvantage.

'Under the item for re-election of officers there was a vacancy for a member of the committee, actually of some longstanding. Kyle put himself forward. He came prepared – he handed round a little biography. He was proposed and seconded and there was no objection. I processed the admin afterwards. I can supply you with a copy of his appointment – I don't suppose one can breach the data privacy of a person deceased?'

DS Jones is nodding, treating the caveat as rhetorical.

'Did he have a specific role?'

The woman shakes her head.

'We have only three officers – Chairman, Treasurer and myself as Secretary.'

DS Jones does not respond immediately; it seems she allows a pause in order to reorientate her line of inquiry.

'There's been a suggestion that Mr Betony did ruffle a few

feathers?'

Georgina Graham appears untroubled by the suggestion.

'I think that was just his nature – a bit of an 'Ideas Man' – that's how he saw himself. ENTPs, we call them in my field. Myers-Briggs.'

'The Debator. Don't try to out-compete them.'

'Correct!'

The woman regards DS Jones with a look that might almost be one of congratulation; certainly there is satisfaction, the small endorsement of a technical aspect of her profession.

Skelgill looks on, a little bewildered – perhaps it is the revelation that it is possible to pay attention to police management training courses.

DS Jones takes the point further.

'Did that pose any problems?'

'Oh, I don't believe so – just healthy discussion. There was nothing wrong with Kyle putting forward proposals – but the DAA is not a public company charged with maximising the returns for its shareholders. It is a conservative organisation concerned with maintaining the status quo. So there is no great appetite for innovation. I think it was his tendency to apply his entrepreneurial principles in other walks of life.' She hesitates, but inhales as if to continue speaking, and her gaze falls reflectively upon the coffee table before them. 'I'm sorry to hear that he leaves a young widow. But I believe at least there are no children?'

She looks up as DS Jones is about to reply; but it is Skelgill that interjects.

'Mrs Graham, how did you come to be involved in the DAA?'

There is another seemingly informed smile; she is neither wrong-footed by the sudden change of tack, nor perturbed by the thrust of Skelgill's question, the implication that she makes for an unlikely Secretary of a fishing club.

'If I may quote Hamlet, you might say it is a case of to the manner born.' The pale blue eyes lock with Skelgill's and it takes all his effort to maintain the contact. Then something in her expression relents, and she speaks more offhandedly. 'We have a family beat on the Greta, at Fosthwaite. I have fished since I was a child. My father was for many years Chairman of the association; we like to show our support.'

Skelgill folds his arms and nods; he looks like he is putting two and two together – and when their interview is shortly concluded, and he is back in the privacy of DS Jones's car, he shares his thoughts.

'She must be Lord Fosthwaite's daughter.' As DS Jones performs a three-point turn, he casts a hand up at the property. 'That explains all this. This'll be their land hereabouts. It stretches right up to where the Greta meets the Derwent. No wonder she's hobnobbing with Sir Montague Brash. These families – they're birds of a feather.'

DS Jones concentrates upon manoeuvring judiciously around a series of steep hairpin bends that bring the neat tarmac driveway to its junction with the fellside lane above the property.

'Clear.'

Skelgill checks for her to their left. She brings the car up to speed and now responds to his observations. Anticipating his point of view, she begins with a little devil's advocacy.

'Between Uber and Alexa, she left a verifiable alibi.'

Skelgill – it is true, unduly influenced by the recency effect and striking appearance of the woman – turns sharply to regard his colleague. She has brought him up short – but he stifles any objection and sinks down into the passenger seat.

'So, we can knock that one on the head, eh, lass?'

But despite his words there is more to his statement, and DS Jones knows it. She turns her own argument around.

'Well – she could have simply driven herself back to The Partridge – any of them could. But if there were a Mrs Smith – there's no saying it has to be one of these three.'

Skelgill emits a hiss of frustration. For him there is the sense of drifting rudderless and with a single broken oar down a great broad river, amidst an unfamiliar landscape, the sky overcast with not even the sun to provide a bearing, and no recognisable landmarks on the horizon. Becalmed inlets where mysterious fish rise provide tempting harbours, but promise little progress.

'Don't forget you started out with the idea that Betony were the one playing away.'

His criticism is perhaps unfairly aimed at his colleague – for he did not demur to the idea in the first place. But she chooses not to argue the point.

'We at least have more on Kyle Betony – at ten thirty he was exercised by some matter – and that may also be the point at which he disappeared. Georgina Graham walked through and didn't see him.'

Skelgill rubs the knuckles of his left hand pensively against a weekend's worth of stubble, his front teeth bared. This much is true – although Georgina Graham in her own words was both uncertain about the time and vague about whom she saw. And he doubts she checked each public room. He inflicts a small ascetic punch upon his belligerently jutting jaw.

'Let's hope Leyton changes the habits of a lifetime and surprises us.'

FELLVIEW NURSING HOME, BOTHEL – 5.30 p.m.

'Thanks for hanging back, sir – much appreciated. I'm running a little late.'

'Oh – it's no bother, Sergeant – I'm not a clock watcher. Where vulnerable elderly people are concerned, there's no room for a nine-to-five mentality.'

DS Leyton is seated opposite the man to whom he has been shown through by a friendly young receptionist who, in the small window that they had conversed, had told him she was from Rwanda (or did she say Uganda?). A smiling Anthony Goodman sits relaxed at his desk, besuited but tieless, a tall, heavily built man of forty-five who around his neck and jowls alone carries a good few excess pounds, a phenomenon that makes his features – rosebud mouth, upturned nose, small blue eyes beneath pale eyebrows and receding thin light-brown hair – collectively seem all the more recessive, giving an overall impression of a child's sketch, the outline of the head drawn first and the contents inserted as an afterthought, prompted by the teacher. Moreover, in keeping with this cartoonist evolutionary theory, are round ears which, if not overly large, protrude at right-angles from the head – it is a distinctive look that, transporting DS Leyton back to his youth, in the playground would attract for those so afflicted cruel nicknames such as 'wing nut', 'FA Cup' or 'jug ears' – the latter tautological in his Cockney neighbourhood, where 'jug' is synonymous with 'ear'.

So distracted, he finds the man looking at him, perhaps with the beginnings of concern (does he read his thoughts?). DS Leyton starts, and throws out a question.

'But – you're not on the clinical side, sir?'

The man responds with a patient smile and a languid hand gesture that indicates the computer at his side; he is well spoken and his low voice carries hypnotic undertones.

'No, no, Sergeant – I'm in charge of finance. But it is a role that inevitably brings me into contact with our residents. Without due consideration to funding, their welfare could be adversely compromised.' He leans forward and rests his elbows on the desk, interlocking hands that are small and short-fingered for his size. The pose makes DS Leyton think of a well-fed praying mantis – another image that he tries to dismiss as the man continues. 'For some care homes it is a just a numbers game. Here at Fellview, we are first and foremost a community.' He smiles in a marginally sickly way; nevertheless, DS Leyton finds himself nodding. 'For our charges, their time here is the most precious of their lives. We have a collective responsibility to get to know them as individuals, whatever their condition. Our nursing staff are stretched – and some of our residents, would you believe, receive no visits. So I say to the admin staff – and I'm not always popular – sacrifice your cigarette break and go and have a chat.'

He leans back in his sprung chair – and for a moment, in a way that contrasts with his manner to date – there is a sudden contortion of his features, as though he has been beset by a spasm of pain. But it must pass quickly, and he makes no mention of it, and merely smiles in a way that might be seeking approbation. DS

Leyton is momentarily alarmed – but he too refers only to the man's stated philosophy.

'Very good, sir – I reckon that must be very reassuring for relatives.'

Anthony Goodman nods regally, but does not comment further.

DS Leyton is thinking about the time, and that he should make progress. There is no obvious segue, and so he has no choice but to launch directly into his brief. He opens his notebook as a sign of his intent.

'As my colleague DC Watson will have explained on the telephone, sir – we're speaking to the members of the angling committee who were at the dinner on Saturday night. We're trying to understand just what happened to Mr Betony.'

Now the man raises both hands and places the tips of his fingers against his doughy jowls; to DS Leyton's eye it is a rather Munch-like gesture, of underlying dreadfulness, and the silent scream.

'Terrible, terrible thing.' His tone is certainly anguished. 'How is his poor young wife? It must have been so distressing for her – and for your officers, having to break the news – and for you to investigate Kyle's demise.'

DS Leyton looks a little self-conscious, that he has garnered some underserved sympathy.

'It's all in the line of duty, sir. Any sudden or unexplained death – the Coroner's Office wants a report before they'll issue a certificate. I guess you'd know about this, sir.'

The man nods reflectively – he turns his head and DS Leyton follows his gaze through a side window – across a courtyard, in the growing gloom, lights are beginning to show in the old manse that is the main residential building – ghostly shadows shift about and death needs little explanation – it is routine, expected, welcomed by some.

DS Leyton involuntarily inhales more deeply – and he detects the hospital smell of disinfectant that pervades even this separate administrative block. It is like a small dose of smelling salts, and it provokes him to press on with his questioning.

'So – it's really just a case of identifying Mr Betony's last known movements – and whether he said anything to anyone that might cast light on why he went down to the river.'

DS Leyton looks up from his notebook to see that Anthony Goodman is staring at him; there is curiosity in his eyes – a look that seems to convey surprise (or is it doubt?) that the police are short of some significant intelligence.

'He was a bit of a strange character.'

There is a questioning inflexion in the man's voice. He is sufficiently diplomatic to present the idea as optional.

DS Leyton is careful not to climb on the bandwagon set in motion at his previous two interviews.

'My Guvnor would probably say that about me, sir.' He chuckles self-deprecatingly (despite that he is thinking the exact opposite would be closer to the truth) – but the point being there are plenty of strange characters who do not end up drowning at midnight – and certainly not committing suicide when it seems their head is full of plans. He does not iterate this perspective, however, and Anthony Goodman is inclined to elaborate. Again he intertwines his fingers.

'Well, of course – we all have our foibles, I don't doubt – but, well – I would venture he was troubled – some longstanding issue – an insecurity perhaps stretching right back to his early childhood.'

DS Leyton regards the man pensively; he is pontificating as though he might be a clinical psychologist – across the desk in this well-appointed office, with his well-tailored appearance and calm, confident, pleasant bedside manner, he entirely fits the bill.

DS Leyton takes the pragmatic line.

'Did he seem particularly troubled on Saturday night, sir?'

Now Anthony Goodman displays open palms – a sort of man-to-man gesture that says, "You know how these things are – we take people in our stride."

'He was edgy – a little erratic – I'm sure the others would tell you the same – and that was his regular demeanour – like there's an engine running beneath the surface, too many revs – a little voice on repeat in his head – *"do this, do that, do this"* – you know?'

DS Leyton furrows his brow and tries not to think of his wife. He sticks to the facts.

'Your associate Mr Chaudry mentioned that Mr Betony said something about a merger of the fishing club with your local rivals?'

Anthony Goodman seems rather bemused by the suggestion.

'Well, he may have said that – I really don't know. I can't say I had an actual conversation with him about anything in particular.'

DS Leyton glances at his notebook.

'I believe at the dinner you were seated opposite to Mr Betony?'

'Yes, that's correct – and I would never have imagined that would be my last encounter with him. It is extraordinary to think of it.'

'That was the last time you saw him, sir – at the table?'

'Oh, no – no, it wasn't.'

DS Leyton is surprised by the peremptory contradiction. The man seems pleased that he has more information, and revels in the moment, causing DS Leyton to prompt him.

'So, what time was it, sir?'

The man gives another slight grimace, less extreme than before, but still indicative of some inner jolt of discomfort. It delays his response for a couple of seconds.

'Hmm – well, I'm not sure about the time. But Jay Chaudry and I had taken our coffees into the Snug, beside the open fire.' He smiles, as though vicariously to enjoin DS Leyton into what was a pleasurable experience. 'After a while I went to the bar to get us a nightcap. Just as I turned with our drinks Kyle passed across in front of me – along the corridor.'

'Moving which way, sir?'

'He was heading towards the toilets – I assume.'

DS Leyton nods. This he notes down carefully.

'If you had to make a stab at the time, sir?'

The man's pasty complexion gains a little colour, pale pink blotches appear where his cheekbones would be, were there less flesh on the face. The small eyes seem a fraction disconcerted – as though he is mildly irked that the policeman has not taken him at his word first time.

'Well – I – I really wouldn't like to be definitive. I mean – I shouldn't like to put you on the wrong track – when I'm not sure. Have you spoken with Jay – he might remember what time it was when I went for the drinks?'

'He did mention you went to the bar, sir. And funnily enough he suggested that you might have seen Mr Betony – since he didn't see him, himself.'

DS Leyton presses his pencil against his notebook; it is perhaps a sign of resignation. Of course, he did not quiz Jay Chaudry on what time this was – because he would have been asking him if he saw something when he was doing nothing.

'Well – perhaps it was half-past ten?'

DS Leyton glances up – a sudden change of heart? The man is smiling hopefully. DS Leyton wonders if he has made him feel obliged to provide an answer. Perhaps his first proposition – that it is better not to guess – was more suitable.

'Why do you say that, sir?'

'Well, actually, there is a clock – up behind the bar – above the whiskies. And now I think of it, when I was choosing a malt I have an image of the clock – yes – I think it was reading ten thirty – and I wondered if they were about to call last orders.'

DS Leyton takes a further note.

'Did you happen to notice Mr Flood – seated in the bar?'

Anthony Goodman looks a little alarmed by this question – as if he might have been remiss in some way. However, he offers an assured vindication.

'Oh – no – but you know the layout? When you go in, the counter is on your right, flush with the door – so you stand with your back to the rest of the room. My mind was on what to order – they stock so many single malts.' He smiles engagingly. 'Actually, if I'd seen Stephen Flood I would have sought his counsel.'

DS Leyton ponders. The answer is candid enough – but it strikes him that the man would surely have noticed were his Scots counterpart still there. DS Leyton does the sums: Stephen Flood says he left at about ten thirty, and thus Anthony Goodman's sighting of Kyle Betony passing along the corridor appears to be the last sighting among his three interviewees.

He feels satisfied with this deduction.

But he should see events through to their conclusion.

'And after you'd got the drinks, sir?'

'I repaired to the Snug – we remained there until last orders – which turned out to be eleven for non-residents. But Jay wanted to get away – he said he had an early start for Manchester. And Lucy arrived to give me a lift.'

'Lucy, sir?'

Now the man's smile has a decidedly proprietorial quality.

'Yes – she's my fiancée. She's actually on the committee, as well. But she's a GP and was on call – she couldn't make the meal. But she'd offered to pick me up – you know, the price of taxis these days?'

DS Leyton sets his features evenly, when a little bafflement lies beneath. It seems he has discovered someone hitherto unmentioned in their inquiry who might fall into the category of 'persons of interest'.

He decides he ought not to reveal any signs of ignorance.

'What time would that have been, sir?'

'Ah, well – that I do know for certain. When Jay left I was quietly sipping the last of my Laphroaig when I saw headlights swing round outside. I went out to check, and sure enough it was her. She apologised for being five minutes early – we'd agreed on eleven fifteen, so it must have been ten past. I did notice a minicab waiting, if that's any help to you?'

DS Leyton is nodding as he notes down the details.

But now there is an electronic bleep and Anthony Goodman picks up a pager from his desk. He squints interrogatively at the device. Then he regards DS Leyton rather contritely.

'Sergeant – I really ought to attend to this. It's not for me directly – but I can lend a hand. A Good Samaritan.'

'Of course, sir – thank you for your cooperation.'

When DS Leyton might expect the man to rise and leave the room with him, he remains seated.

He clears his throat, and DS Leyton, sensing a question, stops and turns.

'Your inquiry, Sergeant Leyton – are you any nearer?' He makes an open-palmed gesture. 'I mean – I'm thinking of Kyle's wife – she'll want to understand. And I'm going to suggest that the committee does something for her – from our funds. I'm Treasurer, you see. But – naturally – I shouldn't want us to put our foot in it – through ignorance, you know?'

DS Leyton takes a half step towards Anthony Goodman. He taps his notebook against his chest.

'I quite understand, sir. We'll certainly keep you informed – just as soon as we're able to.'

The man plies him with one last smile.

DS Leyton, a little fatigued in responding in kind, reflects that he marginally prefers dourness.

7. RECAP

The Partridge Inn – 6.16 p.m., Monday, 20ᵗʰ September

'What kept you, Leyton? Your mash is going cold.'

'Flamin' heck – I'll take it hot or cold. It's not Earl Grey, by any chance?'

Skelgill's scowl is all the answer his sergeant needs.

'Never mind – I just thought I could do with something perfumed.' He sinks with some relief into the free chair opposite his bemused-looking colleagues. 'I've got the smell of sewage in one nostril and disinfectant in the other.'

DS Jones chuckles as she pours a cup of tea from their shared pot. Though they are officially off duty, Skelgill has opted for seats in the residents' lounge. While it has a serving hatch through to the bar, there is not the temptation of the row of traditional handpumps advertising Jennings' finest ales. Moreover, it is a more central station for the purposes of their discussion.

As to meeting at The Partridge itself, they have been required to backtrack a little from Swinside, but the location of the hostelry saves DS Leyton from trailing over to Penrith, only to return home later to nearby Keswick.

It seems that the inn is quiet; they have the lounge to themselves; what residents there are must already be dining, or still elsewhere in the district. It is not a room that Skelgill frequents. The Snug with its log fire is the best place to warm up after a bone-chilling session out on Bass Lake; otherwise the bar is de rigueur – even he appreciates its olde-worlde charm and the quiet presence of four centuries of spirits; the ghosts of wizened locals and dust-encrusted travellers; of coachmen and ostlers and grooms reeking of horse; a mixed fug of tobacco smoke and haze from the oil lamps; the hubbub, inarticulate, comforting.

The lounge has no such attractions – well lit, it is more suitable for afternoon tea than coffee and after-dinner drinks, and more like an old maid's parlour (whatever either of those are: the old maids in Skelgill's family still wield their battle axes, and their parlours are austere traditional spotless front rooms rarely used but for weddings and wakes).

'How did you pair get on, then?'

It is DS Leyton's prompt. In his tone there is a small hint of eagerness, that he has something to impart.

Skelgill raises a hand. It is an automatic gesture – as if they were in the woods and are stalked by wolves. There is a way to do this and not be overwhelmed.

'Let's stick to the knitting. Not get carried away.' He looks interrogatively at DS Leyton. 'Unless you've got some blinding piece of news?'

Now this puts DS Leyton on the back foot – for it raises the stakes higher than he feels he can call. He rests his palms carefully on the edge of the low mahogany table.

'Not exactly, Guv.'

The ambiguity is enough to cause a moment's hesitation from Skelgill.

Then he doles out the tasks.

'I'll kick off.' He glances at DS Jones to indicate she should follow. 'Concentrate on his movements. Stick to the facts. Then you, Leyton.'

'Righto, Guv.'

Skelgill beckons to DS Jones for the documents that she holds. He selects two pages – the list of committee members and the seating plan. He lays them out so they can all see.

Now he addresses DS Leyton. He jerks a thumb at the ceiling.

'Sir Montague Brash stayed here on Saturday night. Probably not alone.' He flashes his associate a knowing look that generates a small murmur of comprehension. But he skips the explanation. 'They checked in as 'Mr & Mrs Smith' – Mrs Smith remains unidentified.'

But DS Leyton cannot contain his curiosity.

'What did he say, Guv?'

DS Jones leans forward and inhales as if to speak – but Skelgill is quick to retort.

'We didn't ask. He didn't tell.'

'*Whoa*. But, Guv – what does that –?'

Skelgill interjects before DS Leyton can shape his inquiry.

'We think he may have gone to bed at, what –?' Skelgill turns to DS Jones. 'Eleven fifteen?'

She nods. 'Or thereafter.'

But Skelgill grimaces.

'I doubt he hung about.'

DS Jones eyes him warily.

But DS Leyton now has a more fully formed question.

'So, what – the woman – the 'Mrs Smith' – she was one of the committee members?'

Skelgill does not answer immediately – again he consults with his female colleague through a brief meeting of eyes.

'Unlikely but not impossible. We need to find out who checked her in. If she was recognised. If she exists.'

Skelgill sounds decidedly fatalistic – he seems to want to set aside this aspect of their findings. He makes an impatient hand signal; DS Jones understands she is to update DS Leyton – and simultaneously remind Skelgill of what he already knows but may not have paid precise attention to.

'We had already learned from Professor Hartley that Kyle Betony was still at the dining table when he and Alice Wright-Fotheringham left at about ten past ten.' She looks towards the archway where a discreet hand-lettered sign indicates the direction of the Wythop Restaurant. 'We have a bit of a gap until just before ten-thirty.' DS Leyton begins to raise a hand – but decides to hold his tongue. DS Jones pats the arms of her easy chair. 'Ruth Robinson and Jackie Baker came to sit more or less here. The latter was the better witness.' She glances at Skelgill who dips his head in silent agreement. 'She was keeping a close eye on the time and says it was ten twenty-nine.' Now DS Jones indicates with an outstretched hand the open doorway into the main corridor. 'Kyle

Betony appeared over there and looked in. He saw them, then he saw someone else – out of sight in the passageway to his left. But he came in anyway. He said he wanted to talk to them later – then he immediately went off as if to go after whoever it was he had seen.'

DS Leyton is nodding vigorously – his expression a picture of acuity. DS Jones looks to Skelgill for further affirmation. He is drinking, but manages to convey with his eyebrows that she should continue.

'That is actually our last sighting. The two women remained here until ten forty-five, when they left. Georgina Graham, whom we also interviewed, remained in the restaurant with Sir Montague Brash. She says she visited the ladies' at about ten-thirty – although she was vague about the time. She remembered the pair sitting here, and thinks she saw Stephen Flood somewhere in passing – but not Kyle Betony. Sir Montague Brash says he didn't see him either, once he'd left the table – including when he and Georgina Graham came through this way at eleven-fifteen. She had a taxi waiting; it seems he went to the gents' before – we think – heading upstairs – possibly via the external steps beside the garden door.'

She glances again at Skelgill – but now he has a glazed look and does not engage with her. She turns back to DS Leyton. She grins.

'That's our half of the jigsaw.'

DS Leyton seems a little unprepared, and fumbles for his notebook from his jacket pocket. However, he composes himself and begins to peruse a page penned in a tiny, meticulous hand.

'My three geezers then. Jay Chaudry – I reckon we can forget about as a witness. He last saw Betony at the dining table. Chaudry and Anthony Goodman took their coffees through into the Snug. Chaudry left at five past eleven – the Snug's right by the front door, yeah?'

Skelgill is back with them and nods, seeing that his sergeant is checking that he has the inn's topography right. DS Leyton continues.

'I reckon my best witness is Stephen Flood – although you wouldn't guess it, to speak to him. He was sat next to Betony at dinner – and he reckons Betony tracked him down to the bar afterwards. Flood was tucked away in the corner. He says he'd had enough of Betony's prattle at the dinner table, and he weren't too happy. Flood went to the gents' and when he came back Betony was gone. That was at about half-ten, and Flood left.'

DS Leyton takes a pause for breath. Skelgill is listening implacably, DS Jones more intently.

'Then Goodman came out of the Snug to get drinks from the bar. That was also half-ten – although I reckon Flood must have just gone.' Now DS Leyton points as DS Jones has done, his palm crooked to the right. 'Goodman was standing at the bar and he saw Betony walk past – along the corridor in the direction of the toilets.'

DS Jones immediately interjects.

'That must have been after he left this room – having spoken with Ruth Robinson and Jackie Baker.'

DS Leyton makes a two-handed gesture, that the point is uncontested.

But now he closes his notebook.

Skelgill is quick to object.

'What about after that?'

'That's it, Guv – that's the last sighting I've got.' He looks a little defensive. Now he grins at DS Jones. 'At least it all fits together – the jigsaw.'

Skelgill is frowning discontentedly.

After a while, it falls to DS Jones to say what she surely must be thinking.

'Who could he have seen – that he apparently went after?' Again she puts her hands on the arms of her chair. 'It couldn't have been any of the three women. Two of them were sitting here. Georgina Graham was in the restaurant – or would have had to walk through here and right past him. The same for Sir Montague Brash.'

She looks to DS Leyton. He understands he should reiterate his findings.

'Like I say – as far as I can establish, Flood had just left – and

Goodman was standing at the bar and saw Betony go past. That only leaves Jay Chaudry – but he reckons he stayed in the Snug.'

Without warning Skelgill bangs his palm flat on the table, making the crockery and his sergeants jump.

'Hold your horses, Leyton.'

But when his subordinates might expect annoyance, it seems Skelgill's capriciousness is at play – for he plies them with a Machiavellian grin.

'So – which one's lying?'

His intervention seems to have the desired effect. There ensues a pause that seems to please him. That their discussion is progressing too smoothly – and perhaps that it is heading to a conclusion that he deems will be unsatisfactory.

Of the two sergeants, DS Leyton seems to take the objection more to heart.

'Thing is, Guv – and I agree – you could be right.' DS Leyton frowns pensively and runs the fingers of one hand through his mop of dark hair. 'But it ain't easy to lie about something like that – or be forgetful or be mistaken – when you've got all these other witnesses. As things stand, we've not actually got a contradiction.'

However, DS Jones makes a murmur in her throat – she seems to chuckle inwardly, and realises she ought to explain.

'It doesn't have to be just one of them that's lying.'

Skelgill has another take on her reaction.

'Aye – but why's it funny?'

DS Jones shakes her head and gives a shrug of self-reproach.

'Oh, it's nothing – silly – I was just reminded of the plot of *Murder on the Orient Express*.'

Skelgill makes a scoffing sound.

'So – Miss Marple's solved it now!'

DS Jones grins wryly.

'Actually, it was Poirot.'

Skelgill gives a further gasp of exasperation.

But DS Jones is not done with her allegory.

'We've already got Sir Montague Brash effectively lying. If one of the others stayed the night with him, that's two. And – as you say – who else?'

Skelgill folds his arms and sinks back into his seat with a hiss of frustration.

'We're singing off the same hymn sheet.' He inclines his head to indicate the papers on the table. 'We just don't know the words yet.'

'Seems to me we agree on the chorus, Guv.'

DS Leyton seems to have something up his sleeve.

'What's that, Leyton?'

DS Leyton makes a face of pre-emptive apology to DS Jones.

'That Betony was a bit of a pain in the backside. Like I said – Stephen Flood was fed up with him – and tried to find a quiet spot in the bar. And how about this – seems Betony was flying another kite – he was touting a merger between your club and that Allerdale lot.'

Skelgill instantly rebuffs the suggestion.

'Leyton, you donnat – there's more chance of you and me getting wed than the DAA joining forces with the AAA.'

DS Leyton does not take the shooting of the messenger personally.

'Funnily enough, Jay Chaudry – who seems to have a good business head on him – he reckons it would be common sense.'

Skelgill scoffs again.

'Since when did common sense trump politics? Why would turkeys vote for Christmas?'

But DS Leyton gestures that he rests his case – Skelgill's very reaction is the proof of the pudding. Any such proposal would likely have provoked the majority of Kyle Betony's fellow committee members; they are not a crew that desires its boat to be rocked.

A silence descends while they consider the possible ramifications of this line of thought. There is not one of them that thinks seriously that a murder would be committed on the strength of a controversial resolution. But there is no doubting the common thread – the confrontational character and persistent unpopularity of Kyle Betony.

'What's your gut feel?'

Skelgill surprises his colleagues; it is a question that runs against his regular grain. He unfolds his arms and leans forward, as if to indicate he is genuinely open to suggestions.

His sergeants regard one another tentatively; DS Jones indicates she will go first.

'I think we can be confident that the last sighting of Kyle Betony was at ten-thirty. I think he followed someone out through the door to the garden. I think he was probably intent upon buttonholing them.'

Skelgill nods pensively. He might split hairs that these are thoughts not feelings. After a few moments he looks to DS Leyton.

'Leyton – gut feel?'

'Same.' He seems a little flustered by the question, and sends it back. 'What about you, Guv – what's yours?'

Skelgill promptly rises and makes a smacking noise with his lips.

'Cheers, Leyton – a pint of ordinary bitter in a straight glass.'

*

'What's this, Guv?'

'An academic exercise, Leyton.'

While his sergeant has procured their drinks, Skelgill has appropriated the mounted map of the immediate district that normally hangs near the front door, alongside a rather dog-eared but nonetheless imposing antique stuffed perch.

DS Leyton is obliged to deposit their glasses on an adjacent table – although Skelgill avails himself of a swift sup before placing his pint in the deep recess of the small window at his back.

'Cheers, Leyton.'

'Good health, Guv. Emma.'

Skelgill and DS Jones are seated on the settle, facing the bar; DS Leyton takes a chair at the end of their table. He taps the map.

'You don't sound very confident, Guv.'

Skelgill does not answer directly; certainly, his tone has imbued into the phrase 'academic exercise' a pessimistic leaning. He digs into his trouser pocket. He brings out a fistful of loose change. After a moment's consideration he places a £1 coin on the map.

'There's Ouse Bridge.'

Now he selects further coins and methodically lays them out. Finally, he explains.

He begins by indicating four 50p coins in turn; they are all to the north of the River Derwent.

'Ruth Robinson, Kirkthwaite. Jackie Baker, Applethwaite. Jay Chaudry, Orthwaite. They would have driven over the bridge. Sir Montague Brash, too – if he'd gone home.'

His colleagues watch with interest.

Now he points to each of three 20p coins; these are south of the river; one to the west of the bridge, two to the east.

'Stephen Flood, Cockermouth. Georgina Graham, Swinside. Anthony Goodman, Keswick. They would have just turned onto the A66. To cross the bridge would be an irrational detour.'

There are two coppers. DS Leyton touches each in turn.

'How about these, Guv?'

'The Prof – and Alice. Braithwaite and Keswick. You can forget about them.'

It seems as if Skelgill has assigned a monetary value proportionate to some likelihood that he does not choose to explain. Or it might just be a matter of availability.

He stares broodingly at the map.

DS Leyton joins him in looking rather like a pupil defeated by a geography master's question – when asked to point out a church with a spire, a public telephone, or – something he never could quite see the significance of – the crossed-swords icon that marks the site of a battle. But after a few more moments he does raise a tentative hand.

'Where's Bewaldeth, Guv?'

Skelgill regards him reproachfully.

DS Leyton hurriedly enters a plea.

'Yeah – I know we had a case there – but I was on holiday.'

'Why Bewaldeth?'

DS Leyton turns to DS Jones.

'Can I borrow your list of committee members?'

DS Jones obliges.

DS Leyton peruses the page, having to extend his arm and squint in the subdued light.

'Here we go – Lucy Bedlington.' He looks up at his expectant colleagues. 'Anthony Goodman got a lift from his fiancée – I haven't had chance to tell you this. She's on the committee but couldn't go to the dinner because she's a GP and was on call. Look – her address is Bewaldeth. I didn't ask him – but they might have gone to her place. I had an idea it was in this neck of the woods.'

Skelgill takes the page and scrutinises it. Then he hands it back to DS Jones and produces a second £1 coin. He places it on the map, just above that which marks Ouse Bridge.

'It's close.' DS Leyton sounds pleased with himself.

Skelgill has a further question.

'What time did he leave?'

DS Leyton makes a quick check of his notes.

'He reckons she picked him up at ten past eleven. They'd agreed eleven fifteen but he saw her through the window – she arrived early, just after the Chaudry geezer had gone.'

Skelgill folds arms. He seems to be regarding the map rather sniffily, as if it is some amateurish attempt to use Cluedo to solve a crime and he wishes to dissociate himself from it.

'Fact is – the bridge is so close – anyone could have made a detour – or come back. There's not one of them lives more than fifteen minutes away.'

A silence follows. DS Jones makes an observation.

'It must only have taken us a couple of minutes on foot.'

Skelgill nods, his expression rueful.

Then, like a losing gambler in defiance of the croupier he makes a sudden two-handed lunge and scrapes together his chips.

'Talk of the devil!'

DS Leyton's hissed alert does not seem to make sense – but he reaches out and gives Skelgill's forearm a warning rat-a-tat-tat.

Skelgill looks up sharply.

A couple have entered the bar; a tall man in his forties with thinning hair and wearing a slightly creased business suit, and a shorter woman of similar age and of striking appearance that is out of kilter with that of her somewhat odd-looking chaperone. The cliché might be of the not-so-handsome boss and his moderately glamorous assistant. A strawberry blonde with straight shoulder-length hair that curves around a well-proportioned face, she wears a short-skirted suit and comparatively high heels. Skelgill notices that her gaze has swiftly if casually homed in on DS Jones. But she turns and smiles affectionately to the man when he presumably asks her what she would like to drink.

DS Leyton intones such that his voice is inaudible beyond their table.

'That's Goodman.'

Skelgill frowns questioningly.

'There's no mistaking those jugs, Guv.' DS Leyton lifts a hand to one ear.

Skelgill nods.

DS Leyton leans towards his colleagues.

'Want me to make myself scarce? He won't know you pair from Adam.'

But Skelgill shakes his head.

'Why look a gift horse in the mouth, Leyton? Bring them over while I put Charlie's map back.'

Skelgill rises and, toting the framed map, squeezes past his colleague and exits through the nearer of the two doors that give on to the corridor.

But Skelgill does not immediately reappear.

And when he does attempt to re-enter the bar, some ten minutes later, by the door closest to the counter, he has to step aside to allow Anthony Goodman and his companion to emerge, led by one of the waiting staff who bears their unfinished drinks on a tray. The woman blanks him, and instead seems to regard her partner admiringly.

Skelgill reaches for his pint from the window niche, and resumes his seat as if little has happened.

'Where did you go, Guv?' DS Jones sounds concerned.

He studies what remains of his pale ale against a wall light.

'Had to see a man about a dog.' Now he grins at her wryly – it seems no coincidence that he has repeated the phrase they heard earlier. But it is evident he is unlikely to elaborate – and indeed he acknowledges his absence. 'What's the story?'

DS Leyton seems keen to answer – as this is something of a scoop on his part.

'That was our missing committee member, Guv. The girlfriend – fiancée – whatever she is. Dr Lucy Bedlington.'

Skelgill nods as if he already knows this.

DS Leyton gestures towards the exit.

'They've got a table booked. Goodman reckons he's treating her – since she had to miss out on the slap-up committee dinner.'

Skelgill scowls markedly.

'You didn't see the menu, Leyton. Even I'd have picked the veggie option.'

DS Jones appears perturbed.

'You would think he would take her somewhere else – given what happened.'

But Skelgill responds in practical terms.

'He works at Bothel, aye?' DS Leyton nods. 'She's just up the road. If you wanted somewhere local it's the Castle Inn, Armathwaite Hall, or here.'

His colleagues do not look entirely convinced. Skelgill, however, is impatient.

'And?'

DS Leyton has taken the lead.

'Obviously, Guv – being in public – I said we might need to take a statement from her. She seemed fine about that – I suppose with her being a doctor, she understands about the Coroner and whatnot. We asked if she saw anything – anyone – any sign of Betony. She said she didn't – apart from a taxi that was waiting – and that Goodman came more or less straight out. Then they went back to her place. So they did cross Ouse Bridge. You were right about that.'

Skelgill does not comment. He drains his pint and now scrutinises the empty glass as if there is some flaw in its manufacture. Then he rises and grins somewhat mischievously at DS Jones.

'I could get used to having a driver.'

She raises her unfinished drink.

'Just a top-up of tonic for me.'

'Leyton?'

But DS Leyton waves his hands.

'Not for me, Guv – I'm on bedtime story duty. *Stig of the Dump.*'

With an involuntary groan he gets to his feet. He inhales deeply, and surveys the bar as if recovering his balance. With a sweeping gesture he seems to stir the air of their archaic surroundings.

'How important is this, Guv?'

Skelgill regards his colleague with a look of disquiet.

'Leyton – that's just what I'm trying to work out.'

8. RABBIT HOLES

Police headquarters – 7.27 a.m., Friday, 24ᵗʰ September

L ike a fox returning to its lair after a long night quartering the fells, Skelgill halts on the threshold of his office to sniff the air. His hackles have risen and he does not know why. Tod is inured to its own smells, but no interloper – canine, feline, vulpine (especially), or other creature, domestic or of the farm – can pass without leaving some trace of their being. And Skelgill's olfactory equipment is uniquely adapted to such detective work.

Roughly, he raises the venetian blind. The window is ajar, as is customary – to enable him to assess changes in temperature and humidity; to hear what calls of nature may abound – although in September Britain is bereft of birdsong, until the robin finds its melancholy autumn voice. Woodpigeons continue to coo their five-note stanza; otherwise there is just the inane chatter of juvenile delinquent magpies, the impatient ventriloquy of jackdaws, and the hungry *craa* of the carrion crow. Autumn smells are beginning to supplant the cut grass of summer, more earthy, fungal spores on the breeze, leaf mould.

Some would find such aromas unpleasant – but for Skelgill it is a connection with where he would prefer to be. Only a smoker somewhere outside the building – even a hundred yards away if they are upwind – will see him rise from his desk reluctantly to exclude the polluted outdoors. He inhales again, more deeply. Does he imagine hints of cologne and tobacco? Outside, the air is still; the alien presence does not come in on the breeze.

Without touching anything he casts about. His desk looks just as he left it three days ago – this same time of morning, when he called in to collect his papers – not having made it back as he had expected on Monday night. But before he can investigate further, he is interrupted.

It is a Keystone Cops-like entrance that DS Leyton performs, a kind of skidding on ice as if to emphasise the efforts he has made to arrive on time. He looks a little dishevelled. His hair is still damp. And there is a waft of fresh deodorant of a different order altogether, and one that is familiar.

'Phew. How was your conference, Guv? Barnard Castle, wasn't it?'

The query is made out of politeness, but Skelgill regards his subordinate in a way that makes plain he does not wish to relive the three-day residential experience. Skelgill could not be accused of being unsociable – but he is sociable on his own terms. There is the adage, one can choose one's friends but not one's family (albeit in the latter case he is a fascinated observer of some great social experiment) – but for colleagues there is no such equivalent. And anathema to him are faux camaraderie and fawning sycophancy (the latter for which he has a less printable term).

'Hard to see the point of it. I suppose the scran were alreet.'

DS Leyton guesses he refers to quantity rather than quality. And here he finds a little off-ramp.

'On which note, the ever-resourceful Emma is at this very moment cashing in favours in the canteen kitchen.'

DS Leyton sinks into his regular seat and rubs his ample stomach in anticipation. He gives an exasperated gasp.

'Snap, Crackle and flippin' Pop. Mixed up uniforms. Kits under the bed. Missing socks. Packed lunches. The littl'un screaming blue murder. Bedlam.'

Skelgill is watching his associate with widening eyes. DS Leyton is content to continue with his parental lamentations.

'I felt bad walking out the door. Too early for me to drop them off at school.'

Skelgill remains a detached observer. He has no qualms about calling a seven-thirty meeting. He has already been fishing. On his left thumb he nurses a throbbing bite from a spunky jack pike.

He eschews any opportunity to commiserate with his colleague.

'I take it I would have heard if there'd been a breakthrough.'

Skelgill's intonation is of the statement variety; DS Leyton looks like he doesn't want to disappoint his boss, and he makes a 'so-so' hand gesture.

'Nothing earth-shattering. But quite a few interesting snippets – and me and Emma have been brainstorming.' He looks hopefully at Skelgill's desk, but appears not to see whatever it is he seeks. He does however observe Skelgill's frown approaching over the craggy horizon of his brow. 'I'll wait until she gets here – she did all the typing.'

Skelgill might be about to speak – but he is distracted – his keen nose again; he has detected on the draught from the open door the aroma that precedes soft footfalls.

He makes a strange sudden grab and tilts his stack of mail trays and pulls out from beneath it a slim manila folder that is marked confidential, for his attention. He flips through several pages and is poring over the document as DS Jones enters.

He looks up – and he visibly brightens.

It would appear he is happy to see her, after three days away – but this would be a safer estimation were she not carrying a tray of teas and bacon rolls.

For her part, she seems pleased that he is reading her report.

'Oh, good – you found it – I didn't like to leave it on display.'

It is an arrangement they have used before.

Skelgill wastes no time in tucking in – it is his own adage, "never compete with the tea lady" – but hunger once stimulated must be quelled before concentration again becomes feasible. Mid-bite, however, he has a query which may to relate to the concealment of the document.

'Has Smart been sniffing around?'

His subordinates exchange glances in a way that suggests there is something they wish not to admit – but it might be imagined; more perhaps that the subject is a perennial bane, in that DI Alec Smart is always sniffing around.

Indeed, DS Leyton answers accordingly.

'No more than usual, Guv – why do you ask?'

But Skelgill shakes his head.

'Forget it.'

He looks from one to the other, employing an expression of exaggerated inquisitiveness.

DS Jones – perhaps not unwittingly – calls his bluff.

'What did you make of our report, Guv?'

Skelgill takes a hurried bite of food and gestures towards DS Leyton with his half-eaten sandwich. He speaks through his chomping.

'I was just getting into it when Leyton barged in – picking us brains about childcare.'

He flashes a silencing glare at DS Leyton, who shifts uncomfortably in his seat.

It is as DS Jones has suspected.

'Perhaps I should take us through it from the start?' Skelgill gives a nod of approval. She addresses DS Leyton. 'There are a few things I added last night.'

DS Leyton grins appreciatively; this is something of a well-rehearsed routine, the challenge of getting Skelgill to read something that does not have 'fishing' in its title (although perhaps here was a missed opportunity).

DS Jones settles herself and spreads the report on the corner of Skelgill's desk; DS Leyton has his own copy.

'To set the scene, there's no reason to believe that our initial assessment needs to change – that Kyle Betony left The Partridge at ten thirty p.m. – using the garden door – with some aim in mind – most likely that he was either in pursuit of someone, or was following them by arrangement.

'His wife told us he was excited about attending the dinner; all accounts of him are that he was in his usual upbeat mood, his head full of plans. He told Ruth Robinson and Jackie Baker that he would speak with them later. For these and other reasons it seems unlikely that he committed suicide. He wasn't drunk, and there is no logical explanation for why he would have walked alone to Ouse Bridge in total darkness, and suffered an accident.'

She has spoken without reference to notes, and has watched Skelgill carefully. He chews, unblinking, but shows no sign that he demurs. She continues, now picking up the first page to refresh her mind.

'Forensics have produced a second stage report. They ran the analysis of damaged cranial tissue through a computer model that is accurate to the 95% confidence level – in other words it would be wrong only one time in twenty. It indicates that the interval between the head impact and heart failure due to drowning could have been as long as five minutes.'

'It doesn't take five minutes to drown – not when you're out cold.'

It is Skelgill's interjection. He seems to be going along with the argument.

DS Jones nods, encouraged by his reaction.

But she offers a caveat.

'Naturally, I pressed Dr Herdwick on this point. He wouldn't be any more definitive – for example, Kyle Betony could theoretically have floated on his back, unconscious, before becoming waterlogged and drawn under by the current.'

The gravity of this finding, however – presented in the context of DS Jones's opening remarks – does not escape any of the three. It plays into a sinister narrative; put crudely, a five-minute gap between *bash* and *splash*. But none of them now volunteers to iterate such a conclusion.

DS Jones, however, takes a small step in that direction.

'It tips the scales away from the possibility that he hit his head as he fell.'

She puts down the typed sheet and picks up the next in sequence.

Skelgill has started on a second bacon roll. Again, he seems part-entranced.

'If you turn the page, Guv.'

He does so, but it is apparent that his focus has blurred; he munches pensively.

DS Jones persists.

'This is the list of hotel guests. DC Watson has spoken to at least one person from each couple – with the exception of the

'Smiths' – whom I'll come to in a moment. They were all one- or two-night stays who were checking out on Sunday. Not surprisingly, no one paid much attention to the angling committee, who for the most part were out of sight in the restaurant. It was noted that the men were wearing dinner jackets, but no one was recognised, and the majority of residents had gone to bed before the dinner began to break up. However –'

Now she pauses – and the small cliffhanger finds Skelgill turning his gaze upon her.

'One chap –' (she glances at the page) 'Mr Brian Cotswold, 67 – went down to his car to get a pillow for his wife.'

'Pillow?'

Skelgill is bemused.

DS Jones responds patiently.

'Some people travel with their own pillows – either for reasons of comfort or perhaps hygiene.'

Skelgill is frowning, somewhat indignantly.

'I reckon that would rile Charlie.'

DS Jones does not contest his assertion.

'This was at or shortly after ten-thirty p.m. As he was taking the pillow from the boot, a car arrived. The driver turned off the engine. But the person didn't get out. Mr Cotswold thought that was strange. But he was feeling conspicuous because he was wearing his pyjamas under a white hotel dressing gown – so he didn't dwell and went back inside.'

'What make of car?'

DS Jones shakes her head.

'He didn't notice. It drew into the row, a few spaces along – he was dazzled by the lights in the darkness, then when it parked he could only see the back. But he was able to state that it wasn't a minicab – there was no PHV plate.'

'A cab would have parked across the doorway.'

It is DS Leyton that chips in.

DS Jones waits for a few moments. When there are no further comments she resumes, and exchanges the page she holds for another. But when it might seem she will move on to a new aspect, her voice becomes lowered and conspiratorial.

'There is one person who might not have wanted to get out of their car.'

She raises the page illustratively. It is headed 'Mr & Mrs Smith'.

Skelgill makes a noise that might be a small inner protest that has escaped – or it might be his stomach in rebellion at being overworked. But as ever, it is both his instinct and his role to dampen heated speculation, if not pour cold water upon it. It is a fine line the detective must tread between progress and misguided meandering; one could fill one's day chasing idle fancies and tilting at windmills. But neither are there prizes for sitting on one's hands.

Moreover, when most residents had long gone to bed and other patrons were beginning to leave, it is reasonable to consider that a car turning up near closing time might have contained someone of interest. The emergency exit at the top of the external steps, conveniently left ajar, would provide easy and clandestine access to a bedroom. Even the main staircase can be gained in a matter of seconds from the porch without the requirement to pass through a public room or within sight of the generally unmanned reception.

'If there were a Mrs Smith.'

This is becoming an uncomfortable mantra for Skelgill – a sort of Pavlovian response to an unwanted stimulus. But DS Jones can put his mind at rest.

'It seems there is. I interviewed the girl who checked her in. She's a new member of staff – a trainee – a school-leaver, aged sixteen.' She makes a face that acknowledges the limitations of the evidence to follow. 'There was a sudden mini rush at reception. Three rooms checking in at the same time. All she remembers is a woman that she thinks was blonde and well-spoken. She filled in the register and the girl gave her the room key. She said she didn't need any help with bags. The girl also described her as "quite old" – which I narrowed down to being in her thirties.'

'Old!'

It is Skelgill's protest.

DS Leyton joins in.

'Flippin' right, Guv. Late thirties? That's a spring chicken nowadays.' Although DS Leyton rubs his chin pensively. 'Mind you, when the nippers have given me the run around – I'm not so sure. I don't know how the Missus keeps it up. Makes police hours seem like a stroll in the park.'

Skelgill frowns at what might be an unintentional if somewhat barbed comment upon the erratic time management he inflicts upon his team.

DS Jones returns to the matter of hair.

'Each of Ruth Robinson, Jackie Baker and Georgina Graham could be described as blonde – albeit not originally so. But it's hard to see how any of them would risk checking in under a false name. Charlie says he personally knows Jackie Baker through the hoteliers' committee. You would imagine the other two are not unfamiliar faces at the inn, given the monthly meetings.'

She realises her male colleagues are regarding her with matching bafflement. Also blonde – although of an ineffable quality with streaks of natural bronze that gain ascendancy in some lights – is her hair the subject of their distraction? Or is it that she alone knows which of the women have resorted to cosmetic treatment?

She presses on regardless.

'The address and mobile number that 'Mrs Smith' entered into the register do not exist. And she left blank the space for car registration.'

This prompts Skelgill to scrutinise his copy of the page. The address is an obscure midlands town. It means nothing to him – but he frowns all the same. A person would rarely come up with something that is totally random. More likely there is a past association – knowledge that lends the borrowed information some authenticity. And a person may use their date of birth or bank account or some other familiar sequence to construct a telephone number.

DS Jones reads his thoughts.

'It's the kind of thing that might make sense if we ever get halfway to knowing who she is.'

Skelgill nods pensively.

DS Jones wants to keep up her momentum.

'The thing is – if she were outside The Partridge at around ten-thirty, she may have seen something. She could be a material witness to Kyle Betony leaving – and anyone else who did.'

DS Leyton lends weight to their argument.

'And Brash is keeping schtum about it – otherwise that blows the gaff for him.'

Now, however, DS Jones adds a word of caution.

'She may not have mentioned anything to him. She may not be aware that she has seen anything significant.'

There is a silence, but Skelgill signifies they should move on. One degree of speculation is enough. This case offers exponential potential for clogging up grey matter.

But DS Leyton has not quite finished.

'We might have to resort to getting Brash to come clean, Guv?'

He puts the suggestion tentatively, knowing it is not a simple issue, bereft of politics or local loyalties – never mind the intractable moral dilemma of when it is acceptable to drop a bombshell into a person's private life.

But Skelgill has an alternative point of view.

'Brash could probably successfully deny he ever stayed the night. A case of mistaken identity. My word against his.'

Again a pause ensues – but Skelgill is clearly mulling over the situation, for now he provides a small concession.

'I might delegate that decision to the Chief. She hob-nobs in those circles.'

DS Leyton cannot contain a sudden exclamation.

'Hah! At least she's a redhead, Guv!'

Skelgill looks genuinely alarmed. It is a mischievous inference.

DS Jones steers the debate back onto a less contentious course.

'There's more to come on Sir Montague Brash. I think we're right to keep our powder dry about his affair, in case we conclude we should investigate him further.'

The suggestion appears to gain acceptance.

DS Jones moves on.

'I took a telephone statement from Dr Lucy Bedlington. She's based at a practice in Keswick – although she's a geriatric specialist and spends most of the time in community facilities. She told me that's how she met Anthony Goodman – about three years ago.'

Skelgill raises an eyebrow – she elaborates.

'I was curious how come both of them are on the DAA committee. It seems Anthony Goodman enlisted her – prior to their becoming an item. The care home where he works is on her patch. There was a best interest conference to discuss a patient – they got chatting and discovered a mutual interest in angling. At the time the committee had been trying to fill a vacancy for a female member. She agreed to it – although she admits she doesn't make many of the meetings because of her job.

'As we had already established, she was on call on Saturday night and didn't attend the dinner. But she confirmed what she briefly told us at The Partridge on Monday evening. She arrived to collect Anthony Goodman at ten past eleven, and he more or less came straight out to her. She didn't see anyone while she was waiting – other than the minicab – and they drove back to her cottage at Bewaldeth. They did cross Ouse Bridge, but didn't pass anyone on the road.'

DS Jones allows time for any reaction, but when nothing is forthcoming she continues.

'I asked her what she thought about Kyle Betony. I didn't put this in the report. I wondered if being a doctor she might have a sympathetic view of him. But actually she was dismissive. And of his death – although I put that down to her professional familiarity with the subject. She said Goodman found him a pest – because he is Treasurer, and Betony was wont to harry him to get his backing for project ideas. I asked if the view was widespread. She said she assumed so – and she suggested we should speak to Jay Chaudry – because he had made a couple of substantial donations to the club and that Betony was probably pressurising him for more of the same.'

DS Leyton has of course interviewed Jay Chaudry; he leans forward.

'I don't recall he said anything about that happening on the night.' DS Leyton glances at Skelgill. 'Just that merger malarkey.'

But DS Jones is nodding along.

'I think Kyle Betony consistently comes across as a low-level irritant rather than a threat to be got rid of.' She raises a palm to acknowledge that she has touched upon the largely taboo aspect of their investigation. 'I asked Lucy Bedlington if she knew of his merger proposal and she said she did not. She said Goodman didn't mention it – which supports his statement that he wasn't aware that Betony had raised it. Also, she attended the most recent committee meeting – and it didn't come up. It must be a new idea – maybe even one he had on the night, on the spur of the moment.'

DS Jones regards her colleagues in turn. DS Leyton nods in solidarity, but Skelgill merely stares at her, his inner workings otherwise occupied.

But it is DS Jones who now starts.

'Oh – one thing she did say – and I'm not quite sure why she told me this – Anthony Goodman suffers from MS.'

DS Leyton responds.

'Multiple sclerosis?'

DS Jones nods.

'She said stress can be an aggravating factor – it can bring on an attack. I didn't press her on it – but she raised it unprompted. I took it as an explanation for why Anthony Goodman tried to have little to do with Kyle Betony. But on reflection – well, maybe she was being protective of him – almost warning us off. She was quite blunt.'

DS Leyton is reflecting upon his own meeting with the man.

'I had him down as a happy-go-lucky type – although now you mention he did act queer a couple of times – I thought he was getting cramp in his legs or something.'

Skelgill appears to have lost interest and is eating again. There is perhaps the suggestion that they are spending time on the one person who has a solid alibi, including a reputable witness to his departure from the inn, while most of the others left alone. DS Jones regards him reflectively.

'I contacted Georgina Graham. As DAA Secretary she keeps

all the membership admin and minutes of meetings. If you recall, she said Kyle Betony had provided a mini biography when he applied to join the committee. She scanned it and emailed a copy to me. It's in the appendix at the back of the document. To be frank – it's actually more of a personal statement about what a boon he would be to the committee. But there is one aspect that stands out. In it he says he served on the committee of Moulsford Angling Association – on the River Thames in Oxfordshire.'

Skelgill perks up.

'Good stretch for specimen chub. Used to be, anyway.'

Unseen by him there is a meeting of raised eyebrows.

DS Jones regathers her determination.

'The thing is – there is no Moulsford Angling Association – and as far as I can establish there never has been. The nearest I could find – one that has bank rights on that part of the Thames – is the Little Stoke Coarse Fishing Club. Their secretary has confirmed that they have no record of Kyle Betony even being a member, let alone on their committee.'

Skelgill is now more engaged, though he offers a caveat.

'He wouldn't be the first person to lie on his CV.'

But DS Leyton is puzzled.

'If he's made it up – why would he pick Moulsford?'

DS Jones frowns.

'Jasmine Betony said he was originally from London. Is it far?'

DS Leyton grimaces.

'Not even Home Counties, girl – they've even got some posh name for the Thames.'

'Isis.'

Skelgill's intervention might seem entirely misplaced – were he not something of a fount of knowledge when it comes to England's rivers.

But he takes a bite of his bacon roll to indicate that his contribution is closed.

DS Jones raps the page she holds with the back of her hand.

'It's frustrating – that's all the progress I've made on his background prior to Cockermouth.'

DS Leyton is supportive.

'But he was abroad – Thailand. How long was that for? Do we know?'

DS Jones shakes her head slowly.

'DC Watson has submitted a request for his tax records. That might give us some indication of where he worked and lived when he was last in the UK. I called his wife last night – but she said he had told her very little about his life prior to meeting her – other than she reiterated that he was originally from London.'

'Might as well say he's from Timbuktu, for all that means.'

DS Jones is nodding.

'I asked whether he had been previously married. She said she didn't know – which I thought was interesting. She said she pressed him once and he got upset and so she decided she ought to let sleeping dogs lie – my words. She's obviously much younger than he was. I think culturally she regarded herself as subordinate. And she's quite inscrutable in her own right.'

Skelgill has evidently been listening more closely than his demeanour might suggest.

'Have you knocked on the head the idea that Betony was up to no good?'

She understands he refers to an affair of the heart. But before she can answer, DS Leyton interposes.

'What if she were the one that turned up in the car?' He waves his copy of the report. 'We didn't think of that.'

But Skelgill has retained the facts of his own experience.

'Leyton – she doesn't drive. His car was left at The Partridge.'

DS Leyton shrugs.

'That don't mean she *can't* drive, Guv. And she could have got a ride.'

DS Jones seems distracted by the possibility, as if she is recalculating her analysis; but Skelgill is determined.

'Leyton, you've not seen her – you could knock her down with a feather. I doubt she's six stone.'

Skelgill's inference is that she would have been physically incapable of having some role in whatever fate might have befallen her husband. DS Leyton tries again, more half-heartedly now.

'There could have been an accomplice.'

Skelgill's expression is scornful.

'What – the woman he was supposed to be seeing?'

DS Leyton pulls in his neck, hunching his shoulders, tortoise-like.

'I was thinking their disgruntled partner.'

Skelgill folds his arms and shakes his head. 'We're barking up the wrong tree.' He turns to stare at DS Jones.

She is forced to concede.

'I know – it seems less likely. Things might become clear, depending upon what detail we can obtain from Kyle Betony's mobile phone operator. The initial tracking report shows it went out of service at seven fifteen on Saturday night and never rejoined the network. Presumably it lost the signal when he entered the hotel.'

Skelgill gives a nod.

'There's no signal indoors. The walls are four foot thick. You see folk hanging out of the bedroom windows.'

DS Jones concurs.

'Naturally, I've checked with The Partridge – the handset wasn't left on a table or handed in.'

'Happen it's at the bottom of the Derwent.'

Skelgill's remark prompts DS Leyton to emerge from his shell.

'But if he took it to the bridge – don't you reckon it would have reconnected?'

'No guarantee – the signal's patchy all round Bass Lake.'

His long-suffering subordinates might pause to think that especially so his signal. Patchy to the point of vacuity.

DS Leyton, however, remains focused.

'What chance of finding it – in the river?'

Skelgill looks alarmed at the prospect.

'Leyton, between Ouse Bridge and the Colonel's Pool above Isel Bridge you're talking two miles of fast-flowing murky water. Divers could never operate in that current, let alone see owt. It must have been easier to find the Titanic.'

DS Jones offers a more hopeful perspective.

'Isn't it most likely that it would have slipped from his pocket beneath the bridge?'

Her suggestion causes some reflection; but they are each aware that there is no real way of knowing.

She takes up several new pages, but now hesitates and regards DS Leyton with a look of uncertainty; he appears to know what is coming, and responds with an encouraging nod.

She addresses Skelgill directly.

'While you were away we conducted some desk research – just to see what came up for the various DAA committee members. No one has a criminal record – but there are several points of interest – possible motives.'

Before Skelgill can object, DS Leyton weighs in on his colleague's behalf.

'This is the brainstorming I was talking about, Guv – opportunity – and motive.'

It is plain that Skelgill lacks enthusiasm.

But further negotiation is stymied. Skelgill's mobile phone emits a rarely heard but compelling ringtone.

Bat out of Hell.

The Chief.

Skelgill simultaneously rises and picks up the handset; he takes leave of his colleagues – they hear only his opening salutation, followed by a silence for as long as he is within earshot.

*

'What's the news, Guv?'

Whether it is because DS Jones is a more astute reader of Skelgill's demeanour – and therefore holds back – or just that DS Leyton is saddled with indefatigable optimism, it behoves him to be the one that prompts their superior upon his return; albeit he avoids what would be the more perspicacious question, "Bad news, Guv?"

In the avoidance of any doubt, Skelgill responds with a line of

Anglo-Saxon iambic pentameter that ends with "Smart".

'I'll get my coat.'

DS Leyton rises, as if in disgrace – but as he turns he winks at the alarmed-looking DS Jones. He corrects his statement.

'Fresh teas all round, I reckon.'

He does not enquire about further food rations – even Skelgill cannot eat another bacon roll.

DS Leyton's optimism is not dimmed by the ill tidings written across Skelgill's face. He is ever phlegmatic. If DI Smart is up to his usual tricks it will likely not end well for the usurper – and merely galvanise Skelgill to extra efforts – despite that he would deny any such competitive reaction.

Indeed, when the stoical sergeant re-enters the office in short order with drinks (one oversized mug piping hot) Skelgill already looks to have descended from the upper level of anger to a state of grim determination. He even acknowledges the procurement of the beverage with a vaguely condescending nod.

Evidently he has saved the explanation for the return of his colleague.

'Smart's come up with some fantasy solution. Supposedly on the say-so of a snout. A drugs connection to Manchester. Links to some wider investigation – a gang that imports from Thailand.'

Skelgill looks like he wants to bang his fist on the desk – but realises that his tea might become collateral damage – and he is obliged to let off the steam in the form of a pained gurning expression that would be unsettling to anyone unfamiliar with him.

He leaves it to his sergeants to join the dots. DS Leyton makes the first stab.

'What – like Betony was in on it? That it was a drugs deal on Saturday night – that's why he went out to the bridge?'

Skelgill does not answer, but neither does he contradict the suggestion.

DS Jones offers a more reasoned analysis.

'Kyle Betony has the Thailand connection. Jay Chaudry is Manchester-based and –'

She is cut off as DS Leyton interjects indignantly.

'He's flippin' well cherry picking! Taking the bits of our investigation that fit his cock-and-bull story.'

When Skelgill ought to be nodding in accord, instead he stares severely at DS Jones. It appears there is more.

'He's requested that you're seconded to his team.'

DS Jones does not immediately react – at least, not verbally; but there is no mistaking her body language as she crosses her legs and lowers her gaze.

DS Leyton seems to sense he is called upon.

'How come he never asks for me, Guv?'

He wins Skelgill's attention – and perhaps there is a glimmer of amusement in his presently greyer-than-green eyes, that his sergeant has resorted to self-deprecation in an attempt to defuse an awkward moment. Of course, DS Leyton is not blind to DI Smart's supposedly professional interest in their attractive female associate.

DS Leyton sees that he has the initiative.

'I know you're way smarter than me, Emma – but you'd think my worn shoe-leather in the Met would count for something when it comes to urban crime. I mean – Manchester – it's not even Britain's second city, is it?'

Skelgill accedes to the diversion; though his tone is cynical.

'Leyton – are you volunteering to work for Smart?'

DS Leyton is quick to respond.

'Not likely, Guvnor – it's the principle I'm complaining of.' But then he glances again at DS Jones. 'Course – if I could save your bacon – you can count on me to jump into the frying pan. Call me a rhino – but being thick-skinned has its uses.'

DS Jones smiles gratefully – but she transfers her inquisitive gaze to Skelgill. She is anxious to know what is the outcome of his negotiation with the Chief.

Battle of wills might better describe it.

Skelgill folds his arms and rests his elbows on his desk and glowers unseeingly at the papers spread before him. What he has not told his colleagues is of the ominous backdrop painted by his superior – and – he suspects – sketched out to her by the scheming

DI Alec Smart. Smart cannot reveal his sources – but has sworn on his (probably still living) grandmother's grave that the lead is gilt-edged. This is unlikely in any circumstances – but unprovable, and there is nothing Skelgill can do. Smart has no doubt pointed out that Skelgill and his team have made limited progress (no crime scene, no suspect) – moreover, he has clearly insinuated that the root cause of such ineptitude might just be that Skelgill is too close to the investigation for comfort. He is not only a member of the angling club that is effectively under investigation, but also a close personal friend of at least two of its management committee. How can he be expected to act objectively, to operate at arm's length?

Skelgill's immediate counter was of course that this is the very reason why he can and will solve the case. His insider knowledge is no different to the reason that Mancunian DI Smart spends much of his time working on cases with links to the drab metropolis. Moreover, that Skelgill's knowledge of the DAA, its mores and methods – his 'inside contacts' (who have impeccable credentials, by the way) – is far more likely to get him to the heart of the matter. Patient fieldcraft is required – when a swashbuckling Smart would wade in swinging and cause total mayhem.

Skelgill's riposte did at least give pause for thought – but not before he was forced to use what little real ammunition he had. In the crisis he saw looming he detonated his nuclear option and dropped the Brash bomb. And perhaps this was the deterrent that stalled Smart's vicarious advance in the shape of their superior. But it has left his arsenal empty.

The Chief has granted an armistice of sorts – until the middle of next week before she makes (or rather implements) the decision. Skelgill is to achieve progress, otherwise she will temporarily dismantle his team and scale down his involvement in this particular operation in favour of DI Smart's line of enquiry. CID have enough fingers in the dam that holds back a flood of misdemeanours; they cannot afford parallel investigations on a case that appears to pose no downstream threat to the public at large.

Accordingly, Skelgill – without directly responding to DS Jones's obvious entreaty for information – now exhibits what must seem to his colleagues like something along the lines of an epiphany. He sits back in his sprung chair and takes a drink from his steaming mug and indicates with a sweep of his free right hand the papers before him.

'What's this opportunity and motive idea, then?'

But the effort of the change of heart is a little too much for him. He abruptly rises and turns to look at his map on the wall; after a moment he moves across to the window beside DS Jones and stares out at the attenuated clouds that scud across a pale autumn sky, still creamy dawn blue on the southern horizon; small flocks of migrating woodpigeons battle into a light headwind. His agitation is plain: he would rather be out hunting varmints than indoors chasing shadows.

His colleagues regard him with expressions of mild suspicion mixed with limited optimism.

But DS Jones wastes no more time; Skelgill might change his mind.

'Guv – the premise is that if Kyle Betony knew something – had discovered something – then that knowledge might have made him a target.' She holds up her hands in response to Skelgill's deepening frown. 'Kyle Betony had a deficit of tact – and a big mouth – and might have put his foot in it to someone else's detriment.'

Skelgill is perhaps mollified by her creative use of the idiom – he grins, though there remains a certain pained edge to his expression. However, he resumes his seat and buries his nose in his mug; it is a sign of grudging attention being paid.

DS Jones references the report.

'Based on what we know from our interviews, and what we've subsequently found out, the obvious person to start with is Mr Smith – aka Sir Montague Brash.'

She pauses to gauge Skelgill's reaction – but he remains deadpan.

'Actually, it has been apparent from the start that he has a potential motive. He spent the night with someone and doesn't want to admit it.' She glances at DS Leyton. 'Setting that aside for

140

a moment, we looked into the incident with the poacher who was burned – remember, that Ruth Robinson related to us?' (Skelgill appears to nod.) 'The case was settled out of court. We couldn't trace the victim – and there are no official records beyond hospital notes that were taken at the time of his admission to A&E. But they are potentially significant. The man had other injuries consistent with having suffered a beating.'

There ensues a silence – but eventually Skelgill speaks.

'You met him.'

DS Jones understands his shorthand – the suggestion that she would have some insight. She recalls the steely blue eyes beneath the wolfish covetousness.

'I imagine you wouldn't want to get on the wrong side of him.'

Skelgill gives the slightest nod; but he plays devil's advocate all the same.

'If it meant that much not to get caught – why would he take the risk of meeting her at The Partridge?'

DS Jones answers quickly, almost by reflex.

'Isn't that part of the fun? The high.'

Skelgill regards her implacably.

She continues, returning his gaze with a hint of insouciance.

'Kyle Betony saw someone at around ten-thirty p.m. If that was Mrs Smith and he recognised her – or for whatever reason was able to put two and two together – then he might have approached Sir Montague Brash. We know from the hotel guest Brian Cotswold that someone did arrive at about that time of the night. The only witness we have to Sir Montague Brash's movements during the latter part of the evening is Georgina Graham – and she did leave him alone for a short period at roughly ten thirty.'

'There's French doors from the Wythop Restaurant into the kitchen garden. You can get round either side of the building from there.'

It is Skelgill who, perhaps to his colleagues' surprise, supplies this supporting information.

DS Jones looks encouraged.

'If you add into the equation Georgina Graham – I mean, that she is Mrs Smith,' (she looks at Skelgill in a way that acknowledges that this is more of a leap in the dark) 'then we would have to disregard as false anything she has told us. While I'm pretty certain she can prove she went home at eleven fifteen, she could easily have driven back. But there are caveats. Clearly she was not the person who arrived in a car at ten thirty. Nor would she would cause Kyle Betony any surprise – unless perhaps he saw her heading up the stairs with an overnight bag – something like that.'

They wait, and after a few moments Skelgill speaks again.

'I let the Chief know about me seeing Brash – and him stonewalling you.'

When he is no more forthcoming, DS Jones seeks reassurance.

'She wouldn't tip him off – without telling us first?'

Skelgill instantly shakes his head, his jaw set.

'But we need to find the woman.'

'That's exactly where we came out, Guv.'

It is DS Leyton that interjects – but he signals to DS Jones that he appreciates she has not quite finished her account.

'As regards the backgrounds of the three women who attended the meeting, nothing particularly controversial has come up. The DAA seems to be running to their satisfaction. Georgina Graham has a longstanding position as Secretary. The Robinsons' farm gains from a share of permit fees, and Jackie Baker's guest house attracts angling visitors because of its allocation of fishing rights. They seem content with the level of activity – if they wanted more money, why not actually support Kyle Betony's scheme to expand permit sales? So it's harder to see what they might have against him – other than just his nuisance value, and the suggestions they have made that they're content with the status quo.

'While we've considered Georgina Graham's probable movements, Ruth Robinson and Jackie Baker we can be less certain about. They left at the same time, ten forty-five, and both drove over Ouse Bridge. Ruth Robinson told us she slept in the spare room, and didn't wake her husband. Jackie Baker's return home, we haven't yet verified. I don't think we can read too much into these points – but we should just keep them in mind.'

Once again, Skelgill gives a tight-lipped nod.

DS Jones hands over to her fellow sergeant; DS Leyton tentatively clears his throat.

'You aware of the River Ellen poisoning incident, Guv?'

Skelgill seems mildly affronted by the question.

'Course I am, Leyton. Killed two thousand wild brownies and set the fishery back a decade.'

DS Leyton taps the side of his nose like a beat copper of old, when asked to reveal some local knowledge. He raises a page from the report.

'Exhibit number one. Stephen Flood. Area Supervisor, Water Quality. It turns out that our Mr Flood is mentioned in despatches. He was over his head in it. And he didn't come up smelling of roses, neither.'

He has Skelgill's attention.

'To cut a long story short – and you probably know much of this, Guv – there was a pollution incident. Silage effluent escaped into the water course. The farm – industrial-scale contract operation – tried to claim it was a one-off leak. But it turns out it had been a systematic thing – they'd got away with it for a couple of years at a lesser concentration. The Environment Agency investigators suspected something fishy – there would have been regular inspections, which suggests someone in authority turned a blind eye. The spotlight fell on Stephen Flood, senior inspector for that area. In the end they couldn't prove anything, and the farm took the rap. They were handed a fine, and Flood escaped with a slap on the wrist. The local press reported that the fine was small beer compared to the money the farm must have saved, and the insinuation was that *someone* took a bung.'

DS Leyton pauses, both for breath and to take a drink of his tea, and to allow Skelgill to absorb the implications; the latter sits stern-faced, however.

'Point being, Guv – looks like our man Flood's got a skeleton rattling in his closet – and it being angling related it might be just the sort of thing that Betony would come across. He was obviously inquisitive by nature – and didn't he tell Jay Chaudry that he'd been doing his homework – which was what had prompted him to come up with the idea of the merger?' The question is rhetorical, and DS Leyton continues swiftly. 'Now – if you had to ask me, of the geezers I interviewed, who's the likely nasty piece of work – then Flood stands out like a sore thumb. He's hard-faced in looks and manner – and we know that Betony was hounding him on Saturday night. He admitted as much and that he wasn't happy about it.'

Skelgill shifts in his seat, as if to object, but again DS Leyton keeps up his narrative.

'Yeah – I know – that arguably works in his favour – but the others knew as well, so he could hardly say otherwise. But what he also admitted was that he left at exactly the same time that Betony seems to have seen someone – and disappeared. We've only got Flood's word that he went to the gents' and that Betony was gone when he got back to his table in the bar. What if Flood had left directly from the gents' – out through the garden exit – and then Betony followed him? Or vice-versa, even.'

Now there is a silence; and an air of plausibility. However, DS Leyton presses home his point, for Skelgill always keeps a little scepticism tucked away like a spare cigarette behind his ear.

'The thing is, Guv – something like this must have happened.'

Any counter that Skelgill might bring to bear is confounded. In these plain terms, his sergeant is right. Kyle Betony slipped from the inn while his associates were all going about their own business. Yet surely one of them must have been involved. Who – exactly where – and how – these are questions that remain tantalisingly beyond the detectives' grasp. He nods for DS Leyton to continue.

His sergeant again appears to confer silently with his female colleague before he begins afresh.

'Righto – Jay Chaudry, then. On the face of it – a decent cove – a bit of a mini-philanthropist. He seems to be trying hard to ingratiate himself with the locals – and he's not been shy of opening his wallet. The others speak well enough of him. But how about this – it's what Emma was about to say when I interrupted – unfortunately, this is the thing that might play into DI Smart's hands.'

DS Leyton seems for a moment reluctant to expound.

'Out with it, Leyton.'

His sergeant seems to steel himself.

'He's built a successful tech company – but that stands on the foundations of several bankruptcies and phoenixes. Okay – that's not illegal, or unusual – especially in IT where it's all boom and bust. But his current incorporation is involved in litigation with Greater Manchester Police. His company has developed a secure communications app that's being used by – among others – drug dealers. On the advice of its solicitors the firm has refused to divulge the encryption code – using the argument that hundreds of other bona fide organisations that bought it would be compromised.'

Skelgill looks like he has put two and two together, but DS Leyton spells it out, raising the fingers of one hand in quick succession.

'Manchester – drugs – Chaudry – Lakes connection – too good to be true for DI Smart. He'll be all over it like a rash, Guv. He'll pin Betony's death on Chaudry before you can say Jack Robinson.' In a sign of frustration, DS Leyton lays his papers on his lap and with both hands tousles his hair, rendering the proverbial 'hedge backwards' look. He sighs. 'Thing is – I don't reckon we can ignore it, neither. What I've told you is public information – it's all reported online. Betony could easily have dug it up. He was a financial advisor – I wouldn't have been surprised if he researched the backgrounds of people he came into contact with.'

Skelgill is listening pensively. He places a palm flat upon the report on his desk and turns to DS Jones.

'I take it this is just a rough draft?'

She nods urgently.

'Purely work in progress. I don't think we need to load anything onto the system until we begin to approach the committee members again.'

Skelgill folds his arms and exhales broodingly.

Surely DI Smart cannot really have struck a seam. He must be operating in the dark – guessing – or, as DS Leyton has put it, cherry-picking from their preliminary report. But now there is a limit to which they can investigate this new Manchester angle without informing the Chief. And she would be inclined to hand it to DI Smart, along with DS Jones. Her job is to get from A to B by the fastest, most efficient route – not to make it a favourable ride for a journeyman like himself.

DS Leyton seems to read his thoughts.

'Guv – I'm not saying there's something in what DI Smart's come up with. It's like a TV crime drama – a deadly double-cross on the bridge under the cover of darkness. But hype aside – Chaudry was left alone in the Snug for the time it took Anthony Goodman to fetch their drinks. He could easily have nipped out of the front door without being seen – and the time was ten thirty. Later – at just after eleven – he left on his own – also unwitnessed, as far we know.'

DS Leyton waits, but when there are no further comments he turns the page.

'Last of my bunch – Anthony Goodman. Like I said – he's a cheerful sort – tries to please – seems perfectly above board. But there was a bit of a scandal a few years back. A resident had changed their will at the eleventh hour in favour of the care home. The relatives believed she would never have done it. When the Care Quality Commission investigated they found at least two other instances. Now, there was no suggestion of impropriety. No personal connection or benefit to Goodman. And it does happen – some people are left alone by their relatives and decide they want to bequeath to those who've treated them well. But he's Director of Finance, and it was on his watch. His name was in the press. An article by our old pal Minto, no less.' DS Leyton glances at DS Jones, but she keeps her gaze lowered. 'Once again, it's all public information that Betony could have found on the internet. And I wouldn't be surprised if that's why Goodman's girlfriend was so touchy – she's concerned about his medical condition and she don't want these old coals raked over, if they've caused him grief once before. That might not have bothered Betony.'

DS Leyton glances at his fellow sergeant, as if this latter point has been the subject of specific debate – and now there is tacit agreement to share their suspicions with Skelgill.

'As Emma touched upon, Guv – what no one on the committee really wants to admit to – is the suggestion that Betony was more than just pushy. What if he weren't averse to digging up a bit of dirt? His regular MO – to win friends and influence people. Find their Achilles' heel. He was clearly ambitious – wanting to make his mark on the DAA. Twist a few arms, get some wins under his belt. Claim the credit and stand for election for one of the bigger jobs. One way or another, that kind of behaviour could put someone's nose out of joint.'

DS Leyton methodically folds the cover over his copy of the report; he regards Skelgill earnestly.

Skelgill rocks a little from side to side, as if buffeted by an unseen wind, but without revealing which way it blows.

'You've been busy.'

When his tone – using such words – might ordinarily be sarcastic, it is possible to draw from his observation the semblance of a compliment, that his team have done a thorough job in unearthing possible leads in trying circumstances. However, he rests in contemplative silence, exhibiting neither marked enthusiasm nor outright despondency. In his mind's eye, however, there plays out a most peculiar daydream. Where the old coaching inn ought to stand against the rising wooded fellside, it is as if he faces a wild bank that is excavated in places, small entrances recently dug, well trodden and marked by fresh spoor. But which of these holds their quarry? Does he bite into the mushroom and take his chance? To venture randomly down a particular rabbit hole is a risk in itself; to become lost in the dark twisting labyrinth of a warren would be doubly foolhardy.

9. WONDERING WITH ALICE

Bassenthwaite Lake – 5.38 p.m., Saturday 25ᵗʰ September

'I should say that actually catching a fish is rather like the cherry on top of a cake, wouldn't you agree, Daniel?'

Skelgill looks distinctly uncomfortable with this notion. He has in one hand a piece of the plain but delicious home-baked ginger cake that his angling companion has supplied. After a few moments' consideration, he offers a reluctant compromise.

'Aye – maybe the icing.'

Alice Wright-Fotheringham gives a knowing chuckle.

'Do I take it that your competitive spirit is undampened?'

'We've still time, if you like?'

'I think my aged wrists have had enough for one afternoon. Your plugging method is demanding.'

Skelgill frowns.

'It's not often the paintbrush draws a blank. I'll give you the pool cue, next time.' He refers to his improvised lures, which dangle from the pike rods that extend from the stern of the rowing boat, beached a few yards along the shore from where they sit. He tilts back his head and examines the sky; there is high cloud of indeterminate form, beginning to reflect hints of evening. 'This high pressure – it can play tricks on the fish – interferes with their lateral lines – they don't seem to recognise the vibrations as a sign of distress.'

He senses that the retired lawyer and judge is examining him as though he might almost be alluding to his own condition; a state of being partially enfeebled. He resolves not to appear downcast. Besides – he would fish on. It is a long-promised expedition –

albeit that she has had to call to remind him. And then he had suspected she was just a little peeved that he had not been to interview her about the present investigation into Kyle Betony and the DAA.

'There are times when the catching of fish spoils an angling expedition. A rude interruption of what can be a transcendental experience.'

Skelgill looks a bit baffled – does she suggest that this might have been one such event? To his mind, the time has passed fitfully, as he has manoeuvred from place to place in search of some action. He would feel more revitalised had they wetted the landing net, and that it was hanging out to dry. He gazes pensively across the silvery meniscus; at roughly half way there is the inverted skyline of Sale Fell, curiously distorted by invisible undulations in the lake surface. A couple of migratory black terns dip for fry, and he wonders what they might be feeding upon.

'This is Scarness Bay, am I right?'

Skelgill is jolted from his empty reverie.

'Aye – it is.'

'I must enquire of Jim about the etymology. I would have thought the Vikings were within his ambit; their time here was medieval, was it not?'

Now Skelgill turns upon the distinguished elderly lady an expression of more complete bewilderment – that this could possibly be a question intended for him. However, she regards him searchingly – and with an effort he hews a reply from the abandoned quarry of his historical knowledge.

'Arthur Hope reckons the Herdwicks have been here above a thousand years. They say they came with the Vikings.'

'It conjures an image that rather belies their macho reputation.'

It could almost be a mischievous remark, and Skelgill feels a blush on his cheeks. Unsure of how to reply, he stretches forward with an involuntary groan and gives his Kelly kettle a shake. There is a modest sloshing sound.

'I can put on another mash.'

Alice Wright-Fotheringham seems to understand his diplomacy. She raises her tin mug to indicate it is not empty.

'You have what is left. I should probably get back soon. I have to pick up Justitia from the vet – she has an ingrowing dewclaw. The dog, that is.'

Skelgill cannot suppress a short laugh at the unexpected quip. He notes a sparkle in the still-vital pale blue eyes.

'Good luck with your bank balance.'

'Oh, I believe the insurance covers it as standard – rather like a cracked windshield on a car.'

Skelgill makes a face that is revealing of some failing on his part in this regard.

Again Alice Wright-Fotheringham is sensitive to his predicament.

'Cleopatra is well, I trust?'

But Skelgill remains just a tad on the defensive.

'She's with next door. It's her second home. They spoil her rotten.'

'I hear she made another arrest.'

Skelgill has taken a drink from his mug and now almost spits out his tea – but he emerges grinning – for he gets that humour is intended.

'She's daft as a brush. Thinks everyone's her marra. She wouldn't know Snow White from Dick Turpin. But flattens them, all the same.'

'Yes – Jim was telling me – the Canine Cannonball. I suppose it avoids the wrong person being bitten – when a convivial head-butt achieves the same effect.'

'Comes in mighty handy.'

'And yet Jim was saying she behaves impeccably whenever you visit.'

'Aye, that's because he's always got a tray of scones on the go.'

The woman regards Skelgill as though she is thinking it is likely not just the dog.

'Nevertheless, a feather in your cap.'

Skelgill seems reluctant to bask in any such praise.

'You're only as good as your next case. When the powers that be have the memory span of goldfish.'

He picks up a pebble and flicks it into the shallows. It must land amidst a shoal of fry, setting off a swishing panicked chain-reaction. There is a small hiatus as they watch the ripples extend and fade.

'Do I deduce that you face some challenge with the present case?'

Skelgill throws another, larger stone – an act of some resignation. He simultaneously exhales in frustration.

'Aye – a colleague of mine. Some story he's fed to the Chief. That I'm too close to see the wood for the trees. Wants to jump in with his size twelves.'

But Alice Wright-Fotheringham – a long career of prosecuting behind her – is far too shrewd not to see through his superficial excuse.

'This is hardly witness tampering, Daniel. Show me the rule that says how evidence must be collected. If you draw the inside lane it is your prerogative to run in it.'

Skelgill nods ruefully. That he is part of the fabric of the land is, in his mind, undoubtedly a strength – and his wise companion seems to be reflecting this view. Moreover, if anyone were to tear up the rules it would be Smart – who would in a heartbeat resort to thumbscrews, lies and deviousness to achieve his ends – and who, as an outsider, bears no burden of loyalty to the community and no qualms about laying waste to all in his path, nor the destruction and resentment that would lie scattered in his wake.

Skelgill gets a sudden flash of clarity – that Smart might either solve it completely, or completely queer their pitch – and he is not sure which he dislikes the most.

Alice Wright-Fotheringham interrupts his thoughts.

'You are right to be judicious in your approach. It reminds me of when Mrs McGinty died.'

'Come again?'

Is this some infamous felony he has completely forgotten – or perhaps one drawn from her extensive personal canon of case law?

'Agatha Christie – surely you have read it?'

Skelgill cannot help digging the beginnings of a small hole for himself.

'Er – there's so many – I struggle to remember. Er … Miss Marple –'

'It was Poirot – but an uncharacteristic authorial flaw if you ask me. The great detective arrives at the village broadcasting to all and sundry that he knows 'whodunit' – when in fact he has no idea – and hey presto there's another murder as the killer panics to cover their tracks.'

With a prosecutorial flourish of one hand, she rests her case.

There ensues another silence while she allows Skelgill to process the aphorism. But she clearly senses that he is willing to talk. Eager, perhaps, though he will not admit it.

'You have enough to be suspicious of foul play?'

But Skelgill begins with a sharp intake of breath in lieu of explicit self-reproach.

'We've got no suspect – we've got no crime scene. But one minute Kyle Betony's there – the next he vanishes into thin air. He washes up at the Colonel's Pool with an injury that could hardly be self-inflicted.'

'Then you are right to speak to me.'

Skelgill regards her with a look of surprise.

But now she rows back a little. She holds up a palm.

'I mean rather than keep me at arm's length out of misguided loyalty or lip service to police protocol. And it is true – neither Jim nor I were there at the crucial time. I have little to add that is top of mind – but if you were to prompt me, who knows?'

Skelgill appears a little reluctant to respond; it seems now he is on the receiving end of a fishing expedition.

'Daniel – to illustrate – can you name, let's say – an American baseball player?'

He is entirely perplexed; this comes from left of field.

'Nay – don't reckon I can. It's not exactly cricket, Alice.'

She is undaunted.

'Have you heard of Joe DiMaggio?'

'Aye, of course.'

'And what do you know about him?'

Skelgill screws up his features, revealing his front teeth in the effort of concentration.

'He was in a song.'

Alice Wright-Fotheringham chuckles. She wags an index finger.

'I think my point is proved.'

Now Skelgill nods slowly. She has tempted him out from the security of his lair. He inhales more philosophically now.

'We know it's no secret that Kyle Betony rubbed folk up the wrong way.' He glances sideways and receives a nod of confirmation. 'But he might have gone further – taken it too far. Perhaps for a reason – perhaps just because he was tactless and nosy. But he might have said something that was perceived as a threat.'

She does not answer. When he looks there is a glaze to her expression that he recalls from her days on the bench. But she issues a terse command.

'Go on.'

Skelgill decides he can show something of his hand. He plays what he considers to be his safest card.

'Mentioning no names. We know that one of committee stayed over and spent the night with a member of the opposite sex.'

Now a more prolonged silence ensues. They both gaze out over the silent lake. It is only when an iridescent-green-headed drake mallard makes an ungainly splashdown some twenty yards offshore that Alice Wright-Fotheringham pronounces.

'It is usually close to home, is it not?'

When Skelgill turns to look at her, she expounds upon her judgement.

'I have overseen many cases of divorce. Affairs – or indeed more legitimate relationships – they rarely drop out of the blue. Colleagues, neighbours, in-laws, old flames – they would account for almost every instance.'

Now Skelgill appears to be the one that is distracted.

'Daniel?'

He starts.

'Aye – they do.'

'So that would be my advice – at least on that account.'

He nods.

'It might be a red herring, Alice. Just a coincidence.' The wrong rabbit hole.

'Of course – you are right to be cautious.'

Now Skelgill is a little more forthcoming.

'Trouble is – we don't know much about Kyle Betony. There's a stepping stone missing between him and the next person.' He pauses for a moment – and then perhaps her maxim sinks in and he poses a specific question. 'Seems he was touting the idea of a merger between the DAA and the AAA. Did you hear talk of that?'

Alice Wright-Fotheringham raises an eyebrow, but remains unflustered.

'At the dinner I was not seated beside him. And I am not aware of any such discussion previously.' She ponders for a moment. 'I believe there used to be an annual match.'

Now Skelgill is surprised.

'You know about that?'

She smiles patiently.

'I was in London back in those days, of course. But, Daniel – don't forget that I hail from a long line of Cumberland anglers.'

Skelgill nods reflectively.

'I fished in it once.'

'Really?' She sounds intrigued. 'That does not seem to be your style.'

He gives a shrug of his shoulders.

'I were nobbut a bairn. A last-minute sub for the arl fella – he were – indisposed.'

She regards him with pointed amusement.

'In the doghouse.'

'You know that, an' all?'

Skelgill sounds a little alarmed.

'Daniel – Ah kent tha' father.' She assumes the accent in which she perhaps once spoke. 'We were contemporaries of a sort.'

Now she gestures to the boat.

'Did you change the name?'

Skelgill looks momentarily disquieted.

'It's supposed to be unlucky. I call her all sorts of things – as the fancy takes me. *The Doghouse* just wore off in time.'

But now Alice Wright-Fotheringham picks up the former thread.

'So you fished in the match. There cannot be many who can say that.'

Skelgill sighs ruefully.

'Must be the best part of thirty years ago. Apparently it were the first time the DAA had won. There's a framed press-cutting in the bar at The Partridge. Under the Northern Counties team that beat the All Blacks.'

'Fine company to keep.'

Skelgill looks a little awkward.

'Not exactly in the same league. I suppose it were more of a regulars' local in those days.'

Again the retired judge seems to deliberate.

'I wonder when the schism occurred.'

Skelgill shakes his head.

'I only did it the once. I've only ever been a lowly member. I leave politics to the troublemakers.'

She chuckles, since it seems she takes this as a small if back-handed compliment.

'A man who ploughs his own furrow.'

The conversation seems to have run its course. Alice Wright-Fotheringham offers the ginger cake. It is a large tin, with moist dark squares nestling among crisp baking parchment. Munching contemplation ensues; it is often the most productive sort.

'So, Daniel – what is your instinct?'

Skelgill squints over the calm water; while his jaw moves steadily, his gaze finds the point on the distant shore that marks the hidden entrance to Peel Wyke, and beyond, concealed by trees, the old coaching inn.

'I can't see past The Partridge.'

'Then follow your heart, if that is the locus.'

Skelgill is unmoving – until he suddenly starts.

'What is it?'

He looks at his watch with a small expression of horror.

'I'm supposed to be meeting someone there – ten minutes ago.'

Alice Wright-Fotheringham laughs knowingly. She drains her mug, and puts the lid on the tin, and hands them together to Skelgill.

'Take the ginger cake – it will keep for elevenses tomorrow.'

She grins further when she sees that she has set him an impossible challenge.

*

'There was no signal – else I'd have warned you. And what with Alice yattering on – trying to be helpful, mind. She came up with a couple of good ideas.'

There is something about Skelgill's multi-faceted and yet disjointed excuse for being late that has DS Jones regarding him with what might be described as a "why am I laughing?" expression.

But she is more conciliatory in her words.

'It's okay – I saw your car. I knew you'd be along.' Still seated in her yellow VW, she holds up a paperback. 'I brought my training manual.' Skelgill sees it is *Miss Marple's Final Cases*.

She raises her driver's window and clambers out.

Skelgill takes a step back. While not dressed to the nines, she has a way of being eye-catching with small effort. And it is Saturday night.

For his part – literally hotfoot from Peel Wyke, the cake tin tucked under one arm, having declined Alice Wright-Fotheringham's lift of a few hundred yards in order to stow his gear and secure his boat – it is plain that he suddenly registers the contrast between his colleague's well-groomed appearance and his own dishevelled condition. With both hands he claws back unruly hair to expose more of his craggy and slightly uneasy countenance.

He indicates to his shooting brake, parked some distance away; there had been a wedding party at The Partridge when he arrived to fish.

'I could get changed – but I don't want to keep you hanging about.'

DS Jones grins.

'I think the phrase is, "I could murder a pint" – yes?'

Skelgill has little recourse but to look sheepish.

'Aye – well – we'll get settled and I'll pop out for my stuff. I'll get changed in the gents.'

He reaches ostentatiously for his wallet – as though he thinks he had better make some redeeming gesture.

As they enter – beneath the rustic porch and into the short hallway with the Snug on the left and the bistro on the right – DS Jones notices the famous stuffed perch.

'Did you catch anything?'

Skelgill heads on, rounding left into the corridor and turning right into the bar.

'Let's say I'm still working on it.'

He glances about, momentarily preoccupied. The small bar seats only a score of drinkers at a push, and is about half full – but he spies that the table tucked into the far corner recess is free. A couple who were descending the stairs have followed them into the room.

Skelgill speaks from the side of his mouth.

'Grab the alcove.'

DS Jones understands.

It is a few minutes before Skelgill joins her – but she immediately picks up the conversation they have left off.

'So – you didn't catch any fish but Alice had some good ideas?'

Skelgill now distracts; he tears open a bag of crisps and lays it flat so they can share. He starts munching so that any answer is more difficult. But DS Jones waits patiently.

'Not exactly ideas – not like –' (Skelgill casts about for inspiration) 'not like – Colonel Mustard in the library with a candlestick.'

DS Jones laughs.

'More like sentiments?'

His colleague is closer to the mark; but now the answer, with its personal connotations, seems embarrassing. And what exactly were these sentiments? While they have left an impression upon him, they are clichés, really. Close to home. Follow your instincts. He finds himself turning to look vacantly at his companion.

'What is it, Guv?'

Skelgill waves a hand – he could almost be standing before an invisible rock face that bars his path and he feels its presence.

'Aye – well – she's long experienced – she were a barrister before she were a judge – you know that?'

'Yes.'

Scrabbling about, now Skelgill finds a small handhold.

'She thinks we're dead right about Smart.'

But this is vague – it could mean several things – and DI Smart is transparent despite his artful smokescreening.

'That he's a chancer?'

Skelgill produces a pained grimace; no way is he going to cite Mrs McGinty! But he finds an alternative form of words.

'More that if you treat them all as suspects – you show your hand – to the one that you don't want to know.'

DS Jones nods in accord.

'Besides, it becomes an impossible jigsaw – suddenly it's multi-dimensional – when you're asking everyone about what everyone else did.' She gestures loosely about the room. 'It's been hard enough just trying to establish Kyle Betony's movements.'

Skelgill is drinking. He puts down his empty glass with a habitual clunk and a small gasp of satisfaction.

DS Jones exclaims.

'That didn't touch the sides!'

'I ran out of tea.'

DS Jones shakes her head, unconvinced. It seems unlikely; Skelgill has spare teabags sewn into his hems like convicts keep hacksaw blades; and there would be no shortage of water.

'I'll get you another.'

Skelgill begins to protest, but she insists, placing a hand on his arm and rising herself.

He watches a little uneasily. He is wondering if he should go for his change of clothes – but the bar is filling up; with no Cleopatra to play sentry they might lose their table. He sees that Charlie has been summoned – all hands to the pumps – to cope with the mini-rush of residents wanting a drink before dinner. He notices a couple of middle-aged men who have their eye on DS Jones.

He distracts himself by thinking again of fishing with Alice. But there is the irksome fact that the trip was unsuccessful; and he has so often talked up Bass Lake.

Close by on the wall hangs a cabinet holding a trout with its record-breaking weight and his name inscribed on an inconspicuous plaque. Though in the lamplit bar it blends with its surroundings like a pike lurking in the reeds; so much paraphernalia has accumulated over the decades and more.

Farming implements; keepers' traps.

Hunting scenes; John Peel, indeed.

The rugby photograph. The famous victory.

Beneath it …

Skelgill freezes.

He stares for several moments at the wall.

Then he stands up with a jolt and calls out.

'Charlie!'

Charles Brown is serving DS Jones – just about to pass their drinks over the counter. He looks across at Skelgill. Skelgill beckons him urgently.

The landlord says something to DS Jones – holding onto the drinks he rounds the end of the bar – it seems he thinks he might as well provide table service.

Skelgill remains standing.

DS Jones can see that he is actuated – she can read the green light in his eyes; the hotelier knows no such nuances.

'Danny? Are you that thirsty?'

But Skelgill ignores the offered pint and points into the corner.

'Charlie – where's your press-cutting?'

There is a vacant rectangle about six inches high by twelve wide – a different tone of wallpaper, and cleaning marks, and two rough holes showing the splayed ends of Rawlplugs.

Charles Brown looks baffled – this might be as much that Skelgill can seemingly be so concerned, as if the small incongruity is spoiling his evening's pleasure; for he cannot be expected to appreciate any significance of the missing item itself. Skelgill has to spell it out.

'Your framed picture of a fishing match. The team. From back in the day.'

But it is plain that the landlord – an incomer by this timeline – lacks any great knowledge of the decades-old wall-hangings that are handed down with each change of ownership. Indeed, he explicitly employs this defence.

'Danny – most of these things were here long before I took over.' But the statement in itself seems to rouse within him a sense of indignation – that someone might have stolen what is part of a community asset, an irreplaceable heirloom, a small piece of the inn's heritage. He begins to bristle, but is at a momentary loss for words.

Skelgill supplies a further prompt.

'When did you last see it?'

But Charles Brown is plainly nonplussed. It is like asking a countryman in November when did he see his last swallow; the birds having been gone two months and the last never announcing itself quite in the way of the first. But he does seem to appreciate now that there is more to Skelgill's interest than concern for his traditional surroundings. He puts down the drinks on their table and pulls a portable landline handset from his back pocket.

'I'll ask Edna.' He turns to glance at the clock above the bar; then he presses out a short-code. 'She's our cleaner. She'll be watching the Ennerdale omnibus.'

'Here.'

He puts the phone on speaker and they crowd around. Amidst the growing hubbub it is not loud enough to be overheard.

A slightly creaky woman's voice answers – and plainly she recognises the caller's number.

'I can't come in tomorrow – if that's what you want.'

It is a local accent, the tone a candid mix of deference and belligerence. The latter would refer to the interruption and what must surely be an unwelcome call to arms for a Sunday.

'Edna – it's a just a quick question.' Charles Brown flashes a look of exasperation at the detectives. 'The police are here. There's a picture gone from the wall in bar – in the alcove – a press cutting of a fishing match. We thought you might have noticed when it went missing?'

They hear Edna inhale – and for a moment it seems she will punch back, there being some hint of an accusation. Her employer adds a hurried rider.

'I know how nothing gets past you – and you've been here longer than anyone.'

The remark seems to achieve some mollifying effect.

'T'were there on Saturday afternoon. T'were gone on Monday morning. I thought you must have took it to be fixed – because the glass were a bit cracked.'

Charles Brown looks at Skelgill; he nods approvingly. It answers the question, albeit with a longer window than they would like. But Edna has not finished. She has already made up her mind.

'Must have been them that chored me steeyan.'

The downshift from accent to dialect leaves the landlord looking baffled.

Skelgill leans in. His eyes again are alight.

'Edna, what stone?'

The woman is unfazed by the new entrant to the conversation.

'From int' gents' – I use it to prop t' door open when I mop t' floor. There's one int' ladies' an' all.'

'And it's gone – at the same time?'

'Aye – it weren't there when I cleaned on Monday. I've been using t' ladies' one.'

Skelgill stares for a moment at DS Jones; she too has a glint of anticipation in her hazel eyes – though it is clear she lacks Skelgill's complete understanding of these circumstances.

Then Skelgill nods to the landlord – that he may end the call.

While Charles Brown is thanking his employee, Skelgill drops to his hands and knees and crawls beneath the table. To wide-eyed amazement he emits a groan as he humps the heavy oak settle and lifts it by a couple of inches. Then perhaps there is a muffled sound of triumph. He emerges, shrugging his shoulders, and he presses his fists into the small of his back. Then he brings one arm around and opens his palm before them – to reveal two old brass screws.

'Looks like someone took it in a hurry.'

The landlord puffs out his cheeks.

'Want me to ask the others? Saskia's not on tonight – but I can probably track her down.'

Skelgill nods.

'Aye – owt you can find out.'

'Thing is, Danny – any member of staff seeing something – they would have intervened. We lose towels left, right and centre – and those Smiths took a woman's bathrobe. But in the public areas things are mostly screwed down.' He gestures in the direction of the missing item. 'I'd understand that rugby photo – there's a market for sporting memorabilia. But a local fishing press-cutting. And why would anyone take an old rock door-stop?'

Skelgill grins somewhat ironically.

'You'd be surprised at how many anglers are closet geologists, Charlie.'

The man looks perplexed – perhaps in case Skelgill is not joking – but now he receives a plaintive entreaty from the bar; the queue has grown and help is needed. He inclines his head and makes a face of apology.

'I'd better pitch in.' And he indicates to their drinks. 'I'll leave you in peace.'

Skelgill takes a moment to examine the brass screws; the average penknife would do the trick. He pockets them and he and DS Jones resume their seats.

They remain in silence for a minute or two, taking pensive sips of their drinks.

It is DS Jones that speaks first.

'From what we know – this is where Stephen Flood was sitting – and where Kyle Betony came to join him.'

Skelgill nods but does not reply.

DS Jones continues.

'And then a what? A fishing article disappears. It seems like a connection.'

Skelgill makes a choking sound. She looks to see him regarding her sideways as he takes a great gulp of beer.

'There's something you're not telling me.'

Skelgill pauses for breath and nods.

'Is it the stone?'

His answer is to stand and drain the remainder of his pint.

'Come on lass, drink up.'

DS Jones flashes him a look of alarm.

'Where are we going?'

'First stop – the ladies'. Second – Buttermere.'

*

'We'll need to have some tea, lass.'

'You mean – like, dinner?'

Skelgill glances over his shoulder – he is just about to push open the back door of his mother's house.

'Aye – whatever.'

'I don't mind – although I suppose you could say you've already eaten – if you count that cake. If you don't want to spoil your appetite?'

Skelgill looks like this suggestion does not compute.

But as they enter the old terraced cottage in the growing gloom there is the sense of no one being at home. A faint glow emanates from the kitchen hearth, and a cast-iron pot simmers on the range.

'She must be round at Renie's. They'll be watching Ennerdale and caning the port and lemon.'

Skelgill lifts the lid of the pot and with the spoon that has been used for stirring takes a taste.

DS Jones watches with interest; he seems entirely inured both to the heat of the metal lid and the food itself – until he gives a sudden sharp intake of breath.

'Hot?'

'Spicy, aye.' He puts the lid back in place. 'She's discovered chilli powder in her old age. She calls this Texican Hotpot.'

Skelgill makes a sound of further discomfort and moves across to stick his head under the cold tap. He gulps thirstily, and pronounces with some admiration as he comes up for air.

'That makes the Taj Mahal's vindaloo taste like korma.'

DS Jones is grinning, shaking her head.

'Are you going to tell me why we're here, now?'

He looks uneasy, as if the little pantomime with the food is just to put off the inevitable, whatever that might be.

'Reet. This way, lass.'

He leads her from the kitchen into a narrow hallway and immediately into a small room on the right. It is a traditional front parlour, set aside for formal use. DS Jones does not have much time to take in her surroundings – there is the sombre ticking of a casement clock – for Skelgill crosses to a walnut sideboard and from its middle drawer brings out a large flat book of the family album type. He places it on the mahogany drop-leaf dining table and turns quickly to a spread that he obviously knows well. He shifts partly aside, but rests the index finger of his left hand upon a press-clipping held in place beneath yellowed cellophane.

DS Jones understands she is to step forward.

'Alice reminded me of this. That's why I noticed in the bar.'

DS Jones pores over the article.

The cutting is rather untidily cropped – torn by hand, in fact. There is a headline and two columns of text, and a photograph that looks like it was of a group but now shows only a boy at the end of a row with half an adult at his side. They stand to attention, like sentries with fishing rods for rifles.

'Is that you?'

Skelgill's embarrassment now increases.

'Aye – I were beaky-looking then.'

She chuckles. She leans over to peer more closely.

'How old were you?'

'Nine.'

Now she reads aloud.

'"The Derwentdale Anglers' Association scored its first-ever victory over local rivals the Allerdale Angling Association in their annual match, staged this year at Bassenthwaite Lake. A last-gasp catch by junior member Daniel Skelgill of Buttermere, a specimen perch of two pounds thirteen ounces taken on a brandling minutes before the hooter, tipped the scales in favour of the jubilant DAA, pictured here."'

DS Jones hesitates for a moment, and then she looks up at Skelgill.

'This is what was taken from the inn.'

'Aye – except in The Partridge it were the full version. The photo of the whole team – not just what me Ma's ripped out.'

DS Jones looks again at the article; but now it is plain that she is making some calculation.

Skelgill waits patiently for her to pronounce.

'Kyle Betony recognised someone.'

She looks up again to see he is nodding.

'Do you know which newspaper this is?'

Skelgill grimaces.

'The arl lass might know. We didn't get a paper – happen it were a local freesheet. Most of them have gone bust.'

DS Jones presses a finger on the page of the album.

'This lists the team line-up.'

She leans closer again and begins to read out the names. Skelgill being on the right of the picture, she ends with "D. Skelgill".

She regards him hopefully – he understands her unspoken query. But his reply does not reciprocate her optimism.

'You can see for yourself – I were a bairn. I were hoyed in at the deep end.'

DS Jones grins.

'It seems you swam.'

Skelgill cannot prevent a modicum of swagger from fleetingly possessing his demeanour. But he does at least move to play down his success, albeit after the fact.

'Aye, well – it were Bass Lake. My home turf. Some of their lot were fishing with maggots.'

DS Jones declines to advance any debate over the merits of various baits; instead she reverts to the crux of the matter.

'If not by name – would you know any of them by sight?'

But he shakes his head.

'I had nowt to do with the team – it were a total one-off for me.'

She nods reflectively.

'Would the club have a copy – maybe of the photograph? Someone must have supplied it to the newspaper.'

'I reckon you're talking Georgina Graham's department. Secretary keeps the archives.'

There is a note of warning in Skelgill's tone that DS Jones entirely appreciates; if it suited the woman's purposes, it would be only too easy for Georgina Graham to report that there is no such item.

They stand in silence for a few moments, both gazing at the press-clipping as if, like a 'magic eye' picture, the missing portion of the photograph will materialise and reveal its hidden content. Eventually DS Jones slips her mobile phone from the hip pocket of her jeans.

'I'll take a shot of it – maybe we can get an online match.'

Skelgill makes a disapproving growl.

'Can you miss us out.'

She chuckles.

'Don't worry – I shan't post it on my Insta.'

10. DYNAMITE

'That's just the right size, Guv.' DS Leyton weighs the hefty river-pebble in his right hand. 'It's smooth – but it's got enough of a point. What does the Doc reckon?' Skelgill makes a face that is on the whole disparaging and only a small part optimistic.

'Hedging his bets.' He takes a drink from his mug as if to illustrate this concept. 'The impact area matches up – assuming the actual stone was more or less the same size and shape.'

'So it ain't ruled out.' DS Leyton rehearses a series of aggressive strikes. Then he pronounces more thoughtfully. 'A geezer?'

Skelgill regards his subordinate without divulging whether or not he agrees with this diagnosis.

'It were taken from the gents' – I'll give you that much.'

DS Leyton nods and contemplates the egg-shaped door-stop. If not perfect, it is certainly an adequate weapon for despatching an unwary opponent.

'Suggests spur of the moment – don't you reckon, Guv?'

Now Skelgill narrows his eyes. He has not allowed himself to speculate inordinately since the revelation of the rock. However, he gives a twitch of his head which his sergeant takes as a green light to expound.

'Betony last seen heading in the direction of the gents'. We know he's agitated about something. Has a bit of a barney. The other geezer says let's go outside and discuss it.' Now he raises the stone. 'Picks up the nearest weapon. Coshes him from behind.'

Skelgill listens implacably.

'Reverses up to the side gate – there's hardly any lighting. And it's not like Betony was a big bloke – what was he – about nine stone? Lumps him into the boot of the car – dumps him over the bridge. Two minutes – job done.'

There ensues a silence; Skelgill and DS Leyton stare at one another, as if in a game of who will blink first – until they are both distracted by the appearance in the doorway of DS Jones. Her cheeks are flushed and she clutches a sheaf of papers to her breastbone, as if they are of special importance.

But DS Leyton takes the opportunity to restate his case. He addresses DS Jones.

'I was just saying – if some geezer whacked Betony and drove him to the bridge – he could be back in the time a person might spend in the toilets.'

DS Jones passes between her colleagues and takes her regular seat before the window. She is alert to the possibilities.

'There was the car that arrived at just after ten-thirty – the driver who was reluctant to get out while the hotel guest was retrieving his pillows. There aren't many spaces along the front of the inn – yet it was able to park in a vacant one – as if it were returning.'

She intones quite casually, and does not press her point with any insistence, or imploring glance at Skelgill. DS Leyton, however, is nodding with satisfaction.

Skelgill folds his arms onto his desk and rocks forward on his elbows. It is body language that combines the urge to act with self-restraint. But his brow is furrowed; a suggestion that uncertainty still holds the upper hand.

DS Jones now brandishes her papers.

'This might be something – for your next meeting with the Chief.'

She hands out a stapled set to each of her colleagues. The first page is a print of the photograph she took from the family album at Buttermere. She is about to speak when DS Leyton interjects.

'S'cuse me, Emma – but – this article reminds me. I should say this first.' He tugs his notebook from his jacket pocket and quickly thumbs through it. 'Here.' He reads silently for a moment and then regards his colleagues, his gaze settling upon Skelgill. 'When Jay Chaudry told me what Betony had said – I took it that the controversial point was the merger. So that's what I conveyed to you, right?' Skelgill nods, accepting this logic. DS Leyton raises the notebook and prods at it with a chunky index finger. 'But Chaudry preceded that by saying Betony had got the idea because he'd discovered there used to be a fishing match between your lot, the DAA, and the AAA.'

There is the impression that DS Leyton feels somewhat remiss for this late entry. But Skelgill merely snaps out a question.

'When did he say it?'

DS Leyton checks his notes.

'This was at the dinner. Jay Chaudry was the only one who could remember the conversation.'

'The only one prepared to admit it.'

Skelgill's caveat is swift.

But now DS Jones has a point to add.

'Remember – one of the waitresses told us Kyle Betony was late arriving at the dining table. But we know he left home early to get to The Partridge.' She displays the partial image from the newspaper. 'Maybe he was in the bar beforehand and saw this?'

Skelgill seems to accept that he is the oracle as far as the legendary fishing match is concerned.

'It's not widely known – Alice remembered – and Jim Hartley would recall it.' He taps on his own copy of the clipping, before him on the desk. 'I knew this were on the wall – because I'm in it. But you'd have to go out of your way to notice it amongst all the gubbins – it was in cobweb corner.'

His phrase is suitably graphic, if unfair to charlady Edna.

More silence ensues. But DS Leyton can contain himself for only so long.

'It fits again, Guv. Betony's gone and said something, ain't he? And he's trod on someone's toes.' He too displays the page in question. 'And that person's even sneaked back and removed the evidence.'

The logic is powerful – but clearly so is the weight of conjecture that Skelgill in particular feels to be circling their little clique. He shakes his head slowly; but it is an act of ruefulness rather than outright rejection of his sergeant's proposition.

DS Jones, having patiently stayed her own news, sees that the moment is opportune. She reaches across and turns the first page of Skelgill's copy of her report. She indicates a column of sub-headings, with annotations alongside each – at a glance several are marked "deceased".

'These are your erstwhile teammates.'

Skelgill glowers at the list. There are seven names, his own omitted.

He casts a sideways glance at DS Jones.

'As you can see – four of them are no longer with us. Two are in their late seventies and have left the district.' There is a sense that she speaks with intentional understatement. 'The last one is interesting.'

She sees that both her colleagues are staring at the name, "T. Jubb".

'PTO.'

They do as urged – the final page is a copy of an official report and is covered in dense type; Skelgill immediately sinks back into his chair. DS Jones grins and begins to recite – it is plain she knows the content – for she paraphrases with ease.

'Jubb is an unusual name. I can't find any others in the county. But twenty-four years ago a Toby Jubb from Carlisle – and aged twenty-four at the time – was involved in a car accident in which his newly wed wife was the only passenger. He was driving a red Vauxhall Vectra. He swerved to avoid a deer in the Whinlatter forest and plunged off the road and hit a tree. He was thrown clear but knocked unconscious. When he came round, the car was engulfed in flames. His wife perished. He was badly burned trying to rescue her. It is possible that she was killed by the impact of the crash – she was certainly insensible, and would have been overcome by smoke before the fire took hold.'

DS Jones pauses to allow her colleagues to envisage fully the picture she paints.

'It was considered whether Toby Jubb should be charged with any offence – right up to causing death by dangerous driving, for which he was initially cautioned. The investigators concluded that he was travelling too fast for the conditions, but it was a sixty-limit road and he was within that. Under the circumstances – the loss of his wife – the CPS eventually decided it was inappropriate and the charges were dropped.'

DS Jones glances up at DS Leyton to see that he is gazing at Skelgill with a puzzled expression. When she looks at Skelgill she realises she has lost his attention entirely. Nostrils literally twitching, he is staring at the open door with concentration that she has only seen from the opposite end of his boat when he detects a bite and is preparing to strike.

And suddenly he does strike.

In a blur he leaps from his chair and launches himself through the open door.

There is a loud exclamation – a male voice – not Skelgill's – and Skelgill backs into his office wrestling a struggling hooded tracksuit-clad figure.

'Skel!' (There is an accompanying entreaty, less printable. *FFS*, the digital version.)

The voice belongs to DI Alec Smart.

Skelgill – evidently now realising – lets him go, but not without a shove against the wall.

DS Leyton has risen; DS Jones watches on, wide-eyed.

DI Smart looks like he is expecting a duffing. He shrinks against the wall and raises both hands.

But his survival instincts kick in, and he swiftly turns his wrong-doing into a virtue.

'A fine welcome.'

He folds back his hood and straightens the garment. It is apparent that the sporty outfit he wears – designer trainers included – is brand new. He makes eye contact with DS Jones.

'I've only come to ask Emma what time's the fitness class.' He smirks, his weaselly features sharpening; but his tone remains excessively injured. 'If I'd wanted judo I'd have signed up for it.'

Skelgill has slowly retired to his seat. DS Jones can see from his taut demeanour that he is still in a state of battle. When it might actually be appropriate to offer, if not an apology, then at least an explanation for his manhandling of a fellow officer, she knows that none will be forthcoming. Were Skelgill seeking an excuse for his precipitousness, it would not be unreasonable to suggest that DI Smart had been mistaken for some interloper who had absconded from the custody suite, hoping to make good their escape along the ground-floor corridor. But Skelgill is fizzing, and incapable of speech – which is never a good sign for an opponent.

She takes it upon herself to address the issue.

'There's nothing at lunchtime Mondays. It's body balance at six p.m. – and then, tomorrow, spin at seven a.m.'

DI Smart contrives a conspiratorial grin. He sidles to the open door.

'I expect I'll see you there – I like to be the fittest in my team.'

'I don't –'

But before DS Jones can express any dissent or cast doubt upon the suggestion, DI Smart is gone. Now they hear his rubber soles squeak on the tiled floor (when before they were surreptitiously silenced). Skelgill sits in total stillness until there comes the closing click of the catch of the sprung fire door.

Now he exhales audibly, attracting the attention of his colleagues.

DS Leyton, resuming his seat, is first to speak.

'Funny – how you didn't recognise him, Guv.'

Skelgill glares implacably.

'Leyton – of course I recognised him.'

DS Leyton glances sideways at DS Jones to see that she is trying to suppress a laugh, pressing the side of her hand to her lips. But he thinks the better of prolonging the matter. Instead he raises the question that refers to the more rational aspect of Skelgill's reaction to the eavesdropper.

'Reckon he overheard us, Guv?'

Skelgill does not immediately answer – not least that he cannot know.

But DS Jones enters the conversation.

'If he heard what I said about Toby Jubb – I don't think it will help him. You see – there is no trace of the man. Nothing since shortly after the accident. It's as if he disappeared – though I imagine emigrated is the probable explanation.'

Skelgill appears just a shade more relaxed.

'What about the woman – this Jubb's wife?'

DS Jones makes an open-handed gesture.

'I've got DC Watson looking into it – she's submitted a request for the release of the complete file. At the moment we don't have the wife's maiden name. Just Lynette Jubb.'

While Skelgill listens, he shows little reaction. It is DS Leyton who – with due politeness to his female colleague – puts to her the obvious devil's advocacy.

'Call me thick, Emma – but – other than a possible match with the name Jubb – what's the significance here?'

DS Jones glances at Skelgill.

'Should we close the door?'

But Skelgill shakes his head. He prefers to know what is going on out there – and he won't be caught out the same way a second time.

DS Jones addresses her colleagues in somewhat hushed tones.

'While the nature of the accident is unusual, it isn't unprecedented. But it is odd that he has disappeared and left no records after the date of the police proceedings. It prompted me to look at the background case notes that were not filed with the final report to the CPS. The officer who investigated was checking for foul play. He queried whether a car would spontaneously catch fire under the circumstances – the accident occurred during torrential rain. So there was some doubt over that. Moreover – and I thought this was interesting – at the same time the next day they set up a traffic stop – to see if there were any witnesses to the crash – which was unlikely given the isolated location, and in fact there weren't. But –' And here she pauses, clearly conscious of the inquisitive eyes upon her. 'A farmer from High Lorton remembered that a few days earlier he was towing a trailer of sheep and had to swerve around a stationary saloon – in the same stretch of road. He glimpsed in his rear-view mirror a man climbing back up the embankment – he assumed it was a case of the call of nature – but remarked that it was crazy to park on a steeply sloping bend with no verge. He didn't get a good look at the male driver – but the car matched the description of Toby Jubb's red Vauxhall Vectra.'

DS Jones looks up to see that Skelgill has shifted from slumped to ramrod erect. He seems to be staring past her out of the window – but his gaze is fixed and plainly unfocused.

'Guv?'

Without warning Skelgill rises and pulls down his jacket from his row of blunted fish-hook pegs.

He turns and looks at DS Jones as if he is surprised to see her there.

'Better get your coat.'

Then he turns to a somewhat bamboozled DS Leyton.

'Hold the fort.'

He plunges into the darkened portal; to his subordinates it must seem that he has finally chosen a rabbit hole.

COCKERMOUTH – 12.59 p.m.

'What were we *actually* looking for, Guv?'

Skelgill has assumed a curious pose, hands gripping the steering wheel of his car, head forward almost pressing upon the windscreen; he looks to DS Jones like his own impression of a Sunday driver, who dawdles along in blissful ignorance of the line of traffic held up in his wake. Except they are parked outside the Cockermouth property that is now in the sole ownership of Jasmine Betony. Their brief visit is over, and Skelgill – having left empty handed – has come on what was obviously a pretext (supposedly to check some point in Kyle Betony's DAA committee file) while she was tasked with keeping the young woman talking downstairs. It had been a rather awkward moment, and she sensed that Jasmine Betony had detected their disingenuity. She had hovered anxiously about the small kitchen, making unnecessary adjustments to a large glass vase of lilies that might have been sent in commiseration. Still, at least Skelgill had not had the temerity simply to knock and ask to use the bathroom.

Thus, however, his colleague's probing question.

'I figured if you didn't know, it was one less person to give the game away.'

'Fewer.'

'What?'

But before DS Jones can reply there is a loud blast from behind. The section of narrow, sloping street, known as Castlegate has an alternate one-way system where individual motorists are left to work out whose turn is next. Skelgill curses and checks his mirror – but it is a legitimate complaint, given that stopping is prohibited, a supermarket lorry that has no prospect of squeezing by. Skelgill sticks a hand out of the window and moves off.

But he conducts them only a few hundred yards; they cross the humped bridge over the River Cocker and pull up towards the end of Main Street.

'Plan B.'

Without further explanation he exits the car.

DS Jones gathers she is to stay put. She watches as he strides across the broad pavement, assuming right of way and causing an illegal electric scooterist to swerve and almost fall off. He disappears into what is an antiquated combined Post Office and newsagents; a legend over the door reads, "Proprietors: Mathilda & Elizabeth Counter." The rather dark dingy dusty shop window displays wares that look like they are from a former era; a faded poster for Cadbury's Aztec bar, old-fashioned stationery, and yellowed periodicals that are surely no longer in print.

Skelgill emerges in short order. There is perhaps just a spring in his step. He wields a folded copy of Angling Times.

But upon resuming his place he casts the fishing newspaper into the back seat, without a second glance.

'Oh.'

DS Jones's exclamation is not, however, in response to this act. For she sees that he had the fishing journal wrapped round a glossy magazine – and it is one she immediately recognises. True Crime

Hunters Monthly. It is the edition about which they had remarked on their last visit to Cockermouth, with the Moors Murders splash on its cover.

'Couple of months out of date. I thought they'd still have it.' Skelgill hands it over. 'Turn to page thirteen.'

DS Jones does as bidden.

For several minutes she reads intently, her expression one of growing alarm.

Eventually she looks up.

'Tobias Jubb. He tried to murder his wife, Jolene – in the United States.'

Skelgill does not react; he is staring diagonally across the street, in vacant or in pensive mood, at the ancient ochre distempered walls of William Wordsworth's childhood home.

'Guv.'

Skelgill starts.

'Aye?'

'This is him, isn't it? This is our T. Jubb of the fishing team. Toby Jubb of the accident that killed his wife – his *former* wife, Lynette.' She taps the page. 'It's a carbon copy.'

Skelgill purses his lips.

'Toby Chub.'

'Pardon?'

'I've just got the faintest memory – so faint, I could be making it up. A good name to take the mickey out of – in angling circles. A toby's a kind of lure. Chub's a coarse fish.'

'That's what they used to call him?'

But Skelgill compresses his features.

'Like I say – I could be making it up. Happen I heard the arl fella say it.'

DS Jones closes the magazine and gazes serenely at the cover. However, like the proverbial swan, her feet are busy beneath the surface.

'But you read this – when we first interviewed Jasmine Betony.'

Skelgill gives a marginal nod.

'Didn't think owt of it. Until you started with your story of the crash, up in the Whinlatter. Thought I was having a déjà vu.' He growls reflectively. 'Didn't help that Smart were nebbing round the door – I lost the thread.'

DS Jones is becoming more animated.

She wields the magazine and employs a phrase out of the lexicon of her absent counterpart.

'This is dynamite.'

*

'This is dynamite.'

DS Leyton's jaw has literally dropped. He looks up from his perusal of the true crime magazine to see that DS Jones is grinning. He turns to address Skelgill.

'Every time you pair go off – you don't half bring home the bacon!'

Skelgill demurs.

'If there were any bacon, Leyton – I'd eat it.'

But the self-deprecating joke reveals he is in good spirits. There is a green light in his eye.

DS Leyton continues his protest. He brandishes the periodical.

'But this explains it, right? Kyle Betony read this before he went to the dinner and made the connection to the name in the press-clipping on the bar wall. Then he recognised Toby Jubb in the photograph – and confronted him. It wasn't about the fishing match or the threat of a merger – or poisoning fish – or drugs in Manchester – or conning old folks. It was none of that. *It was about unmasking a killer!*'

He regards his colleagues imploringly. After a moment, it is DS Jones that plays a somewhat more cautious hand.

'Or – at least – that was the threat that was perceived. But it could have been enough to prompt the murder of Kyle Betony.'

DS Leyton is nodding enthusiastically. He flicks to and fro through the pages of the magazine.

'Half-decent photo – we'll have Jubb bang to rights.'

But his expression becomes thwarted when he realises there is no such thing, in the article, at least. DS Jones responds again.

'I've made preliminary contact with the FBI. They handed over all their files to Interpol. It could take a couple of days to get anything. Meanwhile Jolene Jubb is believed to have moved and remarried – they're doing what they can to trace her. Finally – there's the DAA archive.'

But Skelgill takes a swig of tea and pulls a face, as if the drink is stewed.

'We need to work on the principle that we won't get owt – at least, not in the timescale that matters.'

He looks as though he might elaborate – but when something causes him to hold back, DS Leyton takes the initiative.

'How old would Jubb be, now?'

DS Jones has a ready reply.

'If you recall, at the time of the Whinlatter crash he was twenty-four – which would make him forty-eight.'

She takes her electronic tablet from the corner of Skelgill's desk. After a moment, she has the additional information she seeks.

'Stephen Flood is forty-seven. Anthony Goodman – forty-five. Jay Chaudry – forty-two.' She hesitates. 'And – Sir Montague Brash – fifty-eight.'

There is a short silence; then it is Skelgill who declines to let this incongruity become an obstacle.

'If Jubb's changed his identity you can bet he's changed his age with it. Most folk could pass for five years younger – if you didn't know any better.'

He glances sharply at DS Jones – she smiles reassuringly.

'That would rule out Sir Montague Brash, Guv.'

Skelgill regards her evenly.

'There's no way he could be Jubb. He's lived all his adult life on the Brash estate. He's wed to some Lady or other.'

For his part, DS Leyton has taken down the names and ages on his note pad, and now he peruses them at arm's length.

Stephen Flood, 47
Anthony Goodman, 45
Jay Chaudry, 42

He seems almost to lick his lips.

'So – we're down to three?'

He looks up to see that Skelgill is wearing another from his repertoire of pessimistic expressions.

'If only it were that simple, Leyton.'

DS Leyton looks to DS Jones – but it is plain she is equally perplexed.

They wait; Skelgill is evidently choosing his words carefully.

'Why did Jasmine Betony dispose of the magazine?'

DS Leyton is unaware of this precise detail.

'Did she, Guv?'

Skelgill looks at DS Jones – his intention to reel in her corroboration.

'First time we went – it were on top of the pile. We asked her not to touch his stuff. Today it were gone. All the rest were there – previous editions, his fishing magazines and whatnot.'

DS Jones shifts in her seat, as though she feels it is remiss of her to have overlooked this flaw in the logic – despite that her orders were to distract Jasmine Betony while Skelgill went upstairs alone. And then any such analysis was eclipsed by the astounding revelation that the killer of Kyle Betony might be the elusive Toby Jubb. Now she appreciates why Skelgill approached Jasmine Betony on a false pretence. Ironically, when she had first felt uneasy about the young Thai woman (a sentiment Skelgill had seemingly rejected) – in fact he had registered her intuition. And why would Jasmine Betony apparently conceal a piece of evidence that held the key to her husband's death?

Rather remarkably – but perhaps not so unexpectedly, given his easy-going nature, and the years of surprises under his ample policeman's belt – it is DS Leyton who breaks the impasse, with an elegant volte-face.

'Guv – are you saying Betony could be Jubb?'

Skelgill does not answer, but nonetheless seems benignly interested. He waves a hand for his sergeant to justify the crazy notion.

'He was about the right age. And he went off the radar at about the same time – after the death of Lynette Jubb in the Whinlatter crash – which we now consider suspicious.'

For once, it is DS Jones who has to sprint to keep up.

'But why would one of the committee members kill him?'

'Revenge.'

DS Leyton has responded before he knows it – and indeed seems taken aback by his own answer.

'Revenge?'

DS Leyton sways about a little, from the waist upwards. It is like a game of charades – and he is charged with thinking on the hoof.

'I'm only saying – here's Jubb, come back incognito to his old stamping ground. Then someone connected to his first wife finds out who he is. Takes revenge.'

DS Jones seems exercised by the sharp tangent their line of discussion has taken. However, she offers what is a balanced perspective.

'Jasmine Betony was born in the same year that Lynette Jubb died. As a Thai citizen she has no apparent ties to this area. If she played any part it could surely only have been to reveal or confirm her husband's identity.'

DS Leyton continues in his role as improvisor-in-chief.

'Sounds like she had something to gain – even as a bystander. Any joint assets – and you can bet he had a tidy life insurance policy – given that was his line of trade.'

DS Jones nods respectfully, but in her hazel eyes there are clouds of doubt.

While this exchange has been taking place, Skelgill has watched on inscrutably. He is like a keeper who has speculatively sent his dogs into an unpromising covert, and awaits whatever stringy game they might flush. That his gun is broken over his forearm is perhaps telling.

Now he presents a somewhat double-edged intervention.

'Revenge – it's a fancy theory.' He flashes what might be a reproving glance at DS Leyton. 'But the fact that you pair can debate it tells us there's more to this than we know.'

Skelgill rises and moves sideways to the window, alongside DS Jones. Hands in pockets, he gazes out. Clouds are massing; it is a change in the weather that has been forecast – and it looks like the Met Office have done their homework. When his colleagues might guess he is thinking about fishing he proves them wrong, albeit in somewhat cryptic terms.

'One thing's for sure – we can't take a chance on Jubb being dead.'

When he is met with silence he turns on his heel; his expression is ominous like the sky at his back.

'We can reasonably suggest that Jubb's killed two people and tried to murder a third. But that's just what we know about. Snapshots from a twenty-odd-year career.'

DS Jones is plainly more comfortable with this, the original scenario.

'You mean – why would he stop now? That he might have a plan in progress?'

Skelgill's answer is terse.

'Now might be the most dangerous time.'

DS Jones has duly regained her stride.

'We also have to consider the possibility that he could suspect someone else of knowing his identity.' She glances apprehensively at Skelgill. 'I mean – isn't that where the mysterious Mrs Smith could come into the picture?'

Skelgill grimaces. He is thinking about the allegorical lecture courtesy of Alice Wright-Fotheringham – the tale of the fictional detective – and his bravado that caused an unnecessary death.

DS Leyton swings in behind the central proposition, the brief flirtation with the notion that Kyle Betony could have been Toby Jubb now set aside.

'So what are we saying, Guv – in case Jubb's got someone in his sights – we'd better be on our toes?'

'I don't know about toes, Leyton – but from first thing tomorrow we're treading on eggshells.'

11. NEWS

'**B**ang go the eggshells, Guv.'

DS Leyton's tone carries a mixture of resignation and trepidation as he lays a copy of a crisp half-folded newspaper before Skelgill and simultaneously deposits two mugs clasped by their handles in his other fist and takes one for himself. Skelgill's gaze reluctantly shifts to the periodical, the Westmorland Gazette. However, he picks up his tea and drinks without testing the temperature. When he does not speak, DS Leyton weighs in again.

'Looks like Emma's little pal Minto's been up to his tricks.'

Skelgill frowns. He dislikes the description but the news item has to trump his personal feelings. He is obliged to squint – right now his office is gloomy; heavy rain falls silently beyond the glass; though it is well after sunrise, they could do with lights on.

The headline leaves nothing to the imagination:

EXCLUSIVE: OUSE BRIDGE DEATH BANGKOK DRUGS LINK

He has to admit that if Minto has no other use on this earth he communicates well. And there is a sub-heading:

DECEASED LOCAL BUSINESSMAN SUSPECTED GO-BETWEEN FOR FAR EAST HEROIN SYNDICATE

Skelgill's expression darkens as he scans the body copy.

Kyle Betony, 45, Cockermouth resident and self-employed financial adviser, recently found dead in suspicious circumstances in the River Derwent, was connected to an opiate-smuggling ring with its origins in Thailand, it has been exclusively revealed to the Gazette. It is alleged that Mr Betony fell afoul of a midnight rendezvous at the isolated rural bridge.

Now he produces some colourful local dialect that DS Leyton comprehends only in sentiment. He pushes back into his sprung seat as if to distance himself from the article.

'It's got Smart's name written all over it.'

DS Leyton has read the piece in full.

'It says a confidential source in the criminal underworld.'

Skelgill scoffs, almost choking on his tea.

'Aye, that'll be right.'

But no sooner has he said this than he raises a warning hand – to silence any rejoinder from his sergeant.

In the corridor voices slowly approach – or at least – one male voice that is regaling another person.

They listen. It is the distinctive nasal drawl of DI Alec Smart – and it becomes evident that he is speaking to DS Jones.

'My money's on the Manchester connection – plain as day. Gear coming up the ship canal right into Salford Quays. It's where your man Jay Chaudry lives. He's probably a user himself. He'll crack under pressure.' DI Smart gives a wheezy laugh. 'Get your glad rags packed, Emma. I'll sort it with the Chief. Escape the country bumpkins for a few days, eh?'

They come abreast of the door.

Skelgill swipes the newspaper from his desk and holds it out of sight.

DS Jones makes no pretence that she dives for the safety of Skelgill's office, flashing glances of discontent at her colleagues. She is wearing close-fitting yoga pants and a matching top that are revealing of her figure, and she yanks a sweatshirt from her sports holdall and, seated, pulls it over her head and down as far as it will go. She shows all the signs of having been unwillingly accosted.

DI Smart – despite his new training gear – looks uncharacteristically dishevelled, his lean face beetroot red and his hair plastered down with perspiration. He lingers at the threshold – perhaps just cognisant of his previous roughing-up.

'Alright, cock?' He addresses Skelgill without making eye contact. 'I was just showing the younger ones how it's done.' He cackles, and reaches to pat the seated DS Leyton on the shoulder, and winks at DS Jones as he turns away. 'Course – I'm one of the younger ones – *hah!* Sound.'

And he leaves them.

Skelgill is suitably fuming – even in the truncated salvo is a series of jibes to rile him – not least the parting shot.

Sharing a birth year with Skelgill, DS Leyton takes up the offence.

'He's only two years younger than us, ain't he, Guv?'

Before Skelgill can reply DS Jones moves to pour a little oil upon troubled waters.

'I thought he was going to die. I can't see him coming back to that class.'

Her male associates regard her a little expectantly. But she says no more, and reaches back to pull a band from her hair. She shakes out her fair tresses. Sportswear aside, she shows little sign of having exercised.

Skelgill produces the newspaper and slides it across his desk.

'You might have no choice.'

He has skipped a couple of sentences; but she nods slowly as she reads, lines creasing her brow. She understands her probable fate.

DS Leyton offers some commiseration.

'Guvnor reckons it's a plant. DI Smart. He's leaked it so the Chief has no choice but to open up the Manchester inquiry.'

DS Jones ponders over the fine print.

'At least there's no mention of Manchester in here – nor Jay Chaudry. It's all based on Kyle Betony's Thai connections.'

She looks at Skelgill – his expression is pained – she speaks imploringly.

'In a way, isn't there a silver lining – if we move fast?'

Skelgill seems conflicted, as though in part he grasps her

meaning – but suffers also some inner resistance.

DS Leyton is more unequivocal. He turns to Skelgill.

'Anything that beats DI Smart, surely, Guv?'

Skelgill indicates with a jerk of his head to DS Jones that she should explain.

'The Chief has given us until tomorrow, right?'

Skelgill gives a curt nod.

DS Jones raises the journal.

'Surely this is our excuse to speak to the main suspects? We act like we're investigating Kyle Betony for drugs. We continue to treat them as witnesses.'

DS Leyton claps his hands together.

'Sounds good to me, Emma.' He looks to Skelgill for a response. 'Saves your worry about spooking one of 'em, Guv.'

Skelgill certainly is conflicted. Sure, there is the appeal of thwarting Alex Smart (in more ways than one), but the idea that a second round of interviews might bear fruit does not convince him. A witness engaged under such circumstances is at best a fight with gloves on. And there is always the danger of landing a punch that rouses rather than stuns. It might just provoke the adverse reaction he fears.

DS Jones is first to read his reluctance. She knows him well enough to understand his ambivalence; there is a distant look in his eyes. She has watched him, aboard his boat, becalmed, surveying Bass Lake, absorbing those subliminal signs that will coalesce and lead him to where it is most propitious to fish. There is no gain in casting into barren waters; and right now he does not look ready to drop anchor.

She offers a concession.

'Guv – do you want me to contact Kendall Minto – to find out exactly what he knows?'

Skelgill emerges from his little trance. He folds his arms. His gaze drifts across to DS Jones, though he seems to be contemplating the rain that falls beyond her; the wind has strengthened and rivulets are running down the pane.

'Aye. Speak to Minto – see what's behind this story.'

Then Skelgill turns to DS Leyton.

'Leyton. I'm not holding out any hopes – but while we're waiting for Interpol – like you said, the photograph would be a game-changer. You call on Georgina Graham. Don't give her any warning. Ask to see the archives. She must keep them at her place – there's no base for the DAA beyond that they meet at The Partridge. Don't mention what you're actually looking for.'

DS Leyton looks just slightly panicked. The task seems something of a poisoned chalice. But he knows it is no good asking what he should say he is looking for. He swallows.

'Righto, Guv – I'll do me level best.'

DS Jones is regarding Skelgill questioningly.

'Guv – do you still think Georgina Graham had some role?'

Skelgill returns her scrutiny, but his eyes still have something of a vacant cast, despite that he has dispensed orders.

'I'll maybe know more when I've seen Brash.'

She is a little taken aback.

'Sir Montague? But – he saw you – at The Partridge.'

Skelgill shrugs.

'I'll have to take a chance on it. He only glanced at me. I'll play it chummy. I'll tell him straight out that I'm in the DAA – that we've crossed paths once or twice without speaking. I probably know Jim Hartley and Alice Wright-Fotheringham better than he does. Even if he recognises me, he'll think I'm in his camp – that I've come to brush it under the carpet.'

DS Jones does not hide her alarm. Despite his angling credentials, she doubts that Skelgill will pull off such optimistic subtlety – she has been subject to the penetrating intelligence of Sir Montague Brash. And as to what he might discover that will move them forward, that is difficult to envisage.

She casts a worried glance at DS Leyton, but he merely twitches his shoulders in time-honoured fashion.

Skelgill, however, seems to understand that he should make some form of valedictory pronouncement. He checks his wristwatch.

'See where we're all up to at about eleven. We'll meet

somewhere in the middle.' His expression stern, he looks at each of his colleagues in turn. His gaze lingers on DS Jones. 'That still gives us plenty of time to try out your silver lining.'

12. LEADEN SKIES

Morning, Tuesday, 28th September

BRASH HALL, 9.19 a.m.

'May I help you?'
Skelgill starts.
As always in heavy rain, he feels invisible, knowing that most mortals do not venture out. Though he is not best equipped for these conditions; just a thin shell cagoule that affords some protection for his upper half, and he does not even have the hood raised – another of his *mores*, that makes him less likely to be caught unawares.

Yet he has been caught unawares.

For a second he continues to peer into the passenger window of the vehicle which he has parked beside. It is a smart Land Rover Defender 110 in Coniston green. His arrival at Brash Hall has brought him past the long seemingly vacant sandstone frontage and round into a substantial cobbled stable yard. The Defender bristles with extras – a winch, a snorkel, roof-mounted spotlights – it is a machine as far from his financial reach as ownership of the great Georgian pile itself; the registration plate alone probably cost more than his annual salary – *MTY 1* – leaving little doubt over to whom it belongs. But without any sense of envy he has afforded himself a look to admire whatever interior modifications there might be. The key has been left in the ignition – a country habit and a statement to boot. Besides, the car is being watched.

He pulls away, leaving a distinctive nose-print on the glass, for the forensic team should he be abducted, dismembered and fed to the pigs.

But kidnap seems unlikely. The voice is friendly, well spoken, and female.

It emanates from a section of what is a converted coach-house that has its frontage replaced with a large window from waist level up to the stone lintel; framed in the open doorway a slender young woman. Of about medium height, shoulder-length blonde hair and regular features, she regards him with an enigmatic smile and dark eyes that convey additional curiosity.

'Pandora!'

The woman's exclamation is not an invocation of spirits but a vain entreaty to an elderly overweight chocolate Labrador retriever that slips out from beside her and hip-sways towards Skelgill. Instinctively he drops to one knee to intercept the creature – it seems affable enough – but it performs an about-turn when no treat is forthcoming and the realisation of the downpour sinks in. Skelgill remains in his knight-elect pose. He notes that the woman wears stylish Dubarry boots and a Derby tweed skirt; but just a Tattersall shirt, and with arms wrapped protectively she is patently unwilling to step out into the rain.

'Would you like to come into the warm?'

Her offer confirms his assessment; for his part, he does not consider it to be cold; the prevailing Atlantic depression is typically mild and humid. But evidently his reception of the dog has seen him through the first stage of gatekeeping. He supposes she might think he is a sales rep – though neither his outdoor apparel nor his well-travelled shooting brake would really pass muster; more likely a tradesman with some line in country sports.

He decides he ought to show his credentials.

But she is trusting and before he can retrieve such she turns and leaves him to close the door.

'Coffee? It is freshly percolated.'

'Aye – please.'

He finds himself answering in the affirmative despite that he does not fancy coffee.

As he waits, he casts about. The room is not what he would expect of a traditional estate office – old oak and worn leather; the smell of tobacco and fish and feathers and dogs; paraphernalia, tack, tackle and bills and reminders tacked to an overflowing noticeboard. There is little of the sort. It is modern, minimalistic, more like the reception area of an upmarket legal practice. On the woman's desk is just a small silver MacBook, the latest model iPhone, and some mail that she is mid-dealing with. A further internal door at the rear is closed. To one side, where she has moved, upon a cabinet stand creamy white lilies in a vase; perhaps the sight of them alerts Skelgill to a vaguely familiar fragrance – a flash of something uncertain – and oddly redolent of Parma Violets and the memory of childhood, those disliked purple sweets that he occasionally came by, that were just slightly better than no sweets at all.

Beside the vase the coffee pot is plugged into a wall socket, and there are the other accessories, and some newspapers and magazines laid out, perhaps for visitors' convenience.

'Have a seat, please.'

She speaks without looking back; Skelgill senses she is unfazed that he might be appraising her form; her outfit is closely tailored and her figure worthy of such self-assurance.

'Milk and sugar?'

Skelgill hesitates, but ends up repeating himself.

'Aye – please.'

He will have to take it as it comes.

The woman places a stylish cup and saucer before him; does he imagine that she leans closer than is entirely necessary? In her disturbing of the air he detects a comingling of aromas, the cloying violet and the rich coffee.

She rounds to her side with a drink for herself. The Lab lies beneath the desk.

Now she sits and carefully brushes back her hair with a small sweeping movement at her temples; it might almost be an act designed to draw his gaze to her own.

'What can I do for you?'

Skelgill feels awkward in displaying his warrant card – but she seems to react only with intrigue, the chestnut eyes questioning.

Now he remembers his fleeting sighting of the young woman

on horseback.

'Madam you're – er, Miss Brash – Sir Montague's daughter?'

Her voice is not deep – indeed light and girlish – but now she gives an involuntary throaty laugh.

She opens a slim drawer at her side and produces a calling card.

'I am Fenella Mansfield – Sir Montague's personal assistant.'

Skelgill is tongue-tied – but she quickly reads his misery.

'Inspector, why would I take offence to be mistaken for an eighteen-year-old girl?'

He resorts to drinking from his cup, when a misguided compliment is surely in the offing. But he realises now that she is at very least of an age with DS Jones – perhaps even closer to his own.

He is not where he had anticipated being. Here to interview Sir Montague Brash, instead he is settled in the company of the landowner's attractive PA. She does not make the obvious suggestion that she will telephone through to her employer. Yet nor does he move to state his specific purpose.

The chair is comfortable and the room undoubtedly warm; there must be a concealed heat source. And though it is not cold outside the downpour to which he was a few minutes ago inured now seems like a prohibitive barrier. And there is the cloying, heady, mildly intoxicating scent of violet. Together these sensations contribute to a sense of well-being – that he has arrived for some appointment and is ready to let others take charge. He is compliantly hijacked.

'Would you like to take off your waterproof?'

His inquisitor seems to appreciate his predicament.

But now he experiences a small flicker of resistance.

'Aye – well – I hadn't better hang about.'

He takes a further drink, which perhaps only serves to emphasise his ambivalence.

'I expect you are here to see Sir Montague?'

He wonders why she is the one asking questions.

He summons further resources, his better judgement battling with less sentient forces. But now he must improvise. His half-arsed spiel intended for Sir Montague Brash is no longer valid.

'Aye – I were just passing. There's a little bit of news – concerning the incident by the Derwent.' He holds back to gauge her reaction, but she merely bows her head in understanding – and that he should continue. 'I just wanted to bring him up to speed.'

Fenella Mansfield exhibits no trace of guardedness or suspicion. Nor signs of indifference or contempt. And yet there is a certain professional detachment from what might be considered a matter for commiseration, however indirect.

'He isn't here today – but I can certainly pass on any message.' And now she surprises Skelgill. Like a girl in a bar might share a confidence with a friend she leans forward and stretches out her hands, one flat over the other, her fingers ringless. Her shirt is not fully buttoned and a scarlet shoulder strap is revealed to Skelgill before he can make the eye contact that is almost equally disconcerting. Her smile is coy. 'If I can be trusted.'

Skelgill feels unnerved, though he fights not to show it. The heat is becoming more intense and a bead of sweat trickles disconcertingly down his spine. He cannot tell if his urge is to recoil or just the opposite. For a moment the room seems to swirl and he suffers an uncomfortable sense of suffocation – and in grasping for something tangible he resorts after all to a version of his poorly planned patter.

'I'm a member of the Derwentdale Anglers' Association myself. There was some concern – given the timing of Mr Betony's death – that there could have been a connection.'

Fenella Mansfield's eyes have become large dark pools.

'There has been a development?'

Confronted with the opportunity, Skelgill discovers himself unwilling to relay what he deems to be a fabrication by DI Alec Smart. He hears his voice, curiously disembodied, trotting out a platitude.

'It's looking like there's an alternative explanation.'

The young woman's eyes seem to sparkle now.

'So, we are in the clear?'

It is a slightly shocking rejoinder – and, not least that banter on the hoof is not Skelgill's forte, he cannot discern where on the spectrum between flippant irony and genuine relief her remark lies.

Certainly, she is smiling – and while it seems improbable that she would joke – her manner is such that they (and 'they' includes her employer and the Brash family institution and she herself and the DAA and indeed Skelgill) are intimates one and all.

And yet now a small quip does come to Skelgill's aid.

'You wouldn't say that if you knew my boss.'

It makes her laugh – again the unexpected throatiness. But it only serves to reinforce his impression that she holds there to be some common understanding. Indeed, now she reaches further and takes up his cup and saucer from under him.

'I'll get us a refill.'

Before he can object, she is moving accordingly.

And she speaks again.

'Inspector, I really think you should take off your cagoule.'

There is the clear impression that she is aware of his discomfort. He rises – but he struggles to shed the garment. Apart from that it is damp and clammy on its inside, it is a size too snug – a spare smock-type that he keeps in the back of his car for others; his own newest incarnation suffered an irreparable rent on a recent impromptu fly-fishing jaunt when he was too impatient to dig out his Barbour.

'Here – let me help.'

From behind, she reaches on tiptoes to tug the waterproof over his head, and turns him like in a game of blind man's buff to pull off the sleeves. The jacket is entirely inverted and in the process his shirt is briefly rucked up around his chest.

He feels a flush come to his cheeks.

'Aye – it is quite warm in here.'

The woman stands before him for a moment – then she hands over the jacket and turns back to her coffee making.

'We have a small leisure facility – through the door there.' She gives a light toss of her blonde hair towards the rear of the office. 'A sauna – that's probably what you feel – and a plunge pool – and a modest gym – though it has all the essentials.'

When he would normally voice his regular antipathy – why pump iron within four claustrophobic walls in conceited company when a free natural gymnasium abounds – Skelgill is uncharacteristically circumspect.

'Must be handy – if you like that sort of thing.'

Her response is swift.

'But you obviously work out.'

She speaks without turning. It is plainly not a question – her intonation making plain that it is a view based upon recent observation.

Skelgill makes an unconvincing attempt to downplay the flattery.

'Aye, well – I do what I can.'

'What is your fitness routine?'

And now he hears himself again – and this time also a second, inner voice that tells him the words are factual, even if the impression is misleading.

'Well – there was Pilates last night – and spin this morning. Problem is fitting it in – I'm normally out and about.'

She turns with his coffee and another for herself. She places the cups so that they may resume their seats. Now she speaks casually.

'You could come here – you would be welcome. Monty's fishing guests find it a good antidote to a day spent cramped in a boat. You might be pleasantly surprised.'

Her familiar use of her employer's name and her largesse with his private facilities catches Skelgill off guard; and there is the rider that hints at something more.

'What – like – just rock up?'

She smiles; she seems to detect his discomposure, and perhaps just slightly revel in it.

'Certainly – you can try it now, if you wish.'

'Aye – well – I've got no kit.'

Skelgill grimaces theatrically, though he senses it is a weak objection.

Now there is the throaty laugh.

'We have towels – that's all you need for the sauna.'

Skelgill is dumbfounded and in the muddle he more or less completely drains his coffee. The woman watches him with undisguised amusement.

But it is an alert from her mobile phone that comes to his rescue. It diverts her attention. She leans to look at the screen – and then picks up the handset and holds it such that it is facing her, almost a little secretively. She reads the message and it brings a smug smile to the corners of her mouth. However she does not reply, but instead carefully places the handset face down.

The hiatus has allowed a small tide of unease, hitherto held back by events, to flood Skelgill's mind.

'Something urgent?'

There must be a hopeful note in his voice, for Fenella Mansfield glances at him as though suddenly she sees him in a different light.

She answers, speaking slowly, a note of reluctance in her voice.

'Yes – there is something I perhaps ought to attend to.'

Skelgill drains the last of his coffee and rises. He lifts his waterproof from the back of his chair. Then he steps across to the sideboard to return his crockery to its place. He hesitates for a moment before he swivels to look at her.

'Me too – now you mention it.' He makes a face of exaggerated resignation. 'No rest for the wicked, eh?'

Though the Labrador senses change and struggles to its feet beneath the desk, Fenella Mansfield remains unmoving. Despite Skelgill's abrupt action she smiles and regards him with look of considerable satisfaction.

That she does not speak, however, is disconcerting, and before he knows it he has blurted out a farewell of sorts.

'Next time – I'll bring my bathers.'

She holds his gaze.

'Good morning, Inspector.'

Coatless, Skelgill has to make a run for his car.

Inside, he sits for a moment. In discerning sounds, he realises that distinct from the drum of the rain on the roof is the beat of his racing heart. It cannot be the short dash – it must be the extra caffeine; coffee is largely alien to him, and it seems to have a strength of its own, despite what they say about tea.

But there is more to it – albeit he is unwilling to explore sensations that at once massage and confront his ego – the former desirable, the latter discomfiting. The signals were surely plain, and yet he is left with the uneasy feeling of having been processed and shelved for future use.

Such introspection, however, does not come easily – his radar is on the wrong setting to detect the subtleties of the fairer sex, and his standard default is to proceed with caution and self-doubt, and the odd flirtation with vainglory. He knows this, at least – and now he rather cringes at his ill-considered parting remark. But in so kicking himself he shakes off the passenger's lethargy that had lulled him with its subliminal rhythm – and into the forefront of his mind comes an image, a small shock that had not been enough to derail him a moment earlier, but which now assumes tangible import – as though he had witnessed a murder from the window of his train and only now realises what he saw.

In replacing his crockery he had glanced at the adjacent arrangement of periodicals. There was Country Life, today's Daily Telegraph and – with its Minto-inspired headline in clear view – this morning's edition of the Westmorland Gazette.

The car is steamed up. He turns on the ignition, and pulls levers for wipers and heater.

The screen clears to reveal – just visible, standing back but looking his way, undoubtedly watching – the blonde-haired form of Fenella Mansfield.

A woman who thinks strategically.

He selects first gear and slews away.

SWINSIDE BARN, 9.52 a.m.

'Your great-grandfather?'

'That's right, madam. Wing Commander Edward Leyton, DFC. Stationed nearby in the war – RAF Kirkbride. Proper dedicated angler he was. We believe he was a big fish in your

DAA, if you'll excuse the pun.'

Georgina Graham looks somewhat flummoxed. She is unprepared to receive a visitor, being dressed only in loose-fitting pale pink loungewear, without make-up and her blonde hair still damp from showering.

For his part, DS Leyton has followed Skelgill's orders to turn up unannounced. Not daring to fail, and having got no answer at the main door, beneath dripping eaves he has doggedly skirted the converted property and found a second entrance on the upper level. With some persistence he has gained admission into the no-man's land of a small stone-flagged hallway between a laundry room and the kitchen. A narrow staircase fitted with a hessian runner rises ahead and curves out of sight.

The householder could hardly have left him standing in the rain – but now she seems unwilling to entertain him further. Not least there is his drenched condition. Sensing borrowed time, DS Leyton has launched into an opening salvo that has her regarding him doubtingly.

'But Sergeant – someone who lived in the area three generations ago. How will this advance your investigation?'

The situation has the makings of a stalemate. In the cold light of day, DS Leyton's contrived excuse to examine the DAA archives appears to have its limitations.

He shifts uncomfortably from one foot to the other, and smears the fingers of one hand across his eyes, as if to clear his vision of raindrops. He would appear stymied – until a small rabbit is produced from the hat.

'If only I knew, madam.' He makes a face that combines resignation with contrition. 'But you've met my Guvnor. Stickler for detail if ever there was one. Back at the station they call him "Inspector Perfection".' Now DS Leyton retracts his head into the shoulders of his raincoat. 'I wish I'd never mentioned the war. But, once I did – he was onto it like a terrier with a rat. He reckons if there is some connection, we need to know about it. Come clean in any report we write. Conflict of interest, you see, madam?'

Though still bewildered, the latter point does evidently strike a chord with Georgina Graham. It is something she understands in her own professional capacity. She begins to yield some ground.

'So, you would like to look through the entirety of the DAA's records?'

That she emphasises the word "entirety" might be a small rearguard attempt to deter him.

'Soonest done, madam. And I'll be able to get back to catching criminals.'

And now perhaps an element of pathos plays its part; something about the bedraggled man and his hangdog stoicism that counters the unconvincing logic.

But just when it seems she is about to soften, a thought must strike her.

'I take that you don't have a warrant for this?'

DS Leyton affects startlement, theatrically flashing the whites of his eyes.

'I shouldn't like to do that, madam. It's bad enough me turning up here – disturbing your – your work.' He has gestured towards her before he knows it – in her flimsy leisure outfit she does not look like she is at work. He continues, hurriedly. 'Now, a warrant – that would suggest some kind of jiggery-pokery. And you with your important position, an' all.'

The respectful answer seems to have a mollifying effect.

'Oh – well – yes, of course.'

Without making clear his meaning – it might be that he refers to her occupation, or her senior role on the committee, or indeed her social status – DS Leyton doubles down.

'That's probably why the Guvnor sent me – someone inconsequential – keep it low key.'

His lack of hubris seems to do the trick – despite the small risk of offence, that a minion has been despatched to visit her.

She indicates to the open door of the laundry room.

'You had better hang your mackintosh on the dryer in here.'

She moves ahead and lowers a pulley. DS Leyton divests himself of the sodden garment.

'Much obliged, madam.'

'You're welcome, Sergeant.'

Now she leads him out and begins to mount the staircase.

'I have all the current files in my study. And many of our communications are digital. But there is an archive of sorts. Though I have not looked at it for some time. A great wooden chest in the attic – it would take four men to bring it down.'

'I'll do whatever's the least disruption for you, madam – just show me where it is, and I'll have a sort through. No need for you to trouble yourself.'

They have reached a small landing. The woman moves easily, but DS Leyton pauses beside a window to catch his breath. There is a sense of elevation – on the lake side of the building, set on the steep hillside, this is the second floor – but while there ought to be a spectacular view of Derwentwater and the fells beyond, just a grey amorphous curtain hovers somewhere in the middle distance. DS Leyton is reminded of Skelgill's local lexicon for degrees of rain, and he decides to try one out.

'It's stotting down out there.'

Georgina Graham looks back, a hint of amusement in her eyes. In this one moment DS Leyton, hitherto subsumed by his anxiety in accomplishing his task, and half-drowned by the rain, suddenly realises what an attractive woman she is – and there is more. Despite the doubt and suspicion that circles the characters in this case (including Georgina Graham) – and notwithstanding her reticent reception of him, he detects only ingenuousness, and he is sure in this instant that she is entirely innocent in the matter.

It is rare for such an insight to strike him – and he can put no finger on exactly why – unless, perhaps, she has taken a liking to him.

'There may be floods if the forecast is accurate. I am lucky here, of course. Although there is a small beck that runs past the side of the barn – during Storm Geronimo it burst its banks and swamped the boiler room.'

DS Leyton makes a sympathetic face – but now she turns and continues to climb, a cramped uncarpeted staircase that brings them directly to a small bare oak door with a traditional cast-iron latch. He has to wait a couple of steps below while she pulls it back and ducks into the dark opening.

'Mind your head, Sergeant.'

'Not usually my problem, madam.'

He says it flippantly and she seems to murmur a chuckle; certainly the woman is at least his own height.

She feels to one side – there is the click of a switch – a brief moment of light – and then *splink* – and darkness again.

'Oh, how inconvenient. And I have bulbs on my shopping list.'

DS Leyton does not permit himself to think it might be convenient.

'This should do the trick, madam.'

He has the light from his phone at the ready. He steps cautiously alongside her. The old boards creak underfoot. The bulb is bright, but it has little penetration. In the immediate vicinity he can make out objects that would be expected, plywood packing cases, small items of furniture, lamps, paintings, suitcases – and a collection of sports gear, golf clubs, skis and what might be a surfboard. Just inside the door is a tea chest from which protrude boxes of board games and suchlike; he recognises Monopoly, and Mousetrap.

The deeper recesses are not discernible – though tiny chinks of light give a sense of considerable distance. The attic appears to be long and narrow – beneath a pitched roof of old beams it must run the entire length of the property.

But now Georgina Graham draws his attention to an enormous steamer trunk, covered with worn leather and reinforced with cane bands.

'Here it is.'

She hauls back the lid and rests it against the sloping rafters behind.

DS Leyton plays his light over the interior. It is brim full – but the contents at least look neatly ordered – eight piles of documents, each of about two feet deep. He resists a calculation of page numbers – though at two inches per ream he knows it will number in the tens of thousands.

Georgina Graham, however, seems to be thinking about a different aspect of his task. She reaches down and takes up a document. She angles it into the light.

'Yes – this takes you up to at least 2010 – see – these minutes. As I say, I have more recent documents downstairs – but you want something far earlier. I wish I could say these stacks were in chronological order – but I think they have become mixed over time. I think to find the 1940s you will have to sift through it all. Are you sure you want to do this?'

DS Leyton, however, is breathing a surreptitious sigh of relief. All that matters to him is that the period of these documents spans that of twenty-eight years ago – which, thanks to a junior Skelgill's participation in the fishing match, his present-day incarnation has been able to nail down to the month.

'Not to worry, madam. I'm well versed in these dogsbody jobs.'

She seems a little unwilling to leave him – perhaps now sympathetic to the confinement in which he must work.

'Sergeant Leyton, how about I bring you a cup of tea or coffee?'

DS Leyton demurs.

'Nah – don't you trouble yourself, madam. Thanks all the same. You must have stuff to be getting on with. And I'd probably only spill it and make a mess.'

The attic is chilly. However, much as he would appreciate a hot drink, he is thinking she may return at some inopportune moment.

Rather reluctantly, she begins to step away.

'Well – I do have emails to attend to. They start early in our New York office, and I like to have last night's queries answered.'

The door has swung to without DS Leyton noticing; it must be the way it is hung; Georgina Graham now props it open with a handy golf driver. It must be a regular hack. To his surprise, she now laughs – it seems by way of explanation.

'I shouldn't like to leave you alone in the dark.'

'What's that, madam?'

His question comes quickly.

She must sense some anxiety in his tone, for she seems to adjust her response.

'Oh – just my little joke.' She waves a hand, indicating the property around them. 'A small claim to fame – by repute, Mary Queen of Scots rested here during her flight from the Battle of Langside. Unfortunately, it did not end well, and she lost her head, as you will know. But at least the DAA's records do not stretch back that far.'

DS Leyton taps the rim of the chest.

'Let's hope they go far back enough.'

'Quite so, Sergeant – I shall leave you in peace.'

He waits until the sound of the footfalls on the stair have faded before he takes stock of his situation. When all is quiet he casts about. Although silence would not be an accurate description because there is the rumble of rain falling on the slate roof-tiles; a curious sound, neither a pattering – the precipitation is too dense – nor a single pure note; but a sustained susurration. He has heard Skelgill use the term 'syling' – perhaps this is it? There are other faint noises, too – although ineffable disturbances in the air at some distance. He covers the bulb momentarily, but in the sudden change the depths of the attic seem darker still – and the pinpricks of light where tiles must be chipped or there are ventilation gaps at the soffits are of no help.

He shines his diffuse beam once more on the trunk.

The piles of papers are tightly packed, and it takes him a couple of minutes to remove the first stack piecemeal. He reinstates it as a single column on the rough boards of the floor. Now it is easier to gain access to the remainder, and he is able to extract these half a stack at a time. His plan is to return them to the casket as he works through them.

Without particular analysis of the kind a workflow consultant would perform, a certain innate common sense tells him there are two key aspects that will make this ostensibly impossible task possible. The first is comfort. He drags a heavy suitcase into position as a low stool that puts both the papers and the trunk within arm's reach. Then he jams his mobile phone into a crevice between a batten and a loose tile to produce a hands-free overhead light.

Second are the odds. Having grown up with an influential if somewhat disreputable bookie in his family he is familiar with the concept that maths – or arithmetic, at least – can be an ally of the hard-pressed police officer. Provided these documents have not been totally randomised – which seems an outside bet – while they might be out of broad sequence, individual years' worth of papers ought to have been kept together. He eyes the nearest stack. Each pile is worth roughly a decade, which means that every two to three inches represents a year. All he needs to do is to take 'core samples' at such intervals.

His hunch proves correct – no more than ten minutes have passed when – bingo – halfway down the third stack he locates the era he seeks – and, indeed, he quickly isolates the documents of twenty-eight years ago.

He sits back, giving an involuntary groan – which seems to echo from the far end of the barn roof. The sound distracts him for a moment, though he can see no further than the little cone of light that envelops him. He feels his heart is beating faster than normal – but it must be the small excitement that he is closing in upon his quarry. Perhaps this is how Skelgill feels when fish are circling his boat.

Now he proceeds more carefully. The Monopoly game is just within reach, and he pulls the old worn box across his knees. The pieces inside rattle, and for a moment he feels a thrill of pride, remembering that his very own Old Kent Road is first square on the board. With its familiar red-and-white livery and tiny grinning banker brandishing a wad of sterling notes, it serves as a makeshift desk, and now with a teller's attention to detail he leafs methodically through the pages, peering as close in the pale light as his unwilling focal length will allow him.

The papers include minutes of monthly committee meetings and the same year's AGM; angling reports; correspondence; audited accounts; club rules; details of fees and permits; and blank membership forms.

But there are no press cuttings, and no photographs.

The fishing match took place in July. He returns to the minutes of that month and those of June and August. There is no mention in June, but in July, under 'AOB' he finds the item: *"Fishing match v AAA. Bassenthwaite Lake, 22 July. Team captain Mick Heckmondwike making arrangements."*

For a fleeting moment his already busy pulse gives another little leap – for he recognises the name – but then he further realises it is one of those identified by DS Jones as deceased.

He moves to the August minutes.

Given the apparent newsworthiness – that there was the press article, as stolen from The Partridge – the committee, or the author of the minutes, seemed to downplay the event. This month's entry, again only meriting coverage under 'AOB' reads: *"Fishing match: DAA beat AAA."* There is no mention of the team captain, of Skelgill's exploits, or even any hint of triumphalism.

DS Leyton sighs. Again, there is the sense that his own sounds are being reflected from somewhere in the darkness. He holds his breath for a moment – but he is met only by silence, beyond the persistent syling, as he has settled upon calling it.

He checks the names of attendees and apologies for the July committee meeting. Nothing stands out, but now a thought strikes him. He sets aside the Monopoly box and takes up a slice of papers contiguous with the section he has just interrogated. Flicking through quickly, he alights upon exactly what he seeks: a stapled document of half a dozen pages, headed "Membership List."

His heartbeat is back on the case – so much so that he ignores a definite noise from the far end of the roof space.

And there it is.

Turning to about midway, he finds the entry. *"Mr T. Jubb. c/o Derwentside, Spital Ing Lane, Gote, Cockermouth."*

Inexplicably he suddenly feels like a small boy with apples stuffed up his jumper when voices are approaching through the orchard – but he fights the panic and hurriedly gets down his mobile phone. He drops it in the process and the torch switches off – but it is an intelligent enough device to flash accordingly as he photographs all the pages of the address list, and those of the July and August minutes.

Trophies safely captured, he pauses to take stock.

He has not found the group photograph. Still they have no immediate means of identification – but at least he has the address. It is something that could take them closer to the identity of Toby Jubb.

He also senses – despite that he has taken perhaps only half an hour – that he will be outstaying his welcome. Perhaps now that he has found something, he subconsciously feels he will give cause for suspicion. He sets about reinstating the contents of the chest – but not before putting the pertinent documents in first, so that they will be at the very bottom of a pile and easy to retrieve should there be a requirement.

The lid is heavier than he expects. It slips through his fingers and makes a loud crack. Once again – and this time he registers it – the sound that he makes seems to be reciprocated by a vague hushing from the far end of the loft, with too much of a delay actually to be some kind of echo.

He has managed since dropping his phone without the assistance of the torch; his eyes gradually acclimatising to the light that filters in from the open door at the top of the stair.

He stands and straightens cautiously, conscious of the tiles close above his head and the likelihood of protruding nails. He squints, frowning, along the length of the roof space.

Now he can appreciate the steep pitch and the ancient construction of hand-hewn rafters and purlins.

Now the pinpricks of light are indeed illuminating small areas.

And now he realises there is somebody there.

Standing in the distant gloom – no more than a slightly paler form against the darker gable – a figure.

A woman in a long dress.

His heart, already taxed, inches further up inside his chest.

Does Georgina Graham have some other secret means of access?

Has she been watching him?

He has learned from stakeouts with Skelgill how better to see in the dark, by using the extremities of one's retinas. He turns his head from side to side.

And the ghostly shape takes a little more form – yes, a woman in a long dress – but a woman... *with her severed head held under her arm.*

And – what is it – a fluttering sound? A death rattle?

DS Leyton is on his way down the little staircase before he can mutter Mary Queen of Scots.

At the halfway landing, however, he halts to gaze out of the window. He resolves to pull himself together; though there is little tangible upon which to fix his mind; the conditions have worsened if anything and there is nothing to see beyond the pale mist of rain.

'Lumme.'

The word, spoken under his breath, seems to do the trick.

He inhales deeply, several times.

More composedly now, he descends to the hallway between the laundry and the kitchen.

'Hallo?'

He waits for a moment, but receives no reply to his entreaty.

He looks first in the laundry. As he expects, it is empty – but he tugs down his coat and with a little difficulty shrugs it on. The gabardine fabric has seen better days and has lost much of its water resistance; and there has not been sufficient time for it to dry out. Skelgill scorns the style for use in rural Cumbria and calls it his "Columbo coat".

The kitchen door is ajar. Tentatively, DS Leyton pushes it open.

'Mrs Graham?'

It is an imposing space, bright, with windows on both sides, and a further door that passes through a choke point into what might be a sitting room. And it is impressively appointed – there are Belfast sinks at both windows; an expansive range cooker; an American refrigerator; many small appliances; and shining stainless steel utensils hanging in good order.

In the centre is a table that seats ten. At one corner are the traces of recent occupation. A side plate with toast crumbs. A coffee mug, about one-third full. And a laptop computer, open.

Much in the same way as a man locked in a room with a mirror and a tea-cosy would sooner or later try it on, a detective in similar circumstances and an adjacent laptop must inevitably be drawn to such a device.

Showing comportment that belies his stocky form, he glides effortlessly across the polished floorboards and casually observes the screen.

But now he feels his eyes widening and he leans closer.

Then comes the sudden distraction of activity near at hand.

He realises that in the short passage between the kitchen and the sitting room there must be a lavatory. A cistern has been flushed and there quickly follow the additional sounds of a tap running and then a bolt being drawn.

When Georgina Graham emerges, she experiences a small reaction of surprise. It is to see the detective standing in the kitchen, facing one window, looking at his mobile phone.

He turns and waves the device and slips it inside his mackintosh.

'Headquarters – the Guvnor's chasing me.'

'Oh.' She sounds uncertain. She sees that he has on his coat. 'You are leaving?'

DS Leyton also makes observations. She has changed into more formal attire and has applied make-up – and with it she seems to have acquired a somewhat businesslike manner.

He notices now that she steps over to the laptop. As she looks at it, the screensaver displays a photograph – of her with wild sunbleached hair, wearing a yellow bikini and wielding a blue cocktail. She makes an embarrassed murmur and presses down the lid. She looks pointedly at him, however. And her features take on an expression of concern.

'Are you alright, Sergeant? You are looking a little green about the gills.'

'What's that? Yeah – *nah* – I'm fine, thanks, madam. I reckon being in the dark – and then coming out into the light all of a sudden – ran down the stairs too quickly –'

He does not finish – and in fact a smile creases the woman's face – not just in the superficial curve of her now-crimson lips but genuinely in the glisten of her pale blue eyes set within contrasting borders of mascara. It is an expression that DS Leyton reads as both amused and sympathetic, as though she feels some responsibility for his condition.

'I meant to say – I remembered after I left you. My young nephew and niece were playing in the attic last weekend. There's a dressmaker's dummy – and a dressing-up box. It seems they made an effigy of Mary Queen of Scots, *after* she had lost her head. They abandoned their efforts – we have bats up there – a protected colony of Daubenton's – I think the fluttering scared away the children.'

DS Leyton makes a face of some trepidation – but he is plainly too embarrassed to admit to any such encounter.

'Well – I don't know, madam – I was just concentrating on the archives. That's some amount of material you've got there.'

Georgina Graham shows just a slight hesitation – as though she would wish to reassure herself about his condition. But she picks up his point.

'And did you succeed – find your great-grandfather?'

'What's that?' DS Leyton has answered before he knows it – if potentially to show his hand is to answer – and he scrambles to recover. 'Ah – well – I tried my best. But I couldn't find anything dated before 1947 – and there was no mention of him.'

What might be two white lies are, as it happens, factual.

But the woman furrows her brow – she takes a step towards DS Leyton. She is both perplexed – and evidently annoyed – but perhaps it is with herself.

'Are you sure your great-grandfather was in the DAA?'

DS Leyton makes a determined face.

'As sure as I can be, madam. Naturally, I'm relying on hand-me-down information.'

He is less convincing when it comes to actual white lies – but Georgina Graham seems uninterested in questioning the basis of his claim.

Instead she folds her arms; it is the posture of a schoolmarm, trying to coax an answer from a confused pupil.

'Could he have been in the *AAA?*'

'The AAA?'

'Yes – the Allerdale Angling Association. Our territories overlap.' She raises a hand to her chin. 'I should have thought of this in the first place. But now that you mention 1947.' She holds out her other hand, palm upward. 'You wouldn't have found anything earlier. The DAA was formed in 1947 – two years after the war ended.'

DS Leyton turns out his pliable bottom lip and reaches for his hair, in a passable impression of Stan Laurel, caught out once again doing a dumb thing that is hardly his fault but for which he knows he is assigned the entirety of the blame.

'Stone the crows.'

The woman, however, regards him with a look of optimism.

'But doesn't it answer your issue?' When DS Leyton remains evidently puzzled, she elaborates. 'Surely it eliminates the conflict of interest that was of concern to your Inspector?'

For a second DS Leyton exhibits a kind of childlike glee – the first discovery that inside inedible silver foil lies delicious chocolate – until he perhaps senses he ought not to overact.

'Quite right, madam. I was just thinking that, myself. But I'm sorry to have put you to the bother.'

She presses her hands together in mid air.

'It has been no inconvenience, I assure you – but – would you not like a coffee before you leave? It must have been cold up in the attic.'

Now he wonders if she is actually trying to delay him – and why that might be. Might it be to find out more of what he knows? He doubts he could withstand any clever questioning. He has achieved his goal – and he should get out of here. There can be too much in one morning for a bear of very little brain.

'Thanks all the same, madam.' He taps the breast of his overcoat as a reminder of the presence of his mobile phone. 'Like I was saying – Inspector Perfection, an' all that.'

She yields gracefully.

'Of course, I quite understand.'

He moves again – but now she checks him.

'Oh – I can take you out via the front door – down the main stairs – it will be closer to your car.'

But he waves away her offer.

'No problem, madam – this old coat's pretty sodden, anyway.'

When the back door closes after him he finds himself facing it for a moment, his eyes cast down in thought. He seems not to notice the teeming rain or the lines of drips that cascade from the overflowing gutters.

It takes several moments before he does become aware of one particular stream of drips; it splashes directly upon a large oval pebble that is propped against the wall just where the door might reach to when opened; a doorstop, perhaps.

A doorstop.

His features become alarmed and his heart once more makes a little leap – until he notices, arranged in a continuous line dividing the gravel of the path from a narrow herbaceous border, a whole array of similar pebbles.

'Flamin' Alan Whickers.'

MOUNTAIN CAFÉ, KESWICK, 10.27 a.m.

'It is complete BS, as the American euphemism goes.'

'Right.'

'My editor forced me to write it.'

'Are you allowed to do that?'

DS Jones's tone verges upon admonishment.

Kendall Minto, reporter for the Westmorland Gazette, erstwhile schoolmate, actually seems quite pleased with himself. He has perhaps not detected that there is the underlying suggestion of having wasted police time.

'We were short of a scoop – short of any news of merit. For weeks. It was a message left on the answerphone late at night. I swear the voice is your Detective Inspector Smart – making a poor fist of a Liverpool accent.'

'Ah.'

DS Jones relents somewhat. If not fiction on behalf of the esteemed publication, then just wishful thinking.

Kendall Minto, however, rather doubles down on his employer's misconduct.

'I suppose if he's got a reliable snout – who is unwilling to stick his head above the parapet – he feels entitled to step in as spokesperson. He claimed to be a worker at the customs office at the mouth of the Manchester ship canal – Eastham, on the Wirral. Perhaps you can track down the real man?'

DS Jones hesitates. Rather pensively, she stirs the creamy froth that tops her cappuccino.

Kendall Minto watches; he seems a little perturbed that she destroys the heart of sprinkled chocolate powder.

'Try your cake.'

She is jolted from her little moment of reverie.

'What is it?'

'It's called Westmorland pepper cake – their new signature dish.'

She regards him, now with just a glint in her eye.

'Can you have a new signature dish? Isn't that like a reliable snout? Or pepper cake, come to that.'

'Good point – but, oxymorons aside, at least you can see I have spared no expense.'

She does not bite, except at the cake.

'You and your expense account.'

He flushes, and glances about sheepishly, as though he thinks they may be overheard.

But she nods approvingly, endorsing his choice of snack, at least.

He seems a little encouraged.

'But I take it I can help. Unless you *are* just here to see me.'

'My boss forced me to do it.'

His face falls a little; but he remains resilient.

'Touché.'

DS Jones does not react; she continues to eat, looking pleased.

'It's really good.'

'That makes two of you.'

Kendall Minto grins boyishly; there is no doubting his winning looks, and there is something in his irrepressible persistence that keeps him just on the right side of bothersome. And perhaps there is the novelty of unbridled flattery.

He must detect a softening in her manner.

'You see – you get to have your cake and eat it, too.'

She cannot suppress a chuckle.

'You mean – I could have just phoned you?'

Now he acts more casually, taking a mouthful of his own portion.

'Well, there is that.' He raises his fork over his shoulder. 'Isn't this place a bit close to home?'

DS Jones flashes him a glance that may be conspiratorial. He refers to what is the attic café of Skelgill's favourite outdoor gear emporium.

'Call it hiding in plain sight.'

The idea seems to intrigue him, and he tips back his head in a knowing way. Clearly, he is torn between wishing to believe he is favoured, and past experience that tells him he is usually outwitted by present company.

He opts to revert to the surer ground of their professional interests.

'Is there some juicy morsel that you have to trade?'

Now she flashes him another look of reproach.

He raises his palms; the affable dog that knows a small, sleek feline bristles with a hidden armoury.

But his rolling over does the trick.

'There's something that would help us get to the bottom of this case.'

While she pauses – and eats – he offers a suggestion.

'I take it your Inspector Smart is playing agent provocateur?'

DS Jones nods thoughtfully.

'As my colleagues say, he's a one-trick pony.'

Kendall Minto frowns – a little reservedly, as if he cannot quite conceal some affinity with such methods. Indeed, his response suggests so.

'There are times when one must stir up the hornets' nest.'

'Even if it involves someone else being killed?'

Her sharp rejoinder is a shock tactic.

He rocks back, realising his misstep.

'Ah, well – of course – I don't know the precise circumstances.' And he makes a face of contrition. 'I hope we have not put our foot in it?'

She allows him to stew for a moment. Then she grins.

'I should say don't worry. If anything, you've set an entirely different hare running.'

He is intelligent, quick, and gets it.

'A red herring, indeed?' He regards her optimistically. 'Helpful?'

She considers this proposition. As Skelgill has tacitly agreed, there is a silver lining to the apparently bogus Manchester drugs connection – but the clock is ticking.

Rather peremptorily, she finishes the last of her cake, and drains her cup.

Kendall Minto watches on with an expression of growing alarm – she appears to be readying herself to leave. And she does indeed rise. She checks the time on her mobile phone. But rather than take her waterproof from the back of the chair, she reaches down and places her shoulder bag on the seat. She produces a foolscap envelope, unmarked. She hands it over.

'If you can trace the complete version of this, you could be an overnight sensation.'

His eyes widen as he takes the envelope. He seems to understand he is not to open it in public view, and merely gives an exaggerated wink and slips it inside his jacket.

'My meter expires in five minutes.' DS Jones smiles disarmingly – and he has no recourse but to bow his head. 'Thanks for the pepper cake.'

As she descends the open curving staircase down onto the second floor, DS Jones is too deep in thought to notice, across in a section to her left, beneath a hanging banner that reads, "Autumn Sale – Men's Waterproofs" a tallish individual is trying on a black cagoule, rather fighting with it, in fact. The hood is raised, and the figure turns away as she passes, and only a prominent protruding nose might give a clue to the prospective buyer's identity.

A minute later, as she is adjusting her own garment for better protection, hurrying past the churchlike edifice of the Moot Hall, her mobile phone rings. She picks up, and slides the handset inside her hood.

'Guv – hi.'

Skelgill does not trouble with pleasantries.

'Where are you?'

'Keswick – I'm running to avoid a parking ticket.'

There is a slight pause.

'Stick in another hour. We'll meet at the Mountain Café. Leyton's on his way.'

*

'Oh – what's this?'

Skelgill, already queuing at the counter, has directed DS Jones to claim a secluded corner table. Now he joins her with a loaded tray. He grins, wryly it seems.

'They're calling it Westmorland pepper cake. I reckon it's not selling.' Rather defiantly he puts down a plate that holds four slices. 'Two for the price of one. No point getting three.'

Before DS Jones can remark upon their good fortune they are disturbed by the arrival of a panting DS Leyton, damp and dishevelled. He seems, however, to be in good spirits.

'New cagoule, Guv?'

'What?'

Skelgill has not yet divested himself of his waterproof; his reaction suggests a certain defensive embarrassment – a familiar Skelgillism, that anything concerning his attire and shopping habits is a matter to be kept shrouded in secrecy. Or perhaps it is just the small ignominy of being caught buying in the autumn sale.

DS Leyton reaches and gives a tug to the back of the jacket.

'You've left the price tag on.'

But DS Leyton does not seem bothered, and he settles, eyeing the cake. Perhaps to his surprise Skelgill slides a mug of tea in his direction, and offers around the Westmorland pepper cake. Skelgill watches DS Jones as she rather gingerly accepts a slice and puts it on her side plate without attempting to try it.

But DS Leyton now pre-empts any further small talk.

'I just saw Minto – he went into the Keswick Chronicle office. That's his lot's sister publication, ain't it?' Though he looks at his colleagues he does not wait for an answer. 'Seemed deep in thought. Walked right past and blanked me.'

DS Jones can feel Skelgill observing her; she opts to explain.

'I've put him on the trail of the photograph – as back up.'

She turns hopefully to DS Leyton – he understands she is querying his success – but he responds with a face that conveys otherwise. She continues quickly.

'Most of the media use a central agency that sources stock and archive photography. They're probably our best bet, under the circumstances. I gave him a photocopy of the incomplete article.'

DS Leyton chuckles.

'Looks like he's straight on the case. Must be trying to impress you, Emma. *Hah.*'

She dares to look at Skelgill. His expression is as anticipated, largely disapproving – not least that she has handed over a photograph of him as a 'beaky' kid. But she quickly heads off what can be his only professional objection.

'I said nothing about our line of inquiry – that we're trying to identify Jubb. And he came clean about the Manchester drug story – he says he's sure it was DI Smart that left the message on their out-of-hours voicemail.'

Being proved correct seems to mollify Skelgill. And as DS Jones relates the reporter's account of the purported customs worker, he silently eats cake. Indeed, he even appears to give consideration to the explanation, now that flesh upon the bones give it a ring of authenticity. If he is unnerved, however, he shrugs it off, and turns abruptly to DS Leyton.

'No joy, then?'

DS Leyton makes another face of frustration, though he flashes a grin at DS Jones.

'Not unless you count the spirit of Mary Queen of Scots.'

Skelgill regards him as though he will tell him he is tapped – but DS Jones is amused.

'Was that your excuse – that you're a ghost hunter?'

DS Leyton chuckles ruefully.

'Cor blimey, Emma – I should have thought of that.' He glances at Skelgill, checking how far flippancy can go. 'Nah – I invented a wartime ancestor – I reckon it did the trick.'

But for a moment he halts and frowns introspectively – before moving again, pulling out his mobile phone.

'No photo or press article – and, to be honest, no way of knowing if the documents had been tampered with. And your fishing match only got a brief mention in despatches. But I did get an address for one Mr T. Jubb.'

He has Skelgill's attention – indeed his superior takes the handset and devours the information as hungrily as he has despatched his first slice of cake.

'From their list of members in the same year as your fishing match, Guv.'

Skelgill stares hard at the little screen.

Then, without speaking, he passes the phone to DS Jones.

It is she that raises the question of him.

'Does this mean anything to you? He would have been single – four years before the car accident.'

Skelgill, who knows Cockermouth better than most, is pensive. He pictures the locality. Gote is the settlement on the north bank of the Derwent, and Spital Ing Lane a rather curious backwater – almost literally so, an *ing* being a water meadow.

But he shakes his head.

DS Jones speculates further.

'It gives the impression that he was in lodgings – that it says "care of" the property. I wonder what chance it's still in the same hands. If he lived there for a while, someone might remember him – or a neighbour, perhaps.'

Her tone is neutral, and Skelgill looks even less optimistic. A lot can change in twenty-eight years; the property may not even be there. But they can all agree without needing to discuss it that it is something they will soon investigate.

DS Jones returns the mobile to DS Leyton. For a moment he, too, seems a little deflated – but then he remembers he has another small card up his sleeve.

He looks inquiringly at Skelgill.

'What about this DAA committee meeting tonight, Guv?'

'How do you know that?'

There is something about Skelgill's reaction – quickly disguised – that hints at consternation.

DS Leyton contrives to continue evenly.

'Georgina Graham – she'd left her laptop open. She must have been finalising the agenda before she circulates it this morning.' He picks up his mobile phone. 'Here – I photographed it, an' all. You'll have to fiddle about, to read it.'

Skelgill grimaces as he manipulates the too-large image. He sees, however, that his sergeant is right. Today's date. The Partridge. Seven p.m. in the Smoke Room.

Skelgill's gaze drifts away, through the skylight window that would give a view of the distinctive summit of Grisedale Pike on a clear day – but he is as unseeing as the elements are unrevealing. Why did Fenella Mansfield not tell him? As Sir Montague Brash's PA she would certainly know about the meeting. Yet all she said was that he was away today. He reaches no conclusion, but feels deeper stirrings that disturb his equilibrium. Eventually, he addresses DS Leyton.

'Did she mention it?'

DS Leyton seems to understand something of Skelgill's concern – but he plays down any underlying suspicion on his part. 'Nah – she didn't, Guv. But don't get me wrong – she wasn't cagey – just the opposite. I noticed the agenda on her screen and snapped it on the spur of the moment. To be honest, I'd got that address and I wanted to get out of there before she blew my cover.'

Skelgill seems unmoved by his sergeant's explanation. Now, rather than attempt to read the small detail, he passes the handset to DS Jones.

More adept in such matters, she quickly analyses the agenda.

'It's mainly standard items – Apologies – only Lucy Bedlington – previous minutes, Chairman's report, Treasurer's report – but there's this.' She has enlarged a section and turns the phone so both her colleagues can see.

Under 'AOB' is the wording: "Mrs Betony – condolences/flowers".

'It must have been submitted for inclusion.'

She glances at Skelgill to see his expression is again showing some concern.

'I take it Sir Montague didn't mention the meeting, either?'

Skelgill seems to start – as though he were deeper in thought than was apparent.

'What?' He folds his arms and leans back in his seat. 'He weren't home. I'll need to go back.'

It seems he has nothing to add; though it is clear he is discomfited.

DS Jones makes an effort to lighten the issue.

'I don't suppose we should read too much into the committee meeting. Given your contacts, Guv – it's hardly something they would think they could hush up. In fact, didn't Charlie say it's the last Tuesday of the month?'

A pause ensues. Skelgill has finished his cake and is looking at the spare slice; however DS Jones only prods at hers, and he seems distracted by the duality.

DS Leyton, however, is eager to come to the greater point.

'What next then, Guv – turn our fire on the big guns?'

Skelgill does not answer, but remains staring at the table. DS Jones, as though she knows how to unlock the impasse, hands Skelgill her plate.

But she simultaneously interjects.

'Since there's a committee meeting – then assuming he attends

'– at least it means Jay Chaudry won't be down in Manchester.'

Skelgill nods at this. He recognises some crumbs of comfort. For the unity of his team in the short term, this is a small benefit.

But still he is preoccupied.

It smarts, his failure to discern that there is a meeting tonight. What was he up to, in that impromptu encounter with Fenella Mansfield? It was a golden opportunity to dig beneath the surface of the life of Sir Montague Brash – but she walked all over him.

And then there is the DAA committee meeting itself. Yes, it might be scheduled – but the sudden knowledge, and its proximity to the writhing netful of promising leads and puzzling unknowns, trawled up but not disentangled – and the imminent threat of DI Alec Smart diving unrestrained into the midst – these factors unnerve him out of proportion.

For what?

No – not for *what* – but for *whom?*

Who is in danger?

And who is the threat?

13. ELIMINATION

Derwentdale – 12.30 p.m., Tuesday, 28th September

Skelgill is under pressure. The feeling is nothing new – but the type of pressure is. He might be about to meet a killer – a serial killer, indeed. And one with whom he may have interacted before. Twenty-eight years ago, as a nine-year-old boy unobservant of his peers, when most grown men looked and smelled the same. A man who would have been twenty then and is aged forty-eight now, possibly changed beyond any hope of recognition.

He is glad for the company of DS Jones – yet in certain respects a showdown might be more productive were he to be alone. Two men meeting are finely attuned to one another's body language; the presence of a third party alters the dynamic in a thousand little ways; and in several big ones when that person is a desirable female.

But the detective trio has discussed the pros and cons.

A stay was the first option – but this was dismissed almost as quickly as it was mooted. Yes, more background information would surely help them home in on their quarry – but the inevitable delay may render some other prey exposed and helpless. And there is DI Smart to worry about. So, while parallel inquiries can take place – and new information gleaned can be relayed to headquarters for investigation – they will forge on in the hope that, questioned with a new purpose in mind, someone might slip up.

DS Leyton has reluctantly agreed that he cannot best perform these interrogations. There is the matter of credibility, of him repeating questions he has already posed – and, not least, the outside chance that Skelgill might find a memory triggered that he was unaware is in his possession. A singular trait or characteristic, lodged deep in a subterranean crevice of his long-unvisited labyrinth of boyhood experiences.

And DS Jones's presence might well be beneficially disarming, when the alternative is some kind of gunslinger's stand-off. After all – if one of these men is Toby Jubb, that man knows it.

Thus DS Leyton has accepted with good grace what is, on the face of it, a lesser role. He appeared momentarily to rue that he raised with some vehemence the notion of revenge – but at least Skelgill gives his reserve theory some credence, in assigning him to revisit the two females – Ruth Robinson and Jackie Baker – for whom such a motive might just apply. After all, did they not interact with Kyle Betony moments before his disappearance, and unobtrusively leave together shortly after? Both passed over Ouse Bridge on their routes home; neither was particularly sympathetic to his loss. Hitherto treated as minor witnesses, it would be negligent not to understand any possible connection to the late Lynette Jubb.

There is also the task for DS Leyton to follow up his own well-found lead that Toby Jubb once lived – or lodged, at least – at the Cockermouth address on the Derwent's northern bank.

It is the Derwent that immediately figures in Skelgill's calculations.

Their small convoy having headed westwards from Keswick, while DS Leyton has continued on the A66 as the most direct means to Cockermouth, Skelgill and DS Jones have pulled off through falling wet leaves to park her car conveniently at The Partridge. DC Watson, tasked with setting up interviews, has quickly and efficiently informed them that Anthony Goodman is available during his lunch break; the road to Bothel takes them from the old coaching inn over Ouse Bridge.

No sooner have they set off again than Skelgill veers from the road.

He bumps his shooting brake onto the rough verge just short of the bridge turn, ploughing through a bed of decaying thistles and crispy chocolate-brown docks and late-flowering stinging nettles. The car slides about, sinking and slipping in the squelchy ground.

'You're not getting out in this?'

Skelgill grimaces, as though there is some unpleasant call of duty.

'Better test this new cagoule while it's still got the label on. Case I need to take it back.' He shoulders open the driver's door and tumbles out. 'Besides – someone needs to check the level.'

DS Jones, for a moment, thinks it is simply his incorrigible habit – the inability to cross a river without some form of inspection. But it seems an especially unattractive prospect in the pouring rain. However, she offers her support.

'Do you need me to come?'

Skelgill leans in and indicates to a brown paper bag in the central console.

'Finish off your cake – else I shall.'

He smirks and slams the door.

DS Jones watches his dark shape become disfigured as rain streams down the windscreen, little waves that distort the view. But she reflects that he seems now in good spirits – back with her – on the hunt. She feels happy – but anxious.

For Skelgill's part, the regular quip about checking the level is today no joke. He has heard from Arthur Hope that six inches of rain have fallen over Seathwaite in twenty-four hours, and the vast slow-moving depression seems to have shuddered to a halt over Borrowdale, the Derwent's basin. Rivers and becks will be bursting their banks. They are in the early stages of a potential threat to public safety. And there will be difficulty in getting about the county.

He makes his way to the gentle apex of Ouse Bridge.

He stands on the downstream side.

The grey Derwent is shifting beneath like the roof of an express train; bulging, inexorable, a frightening speed, an irresistible force of current. To fall in, one's only hope would be to cling to the meniscus like a stowaway in a Bond movie and pray to be cast off by centrifugal force on a sharp bend; but already shingle banks are subsumed – the spot where nine days ago they had breakfasted is gone – the river has doubled in width and is about to spill over its artificially raised bank into the narrow grassy ing beyond. Sheep move about uneasily, their bleating mournful.

He leans over and looks directly below and reflects again on what fate might have befallen Kyle Betony. The idea that he was whacked at the inn and brought by car and heaved over the parapet now seems to hold most currency. But impact with the central pier cannot be ruled out. It has an unusual shape; spearlike, it protrudes downstream, rising curved with a crest that meets the wall of the arch. Perhaps its design makes it more streamlined, allowing the water to flow with least turbulence, minimising the suction that over time undermines the foundations. But that it juts out by a good five feet means that a slip at exactly this point would not be a clean drop into water – a person would hit the stone structure, possibly the sharp edge.

Skelgill asks himself why he has come back to look at this. Such logic sows inconvenient seeds of doubt upon the barren plain of his mind. He sniffs; though it is rain that drips from his nose, the reflex is instinctive – akin to the primal sense that strength and direction are gained from a return to the essential locus. Just like Alice said.

'How is it?'

Skelgill slides back into his seat and hurriedly slams the door.

'Dangerous.'

'Oh – I meant your new waterproof. It suits you, by the way. It's a better fit than your last one.'

Skelgill is momentarily wrongfooted by the unsought compliment. There is the sense that she has made a specific effort; he grasps the steering wheel and stares ahead, when eye contact might be appropriate. Raindrops are spilling from his newly proofed garment.

'Happen I'll wreck it soon enough.'

FELLVIEW NURSING HOME, BOTHEL – 1.00 p.m.

'Thank you for sparing the time to see us, Mr Goodman. Sorry to encroach on your lunch hour.'

Anthony Goodman smiles, his small blue pupils fixed upon DS Jones; leaning across his desk, his relaxed pose conveys a sense of patient resignation.

'We professionals have to stick together. It must be your lunch hour, too – and I rather feel your task is more onerous than mine.'

Skelgill, sitting a little aside and behind his colleague hears a voice in his head; impudent, insolent even, "Every hour's a lunch hour" – and he feels the urge to echo the words aloud, like some pipsqueak schoolboy who has been overlooked by a VIP visitor to the classroom, and who cannot contain himself from spouting attention-seeking nonsense.

But since their arrival and perfunctory reintroduction his presence might almost have been invisible. Anthony Goodman, Financial Director of Fellview Nursing Home and Treasurer of the Derwentdale Anglers' Association has had eyes for no one but DS Jones.

The man's rather fawning manner cuts no ice with Skelgill. So it is perhaps just as well that he is taking a back seat. Indeed, he ought to be happy with this state of affairs. If he is to approach an understanding of the deeper sensations that trouble him, the last thing he needs is to be thinking up questions and – worse still – paying heed to the answers.

In Skelgill's case, only briefly met in passing at The Partridge, he has just DS Leyton's second-hand account of Anthony Goodman, and now forms first impressions. The man obviously thinks he is both amusing and attractive. Skelgill is a little disconcerted that DS Jones appears suitably endeared, a condition he hopes is affected for the purposes of their interview.

Anthony Goodman writhes as if in sudden pain.

'Are you okay, sir?'

The violent spasm passes just as quickly as it arrived.

'Oh – ah. Yes – thank you. It's nothing, Sergeant. My apologies. Just a minor affliction – I suffer from multiple sclerosis. These little bouts can come as a precursor to a relapse. I try to avoid medication – I prefer to tackle it through a combination of diet and willpower.'

DS Jones seems a little too concerned for Skelgill's liking.

'We could come back another time, sir?'

'No, no – by all means stay. We each have our cross to bear.'

He grins ruefully, and flashes a dismissive glance at Skelgill; there is the implication that he considers him to be DS Jones's.

'If you're sure, sir?'

He presents a hand, palm upwards; the slender pink fingers are unblemished by traces of manual work. It is like an emperor's summons, and he does not deign to embellish the action with words.

DS Jones, for all her outward compassion, promptly takes up the invitation.

'Sir – you have perhaps seen this morning's media – the report about there being a drugs connection to the death of Mr Betony?'

She carries off the question without a trace of the apprehension she must feel; Skelgill, too, endeavours neither to move nor not move for fear of revealing their collective anticipation. But if they are hoping for some telling reaction, then they are disappointed.

'Indeed – it was the talk of the staffroom at breaktime.' Anthony Goodman leans forward, pressing his hands together and intertwining the long pale fingers, further engaging eye contact. 'Thanks heavens you have a lead. I knew it had to be something like that.'

DS Jones, Skelgill notes, evidently decides not to correct the man. The article makes no mention of the authorities as the source of the story. Only they know it might be a police lead – and even then, one that exists predominantly in the mind of DI Alec Smart.

Instead she probes the sentiment underlying Anthony Goodman's remark.

'Why do you say thank heavens, sir?'

Now there is perhaps a momentary flicker; the small mouth in the seemingly oversized face briefly opens and closes – as though he was about to speak but has paused to vet his response.

'Well – I mean – circumstantially – what on earth was Kyle Betony doing? I assume he was pushed over the bridge. Why would he have walked so far in pitch darkness? He must have been up to no good – it would be to avoid being seen, or identified by driving his car there.'

Again the man smiles, and writhes – although now it seems more an act of obsequiousness, and one that Skelgill, reduced to spectating, finds wholly distasteful.

'My apologies, Sergeant – I am doing your detective work for you.'

DS Jones responds with a polite grin that seems intended to convey no hard feelings; but she pursues her point.

'Does your view extend to something about Mr Betony himself, sir? What do you mean when you say it had to be something like that?'

Now there comes a reaction that Skelgill reads as conspiratorial; the man regards DS Jones intently; there is almost a glint of glee in his small eyes, and he slowly rubs together the palms of his hands.

'I am sure I can't say anything that will have escaped your undoubted talents and obvious powers of investigation.'

'Try me.'

Skelgill is a little taken aback by his colleague's rather intimate engagement with the smarmy man, whom he would rather lamp at this juncture.

Anthony Goodman seems enrapt by the challenge. He leans closer, his attention focused exclusively upon DS Jones; Skelgill might as well not be present.

'As I intimated previously to your colleague, Kyle Betony came across as highly strung, almost hyperactive, prone to mood swings – something that I rather generously put down to a deep-seated insecurity of character – some childhood influence perhaps.'

He stops, and regards her intently, beaming upon her a like a professor encouraging a student by powers of telepathy to reveal her nascent thoughts.

'You mean he took drugs himself?'

Anthony Goodman claps his hands together and sits back, as though she has come up with the correct solution.

'Don't all these people involved in the drug gangs? Isn't it the way the kingpins control their foot soldiers?' He watches carefully for her reaction, but continues quickly. 'And Kyle had been living out in Thailand – he found his wife there. I assume you have interviewed her? She still has strong connections, I believe.'

DS Jones does not answer directly; but now she surprises Skelgill by moving the conversation on. She has before her printed notes of DS Leyton's earlier interview, and she makes a brief reference to these.

'You told my colleague that the last time you saw Mr Betony was when you were getting drinks from the bar – and that he passed along the corridor in the direction of the toilets. Given this new possibility, does that call to mind anything else, in hindsight?'

Anthony Goodman seems pleased with the question; once more he intertwines his prehensile fingers and nods slowly several times. Though the action has a certain hypnotic quality, Skelgill is more gripped by the iron self-control of his subordinate; put in her elegant shoes he would never tolerate the patronising manner.

'Yes – that's correct, I certainly don't recall seeing him after that. Of course – you know there is a side exit? That could be when he left – if he had a pre-arranged drugs deal, I imagine he would not have wanted to advertise his leaving. He could have slipped out and returned the same way without being missed.'

Now the man folds his features into what seems to be an exaggerated introspective smile.

DS Jones looks at him inquiringly.

'But I am teaching granny to suck eggs, as the saying goes – and you are as far from a granny as I can imagine.' His gaze lingers upon DS Jones, indeed he looks her over, as though his own statement provides the requisite permission.

Then he turns to a scowling Skelgill. 'We older ones, eh?'

Skelgill's expression blackens, but the man ignores him and reverts to DS Jones.

'Actually, I was forty-five this year – but Lucy insists that I have confounded the onset of middle age.'

He sits back in a preening fashion; he seems to be expecting a compliment from DS Jones.

Unfazed, she simply picks up the link he has provided.

'Lucy – that's Dr Bedlington – your fiancée – she collected you from The Partridge.'

Anthony Goodman blinks a couple of times, as if he has lost the thread of their discussion.

'Exactly, Sergeant. I saw that she had arrived – so I did not dwell outside I'm afraid. I realise I am not a helpful witness in that regard.'

'And you would have driven over Ouse Bridge – but you saw nothing.'

'We certainly didn't notice anything – naturally we would have told you. I imagine the blacked-out Mercedes was long gone. *Hah-ha.*'

DS Jones acknowledges his little aside. She re-orders her papers and brings to the surface a printed form with spaces to be completed.

'Given the possible narcotics connection I'm sure you'll appreciate that we need to eliminate all of Mr Betony's known contacts – in terms of prior acquaintanceship. There are standard background checks that our administrative section performs.' She looks down at the page and moves her pen to the first empty box. 'We have your current details – perhaps if you could give me your former addresses and employers – we normally like to cover ten years, working back from the present day.'

Skelgill permits himself a break from fuming to admire the way that his colleague has pinned the man with what in sales would be known as the 'assumed close'. He looks casually at Anthony Goodman. Does he imagine a reaction – some restraint being exerted – or has DS Jones succeeded in making their enquiry into his personal history seem entirely routine?

But then the man grins, once again in the sickly way he has employed in trying to win her over.

'Sergeant, why don't I just give you my potted history – you can take from it what you need.'

He speaks as though he fully intends to do so – but DS Jones expresses no objection and indicates he should proceed.

He casts about the large, well-appointed office, as if to set up a contrast.

'I hail from humble origins. I grew up in Melton Mowbray. I have a much older sister, Mary – seventeen years my senior. Our parents are dead. I believe Mary still lives in the area – her married name is Lewinksy – her husband is of Ukrainian descent. I lost touch with her when I left for university. As you can imagine, we had almost no life in common – she moved out when I was a very small child. I studied accountancy at Manchester Metropolitan, and after graduation I spent fourteen years in the accounts department of Coronet Paints in Accrington. I lived in the town – my address was 48, Blackburn Street. Accountancy – and watching paint dry – how about that for an invigorating career?'

He regards DS Jones as though he expects her to laugh, that it is a tried-and-tested maxim of his.

She smiles politely, looking up from her writing; he seems to try to steal a glance at her notes, but she uses shorthand.

'Having risen up the ranks, at thirty-five I found my dream job. Crick Biotech at Ellesmere Port. We worked on advanced DNA profiling. I was FD.'

He turns to address Skelgill.

'Financial Director.'

The moonlike visage seems to spin and Skelgill feels the bizarre frustration that there is nowhere to land a satisfying punch – the upturned nose is undersized and not worth breaking; the mouth a miserable target; the chin too weak to crack. When he recovers from the rush of blood and the ringing in his ears subsides, Anthony Goodman is still crowing.

'Share options. International expansion. Executive travel. I bought a substantial house on the Wirral – it was called The Old Manse, at West Kirby.'

Then he seems to suffer some painful memory.

'Disaster struck.'

He does not now speak, and DS Jones understands she is to humour him.

'Sir?'

'Bankruptcy – due to fraud. Five years in, the founder emptied the bank accounts and absconded to Panama. What capital I had accrued and invested went with him. The firm collapsed overnight, along with my dreams. I had to hand back the keys to my property.'

DS Jones nods but does not dwell upon his misfortune.

'That would have been when you got the job here?'

He seems a little perturbed that she moves on so peremptorily.

'Well – yes – a small hiatus. You understand – it took a little time to recover from the body blow.'

But he grins – again, it is his politician's smile, over-practised, hackneyed, unconvincing – and yet it is human instinct to react to such a stimulus within only a permitted range of responses.

DS Jones allows a few moments' pause. Then she taps her pen against a point on the page, like a conductor regaining control of the orchestra.

'You're engaged to Dr Bedlington. Were you previously married?'

Now there is a more considered smile, an expression of smugness – that she might find hard to believe what he is about to tell her, such an attractive prospect as he.

'I have hitherto managed to avoid Cupid's arrow – but Lucy and I – we seem to be soulmates.'

DS Jones appears in two minds over whether to probe further. Then, with her pen poised over a blank box, she strikes a line through it. She looks up – and now speaks in a more conversational tone.

'What made you come to Cumbria, sir?'

'Needs must, Sergeant.' He seems not to notice or care that the expression may cause offence – that he might as well have said, "Beggars can't be choosers". But he continues – and again casts about the large room – as though to emphasise that he has recovered his rightful status. 'There are only so many jobs at my level of experience and competence.'

'And that was five years ago?'

'Correct, in August.'

DS Jones briefly refers to her notes.

'And you joined the DAA – the Derwentdale Anglers' Association – almost immediately.'

He seems to interpret the question as a small slight; he responds in a superior manner.

'Well – one's hobby is always a good way of meeting like-minded people – when you move to somewhere new, you know?'

'What made you pick the DAA over the other local group – the AAA?'

Now he appears momentarily puzzled.

'I felt – and I believe I have been proved right – that the DAA is a smaller, more friendly organisation.'

DS Jones turns to Skelgill – as if she is inviting him to step in with a question. But he looks not a picture of geniality. A small crease forms on her brow. She has made the opening and it seems he eschews it.

She addresses Anthony Goodman.

'Which brings us full circle to Mr Betony. He joined the DAA quite recently – did you know him or have any contact with him before that?'

The man slowly shakes his head, and resumes the slow wringing of his hands, as though he might be revisiting the tragedy in his mind's eye.

'Actually, he appeared out of the blue. I don't recall any procedure. We had a vacancy on the committee – and suddenly one evening he was there.'

'And did you socialise with him – or fish with him – or anything like that?'

The condescending smile is rolled out once more.

'You know, Sergeant – I don't believe he was much of an angler. I suspect his involvement on the committee was more about self-advancement.'

*

'Sixty-four-thousand-dollar question.'

DS Jones has waited until she and Skelgill have moved away

from the building. Now he seems to be leading her in the opposite direction from the area marked for visitors' parking. She has her hood up against the rain and has to hold one side of it to look at him. He seems unbothered by the conditions, his own hood down.

He stares intently, but shakes his head. He does not otherwise answer.

'I thought –' DS Jones hesitates, to rephrase her statement perhaps. 'You seemed agitated. I wondered if you'd recognised him. He's distinctive looking.'

Skelgill swings a left hook at the low-hanging branch of a sycamore – it has not yet cast its leaves and a sudden deluge of oversized droplets descends upon him.

His sole verbal rejoinder is a mild curse, which may or may not be a reaction to the ill-advised punch.

'I mean – sufficiently distinctive that Kyle Betony might have seen the resemblance in the photograph.'

She has tried to mitigate what Skelgill might interpret as a criticism of his own powers of observation. And she goes further.

'But, of course, if it's not him – then there would be nothing to notice.'

Skelgill is striding on at a good lick, and she has to move quickly to keep up with him. They seem to be circumnavigating the building; now they are on spongy mown grass that forms part of the extensive grounds. She takes a different tack.

'Where are we going?'

'Staff car park.'

And Skelgill's sense of direction is proved right; they round a corner to emerge upon a second parking zone. There are about a dozen vehicles in two rows. Those facing the windowless rear wall of the modern administrative block have bays marked by small signs. Skelgill halts at the one that reads, "Director of Finance".

'Looks like his bank balance has recovered.'

A new top-of-the-range white Mercedes coupe fills the space.

DS Jones wants better to understand the purpose of their detour.

'What are you thinking, Guv?'

Skelgill ponders for a moment, his lips compressed, his lashes blinking away raindrops.

'I'm thinking we should have taken all the numbers outside The Partridge.'

'On the Sunday morning?'

'Aye.'

'There's the hotel register.'

'That's residents only.'

'Ah, yes – and I suppose no obligation to complete it – the Smiths left that section blank.'

'This car weren't there when we saw Goodman and his woman on the Monday night. They must have arrived in hers.'

DS Jones is nodding. So that was what he was up to when he disappeared for a short while. She wonders what might be his logic (rarely a good idea, she admits). And there are too many possible permutations – though she understands that not everyone need have travelled home by the same means as they arrived; a vehicle could have been left overnight, blending in with residents' cars, and collected next morning.

'As soon as we're out of the rain – I'll send these details to DC Watson.'

She pats her shoulder bag; she means the information that will corroborate the identity of Anthony Goodman.

Skelgill nods grimly.

He casts about; there are large puddles forming on the tarmac, and across on the lawns water is collecting in small depressions, the heavens emptying too fast for the sodden ground to absorb.

'Flood.'

RUBBYBANKS ROAD, COCKERMOUTH – 2.22 p.m.

When Skelgill said "Flood" it was a dual-purpose term – for Stephen Flood is their second appointment. They have received word that he has the afternoon off, and may be found at his home address.

'Remind us what we know.'

They have parked outside a property in the older part of the town, quite close to the centre, where cramped terraces have Georgian and Victorian origins. This particular sector lies in the obtuse (rather than the acute) angle between the rivers Derwent and Cocker. The latter joins the former like a motorway on-slip, and provides the settlement with its toponym.

They have descended from the north on what Skelgill calls the "top road" – actually passing Spital Ing Lane – a craned glimpse yielding no sign of their colleague's car; and they have not tried to contact him. Skelgill works as usual on the principle that, be there news, Leyton will call.

They have crossed Gote Bridge into a town on flood alert. Many householders and shopkeepers have already erected their door barriers (or piles of sandbags, where no such device has been fitted). Skelgill was conscious of historical nick marks and more formal flood-level plates on walls that would show his car to be entirely submerged as they navigated Main Street. The town has a beauty-and-the-beast quality; the rather magical confluence of the largely benign rivers – and the wrath that a prolonged storm in the fells can unleash upon its unsuspecting denizens. Though flooding is a little more anticipated these days. Once-in-a-century inundations have become once-in-a-decade events. A stoic population hunkers down, like the residents of many a border town in bygone times, as the whims of barons and kings saw marauding armies sweep north and south and back again.

Rubbybanks Road is no exception. Running parallel to the Cocker, and the river forming one side of the street over a low wall, it is a prime flooding spot. So much so that there has been an investment in self-raising flood barriers that rise up out of the wall itself. Skelgill stares at the arrangement – as yet, the innovative contraption does not appear to have activated, despite that the flint-blue water seems ominously high.

It is an interesting choice of address for a man in Stephen Flood's line of work; not to mention his surname.

Skelgill speaks his thoughts.

'Flood by name.'

DS Jones is still trying to locate DS Leyton's interview report on her tablet. She speaks without looking up.

'I was at uni with a girl from Glenrothes called Morna Flood. Think it's a Scottish name?'

Skelgill shakes his head somewhat indifferently. He has met no other human Floods, and two Scots is a small sample.

Now DS Jones finds what she seeks.

'We have his age as forty-seven. Widowed. He has been living in Cumbria for twenty-two years.'

She hesitates at this – perhaps because it is patently fewer years than the incident twenty-four years earlier; the now-controversial death of Lynette Jubb.

Skelgill seems to be thinking along similar lines; his expression is severe.

'When's he forty-eight?'

'Ah – that's October – the twenty-fifth.'

'When's Jubb's birthday?'

'I don't recall the exact date – but it was June – he would already be forty-eight.'

Skelgill's face is severe. These points could of course be academic if someone is concealing their true identity and age – it would seem too obvious for anyone with a modicum of basic cunning to overlook. Nevertheless, Stephen Flood of the three suspect males is ostensibly the closest in age to what Toby Jubb would be.

DS Jones understands what Skelgill is getting at.

'He was one of the last to interact meaningfully with Kyle Betony.' She begins to paraphrase from the report. 'After the dinner, Betony joined Flood at his table in the bar. Flood was irritated by Betony's persistence. Flood paid a visit to the gents'. When he returned Betony was gone. Flood finished his drink and left – and that was at around ten-thirty. If you recall from the other witness statements, it seems likely that this was the point when Betony spoke with Ruth Robinson and Jackie Baker in the residents' lounge – and then returned along the corridor towards the toilets and the exit. That was when Anthony Goodman saw him pass. After that, we have nothing.'

Skelgill remains silent; he seems mesmerised by the flow of the river, his gaze flicking back and forth as he follows successive items of flotsam that sail the stretch in view.

DS Jones offers a prompt.

'We only have Stephen Flood's word that he didn't see Kyle Betony again. He did admit he was riled by him. And they were sitting in the alcove – where the photograph was removed from the wall. When you piece it all together, it makes him sound like someone we ought to look at closely. Flood must have left at more or less the same time Kyle Betony disappeared.'

Skelgill is evidently paying more attention than his demeanour might suggest.

'What time did that car pull up – the car that the pillow bloke noticed?'

'Mr Brian Cotswold?' She checks. 'Well – yes – that was also at or shortly after ten-thirty.'

Skelgill folds his arms and turns his gaze away from the river. Ahead, the road narrows into a pedestrian tunnel where Victoria Bridge spans the Cocker, one of only two road-crossings in the town. The asymmetrical double stone arch calls to mind Ouse Bridge, though the latter is grander and somehow more elegant; perhaps it is the backdrop of Bass Lake and Skiddaw that influences him. His front teeth protrude, an expression of concentration when little concrete is forthcoming. Flood is a neat circumstantial fit. He wonders why he has not seen this so clearly hitherto. But he is aware that the clock is ticking to ill effect. Avoid temptation. To plump for Flood would be like Alec Smart has plumped for Jay Chaudry. Circumstantial evidence has its limitations. Wrong conclusions can be drawn. Twice in a fortnight he has returned home to find his dog had stolen and eaten butter from the worktop. Until – third time around – Skelgill approached stealthily from the rear of the house. Through the kitchen window he observed the cat making a meal of the latest replacement packet – devouring most of its contents and eventually pushing it off the raised surface. Thence Cleopatra licked the wrapper clean around the house, ending up near the front door. Were Skelgill to enter, he would find only the dog capable of looking guilty. The cat has no such capacity.

'Let's keep it in mind.' Skelgill makes to move. This time he pulls up his hood. 'Reet. Same form then lass. You did a good job with Goodman.'

DS Jones does a little double-take, the compliment coming unexpectedly; though there is perhaps a back-handed component, in that she must again put in the hard yards. They have not discussed in any detail their previous interview – agreeing that reflection is better kept for the wider context of having spoken to all three men, along with any information that DS Leyton will bring, or the team at headquarters might unearth.

In answer to her question – what did Skelgill think? – driving away from Bothel, he had merely remarked that "Something didn't smell right" – it had come across as a platitude, deflection – she had been tempted to joke that it was the strong smell of an expensive cologne that she had noticed, but she had decided not to mention it. Evidently, however, Skelgill was impressed sufficiently by her work.

She joins him on the pavement, and for a moment they both regard the building before them. In a street of mainly well-kept properties, freshly painted in pastels of blue, yellow and pale ochre, with window and door surrounds picked out in black or white, number thirty-seven makes an unsightly contrast, even to Skelgill's less discerning eye. It is the end house of a short terrace of very narrow homes, each just a door and a window wide, but three storeys high. It seems to tower diffusely into the mist of the rain. The bare fascia is of stained harling badly in need of attention; it conveys a sense of dereliction of interest, of slatternliness. Within a low wall over which sprawls an unkempt privet hedge a small front garden has run to ruin. Rose bushes have long grown leggy, beyond the redemption of pruning. There are weeds in the path, and decaying fallen leaves gather unswept.

Is this the mantle of solitary living? Skelgill looks askance at DS Jones – as if he fears in some indirect way that the property projects upon him an undesirable quality. But she seems more perturbed by the unrelenting downpour – and he pushes open the unlatched gate so that they may swiftly gain the cover of an open-fronted porch beneath which four steps rise to the front door. A gutter drips from above, a steady splattering upon the algae-stained corrugated plastic roof.

'Hark.'

DS Jones, poised to ring the doorbell, retracts her hand.

Skelgill leans in.

From within emanate raised voices. A guttural male and a sharp, staccato female. It is hard to judge who leads the argument – sometimes they shout at once. Exact words are indiscernible.

The detectives exchange concerned glances – the question is whether they should intervene.

Skelgill gives a terse nod.

DS Jones presses the button – they do not hear the chime – it must be deeper in the house.

But the voices are silenced.

Nobody comes.

The detectives wait.

DS Jones seems to know the optimum interval – she rings again just as Skelgill is about to nudge her.

Still nothing.

Skelgill, deceptively gently, moves her aside. He is just raising a clenched fist when, in the passage at the side of the house there is the slam of a door.

A moment later a man appears.

Short, stocky, wearing a long mackintosh and a tweed cap of the sort Skelgill would associate with a gamekeeper, he rounds the side of the porch and mounts the bottom step.

Hands in pockets, there is little to see of him – thickset, square-jawed, a generously bulbous nose and a contrastingly mean mouth; the expression belligerent – an impression boosted by a diagonal scar that cleaves his left cheek.

'Mr Flood. We're from Cumbria CID. I'm DS Jones and this is DI Skelgill.'

That DS Jones quickly adds their credentials is because she sees suspicion in his reaction – and it would not be the first time they have been mistaken for evangelists of some variety. She has her warrant card at the ready and the narrowed eyes briefly flick over it.

'Aye.'

He seems to accept that they were due to arrive. He makes no move, nor reference to anything that has gone before – not even to the altercation, or to his irregular emergence.

'We are at the correct house?'

'Aye.'

There is a momentary standoff – but DS Jones seems determined to hold her ground.

'Is this convenient, sir?'

She does not elaborate – although it must be obvious that the cramped circumstances of the inadequate shelter form at least part of her meaning.

'Ah'm just going fae the evening paper. It'll keep.'

Skelgill is wondering if the man's standpoint is designed to hurry them off. They are uncomfortably close, two steps apart, looking down upon him. Skelgill edges away to the extent that he can – the man seems perturbed; the inference being that DS Jones will speak. She does.

'Mr Flood – we're having to reassess the investigation into the death of Mr Betony – you may have seen press reports of a possible drug connection?'

'Aye.'

He is no more forthcoming as to how he heard. Then he listens dispassionately as DS Jones explains the routine elimination process and their obligation to verify employment and domestic details.

He stares for a moment longer.

'I was at BNFL Sellafield. Started as a graduate apprentice. Magnox storage ponds.'

'Was that your only employer, prior to Cumbria Water?'

'Aye.'

'You graduated – where did you study?'

'Dundee.'

'University?'

'Tech.'

She has the form on a clipboard and is steadily moving down the page. Though he answers without evasion his suspicion seems to grow; he checks each time he speaks for Skelgill's reaction.

'And are you originally from Dundee?'

'Dourness.'

DS Jones glances at Skelgill, but he remains in impassive mode.

'Could you provide us with an original home address?'

Now Stephen Flood shifts uneasily on his feet – yet blocking their exit there is something of a Tolkeinesque dwarf about his demeanour – that he is torn between cooperation with the forces of good and his orders that none shall pass. Reluctantly he yields name of a farm on the southern shore of the Tay estuary.

Skelgill's ears prick up. He has to refrain from what might be a distracting question. He wonders if indeed the man is a native Fifer. He has uttered *"bark"* for "back" and that he "stayed" rather than "lived". Skelgill's friend Cameron Findlay would no doubt be able to place the rich brogue.

'And when you worked for BNFL, sir?'

Now he provides two addresses in Egremont; one rental, one owned.

'Was there anywhere else in between there and your current address?'

He gives a curt shake of his head.

'This was the wife's mother's place. Ah moved up here before I left BNFL. I wasnae keen on the commute – waste of two hours a day.'

It is the first time he has expanded upon an answer.

In return, DS Jones strives to make it seem like she is nearly done. However, she hesitates, and frowns.

'We don't have anything filled in for your marital status.'

Skelgill affects a yawn; it is perhaps intended to deflect from the white lie.

'I'm a widower.' Stephen Flood answers evenly – then he

makes a strange movement. It could almost be imagined that he has stopped himself from stepping back and looking at the run-down property and the gone-to-seed garden. 'Three years.'

DS Jones seems not to notice anything untoward – she continues to scrutinise her form, as though she is unfamiliar with its contents.

'And – do you have a current partner?'

'Why do you need to know that?'

There is a sudden change in the man's tone – just a hint of aggression when the belligerence thus far has been of a more defensive nature.

DS Jones looks at him in surprise.

'Sir – there's no obligation to provide any information – we appreciate your co-operation.' She half-tilts the clipboard towards him. 'A standard set of data are collected – it's more or less automated.'

Stephen Flood looks unconvinced.

'No.'

'Sir?' She thinks he disagrees.

He seems to harden his stance.

'Nae partner.'

'Ah – right. Perfect.'

It appears she has ticked off her list and is relieved to have reached the end. She lowers the clipboard to her side and regards him in a collaborative manner.

'It's because of the possible drugs connection, sir. There are national procedures that we all must follow.'

The man nods – perhaps he can empathise with the blight of the ivory tower.

Skelgill affects further boredom; he guesses what is coming.

'In view of what we now suspect – did Mr Betony give any hint of what he might have been about to do – since you were the last to see him?'

'Ah wasnae.'

The denial is vehement.

DS Jones blinks a couple of times. She might almost be

apologetic.

'Oh – it's just that – naturally – we have spoken to the other members of the committee. And you mentioned to DS Leyton that Mr Betony joined you after the dinner. When he left you, it seems that was the point at which he also left the hotel. He'd been bothering you – I wondered if that was because you disapproved of what you described as a hare-brained scheme?'

Skelgill is craning up at the stream of drips that batters the flimsy roof; it seems to be gathering force – rather like his colleague's impressive verbatim recall and creative use of DS Leyton's interview.

Stephen Flood, who has hitherto stood with his hands resolutely dug into his pockets, brings them out and folds his arms; what little they can see of his features between his upturned collar and the shadow of his cap seem to become grimmer; he looks like he might be about to lose his temper. Skelgill shifts a little closer to his colleague; a reminder of his presence – they have, after all, borne witness to a domestic altercation that did not sound entirely pleasant.

The response is abrasive.

'Ah wasnae bothered by him.'

DS Jones regards him artlessly.

'Isn't that what you told my colleague, Sergeant Leyton?'

'*Tch.* He couldnae understand us. Cockney yin.'

DS Jones appears concerned – but in a way that seems willing to accommodate the man's point of view.

'Just to straighten the record, then, sir – could you describe what actually happened?'

He glances furtively at Skelgill; Skelgill flashes a forced grin.

'There isnae much tae tell. He came and sat fae a few minutes. He was haverin' – nonsense – like he was killing time. I said I'd get him a drink. He asked fae a whisky. But I went tae the gents' first and when I came oot he was awa'. I thought, good luck tae ye, pal. I didnae bother with another. Finished ma drink – went. I'd planned tae leave then, anyway.'

DS Jones is listening earnestly.

'You said when you left The Partridge you didn't see anyone?'

He begins to shake his head.

'Ah caught a glimpse of Jay – in the Snug – the door was ajar. I didnae speak to him. He was looking at his phone.'

'That's Mr Chaudry?'

'Aye.'

'And outside – no one, no cars waiting?'

Once again – a brusque shake of the head.

'Which way did you drive home, sir?'

Perhaps Stephen Flood realises he has adopted a defensive posture; now he puts his hands back into his pockets. He shrugs, his tone verging on the precocious.

'Usual way.'

'The A66?'

'Aye.' His intonation seems to question why she might imply he would do any differently.

DS Jones appears to have a sudden thought. She raises her clipboard and briefly checks some point.

'You gave us your car registration. Is it in your name or is it a company vehicle?'

'Company car. Why?'

Skelgill finds himself stiffening. But he need not fear, for his subordinate evidently knows exactly where she is going.

'There's an APNR camera on the Cockermouth stretch of the A66. We'll be cross-checking the registration numbers of cars that passed at that time of night. If there were a drugs gang, it's probable they will have used cloned plates – but we can still identify that by eliminating legitimate vehicles, such as yours.'

The man seems to sway a little, but he does not speak.

Skelgill remains tight-lipped; they are letting him stew.

DS Jones folds over the cover of her clipboard and slots her pen away.

'Well – that's all for now, sir. We appreciate your help.'

She looks at Skelgill and they both make to move – but the man does not step back to let them pass.

'Wait. Mebbe I didnae.'

'Didn't what, sir?'

'Go along the A66.'

'Why not, sir?'

Now it is plain that he does not want to answer. He looks at Skelgill – there might almost be a small hint of panic in his eyes – the sense that he is perhaps trying for understanding and leniency, and that the male of the two will provide it.

Skelgill takes up the invitation.

'Which way *did* you go?'

That he does not condemn the attempted deceit, but has merely moved on to the facts, seems to release a response.

'Aye – now I think about it – I took the back lanes.'

'It takes longer that way – especially at night.'

The man shrugs; he is in a cleft stick.

Skelgill waits for a moment more, and then lets him a little off the hook.

'But no coppers waiting in laybys, eh?' He grins wryly.

Stephen Flood lowers his eyes; to the extent that such a hardened countenance is malleable, he winces in apparent relief.

He brings out a hand and indicates a mid-range Vauxhall parked in front of the house.

'I cannae work wi'oot the car.'

Skelgill seems to have discounted the implied misdemeanour.

'What about when you went over Ouse Bridge?'

'I didnae cross the bridge.' His reply is swift. 'That's the turn fae Bothel. I carried on along Bitter Beck Lane – that comes past the castle. But I didnae see oot – if that's what you're getting at. Nae car – nae drugs gang – nae Kyle Betony.'

*

'He changed his story, Guv. Twice.'

Skelgill drives in silence. The town's narrow streets are treacherous; motorists lack visibility, and unseeing pedestrians bent under umbrellas lurch at random across their path.

He seems reluctant to embrace his colleague's enthusiasm.

'There's plenty of folk take the back lanes to avoid the breathalyser.'

DS Jones is dissatisfied with the vicarious excuse.

'If he was over the limit – he got away with it. So why not just tell us he drove past Ouse Bridge?' She raps a knuckle against her folder. 'Besides – he's now claiming he offered to buy Kyle Betony a drink.'

'Reckon our *Cockney yin* got it wrong?'

DS Jones shakes her head.

'No, I don't. Stephen Flood is trying to hoodwink us. He could have gone outside with Kyle Betony and driven him to the bridge – and then just continued on home.'

Skelgill has his attention focused on the road ahead. He seems in no hurry, and hesitates before choosing which way to turn onto Main Street. His voice seems to sound a corresponding note of caution.

'What about the car that came back? And why didn't he cover up in the first place – why tell Leyton he'd fallen out with Betony, when it would put him in the frame?'

DS Jones does not have an immediate answer – but Skelgill's words prompt a literal connection.

'He was best placed to be the person that took the press cutting from the wall.'

Skelgill does not contest this point.

DS Jones turns to scrutinise him, as if to gauge his thoughts.

'Do you think I pushed it too far?'

'In what way?'

'We said we must avoid anything that would cause the killer to act rashly.'

Skelgill exhales lengthily.

'It's a hard line to tread. I reckon you did as good a job as you could. You stuck to the drugs story.' He turns and grins. 'Mind, you spooked him when you said he was the last to see Betony alive. No wonder he's running scared. And that APNR camera's been bust for months.'

DS Jones reacts a little sheepishly. These seem mainly to be

246

compliments. It saves her reminding him that she is a student of his playbook. And now she shifts into her mode of efficiency. She opens her clipboard to reveal the form she has completed.

'I'd better send these details to DC Watson.' She gives a small sigh. "Trouble is, Guv – if his back story checks out, he's not a good match for Toby Jubb. No more than is Anthony Goodman.'

Skelgill does not answer. On the face of it, neither man to date could be the would-be killer, who disappeared – presumably to the United States – in his mid-twenties. Their theory could be a complete fallacy. But he is also thinking – more feeling, perhaps – that it is the nature of police investigations: there are bridges that can only be crossed when they are reached, and the knowledge that they lie ahead is a handy chimera for the apathetic detective. How often has he ignored a 'bridge ahead closed' sign to find the workers long gone, tarmac rolled, advance warning notice forgotten – or abandoned as too much trouble to retrieve. He grins; some farmers even keep them to deter tourists during lambing.

And, Toby Jubb or not, someone surely killed Kyle Betony.

'When's Chaudry due at Orthwaite?'

DS Jones makes a quick check of her mobile phone.

'No advance on four p.m.'

Without warning, Skelgill hangs a sharp right turn.

'Time for some Cockermouth sticky bread.'

CASTLE HOW FARM, ORTHWAITE – 4.10 p.m.

'Sorry to keep you Sergeant, Inspector. My housekeeper should have been in to fire up the Aga. Shall we make a dash for it?'

Jay Chaudry shields his eyes from the rain; he has pulled alongside them in an executive car – DS Jones has lowered her own window by a few inches. She gives a brief wave of assent.

The car – what must be the pride of the BMW stable, a sports sedan with its iconic motorsport badge – emits a throaty roar and slips in front of Skelgill's decidedly less flashy shooting brake.

The house is set directly on the public road – indeed the narrow single-track lane that has brought them here jinks through what is a working yard, lined with a cluster of buildings and gated side-tracks into the farm. It is a relic of the past, when the only purpose of these obscure back roads was to reach and connect isolated homesteads; no need to be further still off the beaten track.

A steady sliding film of surface run-off carries liquefied slurry from the concreted downslope that passes the house on the right. On the left in a walled garden Skelgill glimpses fruit trees – a well-laden apple that looks like Laxton's Superb catches his eye, and conjures a boyhood urge never to look a gift horse in the mouth.

They watch for a moment as Jay Chaudry makes for the front door. The property is Georgian, red brick, big and square with perpendicular lines; it looks more like a small country hotel – and this is an impression reinforced as they are welcomed inside, for no expense has been spared in redecoration and the purchase of restored period furniture.

'Nice place you've got, sir.'

DS Jones shoots a sideways glance at Skelgill – such congratulations are not his forte; even to notice is uncharacteristic.

'I wish I could spend more time here, Inspector – but that, of course, is my longer-term goal.'

Jay Chaudry looks a little mournfully at DS Jones; it seems to be a self-deprecating gesture, though he offers no further explanation and turns away.

'Come through to the kitchen, please. I'll get the kettle on.'

They follow. The kitchen is in keeping with what they have seen thus far, large and well-appointed, with a panelled door and sash window giving on to the fruit garden at the side. He directs them to carver chairs at a solid oak table.

It is warm – the Aga fired up as he had predicted. He fills and places a flat-bottomed kettle on the hotplate.

It seems his housekeeper has further excelled herself – he makes an *"Aha"* of discovery, and together with mugs, milk and sugar, he carries across to them a plate covered by a napkin.

'Sandra – she is the wife of Bill Jackson, my farm manager – he has the next place.' (Skelgill vaguely knows the name, a reputable farming family.) 'She comes in and cleans – does for me, as she puts it. She's a bit of a demon baker. I'm glad you're here – you can help me with these.' He has a scrap of paper on which is written a note. He looks at the detectives questioningly.

'Ginger drops?'

'Aye, I've got an aunt who makes them.'

'She catches me out if I don't eat the last crumb.'

Skelgill grins; it is his kind of challenge.

'You need to get a dog like mine, sir. Eliminates food waste.'

Jay Chaudry has returned to the Aga to fill a large traditional earthenware teapot. He speaks over his shoulder.

'Actually, Inspector, I was thinking whether I should have a pig – if I lived here – with a family.'

Skelgill seems to take the question at face value; he is happy to be the expert in the room.

'I reckon it's a while since farms worked like that, sir. Mind – if you've got some land to clear and fertilise, they're in a class of their own.' He cocks his head towards the window. 'That said, sheep'll prune your garden if you're not careful.'

The man chuckles ruefully.

'Don't worry, Inspector – I learned an early lesson. Who would have thought lupins could be so tasty?'

He carries the heavy pot across and lowers it onto a brass trivet.

'But I am distracting you from your purpose. Please – go ahead, I'll be mother.'

Skelgill lifts a somewhat idle hand to indicate that his colleague will speak. She seems a little unprepared – indeed they have both relaxed in the genial, undemanding company of Jay Chaudry; quite a contrast to the combative Stephen Flood, and the unctuous Anthony Goodman.

DS Jones first accepts a mug of tea – and declines a biscuit while she succinctly outlines the background to their re-visiting of the members of the DAA committee.

Jay Chaudry listens keenly, his dark eyes intelligent, his expression intense but collected – as though he is in a business meeting, being told of an issue and evaluating strategic options as he goes.

When DS Jones concludes he raises a hand to rub what is longer than designer stubble, if not quite a beard – though his jet-black hair creates the effect of a dense covering.

'I did not know that – but I have been in Manchester since – well, since the day after Kyle died.' His tone is apologetic. 'We're mid-acquisition – it has been dawn-till-dusk closeted with venture capitalists and our respective teams of lawyers. I wasn't sure I would even get away today – but we've identified a couple of points of due diligence that require some work in Silicon Valley – they won't be completed until tomorrow morning, Pacific time.'

DS Jones has the copy of the Westmorland Gazette in her shoulder bag. She arranges it and presents it across the table for Jay Chaudry to look at. It seems he quickly takes in the content of the article, scanning first superficially and then with a little more care, working through the layers.

He has his elbows on the table, arms folded – and just when it looks like he might be about to read the fine print, he looks up, first at Skelgill, and then at DS Jones, paying respect to her role as questioner.

'That sounds improbable, don't you think?'

DS Jones has Skelgill at her side – she has to restrain herself from looking at him – for her first reaction is that, *yes*, it is improbable. It is likely a figment of DI Smart's imagination, convenient wishful thinking when he came across the words app, drugs, gang, quay, Manchester, Thailand (in no particular order) and fitted them together into a future custodial sentence. She sees the fingers of Skelgill's left hand drum a silent beat on the table.

'Why do you say that, sir?'

The man regards her questioningly.

'Well – from a practical point of view – is there actually a drugs trade up here? *Out* here? I mean – the sparse population – is it worth their while?'

DS Jones opens her mouth a little before she speaks – it would reveal her assumption to be premature, were the man a mind-reader.

'You'd be surprised, sir. The tentacles of county lines leave few corners uncorrupted. We're only twenty miles from the city of Carlisle – and there's a sizeable population through the West Cumbrian towns – and they all have thriving ports.'

'Yes – good point – I live at one, albeit inland. I do wonder what goes on there, sometimes.'

It seems a further contradiction – that he refers to his home in Manchester in this way – naturally unsuspecting of their disreputable colleague's determination to pursue that geographical line of inquiry. Not to mention his own firm's litigation with the Manchester police force, and the link – if indirect – to the local drugs scene.

DS Jones has agreed with Skelgill that they will avoid this matter – for it can only put him on the back foot, a counter-productive outcome. Stay on track – the routine elimination of contacts of Kyle Betony.

But she makes a mental note: the civil legal action might have been something that he would refer to – and surely by association he knows more about the distribution of drugs than he would wish to admit.

She does, however, pick up on one aspect of his response. She opens her clipboard; she has prepared it with a new interview form to the fore. She lays it down.

'We do have your address in Manchester, sir – and obviously here. How long have you been at Salford Quays?'

He has waited patiently for her question; now he answers without hesitation.

'It's just coming up to eight years – since I returned from India. My flat number has changed a couple of times – I have subsequently bought six more apartments in the same block, as they have come on the market.' He grins, contritely. 'I'm waiting for the penthouse so I can move up in the world, but as yet the owner is sitting tight. Believe it or not it's a Man U footballer – you wouldn't think he'd last so long, given their recent record.'

His expression of personal wealth is conveyed without any hint of conceit.

'And prior to that, sir?'

He looks surprised – his dark eyes widening a little and showing contrasting white.

'Ah, well – I lived in Bangalore – at a variety of addresses. I could probably dig them out with a bit of time spent raking through old emails. The last one, however, was at Purva Zenium – Hosahalli. It's a gated community out towards Kempegowda airport.'

When DS Jones pauses to reflect upon her shorthand, he seems to feel that he ought to elaborate.

'Bangalore is India's IT capital. I got an opportunity there straight after I graduated. It's where I started my business. The UK operation is officially a subsidiary of an Indian-registered limited company – even though it's now by far the biggest part.'

'So – you graduated – in what year, sir?'

'Well – I was twenty-two – so that's –' He makes a pained face, as though the admission of age is uncomfortable to bear. 'Exactly twenty years ago. Wow. Where did it all go?'

DS Jones looks up to find him regarding her thoughtfully.

'So, you were in India for twelve years?'

'That would be right, yes.'

'And where did you study?'

He hesitates for a moment, as if his current thoughts have not quite finished with whatever microprocessor is the brain's RAM.

'Ah, yes – I was at De Montfort in Leicester – I grew up and went to school in the Belgrave district. My parents couldn't afford for me to go away – they needed me to help with the family business.' Now he chuckles reflectively. 'We had online ordering long before anyone had ever heard the word Deliveroo.' He shakes his head. 'I missed a trick there. That said – at least I'm not having to fight with governments and trades unions over workers' rights.'

DS Jones has listened evenly – and she smiles at his small digression. However, she sticks to her script.

'Can you provide an original home address?'

He responds with the name and location of a restaurant; DS Jones detects a small pricking up of Skelgill's ears. However, he makes no sign that he will interject.

She scowls at her form; thus far, it seems to have been a convincing tactic.

'We have a blank for marital status, sir?'

He lifts both palms towards her, but then wraps his hands around his elbows and slumps back in his chair.

'I have failed miserably to find myself a farmer's wife.' He glances at Skelgill, without giving any real clue that he is looking for some moral support. 'Most of the ladies I seem to meet favour the metropolitan lifestyle – a trip to the country for them is shopping for a crocodile-skin handbag in Alderley Edge.'

Skelgill seems to grin a little inanely; but DS Jones regards Jay Chaudry with some interest, a sparkle in her eye.

But she has already noted that the man himself is no stranger to high fashion. There is the subtle embroidered branding of his black merino Hugo Boss sweater, and while he had prepared tea she identified Moschino jeans and Prada loafers, an ensemble running comfortably into four figures.

But she cannot find fault with his unassuming manner.

'Is there a partner – of long-standing?'

He gives a nod as if to show he understands for their purposes this could be of equal significance. Then he shakes his head pensively.

'No, I – am the proverbial bachelor.'

He looks suddenly at Skelgill, more pointedly now – and perhaps his eyes even scan about to see whether either of the pair opposite wear rings. And then he starts, as though he has been led astray and now catches himself trespassing.

'Look, frankly – the reason I went to Bengaluru – to Bangalore – was to escape an impending arranged marriage. Ironic, you might say.'

He brings up both hands and gives a brief vigorous rub of his short beard, like he has in a peculiar way washed himself of some uncomfortable presence. He exhales; he has been unwittingly holding his breath. But now he smiles, showing bright white teeth.

'All history, thankfully. Meanwhile I have been so focused on growing the company – it can be overwhelming. Hitherto, I would not have made a good husband or father.'

Inevitably there is a small and slightly awkward hiatus. Jay Chaudry leans forward and pushes the plate of biscuits towards Skelgill. It seems he has worked out the natural hierarchy.

'Assist me with these ginger drops, Inspector – Sandra could arrive at any moment. She'll want to know if I have urgent laundry.'

Skelgill interprets his entreaty as permission to help himself to a handful. Jay Chaudry generously tops up their mugs from the teapot. DS Jones takes a single biscuit, and places it beside her mug. She glances a little smugly at Skelgill – she can see he is desperate to dunk, but that he is rather thwarted by the inconvenient shape of the rounded sweetmeat.

She brings the meeting back to order. She raises her clipboard two-handed, and then replaces it. It is an illustrative action.

'That's more or less what we need, sir.'

Jay Chaudry nods; though he regards her carefully; he seems to anticipate a supplementary question.

She does not exactly disappoint, although she takes a moment to peruse notes held beneath the standard questionnaire.

'Sir – looking at the information you gave to my colleague, DS Leyton – about the evening of the dinner and your interactions with Mr Betony – is there anything that now strikes you as relevant?' She indicates to the newspaper which still lies on the table. 'In particular with reference to this possible lead.'

Jay Chaudry takes a moment to compose himself. He intertwines his fingers, his forearms resting on the edge of the table. He regards her earnestly.

'Sergeant – I bow to your superior knowledge concerning drugs gangs – and I appreciate you would correctly tell me there is no stereotype for someone mixed up with drugs – but it just strikes me as absurd that Kyle could have been involved. You see – things seemed to be all-consuming for him – and I think it would have done just that – consumed him. It would have been obvious. He shot from the hip, wore his heart on his sleeve.'

DS Jones nods, conscious that the man is only reiterating their understanding, though she cannot reveal such. She endeavours to put to better use his candid attitude.

'I gather Mr Betony was commending a merger between the DAA and the other society, the AAA.'

Jay Chaudry does not seem slighted that she sidesteps his analysis – but perhaps her question is sufficiently on point to hold with his logic.

'Yes – he was. I don't recall that the subject gained any traction. The aim of the night was to avoid talking shop. But I've been reflecting since your colleague mentioned it. From a purely commercial perspective it's a sensible suggestion – I think I said that.' He raises one hand and now rubs at his chin more introspectively. 'But, to be honest, I'm still a relative newbie to these parts – and I imagine there would be many perfectly good reasons why, after three-quarters of a century, there are still two organisations squabbling over the same stretches of water.'

He seems to be implying that he would take a more diplomatic path – and not raise such a controversial subject. DS Jones turns to glance at Skelgill – he has a mouthful of biscuit but he merely scowls, leaving her to read into it what she may. For her part, there is no value in going over old ground – DS Leyton has reported his movements and what little he saw. And she does not wish to expose the true purpose of their visit.

However, Jay Chaudry is perhaps ahead on this score – at least as far as the bigger picture goes. He clears his throat, a little apprehensively. He engages eye contact with each detective before he begins.

'It's not for me to do your job for you – I'm sure you're a thousand times better qualified than I am. But – I take it you don't have any CCTV – that would have recorded Kyle leaving the hotel?'

DS Jones shakes her head.

'There's no surveillance at The Partridge, sir.'

'How about his mobile phone?'

She would like to see Skelgill's expression. But for two detectives to cross-reference one another is too revealing of an unspoken agenda. While the absence of CCTV at The Partridge is a simple matter of public observation, she concludes that Kyle Betony's mobile phone is not up for discussion.

'We are working on that, sir.'

He regards her intently. He nods.

'Actually – I seem never able to get a signal – even outside. I was having to use the Wi-Fi while I was there. Would have been no use tracking mine.'

He gives a somewhat nervous laugh – and then perhaps colours a little, as though he thinks he has revealed that he has been aware all along that he must be a suspect of sorts.

Then his features become confused – such that DS Jones decides she ought to relieve him of the afterthought.

'What is it, sir?'

He is gazing blankly into his mug. He looks up, still puzzled.

'Oh – well. It kind of ran through my mind. I mean – a mobile phone. It's not quite right – what I just said. True – there's hardly ever a signal, and even if there were, the inn and the river are probably too close to use triangulation to establish a person's movements. But these days there's a built-in GPS chip. With location services switched on, one of the apps might have tracked a handset.'

His tone becomes apologetic.

'I suppose most people know this. Sorry – I am rambling. Have another biscuit – please.'

Skelgill appears not to hear. DS Jones turns to see him staring intently at Jay Chaudry – and only when she snaps shut her clipboard does he emerge from his trance.

Then the man's words seem to register.

'Biscuit? Thanks all the same, sir, but we had better make tracks – we have another meeting shortly.'

Jay Chaudry looks a little surprised that Skelgill declines. However, he remembers there is another tack.

'How about a doggy bag? I'd be delighted to offload the balance.' He pats his stomach. 'I'm watching my waistline – and I know Sandra will find them, no matter how hard I try to dispose of them.'

Skelgill grins and shrugs a form of reluctant agreement.

'In the absence of your pig, then, sir.'

DS Jones regards him doubtfully.

As they are leaving, poised on the threshold, preparing to make a return dash betwixt raining stair rods to Skelgill's car, Jay Chaudry seems to remember there was something more that he wanted to say. He addresses neither of them in particular.

'Oh, and Mrs Betony – have you any word of how she is? I feel guilty having been so busy. I know the DAA was only a small and recent part of Kyle's life – but I feel the committee might do something for his wife. I don't believe either of them have relatives in the area.'

Skelgill takes it upon himself to answer.

'We've seen her a couple of times, sir. She seems to be bearing up.'

Jay Chaudry regards Skelgill with a frown, as if this platitude does not really provide the reassurance he would like.

'When Anthony phoned to tell me about Kyle on the Sunday morning, I mentioned sending her some flowers. I don't know if we've got anywhere with that.'

The detectives happen to know it is on tonight's agenda – but decide not to reveal their hand.

*

'Where to, Guv?'

Skelgill frowns.

'If Leyton's where he claims to be, we may as well meet him at The Partridge. Besides, there's your motor.'

Skelgill has started the engine and has the wipers set to max. But it is getting dark and the unrelenting rain makes almost any journey seem undesirable. DS Jones peers out doubtfully.

'How safe is The Partridge?'

'Not all that safe.' Skelgill grins. It seems he will add a caveat. 'I mean – it takes a serious flood. But it's in a channel only a couple of feet above the normal level of Bass Lake. The water comes at it in a pincer movement – from Peel Wyke on side and Dubwath Beck on the other. The A66 normally stays clear – the lowest point is where you cross from The Partridge towards Ouse Bridge.'

'Our nadir.'

Skelgill does not respond.

She questions him once more.

'Do you think we're in danger of a major flood?'

He is pensive, but after a moment he shakes his head.

'I wouldn't mind a look at Bass Lake. But this rain's supposed to ease in the early hours. I reckon we'll get away with this one.'

He slots the car into gear and lets in the clutch.

They remain in silence, but for the various sounds of water; tyres splash through puddles and newly formed streams that percolate through dry stone walls; bursts of heavier rain batter the windscreen; the wipers swish and slosh back and forth, inventing new onomatopoeias. The narrow lanes seem especially treacherous; it would be almost impossible to avoid an obstacle in the road, animal or mineral.

Skelgill is thinking that sometimes driving is easier in pitch dark – at least you can see other cars' lights – when DS Jones interrupts his musings.

'What did you make of Jay Chaudry?'

Skelgill laughs unexpectedly.

'You were dancing around handbags.'

'Really?'

'Aye – he kept leaving open goals.'

She is trying to piece together the two metaphors when Skelgill interjects.

'Nay – you did alreet. I reckon you got what we wanted to know. Plus, he's the first one to admit he was out of the country at the time of the Jolene Jubb incident.'

DS Jones turns sharply to look at Skelgill. It is not like him to be the one that so succinctly propounds the case for the prosecution. But he remains phlegmatic, gripping the helm, craning forward, eschewing his mirrors – abaft is of no significance when all concentration is needed aweather.

'Was there something I missed?'

It takes him a moment to answer.

He sniffs.

'Seems like a decent bloke.'

She is perplexed by his response – it is blatant obfuscation; there is plainly a feeling he cannot yet iterate; small but pertinent, it has sunk in but not yet bobbed back up to break the surface of his consciousness.

She waits a moment longer before she replies.

'Actually, I agree – he does seem to be both sensitive and likeable.'

'Not your average neighbourhood psychopath?'

His tone invites her to contest his point.

'Well – I don't suppose I would go that far. But – for someone who's done so well for himself – he's not even your average neighbourhood braggart.'

Skelgill does not answer – and DS Jones replays what she has said, for fear of it having irked him – when he reveals it has.

'Eligible bachelor, eh?'

DS Jones gives herself a small mental kick in the pants.

'But, Guv – what if his fortune comes from drugs?'

The remark is facetious, but it helps.

14. THE LOCUS

The Partridge Inn – 6.00 p.m., Tuesday, 28ᵗʰ September

'Here he is. Better Leyton than never.'

'Yeah – very funny, Guv. I got stuck in flippin' mud at Ruth Robinson's farm. Her old man had to pull me out with a tractor.'

Skelgill leans from his fireside seat to examine DS Leyton's attire. His overcoat is soaked through, but his footwear looks none the worse for his ordeal. Skelgill has commandeered the Snug. He has talked Charlie into putting a sign on the door, "Private Meeting" – under protest that he will need it for the DAA committee in the Smoke Room a little later.

DS Leyton reads his superior's critical gaze.

'I stayed in the motor, Guv. Lucky I had a signal – so I was able to phone back to the farmhouse. Just as well – the water was rising all the time. You know me and boats.'

Skelgill scoffs. He gestures to a pale-yellow pint in a tall, slim modern glass, coated with condensation and somewhat incongruous in the ancient beamed surroundings and the cosy heat of the blaze.

'Set yourself down.'

DS Leyton gives a token glance at his wristwatch.

'Ah, well – after six – I suppose we're technically off duty.'

There might be a small complaint in his verdict – though he catches DS Jones's eye and winks.

But if it is an attempted wind up, Skelgill does not seem to notice; he takes a decorous sip of his own pint of amber Jennings ale – and he lingers a little, staring into the glass. Its place of origin, six miles hence, the old brewery sited on the isthmus where the Cocker meets the Derwent, is one of the first places to flood.

DS Leyton smacks his lips and rouses Skelgill from his reverie.

'Recognise anyone, Guv?'

There is the sense in his tone that DS Leyton knows what is coming – it would be the first thing they would tell him – but he sees that DS Jones is alert and looking keenly at their boss, as if she hopes he will reveal something hitherto kept close to his chest.

But Skelgill only lifts his glass and takes a longer pull. His taste buds thus occupied, he shakes his head, and then tilts it to indicate that DS Jones should provide a debrief.

She looks a little disappointed. But she raises her electronic tablet; she has been busy on the shaky Wi-Fi while they have waited.

'I'm expecting an update from DC Watson any minute. We got biographical detail stretching back to cover the period from before Lynette Jubb's death – when all three claim they were in England. Likewise Anthony Goodman and Stephen Flood at the time of the Jolene Jubb incident. Jay Chaudry says he was based in India.'

DS Leyton makes another clutch at the original straw, though he must know it is futile.

'But nothing rang a bell, Guv?'

Skelgill, when he might be irked, being asked the same question twice, seems rueful. It is a source of genuine chagrin that he has such scant recall; that he went about in his own little bubble as a small boy.

DS Leyton manufactures some enthusiasm.

'They're like the Ugly Sisters between them – Goodman and Flood – I'd hoped one of them would jog a memory. Surely that's what did for Betony? He recognised one of 'em because you can't change the old dial.'

DS Jones picks up on a technical aspect of her colleague's point.

'Are you saying, therefore, that you don't think it could be Jay Chaudry?'

DS Leyton combs the fingers of one hand through his mop of dark hair.

'Well – he's what you'd call handsome, ain't he? Not exactly the kind of mugshot that would jump out from a grainy old photo.'

The exchange yields a small silence in the group. It is a minute before DS Jones responds.

'One difficulty with Jay Chaudry is his age. He was only eighteen at the time of Lynette Jubb's death.' She glances at Skelgill. 'And only fourteen at the time of your fishing match.'

Skelgill is prompted to comment. There is a look in his eyes that suggests he finds antipathy in the suggestion of some ownership, but he answers without prejudice.

'I reckon I'd have remembered if there'd been another kid – a youth, leastways. It were all blokes. That, I do know.'

DS Leyton follows up with a little more positive spin.

'Besides – the age thing. Like we've been saying – if one of them's using a false identity, we don't have to believe their age any more than their name.'

Nevertheless, another silence ensues.

Skelgill finally turns to his newly arrived sergeant.

'What about you, Leyton?'

DS Leyton nods – and for a moment adopts his superior's distraction technique of taking a sip of his drink. He makes a face as though it is bitter, when it is lager.

'That address – Spital Ing Lane – it's been converted – split up into four flippin' flats. Apparently it's owned by a property company. None of the current tenants has been there above five years. I've ordered a title deed search and historical council tax records – but it's going to be tomorrow at best before we get anything.'

He raises his shoulders like a prop forward preparing to absorb an impact.

'I knocked doors around and about – but I couldn't find anyone who'd lived there at the time we're interested in. It's the end house, and there's only a couple of other properties nearby.'

Skelgill is regarding him critically.

'Did you try the Counters?'

'Counters, Guv?'

Skelgill frowns more deeply; but one familiar with him might recognise annoyance at his own failing.

'Hilda and Betty – they run the Post Office. They've been there donkey's years. I should have told you.'

DS Leyton looks a little forlornly at his wristwatch.

'I can call in tomorrow, early doors.'

Skelgill nods.

'What about the two women?'

DS Leyton has the sudden panicked look of a schoolboy who, having forgotten his homework, his mind now frantically casts about for excuses – my sister spilt gravy on it and the dog ate it; my mother thought it was so good she sent it off to a publisher; I was showing it to a friend in the playground and a seagull mistook it for my packed lunch. It is a curious reaction – and one in fact unworthy of his efforts – but perhaps it is the momentary realisation that he brings back only news of defeat in the race to find a motive for the killing of Kyle Betony.

He gathers his wits, though he sighs audibly.

'I got flamin' chapter and verse – Ruth Robinson, especially – the whole life story. Right enough, she's grown up in this neck of the woods. Jackie Baker, on the other hand, she moved down from Scotland seven years ago with her partner. She has no prior connections in the area – and she's thirty-seven – so she was only thirteen at the time of Lynette Jubb's death. I reckon we can rule her out completely. Ruth Robinson's thirty-nine, so she was fifteen. Her maiden name's Wilson. In the end I got round to mentioning Jubb – but she didn't react and she claims she don't know the name. I asked if she remembered the accident in Whinlatter Forest and she thought she did – that her father had warned her to be careful after she'd learnt to drive – that there was a dangerous bend with an adverse camber where someone had died. But that's about the length of it.'

Skelgill nods slowly – he seems satisfied enough with his sergeant's work.

The subsequent silence, however, seems to prey on DS Leyton's residual sense of guilt for not having made more progress, despite that none of them are knowingly any further forward.

He raises an index finger in the air.

'One thought I did have.'

Skelgill regards him suspiciously.

'Aye?'

'What if it was a case of mistaken identity?'

'What are you talking about, Leyton?'

DS Leyton shifts awkwardly in his seat.

'I mean – if Betony was mistaken for one of the others.' He is hesitant, a little embarrassed to explain his thinking – the reason behind which becomes plain. 'What if there were something in this Manchester drugs business? And then what if Betony was mistaken for Chaudry? They're a similar age. Not much difference in size. They're both dark, clean-shaven.'

Skelgill is looking alarmed.

DS Jones, however, has a practical rejoinder.

'But Jay Chaudry has a beard.'

DS Leyton frowns.

'He didn't when I interviewed him – he must have started growing it since.'

No one seems to want to add to the specific debate – the small possibility that Jay Chaudry might have tried to alter his appearance. But now Skelgill makes a horizontal chopping motion in the air with his left hand.

'This is about Betony.'

However, he puts forward no single killer fact.

DS Leyton sticks out his jaw – although his tone is less belligerent.

'S'pose you're right, Guv. I'm just keen to get us somewhere before DI Smart pounces.' He turns to look sympathetically at DS Jones, knowing that she is in the firing line. 'You're always saying – don't get stuck down one track when there might be others to investigate.'

Skelgill is scowling pensively.

'It's getting late in the day for that, Leyton.'

His colleagues both glance at him sharply. It is not like their superior to talk so openly in such terms.

And Skelgill knows it. It is at times like this when – perhaps a little inexplicably – he realises he could never be the fishing guide that is so often suggested as his retirement plan. The pressure of a paying customer who must have that specimen pike before dusk – when Skelgill's modus operandi is that the pike will still be there in the morning, and no amount of forcing, ground baiting, dead baiting, live baiting (heaven forbid, it could come to that) or random thrashing and guddling will make a shred of difference.

His gaze is fixed if unfocused upon his mobile phone that lies on the table between their drinks. Aye, the pike might still be there tomorrow – but at any moment the Chief could ring to call time. Except – a crumb of comfort – there is no signal. *Hah!* His focus sharpens – and something about the image of the handset strikes a chord – it is too deep within for him to perceive its meaning, yet he feels a small wave of euphoria.

'This must be where Goodman and Chaudry were sitting.'

His colleagues, who have waited patiently for his brown study to pass, see that he is looking at the door – or perhaps through it, more like – to some unseen destination beyond.

There is no particularly appropriate rejoinder to his statement – and, now, an inflexion point in their meeting – for there is an alert from DS Jones's electronic tablet.

'That's DC Watson.'

Her tone is propitious. She swoops then reads, swiping and scanning efficiently. She looks up.

'It's incomplete – but they've done well.'

However, there is a small crease of what might be dismay on her normally smooth brow.

'Want me to run through it – or take the points one by one?'

Skelgill reaches for his glass.

'Hit us with the lot.'

DS Jones nods.

'She's split it into two parts – kind of, for and against. She begins with the against section. Most significantly, all three have National Insurance numbers that match their names and dates of birth. Their corresponding tax records confirm their employment as described to us. Anthony Goodman and Stephen Flood have been in the UK for their entire working lives to date. Jay Chaudry got an NI number when he was sixteen, but there is no activity against it until eight years ago, which would be when he set up his UK operation.'

Skelgill is scowling fiercely.

'Aye – he was working in the family business, mind.'

It seems a grudging remark, a throwaway comment, and leads to something of a depressed silence.

It falls to DS Leyton to play the role of the boy and the emperor's clothes.

'So – they're all who they claim to be?'

Neither of his colleagues seems to wish to confirm the assessment.

Skelgill knows it is for him to rouse his troops – but the small if inexplicable ray of hope of a few moments earlier seems to have been overshadowed by this greater, tangible news that looms like the massed clouds over the fells.

DS Jones, however, sounds a small note of optimism.

'There are points of interest.'

The others look on and wait.

'Stephen Flood – a widower, right?' She does not wait for confirmation. 'His wife died – three years ago, as he told us – but what he didn't say is that it was an overdose of paracetamol. She was being treated by her GP for depression. The Coroner's verdict was misadventure – that it was accidental.' Now she does pause, perhaps for some effect. 'Stephen Flood inherited the property, which had been in her sole name.'

DS Leyton dives in.

'I've thought all along he's a wrong 'un. We know he was more or less last to be with Betony – and look where they were sitting, an' all – right beside the photo. Face like that – I bet you Betony did recognise him – and he lured him outside and made short work of him! And now you're telling me he's trying to change his story – that they were best of pals and he was buying him a drink.'

It is plain that DS Leyton, like them all, desperate to get somewhere, has finally pinned his colours to the mast. It is all in a good cause – and his colleagues do not resent him for it.

But Skelgill has put down his drink and folded his arms.

'He can hardly be Jubb – we've just heard he's worked in Cumbria the last twenty-odd years.'

But DS Leyton is getting into his stride.

'Maybe he's been leading a double life, Guv?'

'What – half in Cockermouth and half in Missouri? Come off it, Leyton.'

DS Leyton scowls and takes a heftier than usual sup of his pint, his malleable features expressively defiant.

'Guv – we're right on this – aren't we?' He gestures around.

Skelgill stares at his colleague. In a curious way he hits the nail on the head. Yes, they are right on it – *it* was the feeling that briefly touched Skelgill. *It* is under their noses and they can't see it. And, if they do not act soon, *it* will happen again – and *it* might be gotten away with again.

He addresses DS Jones.

'Go on – what else, lass?'

She has been like a videoed presenter placed on pause while DS Leyton has held the stage, and she resumes her narrative smoothly.

'Well – that's it at the moment for Stephen Flood. The farm where he says he grew up has changed hands a couple of times – so nothing there, yet.' She scrolls down. 'But the team checked out Anthony Goodman's claim that he grew up in Melton Mowbray – it looks like they managed to find his sister, Mary.' Now she frowns. 'Although there is a small oddity here. Remember he said she had married a Ukrainian by the name of Lewinsky? There was no Lewinksy but they found a Zelenskyy – and that seems to be her, Mary Zelenskyy. They tracked her down. Before her mobile phone ran out of battery she confirmed she was born Goodman, and that she had a younger brother, Anthony. She says she lost touch with him about forty years ago – she had limited contact with the family –' DS Jones stops, her lips parted.

'Aye?'

'She says she thought she'd heard he was in America.'

'What?'

It is DS Leyton's exclamation.

'That's all we've got.'

'America – where in America, when?'

DS Jones shakes her head.

She scrolls back up. Now she bites her lower lip. The contradiction is unequivocal.

'But – his records are intact – Anthony Goodman has paid tax and national insurance in the UK every year for the past two decades – longer. The sister must be mistaken.'

There is a silence before she adds a considered rider.

'If there was a family rift – maybe neither of them wants to know the other – it's not unusual. They don't trouble to inquire.'

But this news has been unsettling. Even DS Jones now pauses to take a drink.

'What about the eligible bachelor?'

Skelgill breaks the silence, on a sardonic note.

DS Jones flashes him a brief glower of reproof.

'They've not had long on this. The family restaurant still exists, Belgrave Road in Leicester. Same ownership – a Mr Ashok Chaudry. They weren't answering their phone – the website has them not opening until seven p.m. Another twenty minutes or so.'

DS Jones pauses for a moment, while she reads ahead.

'This is noteworthy.'

Her audience perhaps leans in a little.

'The case files have been delivered – the investigation into the death of Lynette Jubb. It's all in paperwork format – eight Bankers boxes. They've not been able to go through it in detail – but they've found a reference in the investigating officer's notes – the Jubbs took out a joint life insurance policy about a week after they were married.'

Skelgill regards DS Jones reflectively; it is a question that has crossed his mind; now perhaps, he is a little reticent in receiving the answer. Every case has its red herrings, irrelevant skeletons in closets, loose ends – millions of people act lawfully and unlawfully every day in ways great and small.

DS Leyton can be relied upon for a pragmatic contribution.

'Did he claim?'

DS Jones compresses her lips. She is reading intently.

'We've submitted an inquiry to the insurers. It will take forty-eight hours to retrieve the information.'

DS Leyton raps a knuckle on the table.

'It don't say in the notes?'

Skelgill intervenes.

'Leyton – Jubb would have needed to wait on the Coroner – for a death certificate. That would have closed the case.'

DS Leyton exhales, puffing out his cheeks.

'Thing is, Guv – it strengthens our view – that Jubb's MO was to knock off his missus and clean up whatever he could. That's exactly what he tried in the States.'

Skelgill stands up and circles the small room. He hesitates over a stormy landscape of Bassenthwaite Lake with a brooding Skiddaw looming large and dark. He leans into the square porthole of the window; it might almost be waves breaking from the lake itself that splatter against the old warped glass. The wind is getting up.

He turns, his features conflicted, haggard like a weatherbeaten mariner about to set a course into the wind when flight to harbour is indicated.

DS Jones is on this journey with him.

'None of Flood, Goodman or Chaudry is presently married.'

There is a silence before DS Leyton takes up her point.

'So, what, girl – are you saying you don't think anyone's at risk, right now?'

At his station across the room, Skelgill inhales but then checks himself; having heard the blazing row at Cockermouth, he opts not to let it divert him.

DS Jones seems possessed of a burden of some gravity. She lays down her tablet and takes hold of the edges of the table.

'Actually – it's been going through my mind – whether we should identify all of the potentially vulnerable females and issue them with Osman letters.'

There is no suggestion of doubt in her tone, no rising intonation that makes the statement into a question for debate.

Skelgill looks at her with alarm.

When he might simply gainsay the suggestion – slap it down – were it made by DS Leyton, that it emanates from DS Jones gives him pause both for thought, and to contrive a diplomatic rejoinder. She is right in principle – but he has been there before in practice. An Osman letter covertly warns a person of a purported lethal threat from a partner or close acquaintance.

'Jones – the Chief would never wear it. Too much risk of a backlash from the ones we'd get wrong.'

DS Jones does not seem disappointed; she senses they share a mutual frustration.

And Skelgill offers a small consolation.

'Aye – someone is at risk.'

Skelgill momentarily closes his eyes. He feels it – it is true. But is it the impending threat of DI Smart's clumsy intervention – or that here at the inn lies the very heart of the mystery that surrounds Kyle Betony's death – or simply the many small signs that give cause for concern? Or is it that he has met the faceless killer and knows they will strike again? Like an unfamiliar cat on a garden wall. It will mew and push against you. When you walk on it will murder a nest of fledglings.

DS Leyton, too, is uneasy.

'When you say *someone* – are you talking about one of the committee?'

Skelgill experimentally punches the old black-painted timber door; the iron catch rattles a protest.

'Aye – that – or a witness – or summat.'

The door seems to rattle again, of its own accord – Skelgill yanks it open to reveal a surprised Charles Brown.

'Ooh. Danny – can I get my sign back? They'll be arriving soon.' Skelgill is about to answer, when the landlord leans conspiratorially closer. 'And – can I just show you something?' He gives a jerk of the head.

He leads Skelgill to the left and then immediately right and along to the small reception area at the end of the passage. The great ancient register lies open, on the staff side of the desk. He reaches and swivels it around. He steps back, but keeps a finger on a recent entry.

'We've got the Smiths booked in.'

Skelgill stares at the man.

'You said you get lots of Smiths.'

The hotelier shakes his head.

'It's the same handwriting.'

Skelgill now leans over and reads.

'I'll take your word for it.'

'It looks like our daytime receptionist did the check-in. She's gone off duty. She's not answering her phone.'

Skelgill straightens up; he feels a twinge in his spine and grimaces momentarily. He has not yet shared with his friend their knowledge that 'Mr Smith' is almost certainly Sir Montague Brash.

'Can I borrow your master key?'

The hotelier looks a little nonplussed – but he reaches nevertheless into his pocket and produces a modest brass Yale type. He hands it over.

When Skelgill returns to the Snug his colleagues can see signs of wetness on his face and shoulders.

They look at him – expectantly.

'Still hoying it down. Getting worse before it gets better. Back end of the front.'

He checks his watch.

'Brash's Defender's here.'

DS Jones knows something is afoot.

'Is that what Charlie wanted to show you?'

He stands for a moment upon the threshold. They have lost their rights of privacy and perhaps for this reason he leaves the door ajar.

He resumes his seat and takes a drink.

'The Smiths have booked in. Same room – Skiddaw suite. Same woman's handwriting in the register.'

His colleagues release small gasps of interest.

Skelgill waves the key and drops it into his breast pocket.

There is a respectful silence – it might be that they are each waiting for an idea to land.

But as with all brainstorming – if that is what it takes – there has to be some catalyst. The human mind is ill suited to original thought, but finely honed to see patterns – it might be inventive, but it needs a stimulus.

Skelgill inhales deeply.

It appears to his colleagues that he is sniffing.

He looks about – and fastens upon the doorway. It seems to be the source of what disturbs him.

DS Jones is first to inquire.

'What is it, Guv?'

Skelgill seems reluctant to speak.

He rises and stalks to the door; carefully, he peers out – now he is definitely sniffing. He takes a step into the passage, and disappears for a couple of seconds.

Reluctantly, it seems, he returns and sits.

Now he elaborates.

'When I was at Brash Hall this morning. In the estate office – there was a vase of big creamy white flowers. Loads of pollen dropping. The smell about knocked your head off – it was like Parma Violets.'

Both of his associates are looking perplexed – but DS Jones sticks to logic.

'Do you mean lilies?'

Skelgill shrugs.

'They might have been, aye.'

'I would say lilies smell sweet and spicy – more like a mixture of cloves and cinnamon.'

DS Leyton regards his boss warily.

'Do you smell it now, Guv?'

Skelgill merely looks a little defeated.

'I thought I did.' He cocks his head in the direction of the door. 'There's nowt out there.'

'Maybe someone just walked past with a bunch? It's on the DAA committee's agenda, ain't it? To send flowers to Jasmine Betony.'

He makes a simple practical point.

But now DS Jones seems to be diverted; she raises a hand and rests it upon her crown.

'You know – now I think of it – she had some in her kitchen.'

Skelgill's frown demands an explanation.

'Yesterday – when you went up to Kyle Betony's study to look for the magazine. My job was to keep her talking. There was a vase on the side – I remember she adjusted the stems. The flowers hadn't quite opened – so there was no scent – they must have been fresh.' She screws up her eyes like she is making a wish. 'I suppose I kind of assumed she had just bought them – but there was fancy wrapping paper, folded up – and a gift card.'

If Skelgill were being asked to perform a charade in a party game, from his expression one might deduce that his brief is to act out being on the horns of a dilemma. And there is a dilemma, of sorts. Something that does not fit and yet neither can be dismissed – a matter that has not resolved to his satisfaction. It is the disappearance of the true crime magazine from the Betony house. And now he is reminded of DS Jones's unease on their first visit, a kind of premonition which he thought he had talked her out of.

These points – and the flowers – seem as tenuous as the fragrance itself; and yet a moment ago it had been both powerful and evocative. But evocative of what? Is this the ultimate stage of grasping at straws – when they are rapidly running out of options, and skidding haplessly towards the last-ditch measure which Skelgill has thus far not countenanced, the playing of a wildcard with almost unacceptable risk attached – to suggest to the suspects that they have a witness about to spill the beans.

He speaks quietly.

'It might be useful to know who sent them.'

He glares at his phone.

'Anyone got a signal?'

No one has.

DS Leyton begins to rise.

'Want me to go out in the rain, Guv?'

'We'll use Charlie's landline – he's got a hands-free at reception.'

'Even better.'

When DS Leyton returns, DS Jones has the number ready. She presses the speaker button; the handset makes extra loud bleeps as she types in the digits.

She places the phone on the table; they all stare like it is a ticking timebomb.

'You speak.'

DS Jones leans a little closer at her superior's command.

The recipient picks up.

'Mrs Betony?'

'Hello?'

DS Jones has to repeat herself. There is indeterminate background noise and electronic interference.

'Hello, yes?'

'It's Detective Sergeant Jones. Sorry to disturb you.'

Jasmine Betony seems distracted – or fails to hear properly.

DS Jones decides she ought to cut to the chase.

'When we called round yesterday – I noticed you'd had some lilies delivered. Can I ask whom they were from?'

There is another delay. But then she indicates she has understood.

'The angling committee. Sir Montague –'

The line breaks – there is a moment's silence, but then it reconnects.

'Mrs Betony, could you repeat that? I lost you.'

Now there is either hesitation or just a poor signal attenuated by the bad weather.

But DS Jones seems to sense there is more.

'Jasmine – are you okay?'

There is concern in her tone – and that she uses the girl's first name – but only disjointed noises come through the speaker – until what sounds like a muffled male voice.

Then Jasmine Betony again.

'Sorry – I –'

The line goes dead, and stays dead.

The detectives wait, but nothing more happens.

'Sounds like she's with someone – a geezer.'

It is DS Leyton's observation. DS Jones looks at him.

'What did he say?'

DS Leyton shakes his head, his features twisted.

"That's thee, lass".'

Both sergeants look at Skelgill – it seems he alone deciphered the phrase.

'Reckon she was in a shop, Guv? I've had that kind of thing with the Missus – when she's at the tills and tells me she's ready to be picked up.'

'Sounded more like she was on the move.'

As Skelgill says this a car must swing around outside, its headlights making a sweep that briefly illuminates the low lighting of the Snug. It distracts them for a moment – but somehow seems to reinforce Skelgill's theory.

DS Jones picks up the handset.

'I'll try to reconnect. If she's travelling, the signal might improve.'

She begins again. The handset has no obvious redial feature, so she has to type in the entire number. This time the call is diverted immediately to voicemail. She persists, but successive attempts meet the same outcome. She does not give up, however.

DS Leyton rises and drifts across to peer out of the window.

Skelgill seems to have sunken into a state of brooding; he has his gaze trained on the fire in the grate, his eyes unblinking. The angling committee? So why are flowers on tonight's agenda?

He becomes vaguely conscious of movement just out in the passage. The door is still a little ajar. Of course, odd folk have been coming and going. It is a public house, and there are residents.

Two people must converge.

'Oh, sorry.'

'No, after you.'

DS Jones is persistently dialling without success. DS Leyton seems preoccupied by the weather.

Parma Violets.

And more – Skelgill recognises the voices.

He stands – so sharply that he is fleetingly dizzy – and sways, to the consternation of his colleagues.

He gathers his wits – and strides to the door.

He looks out – but no one is there.

Without a word he turns to his left and takes the little dog-leg into the first door of the bar.

The girl Saskia stands polishing a glass. His expression must be fierce, for her mouth drops open.

Skelgill casts about – and leaves.

He returns to the corridor and pauses – and inhales, lips compressed.

He enters the residents' lounge – scanning about – and without breaking stride on into the Wythop restaurant. More staff look at him, a little aghast. A similar reaction is engendered in the bistro.

Now his pace is picking up – indeed he breaks into a trot along the corridor.

Without knocking, he ignores the "Private Meeting" sign and barges into the Smoke Room.

A bemused Jim Hartley and Alice Wright-Fotheringham break off mid-conversation to regard him, the professor with a look of wonder, the retired judge with a certain knowing smile.

Skelgill merely nods curtly, and withdraws.

After a moment's hesitation, he enters the ladies' toilets – this time after a sharp knock.

Then he checks the gents – though he merely looks inside from the doorway.

For a second, now, he seems stymied – then he inhales again and something seems to come to him. Like a cartoon dog that has picked up the wafting aroma of frying sausages, a curling wraith that is visible in the air, drawing him forth, he lurches nose first back along the passageway and swings left with the help of the banister rail to mount the broad staircase, taking two steps at a time.

He gains the upper corridor – now the violet aroma is palpable.

At the Skiddaw suite he slows and stops and draws a deep

breath.

He tugs the master key from his pocket.

In a single swift and decisive action he inserts the key and pushes open the door.

It might almost be the act of a cuckolded husband come to expose the miscreants.

He stands framed in the doorway, stock still.

There is only silence from within.

But Skelgill stares – there is something to see.

Then, without a word, he reaches for the door handle.

He steps back, pulling shut the door.

He spins on his heel and stands, immobile.

His grey-green eyes have a faraway look.

Then he sees what he seeks.

He takes the stairs down, three at a time now – and crashes back into the Snug.

He has been gone only a minute.

DS Jones is still valiantly trying to connect the call.

DS Leyton loiters at the window.

'That was a minicab, Guv.'

Skelgill stares at DS Leyton as though he does not comprehend.

DS Jones sees Skelgill's animation.

She begins to rise.

'Guv –?'

'Get your coats.'

15. THE BRIDGE

The Partridge Inn – 6.51 p.m., Tuesday, 28th September

'The Defender's gone.'

'But, where to, Guv?'

Skelgill looks rather askance at DS Leyton – as though his colleague should know his thoughts. But DS Leyton is preoccupied with fastening up his mackintosh as high as it will go, under protest around a neck that is more suited to packing down in the scrum than the fitting of couture.

DS Jones, likewise, is pulling up her hood, tucking away stray strands of blonde hair. Her hazel eyes seem to flicker in the swaying light of the rustic timbered porch of The Partridge.

In only partial shelter, they gird their loins. Sheets of rain are blowing in sideways. The wind roars, marauding about the black conifers that shelter the old inn. Skelgill has to raise his voice.

'Jones – you come with me. Leyton – you follow.'

They make a collective assay into the tempest, DS Leyton breaking off to head for his own car.

From her passenger seat DS Jones gazes a little wistfully at the small square window of the Snug, its orange glow inviting, somehow twice as cosy from out here. Skelgill's tyres spin in the surface water, but then they bite and the shooting brake pitches forward. Despite the darkness, she recognises some of the cars lined up along the front of the building – a Mercedes, a BMW, and a more modest Vauxhall.

'They must be arriving.'

But Skelgill does not reply. He simply puts his foot down and smashes through the gears – it seems to DS Jones without let up on the revs – and at the A66 surely he shoots the junction – for in a blink of an eye and amidst the blur of the rain they are snaking along the tree-lined lane opposite, feeling the presence of a brim-full Bassenthwaite Lake close on their right.

Skelgill has thrown caution to the wind.

She prays that nothing lies in their path.

Then Ouse Bridge – he overshoots the turn by a couple of yards – but perhaps it is not his intention anyway to cross the bridge itself.

For, ahead on the soft verge, where Skelgill had parked before, stands the Defender. Registration number, *MTY 1.*

It seems – in the moment that they pause to take in the scene – that a dark figure climbs into the driver's seat. The lights come on, the brake lights flash – and the Land Rover lumbers off the verge and moves away along Bitter Beck Lane.

Skelgill engages gear, when DS Jones cries out.

'Guv – what's that?'

She points across him – through his side window, to Ouse Bridge, the tarmac black and slick in what little ambient light emanates from the car. Where it narrows and rises to a smooth apex, there is a small patch of something white.

Skelgill cranes to see his rear-view mirror. DS Leyton's headlamps approach at pace.

'Wait.'

He jumps out and flags down his colleague.

'Leyton – the Defender's just gone – this lane has no turns for four miles – it's slow going. Take the A66. Head it off. I'll block from this direction. Don't spare the gas.'

DS Leyton grins gleefully.

'I'll imagine I'm on the North Circular, Guv.'

'And, Leyton – call the cavalry.'

'Wilco.'

To the extent that a handbrake turn is possible from a standing position, DS Leyton now performs one. His car disappears, fishtailing into a cloud of spray.

Skelgill leans into the shooting brake.

'Come on, lass – quickly – let's see.'

Despite the conditions DS Jones needs no encouragement. But

as the pair bend into the rain and wind she takes Skelgill's arm for balance.

Skelgill has his torch – he illuminates the alien object.

Twenty yards gained, to the centre of the bridge.

DS Jones stoops.

She lifts a large oval pebble that pins down a sheet of paper inside a clear polythene bag.

Skelgill directs his torch.

At first the intense light reflected blinds them both – he adjusts the beam to make it less fierce.

It is not often that DS Jones swears – but she reads more quickly than Skelgill.

Were a car to come upon the two detectives at this moment, its headlamps would find them statuesque, together like a single black figure, hunched and hooded, a spectre that haunts the scene of some ancient tragedy.

'What does it say?'

Skelgill can surely read it – for there are barely thirty words, clearly printed in large type.

'It's a suicide note – and a confession – *by Jasmine Betony.*'

Skelgill has his feet planted wide; he provides some token lee for his partner. The gale is gusting; powerful eddies surge through the valley, causing bankside shrubs to shiver and shake as if they would up and run, if only they could; at their feet, in the halo of the torch, the tarmac is plastered with pale upturned leaves prematurely ripped from nearby poplars.

DS Jones has to shout to be heard.

'It says the stone is the murder weapon.'

Skelgill has it in him for his intuition to play one last trick on logic.

'It could be fake.'

His colleague seems only half to hear him. The rain batters them both. She pulls back her hood to check that she has understood.

'You mean she has a plan to disappear?'

Skelgill inexplicably upturns the torch so that it illuminates his

280

face, a pale mask framed by his hood that seems to float in the velvet blackness. He inhales to speak – but he only gasps as the wind snatches away his breath – when a sudden sharp sound pierces the air.

'What's that?'

'A barn owl.'

But DS Jones with her hood lowered has superior stereophonic hearing.

'Guv – it came from the river.'

She turns but before she can take a step Skelgill is past her and leaning over the low parapet. He directs his beam downwards. For maybe two seconds he remains frozen – then acts.

'Here!'

He thrusts the flashlight into DS Jones's hand and sprints into the darkness.

In thirty seconds his shooting brake slides to a halt beside his waiting colleague.

In another thirty seconds he has a climbing rope from the back.

He kneels and threads one end around the nearside rear suspension and pulls it through.

He knots the two strands and backs towards the parapet, drawing the now doubled rope.

He steps one leg over the rope and lifts the working end over his head and brings it back under his opposite arm. It is the classic abseil, when no harness is available, or there is no time to fit one.

Now he reverses onto the parapet, leaning away, using his body weight to draw the rope tight.

'Shine the light!'

'It's not safe!'

She can see that Skelgill is not tied on – were he to slip, his body would rotate and the rope would simply unwind.

'I could belay you – with one of the strands.'

'Shine it!'

DS Jones steps forward, and gets down on her knees against the parapet – a precaution against a rogue gust that could toss her over. Her heart is pounding in her chest.

Skelgill begins to lower himself, kicking out two-footed.

Eight feet below, spreadeagled, Jasmine Betony clings to the smooth wet stones of the spear-shaped pier.

The black water is above her knees – it must pull at her, draining her will.

She does not look up; she does not move; she might almost be barely conscious.

This is a human at the very precipice, where life meets death and death holds sway.

Then Skelgill is beside her.

Now he too is part submerged.

He can feel the current sucking at him – it would take him in an instant – it is a miracle that the girl clings on – her tiny frame and survival instinct must combine to give her the strength of a gymnast.

The night is mild, but the water is chilling – the rain has fallen at forty degrees Fahrenheit, easily low enough to incapacitate muscles and induce hypothermia.

Every second is vital.

And she is not secure.

Skelgill, with a last heave of his quads springs out and simultaneously sideways – as he swings back against the bridge he thrusts his left knee between her legs.

She makes a small cry – she is frail, and he knows he knocks the wind out of her, crushing her against the stones of the pier – but at least he provides some support.

And now for the greatest risk.

He must get one strand of the rope around her.

His right hand is controlling the friction of the abseil – if he lets go, he will slide and be gone.

The two ends trail downstream. He reaches behind with his left hand and drags one strand around and up to his mouth. He bites on it, and pulls again, and repeats the manoeuvre until he has a free loop.

His own discomfort is worsening. The emergency abseil is painful at the best of times. Upright, the unsuitable position has the rope cutting into his groin, his back, his neck and his right armpit. The current saps his energy reserves and the relentless rain impairs his vision.

He moves his head close to the girl's.

'Stick your bum out, lass!'

It is a crude instruction – but unequivocal and effective – and he feels her press against him.

With a quick thrust he threads the loop of rope around her slender abdomen and again uses his teeth as a brake until he has enough through. He ties the loop off on the bight – a double half-hitch that is the best he can do one-handed – but it is a good knot that tightens under strain, though he has no means of dressing it.

'You're tied on!'

His mouth again to her ear he feels her nod – and to his relief she grips ever more spiderlike to the rising curve of the stone pier. She might be tied on, but there are several feet of slack.

Now he recognises his own predicament.

DS Jones was right – but would the girl have lasted another thirty seconds?

And now if he lingers he may weaken beyond recovery.

There is no such thing as a reverse abseil – not a climber on earth can invert the force of gravity.

He must literally take his life in his hands.

With a great heave he rotates his body and unwinds himself from the rope.

'Guv!'

He hears DS Jones's despairing wail as he swings out into the current – for a moment it threatens to take him away. She makes a grab at the rope and drops the torch at her feet and he is plunged into darkness.

Teeth bared and features strained beyond recognition – the bizarre thought strikes him that it is just as well that she does not witness such an unbecoming expression. The rope bites into his numbed palms and burns his raw fingers.

But Skelgill has the frame for this moment. He is bigger than the average man, yet his build is wiry, sinewy, more muscle than slack – he is far more powerful than he looks and the ratio of this available force to his lean weight means he is able to haul himself up – slowly, jerkily, heaving and reaching, hand over hand – and as he draws his hips and then his legs from the river, the undertow lessens and he climbs faster.

Above, DS Jones is trying in vain to pull up his strand of rope – but the instant he rises to within reach she has him – unceremoniously – first by the hair and then by the scruff of his neck – and with an explosive heave she has him flopping over the parapet and landing upon her. Laid out in the light of the fallen torch they look at one another agog.

But there is no time for an inquisition.

They scramble to rescue Jasmine Betony. Six stones – Skelgill's casual estimate at an earlier juncture – proves about right – she is not even a flyweight, and they have her up in seconds, a tiny bedraggled figure, her long black hair plastered across her face and caught in her mouth and nose. They lift her by the armpits and lower her down against the parapet – but incredibly she rolls over and struggles to her feet.

She seems ready to flee.

Skelgill seems to understand something.

He picks up the torch to confirm the identity of her saviours.

And he is right – she seems a little reassured.

'I thought he'd come back –'

Her voice is weak and tremulous – but she pulls at the rope tied around her waist – as if the role of captive still troubles her.

DS Jones moves in to help.

Skelgill is digging in the flatbed of his car. He produces an army blanket – he tosses it to his colleague – and then he is biting into the plastic shrink-wrap of a foil survival cape.

While DS Jones fights the wind to envelop the girl, Skelgill detaches the rope from his car's suspension and tosses it into the back. He slams down the tailgate and rounds to the driver's door.

DS Jones looks anxiously across at him – but then she sees beyond – in what distance is visible – through the haze the faint flashing blur of blue lights coming their way.

Skelgill calls out to his colleague.

'Time I made sure.'

And he is gone.

*

'Unconscious – but breathing.'

Skelgill surveys the lane ahead of him – the full beam of his headlights illuminates a scene like a movie set. His sergeant toils towards him, bent into the gale, calling out his news.

Behind DS Leyton the Land Rover Defender, *MTY 1*, lies on its roof beyond the bend in the road, half embedded in a hawthorn hedge, half submerged by the flood that has caused the crash.

'Lucky I've got a signal, Guv – ambulance from Cockermouth reckons they'll be three minutes.'

Skelgill nods, grimly, pensively.

But he cannot speak. Perhaps the drama and effort of the past hour are just starting to take their toll. He knows he ought to commend his sergeant.

But he turns, and begins to walk back towards his car.

'Cor, blimey!'

Skelgill spins on his heel.

'Aye?'

'Your new cagoule, Guv – it's split right down the back.'

16. IDENTITY

Two weeks later

LUCY BEDLINGTON, POLICE HQ, 10 a.m.

'I just don't believe it.'

The detectives wait in patient silence.

After a few moments, DS Jones leans forwards and indicates with her pen. On the coffee table around which they are ringed in the less formal interview room she has placed an enlarged newspaper article. It consists of a photograph of a motley team of men (and a lanky boy at one end) standing to attention with fishing rods, and a small column of print.

'Dr Bedlington – this is him, don't you agree?'

The woman, who looks drawn and worried, leans forward tentatively. Her neat shoulder-length strawberry blonde hair falls across her face and in the act of parting it she might almost be wiping away tears.

But she has her wits about her, and it is plain that she not only scrutinises the image, but also she cross-references the man's place in the line with the list of names.

'It says T. Jubb.'

She is not questioning; merely confirming what she has been told in outline.

'That's right, Doctor. The man you know as Anthony Goodman is Tobias Jubb. The real Anthony Goodman lives in the United States. He emigrated when a British company of which he was a Director was asset-stripped. He had committed no crime but departed our shores to escape potential action by creditors. We believe he sold – or rather, *licensed* – his British identity to Tobias Jubb. This aspect of our investigation is still ongoing – the real Mr

Goodman admits to being befriended by Tobias Jubb in the USA – but he has claimed that Tobias Jubb stole his documents. Neither the FBI nor we believe that. There is evidence of collaboration. The information that Tobias Jubb is in possession of is too comprehensive – ranging from technical data such as a national insurance number, to biographical detail on his upbringing in Leicestershire, his education, and his work history.'

DS Jones pauses to allow her words to sink in.

Skelgill and DS Leyton watch on thoughtfully. The woman is smartly dressed and discreetly made up – but the vivacious persona that Skelgill observed at their first encounter seems entirely crushed. Even he makes an effort to exude sympathy.

DS Jones removes another printed sheet from her file, this time a copy of two photographs juxtaposed. They each are of a couple at their weddings.

'This is Tobias Jubb and his first wife, Lynette. They both originate from this part of Cumbria. Lynette Jubb died in a conflagration that was the aftermath of a car crash in the Whinlatter Forest, twenty-four years ago, shortly after they were married. Tobias Jubb escaped with minor injuries. He claimed a very significant insurance payout, and we believe soon after left the United Kingdom.'

She waits a moment before she indicates again.

'And this is Tobias Jubb with his second wife, Jolene – we think, his second, there may be others. They settled in St Louis, Missouri. Jolene Jubb had begun to experience inexplicable bouts of tiredness. On one particular day – ten years ago – on a family outing she woke in the car to see Tobias Jubb pushing their daughter away, up a forested track in a buggy. There was a can of petrol on the bonnet of the car. She managed to hide – and rescue the little girl. They fled and she raised the alarm at a farm. The FBI later found the car at a nearby airport. Tobias Jubb completely disappeared. We believe he left the USA using the identity of Anthony Goodman. Shortly before the incident in the forest, Tobias Jubb had taken out a multi-million-dollar insurance policy on Jolene Jubb's life.'

The doctor is silent.

They understand that part of her is fiercely resisting these uncomfortable facts.

Quietly, DS Jones ups the ante.

'It was established that Tobias Jubb was drugging his wife Jolene – it appears he was building up the dose, trying several dry runs, seeing to what extent she would fall unconscious on trips for picnics. As for Lynette Jubb – we have managed to retrieve and re-analyse tissue samples that were retained from the autopsy. The forensic laboratory has confirmed they contain abnormally high levels of a proprietary benzodiazepine.'

Dr Lucy Bedlington looks up in alarm.

'Is there something?'

It takes a few seconds for the woman to compose herself. And when she speaks, her words come disjointedly.

'Anthony – he – he had asked me to prescribe him extra diazepam – you might know it as Valium? He said he found it helped with his MS.'

She checks rather nervously about the detectives; though none of them exhibits an expression of reproach.

'Though I didn't like to do it – I am not his GP.' She bites one side of her bottom lip. 'He can be persuasive.'

It is plain that the woman feels a great weight on her shoulders; she literally sags.

DS Leyton clears his throat.

'Madam – we found a stash of it in his car – hidden in the fuse box under the driver's seat. That doesn't seem like the normal place that you'd keep that kind of thing.' He grins amiably, though it is perhaps wishful thinking that it might alleviate her tension. 'Also a bottle of dental chloroform, labelled from the care home where he worked.'

She regards him wanly. Then she looks at Skelgill, who makes a resigned grimace.

She turns pleadingly back to DS Jones.

'Doctor – we were exploring the possibility of meeting privately with you to deliver an Osman letter. Our difficulty was the uncertainty over the true identity of Tobias Jubb. To present an Osman letter to someone whose partner is actually entirely innocent would of course be a grave error. There was also the consideration that you were still unmarried.'

Dr Lucy Bedlington looks like she is seeing some horror unfold before her.

'But – our pensions –'

DS Jones leans forwards reassuringly.

'Yes?'

'Neither of us have close relatives. You know how you can nominate a beneficiary for your personal pension under the new deregulated system? Anthony – I have to call him that – Anthony had proposed that we nominate one another.'

The detectives make a collective effort not to react to the small frisson they each experience.

DS Jones maintains her composure.

'Had you done it?'

The woman inhales deeply.

'I've had the papers in my surgery for weeks. You know we are stretched to breaking point. I just hadn't got around to reading them.' She exhales and breathes in deeply again. 'He did keep asking me – reminding me to bring them home – he offered to run through them with me – as he's got an accountancy background.'

There is alarm in the eyes of her onlookers.

But now she gives a small ironic choked laugh.

'The NHS backlog saves a life! Am I right?'

They don't like to agree – but it is a breakthrough – indeed, the woman reveals she is beginning to grasp the predicament from which she has escaped.

Now she has more to add.

'Recently – he has been suggesting we take drives out on Sunday afternoons.'

'Where to?' It is Skelgill's interjection.

It takes her a moment to recall – her gaze drifts to the window and the landscape beyond; the low autumn sun is in her eyes, and she almost closes them.

'He said he wanted to find obscure places that we could fish – using green lanes – so that we could drive there – I have an off-road vehicle – I need it for my job, to reach isolated farms.' She looks directly at Skelgill. 'We tried to get to Red Screes Tarn – but the track was blocked by a landslide. He was keen to try again – he wanted us to be the first to fish there.'

Skelgill would beg to differ – they would be beneath him on the honours board (and others, he has no doubt) – though he reached the place on foot, a hard-won ascent. But he knows the precipitous track, with a sheer drop of three hundred feet into an abandoned slate quarry. How surprised would anyone be if an off-roader foolhardily drove that way and met an ignominious fate.

He decides not to share his thoughts; he merely nods to indicate his understanding, and DS Jones picks up her script.

'Dr Goodman – you mentioned you are not his GP. We have obtained his medical records – both those since he returned to the UK as Anthony Goodman, and prior to his leaving – as Tobias Jubb. There is no mention of a diagnosis of multiple sclerosis.'

The woman is silent – though her expression, an introspective frown, indicates some degree of self-analysis.

DS Jones continues.

'I'm sure you'll be aware – it is not uncommon for a psychopathic personality to affect a long-term illness – as a means of endearment or manipulation – and of gaining trust. It can also be a convenient practical excuse when a person needs to retreat from public view.'

The woman looks at her sharply.

'Is he doing that now?'

DS Jones glances at Skelgill. He seems relaxed.

'Yes. But our medical team can find no problems with his vital signs.'

'He is overweight – and he smokes.'

The comment seems curious – as though it escapes before she can think about it. But she follows up quickly with a question.

'What is he saying?'

'He is denying that he is Tobias Jubb. He says this must be

some kind of witch hunt – to find a scapegoat for the death of Kyle Betony. Otherwise, he is refusing to cooperate.'

Dr Lucy Bedlington regards the young female detective pensively. Then she gestures to the photographs.

'It looks like him – but – do you have anything more conclusive?'

Again DS Jones makes a quick referring glance to her superior; he gives a faint shrug.

'His DNA is a match for samples retrieved by the FBI from the Jubb car and home in Missouri.'

Now the woman's gaze becomes more penetrating.

'Why would he kill Kyle Betony?'

DS Jones reaches unhurriedly to indicate the DAA fishing team.

'A copy of this photograph was on the wall in the bar at The Partridge. It was removed on the night of Mr Betony's death. We believe that Mr Betony saw a magazine article about the incident involving Tobias Jubb in the USA – the attempted murder of his wife, Jolene. We think he put two and two together and either challenged him about it – or maybe even just joked about the coincidence – the unusual surname, the physical resemblance. Whichever the case, Anthony Goodman seemed to think he was about to be unmasked as Tobias Jubb.'

The doctor is nodding; but her training demands that she follows through the logic.

'And do you know that Anthony did it?'

'From the boot of his Mercedes our forensic team has recovered strands of Mr Betony's hair and further traces of DNA. In our subsequent investigation we have also recovered Mr Betony's mobile phone, and the original framed photograph.' She does not reveal how or where, but in her authoritative tone there is the implication that these were in the possession of the said perpetrator.

The woman has listened carefully – but there is something in her manner that again causes DS Jones to prompt her.

'What is it, Doctor?'

She raises both hands and gently massages her temples with her fingertips. Skelgill watches her, somewhat intrigued. She might almost be coaxing out an unwilling memory from its retreat – and it makes him think of the way a seagull tramples turf to simulate rainfall and tempt earthworms from their burrows.

After a moment, she has it.

'On the night – when I collected Anthony after the dinner. He came out and I began to drive away – but then he immediately remembered that he had left his bow tie – he said he took it off in the bar afterwards. I reversed back – but he made a point of wanting to go in at the side door – he said so that he didn't get waylaid by one of the committee and keep me waiting. But he took a little longer than I expected – he said someone had picked it up from the table and handed it in at the counter.'

DS Jones is nodding encouragingly.

'And did he have anything with him – the photograph?'

Now Dr Lucy Bedlington frowns.

'I suppose he could have had it tucked inside his overcoat.'

DS Jones looks at Skelgill – he nods – they sense they are winning her over – but recognise that she is riding a little rollercoaster of shock and disbelief.

There is a missing piece in their jigsaw – and they are close to it now.

Skelgill slumps back and casually digs his hands into his pockets. He is entrusting matters to DS Jones.

'You couldn't make the DAA dinner yourself, Doctor Bedlington.'

'I was on call – I probably attend less than half of the committee meetings for the same reason.'

'When you collected your fiancé – what was the arrangement?'

DS Jones's tone is conversational – when otherwise she might appear accusative.

But the woman's manner has materially changed; she seems galvanised, and her words come without hesitation.

'I was due to finish at ten. I'd originally thought that I could at least arrive in time for a drink – so I offered to pick up Anthony. We arranged a fallback of eleven fifteen – to give plenty of leeway in case of emergency – and I was delayed, of course.'

'And what was the sequence of events after you left The Partridge?'

'I drove us back to my place. We had a drink – and, er – went to bed.'

She blinks a couple of times as she looks at DS Jones – there is the suggestion of a euphemism at play. She briefly turns down her mouth.

DS Jones smiles understandingly.

'And did – Mr Goodman – stay the night?' She uses the familiar name. 'I mean – what time did he leave the next day?'

But Dr Lucy Bedlington is already shaking her head.

'Actually – it was about two a.m. He said he needed to be in his office at Fellview early in the morning. He was working overtime on the annual accounts – that he had left his files at home. He said it would be easier to go back while he was still awake.' She ends – but then appears to anticipate the next question. 'He ordered a taxi.'

There is a moment's silence.

So that is the answer. Goodman – or Jubb – took a taxi back to The Partridge and removed his car in the early hours – even before their dawn arrival. By the time they had impounded it ten days later, it had been professionally valeted – but in the world of modern forensics there is the maxim "every contact leaves a trace". And it usually does.

Perhaps she perceives the collective reaction, for now she shudders.

'I met you – the following evening, in The Partridge?' DS Jones nods on behalf of her colleagues. 'Anthony said he wanted to treat me because I had missed the dinner.'

They wait.

'It was a return to the scene of the crime.' There is distaste in her voice. 'Like the proverbial arsonist, joining the back of the throng to watch the burning building.'

DS Jones responds.

'Or to check that he was in the clear, perhaps.'

Dr Lucy Bedlington nods, though her gaze seems to lose its focus.

'There have been inconsistencies – I dismissed them as cognitive failings, side-effects of his illness. Things about his past that contradicted, or didn't quite stack up. And he was always rather evasive. He would say there had been some unhappy episodes – things he was not ready to discuss – that we should look forward to our future.'

She swallows, as if the latter promise still troubles her.

'And his MS. Well – I sometimes wondered. He seemed to have symptoms when it suited him – to get his own way. But most of the time – you'd never know. Though it can present in many forms – no two sufferers have the same experience.'

The woman starts a little, as if she realises her monologue has been at the exclusion of those around her. She looks pointedly at DS Jones.

'But an Osman letter – I would have rejected it. I probably would have told him straightaway – that it was preposterous. I would have inadvertently warned him – and perhaps placed myself at more immediate risk.'

She glances about, as if she is trying to gauge the reaction to her admission.

'Doctor – it is entirely understandable. We realise – well – when you have been close to someone – and they turn out to be someone else – literally.'

The woman shakes her head slowly.

'Apologies if I have seemed uncooperative.' She sighs. 'The things you do, when a person says you are special.'

DS Jones shoots a glance at Skelgill; he anticipates her attention and quickly averts his eyes.

When Dr Lucy Bedlington has been ushered out, they sit reflectively.

'She's coming round to it.'

It is DS Jones's assessment – but DS Leyton looks a little less optimistic.

'There's more to come. She ain't going to like that.'

He refers to interviews he has since conducted with the Chief Executive of Fellview Nursing Home. In the first instance, before mention of Anthony Goodman's arrest, she had given a glowing report. He came with first-rate references and top qualifications – frankly, they thought they were lucky to get him. Pay is not high in the care sector, never mind in rural Cumbria. He was good with staff, and had a real knack of engaging with patients – and he would spend time with them whenever he had a spare moment. The controversy of the legacies left to the organisation and challenged by relatives – it could happen to any such institution.

But a minor query had arisen in relation to Anthony Goodman's unexplained absence. A recently admitted resident, an elderly widow, had been asking for him – it seems he had been feeding her cat, left to fend for itself at her empty home. At the property, police officers found evidence of careful ransacking, a copy of the woman's will with the executors, bequest and signature pages missing, and – hidden inside tomato growbags in the garden shed – the framed photograph from The Partridge, and Kyle Betony's mobile telephone.

Initial work by forensic accountants has already identified that Anthony Goodman had siphoned off significant portions from the historical legacies – as bogus solicitors' fees as executors – when in fact he had managed to get himself appointed as sole executor. His closeness to residents, and financial role working with Social Services to organise care plans, meant he gained full knowledge of and access to vulnerable elderly residents' finances, and he especially targeted those who had no close or nearby relatives. At his own home, two more wills made in his favour were discovered.

And then another little bombshell – here the greater source of DS Leyton's disquiet. Understanding the seriousness of the offences, the Chief Executive had expressed concern for Anthony Goodman's nurse fiancée. DS Leyton had countered – surely she meant *doctor?* No, no – a geriatric nurse – a full-time employee of Fellview.

DS Leyton had asked to be introduced to her; she was not Lucy Bedlington.

And now he pronounces.

'Poor old Doc – far from being special – in the eyes of Tobias Jubb, she was simply prey.' He compresses his features into an expression that combines both anger and sympathy. 'And now she reckons she's been taken for a fool.'

Skelgill resorts to an oath.

'In his eyes, we're all fools, Leyton.'

'To a monster, the norm is monstrous.'

DS Jones seems to speak from a daydream.

Then she realises that her colleagues are staring at her.

'It's a John Steinbeck quote.'

They nod.

JASMINE BETONY, POLICE HQ, 11 a.m.

'The man is a monster.'

The three detectives briefly look at one another.

DS Jones, however, nods in exaggerated sympathy. Indeed, she is prompted to reach and touch Jasmine Betony on the hand; they have more shared moments in the storm than the Thai girl can realise.

Jasmine Betony, however, looks up, a little surprised.

'It's okay – I'm fine. I don't allow these things to affect me.'

She smiles reassuringly, a full smile of the wide mouth showing bright white teeth. It would be possible to think she is speaking of a lost purse, or a broken washing machine; though closer scrutiny reveals that in the dark pools of her eyes there seem to swim shadows – and DS Jones is reminded of her idea that these are not the first traumas in the girl's short existence.

But there remain aspects of the knotted case that the police must yet unpick. Not least there is the disappearance of the true crime magazine. And the suicide-confession letter and the events surrounding it – the audacious claim that it was Kyle Betony's involvement in drugs that prompted his wife to kill him and take her own life to escape the attendant shame.

'Jasmine – we have to ask you some questions – for

completeness. It will help cement our final case in court.'

'Naturally, I understand.'

DS Jones slides a polythene evidence folder containing a creased page across the table.

'I take it you have never seen this before?'

If it were a mock interview for training purposes, she might be criticised for phraseology, for asking a leading question; but anything more ambivalent would seem hostile. Besides, they have already matched the paper and printer ink to the office of 'Anthony Goodman' at Fellview Nursing Home, and further analysis is expected to yield a corresponding DNA profile.

Moreover, it is true that Jasmine Betony has not seen the exhibit before. She does not pick it up, but leans over and reads. She takes longer than the limited missive demands – but there is some novelty in reading such a letter, authored by proxy.

Finally, she looks up and merely shakes her head.

'Mrs Betony – when Inspector Skelgill and I visited you – our second call, on the Monday afternoon, the day before the – the bridge?' Jasmine Betony nods inscrutably. 'The flowers – the lilies that we asked you about when we phoned you?'

The woman understands.

'It was earlier – in the morning – I had just finished translating a press release for Air Siam – and I was in the kitchen making tea. He came to the back door – which is unusual for anyone to do.' She hesitates, and takes a moment to look at Skelgill and DS Leyton before returning her gaze to DS Jones. 'He introduced himself as Sir Montague Brash. I had no idea he was actually Anthony Goodman – or –'

'Tobias Jubb.'

'Yes. You see – I have never met any of the committee members – but Kyle had spoken often of Sir Montague as an important person – the Chairman.'

'And what did the man say?'

'He advanced his condolences and gave me the lilies. I offered him tea, but he declined. But he asked if I would mind if he looked at Kyle's committee file. I said I would bring it down from Kyle's study, but he replied that he knew what it looked like and that he would do it – that I should put the lilies in water.'

'Was he long?'

She shakes her head.

'Less time than it took me – I was still trimming the stems when he came down.'

'Did he have anything with him – the file?'

'No – not that I noticed.'

'What was he wearing?'

'It was a shooting jacket – a Barbour type.'

DS Jones senses that Skelgill shifts in his seat. She can almost hear him thinking aloud, "Aye, with a poacher's pocket."

DS Jones produces the true crime periodical purchased by Skelgill.

'We suspect he took your husband's copy of this magazine. It contains an article about Tobias Jubb – an attempt to murder his second wife, in the United States. We believe it was what prompted your husband to suspect – or at least infer – that Anthony Goodman was Tobias Jubb.'

Jasmine Betony appears to absorb the information without question.

'And Anthony Goodman – Tobias Jubb – suspected that I knew, also? Is that why he wanted to kill me?'

DS Jones does not answer directly.

'Did he ask you anything that might suggest so?'

Now she ponders, though her expression remains serene, and perhaps only her breathing quickens a little, a slight flaring of her nostrils.

'His visit was unexpected. But it seemed entirely plausible. He did ask about Kyle – along the lines that he had seemed agitated on the night of the dinner – and did I know why?'

'What did you say?'

'Just that I thought he was excited – by the event itself – that he had been looking forward to it.'

'How did he react?'

Now Jasmine Betony closes her eyes, the long black lashes

settling like the wings of feathered moths upon her prominent cheekbones. It takes her a moment to recall.

'I think he was going to ask more.' She hesitates, and brings fine long fingers up to touch her delicate chin. 'That's right – but the doorbell rang. Actually, I was expecting a delivery of groceries – that's what I thought was odd when there was a knock at the back. I told him it probably was Tesco – and I'd just ask the driver to bring in the crates. That's when he said – apologised – that he'd remembered he had an appointment with a land agent in Keswick. And he left.'

'Through the back – the way he had come?'

'Yes – he automatically went to the back door. I assumed he must have parked in the lane – you can't really stop at the front for any length of time because of the parking restrictions.'

DS Jones is reprising her prepared notes. She glances briefly at her colleagues, who return encouraging looks – as if fearing she is trying to hand over the baton.

'And what was the next contact?'

Jasmine Betony gives a small bow of her head.

'It came also out of the blue – the next day – I would say at about four o'clock. Sir Montague – his impersonator – telephoned on the landline. He asked if I had seen the reports about the drugs connection to Kyle's death.'

The girl's lips narrow and a small crease appears upon her smooth brow.

'I said that I had and that it was ridiculous – it must be fake news – that Kyle would never have anything to do with drugs. I had a mind to complain about the idiot journalist that wrote it.'

DS Jones shoots a reproachful look at Skelgill – for she can see he stifles a chortle.

But Jasmine Betony seems not to notice, and she continues.

'He said that he was worried for me – that he was so sorry, because he thought there might be some substance to the report – and, if it were accurate, that it would be damaging to Kyle's reputation, and in turn to mine – and even that I could be considered by the police to be some kind of accessory.' Without turning her head, she looks sideways at Skelgill. 'That you had already been to examine his file made me think it might be true.'

DS Jones offers a prompt.

'Was he any more specific?'

'He said that there had been a misappropriation of funds from the DAA.'

This time Skelgill cannot prevent a small scoff of indignation from escaping his person. The explanation – their investigations have indeed revealed this point to be half-correct – misappropriation, yes – by ordinary committee member Kyle Betony, no. By Treasurer 'Anthony Goodman' – yes.

Jasmine Betony hesitates – but Skelgill extends a palm, making an upward motion to indicate she should carry on, that she is on the right track, and they are with her.

'He said he suspected Kyle was diverting monies for his own purposes – to buy drugs in order to sell them on. He explained that he now realised – having seen the media report – that there was incriminating evidence in Kyle's DAA file. He told me there was a meeting that evening – he suggested that if I brought the file along to him beforehand – well – his words were, he could square things with the committee. That I had suffered enough.'

Hitherto, Jasmine Betony has presented a largely neutral countenance – but now, for the first time, her features contract into an expression of remorse that makes her seem much younger even than her twenty-four years. She bows her head more deeply, and does not look up as she speaks.

'I realise I should have told you. Come straight to you. I was confused and frightened – I know you don't have the death penalty in England for drugs offences – but it seemed such a great responsibility. And I have no one else to turn to – since the loss of my husband.'

She keeps her head bowed – DS Jones seems to share her anguish – and DS Leyton, in particular looks alarmed.

But Skelgill's expression errs on the grim. She has paid a high cost – she almost paid more – and in his version of justice, she is innocent.

He clicks his fingers, directing the action at DS Jones – that she should move on.

The sharp snap causes Jasmine Betony to look up; she is like a small animal, cornered and unsure of its fate, but resigned to the outcome.

DS Jones addresses her, her tone decisive.

'Jasmine – we consider you acted under duress.' She raises her notebook illustratively. 'There is only one target of our investigation. If you could just explain further – the arrangement that was made.'

There is relief in the dark eyes; she gives a rueful smile.

'He said I should get a taxi to The Partridge – that he would meet me in the bar beforehand – and that I could just wait. It was only going to be a short meeting – he thought half an hour – and that he would be able to confirm to me afterwards that everything was okay. And that he would give me a lift home.'

The detectives are all nodding. It fits. They witnessed her journey. DS Jones made the telephone call. DS Leyton saw the minicab. Skelgill heard her voice in the passage.

And it is now Skelgill that intervenes – for he also bore witness to her disappearance.

'Where did you go?'

'He was waiting at the bar. But he immediately said it was too public and we should look at the folder in his car. He led me through a second door from the bar and then outside through a side door at the end of the corridor. His Land Rover – what I thought was his Land Rover – was nearby. We sat for a moment while he looked at the file. Then he said something like – the best thing is that we dispose of these pages – there will be no more smoking gun. He said – let's do it together – so that I could witness that they were gone. He made a joke about it being no use trying to burn anything on a night like this. So, he said – let's just go where no one will see us. That it would only take a minute.'

DS Jones resumes.

'So his idea was to throw the papers into the river – the Derwent at Ouse Bridge?'

Jasmine Betony nods – but now she bites her lip and suddenly two large tears overflow from the glistening wells of her dark eyes and stream over the curves of her cheeks. DS Leyton, with surprising alacrity for a man of his build, springs forward to press upon her a paper tissue that protrudes from a striped box.

She does not speak – but she nods in answer to DS Jones's proposition.

'That's okay, Jasmine – we know the rest. We don't need to go over it again.'

'Thank f –'

It is Skelgill from whom the stifled ejaculation issues – his colleagues look at him a little wide-eyed. He even appears shocked himself – but Jasmine Betony seems to understand his reaction.

'Inspector, I have not had chance to thank you. In fact, I don't know how ever I can.'

Skelgill rises and turns away to the window. He leans his hands on the sill and seems to be catching his breath. But when he turns back his expression carries hints of self-reproach – that somehow an unexpected emotion had got the better of him. He fumbles for a self-deprecating retort from what is a limited arsenal – but before he can fire one off Jasmine Betony speaks again.

'I don't think I could have clung on much longer.'

She provides the opening he seeks – though he glances sheepishly at DS Jones. She has several times castigated him for not waiting for her tie him on to the second strand. But his argument has been that, were he to have ended up in the Derwent, he would rather have taken his chances swimming for it, than bobbing on the end of a rope; and that she would never have hauled his weight against the current that night.

He grins mischievously at Jasmine Betony.

'You and me both, lass.'

FENELLA MANSFIELD, BRASH HALL, 5.30 p.m.

Skelgill cannot quite believe his eyes. In the early evening gloom he peers through the glass of the side window of Land

Rover Defender registration *SMB 1* – it must be Sir Montague Brash's reserve model. It is the shorter wheelbase 90, rather than the longer 110 – but where it does not differ from the vehicle half-wrecked by Tobias Jubb is that the keys are once again in the ignition. Clearly, old habits die hard.

Skelgill shrugs and turns away.

A light burns in the estate office, and this time it appears his arrival has gone unnoticed – although he can see a damp black nose pressed against the lower glass of the door, surrounded by a small patch of condensation.

He strides across, his boots crunching in the gravel; he carries a large bulging opaque plastic carrier bag.

Fenella Mansfield looks up in surprise when he enters – it seems she has been engrossed in some item on her mobile phone – she puts aside the device with a fading relic of an artful grin. The dog seems pleased to see him, and this time he has a strip of jerky at the ready, which he surreptitiously palms in the guise of a stroke around the muzzle; Pandora enters into the conspiracy, and slips through the door at the rear, which is a little ajar.

'Oh, Inspector.'

His judgement in these situations being prone to bias, Skelgill's assessment is that she too is pleased to see him. There might also be hints of embarrassment, coyness, vulnerability – a potentially volatile cocktail.

He halts a yard short of her desk and casts about. The flowers of his last visit are gone – but the violet aroma is not. As before, the office seems unduly warm – perhaps the heat of the sauna seeps through the open door – and this time he needs no invitation to remove his jacket – a kind of tactical fleecy under which he is wearing only a tight-fitting t-shirt.

He makes it obvious that he is inhaling, without the act seeming too vulgar.

'Nice perfume that you wear.'

If he is honest, he does not actually think so – whether it is too cloying, or simply that it reminds him of the detested sweets, he is not sure – but he brazens out his compliment.

Fenella Mansfield takes it in her stride.

'Oh – thank you – it's, er –' She leans down to one side and picks a small designer handbag and produces a tiny lilac-coloured bottle with a psychedelic design. She holds it up. 'It's called *Ultra-Violet* – the new fragrance from Suivre-Son-Nez.'

Skelgill nods.

'Aye, I suppose it would be.'

She reaches towards a drawer of her desk.

'Actually – somewhere – I have a new bottle, unopened. Here it is. Would you like it? For your girlfriend, perhaps?'

She flutters her lashes. He is reminded why her employer might have created an awkward situation for himself; perhaps not entirely by himself.

But Skelgill grimaces, all the same.

'Do I look like a bloke that's got a girlfriend?'

'Frankly, I'd be surprised if you didn't.'

She is sharp, and smiling she waits for his further denial with a look that says she will remain in any event unconvinced. Skelgill does not answer – he delves into his carrier bag and brings out what appears to be a large fluffy white bath towel, freshly laundered and neatly rolled.

The woman inhales to speak – but he tucks it under his arm and pre-empts any observation.

'I wouldn't mind asking you a couple of things.'

'Anything you like.' She lowers her voice. 'Naturally, I feel – well – a little indebted to you.'

Skelgill narrows his eyes – as if to convey that he is trying to read between the lines. And his question when it comes is at once forthright and cryptic.

'On the night of Saturday 18th – did you see anything that I should know about?'

He waits. Fenella Mansfield looks for a moment like she might not understand. She is wearing a silky blouse, unbuttoned to her breastbone, and now she gazes at him and places a palm over the bare tanned flesh above her heart. She shakes her head slowly.

They each maintain unblinking eye contact – until, it seems,

Skelgill accepts the unspoken answer and shifts on his feet. He gestures to one side of the office and they both follow his indication, breaking the stalemate.

'The flowers that were here when I came last time – lilies – where did they come from?'

Fenella Mansfield seems a little caught off guard by his question. She shows no sign of disquiet in her expression – but she deflects for a moment, repeating his words.

'The lilies – where *did* they come from? Yes – well – actually, it was – Anthony Goodman – well, whatever – whoever –'

Now she regards Skelgill with a frown, as if she acknowledges it is of mutual concern.

'Did he come often?'

'From time to time.' She smiles, knowingly – in a way that suggests he will understand her ambiguity. 'Ostensibly for meetings with Monty about the DAA.'

Skelgill nods, his expression stern, though not reproachful of her.

'Did he ever ask you out?'

'He did, as a matter of fact.'

'What happened?'

'I said I was spoken for.'

There is silence.

Skelgill experiences a tremor of disquiet – it troubles him – and causes a distraction from which she has to rouse him.

'You brought your own towel? We have plenty.'

He looks back at her to see she is smiling broadly.

She stands up and smooths the material of her tight-fitting skirt.

But with a flourish Skelgill unfurls the item under the force of gravity.

'It's a dressing gown.'

On the breast pocket it has an embroidered bird motif.

'The Partridge? But I –'

Skelgill steps forward and presents it into her arms.

'Compliments of the house. I borrowed it when I was soaked the other night. I reckon you'll find it's just Mr Smith's size.'

'You were quicker than I expected.'

'Seeing Charlie?' Skelgill sounds a little unnerved.

'No – at Brash Hall. I thought you might be in for a long interrogation.'

Skelgill gives a sigh of resignation.

'That's one advantage of our turning a blind eye.'

DS Jones regards him pensively.

'We didn't exactly turn a blind eye – you told the Chief.'

Skelgill shrugs. He is tempted to reach for the colloquial term for the act of protecting oneself from subsequent criticism by failing to mitigate against a predictable outcome – but it is a tactic from the playbook of DI Alex Smart, and not one with which he likes to be associated. Moreover, he decides this is not the moment.

But DS Jones does it for him.

'We covered our asses.'

Skelgill is drinking and her phrase causes him to splutter.

'You've been watching too much American TV, lass.'

But she has brought a sardonic grin to his lips. He is a little more forthcoming.

'Goodman – *Jubb* – he tried it on with her.'

DS Jones emits a small gasp.

'With Fenella Mansfield?'

'Aye. He took her the same flowers – lilies.'

'Do you think he suspected her of having seen something – from the bedroom window?'

'I wouldn't be surprised if he was sounding her out – if he knew she was here, that is. Otherwise – happen she was just another female he got in his sights. It wasn't his first visit.'

Now DS Jones is the one to shake her head.

'How many others are there?'

Skelgill gazes broodingly across the small room; his eyes traverse the extensive collection of single malt whiskies that stretches across the back bar, a comforting golden glow in the low warm light.

'That's a long road ahead. Unless he has a change of heart. And I can't see that.' He sniffs. 'At least, as Leyton says, we've got him bang to rights – for what he's done on our patch.'

DS Jones, too, seems to contemplate the middle distance.

'Remember, when we were talking about psychopaths – how endearing they can be?'

'I remember you saying there was no danger of me being mistaken for one.'

She laughs.

'That was you!'

Skelgill, in denial, buries his nose in his pint of bitter.

DS Jones turns to her left and gestures to the empty space on the alcove wall.

'Do you think we ought to give Kendall Minto some kind of minor scoop? He did come up with the goods.'

But Skelgill only scoffs.

'Aye, two days late.'

DS Jones gives half a nod.

'We would have caught him, at least.'

Skelgill does not look convinced.

'Who's to say he's not got another pocket pardon tucked away?'

'You mean another false identity?'

'I wouldn't put it past him. He could have killed Jasmine Betony and been out of the country that same night.'

'I suppose so.'

She drinks, and raises her glass to the light, as if to see what it is that she tastes. She has succumbed to a half-pint of cask ale – a novelty in that there can be so much flavour in a drink that is neither flat nor gassy, neither cold nor tepid.

'When did you know it was him – Goodman, I mean?'

'You know when you see a snake – and your first instinct is to want to kill it?'

'Really?'

Skelgill chokes back a laugh.

'When Leyton phoned me from the crash site.'

But DS Jones is not having it.

'But you knew there was something afoot – you knew to go to the bridge.'

Skelgill turns to look at her, as though it is news to him.

'Did I?'

'Yes.' She is resolute.

Skelgill sits back, silenced. It takes him a few moments to respond.

'Happen a few things came together. Followed my nose.' His free hand wanders to feel the bulge in the pocket of his fleece jacket.

DS Jones chuckles. She inhales to speak – and hesitates for a moment.

'I missed something really obvious.'

'Who didn't?'

'No – I mean about Fenella Mansfield.'

Skelgill shifts his position, uncrossing and recrossing his feet under the table. He waits for her to elaborate.

'The entry in the hotel register – for Mr and Mrs Smith. The house number and street address given doesn't exist, of course – but the town was Mansfield.'

'Notts.'

'Pardon?'

'Nottinghamshire.'

'Ah – yes, I see. Remember – we thought there might be a clue – maybe in the mobile number. It was more obvious than that.'

Now, however, Skelgill seems untroubled. He sinks back against the wooden settle.

DS Jones continues.

'I should also have noticed – when we first spoke to Charlie – he said something like, Sir Montague's secretary made the bookings for the DAA committee. Of course, he meant Fenella Mansfield. But because he used the term secretary and not PA I took it he was referring to Georgina Graham – DAA Secretary.'

Skelgill seems to sigh, though it may be simply that he exhales after taking a drink.

'I reckon you and Leyton had it worked out – what happened.'

'On the night of Kyle Betony's murder?'

'Aye.'

She narrows her eyes reflectively.

'Well – maybe we were close – but not who.'

'It's not easy – when someone's not who they say they are.'

DS Jones glances again at the site of the missing photograph.

'To think that picture was there all these years.'

Skelgill casts a hand randomly.

'It becomes like wallpaper – no one pays attention to the detail. Betony was sharper than most folk.'

DS Jones looks a little perplexed.

'But not quite sharp enough to realise the risk he was running.'

Skelgill shakes his head.

'Happen he just thought it were a funny coincidence. And talk of the merger – it gave Jubb an excuse to pull him aside – discuss it in private.'

'Do you think Kyle Betony challenged Jubb directly?'

'Not in hearing, if he did.' He sips rather delicately at his beer. 'But – now I've seen him – seen Jubb – and what we know about him. I don't reckon it would take that. Even mention of the fishing match might have been enough. Look how easily he got spooked after our second interview with him.'

DS Jones nods, though she makes a brief face of regret, as though she feels they suffered a near thing. But Skelgill is on her side.

'You never gave a hint that we might be onto him. Ten minutes later he's rolling out his same MO to silence Jasmine Betony.'

DS Jones seems to appreciate his support; it perhaps prompts more introspection.

'I was wrong about her.'

But Skelgill frowns.

'What's to say you were? Stuck in a foreign country with a Billy Liar character like Betony.'

DS Jones turns with her eyes widened. There could be much to unpack in his uncompromising assessment.

'She is resilient, that's for sure. I actually think almost the biggest shock to her is being tricked by Tobias Jubb's impersonation.'

Skelgill shrugs.

'Her and all the committee – his employers – a qualified doctor –' He pauses, however. 'Chaudry, mind – I reckon he suspected something. Remember when he was lecturing us on tracking mobile phones. He'd noticed that Goodman had left his handset on the table in the Snug. So that he couldn't be traced going to Ouse Bridge.'

DS Jones does not answer, and Skelgill leans forward to look round at her.

'Chaudry – the eligible bachelor, remember?'

She starts a little – and looks at him with surprise – as though he might indeed have jumped somewhere on board her train of thought. She gestures towards the main door of the bar.

'They're taking a while bringing the menus. Aren't you starving?'

That Skelgill does not immediately agree seems a little out of character.

'The bistro's packed – there's a new girl in charge – she said she'd let us know when a table's free.'

'I'm surprised you didn't suggest the Taj Mahal.'

'What?'

DS Jones pulls at a tress of hair that has fallen across her cheek.

'Well – it's – an anniversary of sorts. Isn't it?'

Skelgill looks baffled. Then an idea seems to strike him. He produces from a pocket a small package wrapped in cellophane, lilac in colour and jazzy in design.

'I didn't get chance to wrap it.'

'Perfume! You shouldn't have. This is expensive. Thank you.'

There are complex nuances in DS Jones's rejoinder – perhaps including a hint of suspicion – but she half rises and catches him defenceless with a peck on the cheek – he is holding his beer and unable to take evasive action other than sway sideways a little.

'Howay, lass.'

But their contretemps is interrupted by the approach of a young woman in staff uniform – although more striking is that she holds a bunch of lilies. They might imagine she is looking for a suitable vase, were the flowers not gift-wrapped. And, indeed, she seems to know to hand them to a confounded DS Jones.

'From a Mr Leyton.'

DS Jones gives a quizzical half-smile – she reaches for the tag, and looks doubly perplexed.

'But – these are not for me – it says – Mrs –'

There might, however, just be the first small hint of realisation in her tone.

The girl stands patiently, unmoved by DS Jones's bewilderment. She turns to address Skelgill.

'That's the champagne on ice – in the Skiddaw suite – as you ordered, Mr Smith.'

***

Next in the series ...

Murder at Caldblow Farm is scheduled for publication in July 2023. In the meantime, books 1-19 in the Inspector Skelgill series can be found on Amazon. Each comprises a stand-alone mystery, and may be read out of sequence. All DI Skelgill books can be borrowed free with Kindle Unlimited, and also by Amazon Prime members on a Kindle device.

FREE BOOKS, NEW RELEASES, THE BEAUTIFUL LAKES ... AND MOUNTAINS OF CAKES

Sign up for Bruce Beckham's author newsletter

Thank you for getting this far!

If you have enjoyed your encounter with DI Skelgill there's a growing series of whodunits set in England's rugged and beautiful Lake District to get your teeth into.

My newsletter often features one of the back catalogue to download for free, along with details of new releases and special offers.

No Skelgill mystery would be complete without a café stop or two, and each month there's a traditional Cumbrian recipe – tried and tested by yours truly (aka *Bruce Bake 'em*).

To sign up, this is the link:

https://mailchi.mp/acd032704a3f/newsletter-sign-up

Your email address will be safely stored in the USA by Mailchimp, and will be used for no other purpose. You can unsubscribe at any time simply by clicking the link at the foot of the newsletter.

Thank you, again – best wishes and happy reading!

Bruce Beckham